The
Nostradamus
Prophecies

Mario Reading is a multi-talented writer of both fiction and non-fiction. His varied life has included selling rare books, teaching riding in Africa, studying dressage in Vienna, running a polo stable in Gloucestershire and maintaining a coffee plantation in Mexico. An acknowledged expert on the prophecies of Nostradamus, Reading is the author of five non-fiction titles published in the UK and around the world.

The Nostradamus Prophecies

MARIO READING

Atlantic Books
London

First published as a paperback original in Great Britain in 2009
by Atlantic Books, an imprint of Grove Atlantic Ltd.

10 9 8 7 6 5 4 3 2 1

A CIP catalogue record for this book is available from the
British Library.

ISBN: 978 1 84887 124 3

Printed in Great Britain by Clays Ltd, St Ives plc

Atlantic Books
An imprint of Grove Atlantic Ltd
Ormond House
26–27 Boswell Street
London WC1N 3JZ

www.atlantic-books.co.uk

For my son, Lawrence, *con todo mi cariño*

AUTHOR'S NOTE

Nostradamus did indeed only complete 942 quatrains out of 1000, representing his intended total of ten centuries of 100 quatrains apiece. The remaining fifty-eight quatrains are missing, and, to this day, they have never been found.

The Will that I have used in the book is Nostradamus's original last Will and Testament (in the original French, with my translation appended). I concentrate particularly on the codicil to the Will in which Nostradamus bequeaths two secret coffers to his eldest daughter, Madeleine, with the stipulation that 'no one but her may look at or see those things which he has placed inside the coffers'. All this is on public record.

The gypsy lore, language, customs, names, habits and myths depicted in the book are all accurate. I have merely concatenated the customs of a number of different tribes into one, for reasons of fictional convenience.

No definite proof of the existence of the Corpus Maleficus has been found to date. Which doesn't mean it isn't out there.

Mario Reading, 2009

EPIGRAPH

'As it had never occurred to him to leave word behind,
he was mourned over for dead till, after eight months,
his first letter arrived from Talcahuano.'

From *Typhoon* by Joseph Conrad

'Our business in this world is not to succeed, but to
continue to fail, in good spirits.'

Robert Louis Stevenson, *Complete Works*, vol. 26,
Reflections and Remarks on Human Life, s.4

'Perhaps proof of how aleatory the concept of nationality
is lies in the fact that we must learn it before we can
recognize it as such.'

From *A Reading Diary* by Alberto Manguel

ACKNOWLEDGEMENTS

Writing and researching a book such as this can be a dauntingly solitary experience, so one is all the more grateful when anybody outside one's own immediate family takes an interest in it. My agent, Oli Munson of Blake Friedmann, has championed the book from the very outset – from larval caterpillar, through pupal, to fully-fledged butterfly. I am profoundly indebted to him both for his friendship and for his steadfast support, and indeed to everyone at Blake Friedmann for their collective and multifaceted accomplishments. Ravi Mirchandani, my editor at Atlantic, also saw early virtue in the book, as did my German editor, Urban Hofstetter at Blanvalet, who was the first major international publisher to get 100 per cent behind it – I am deeply grateful to them both. Thank you, too, to the semi-invisible sales force at Atlantic, particularly in the form of managing director Daniel Scott, whose personal memo praising the book raised my spirits quite remarkably. Also to the nameless *bouquiniste* on the Left Bank of the Seine who spent nearly the whole of a summer afternoon generously sharing with me his insights into the Manouche gypsies. Finally I would like to thank the British Library and the Bibliothèque Nationale de France for their simple existence. Authors everywhere are in their debt.

PROLOGUE

La Place de l'Etape, Orléans.
16 June 1566

De Bale nodded and the *bourreau* began to haul away at the pulley mechanism. The Chevalier de la Roche Allié was in full armour, so the apparatus strained and groaned before the ratchet took and the Chevalier began to rise from the ground. The *bourreau* had warned de Bale about the strain and its possible consequences, but the Count would hear none of it.

'I have known this man since childhood, Maître. His family is amongst the most ancient in France. If he wants to die in his armour, such is his right.'

The *bourreau* knew better than to argue – men who argued with de Bale usually ended up on the rack, or scalded with boiling spirits. De Bale had the ear of the King and the seal of the Church. In other words the bastard was untouchable. As close to terrestrial perfection as it was possible for mortal man to be.

De Bale glanced upwards. Because of the *lèse-majesté* nature of his crimes, de la Roche Allié had been sentenced to a fifty-foot suspension. De Bale wondered if the man's neck ligaments would withstand the strain of both the rope and the 100 pounds of plate steel his squires had strapped him into before the execution. It would not be well viewed if the man broke in two before the drawing and the quartering. Could de la Roche Allié have thought of this eventuality when he made his request? Planned the whole thing? De Bale thought not. The man was an innocent – one of the old breed.

'He's reached the fifty, Sir.'

'Let him down.'

De Bale watched the sack of armour descending towards him. The man was dead. It was obvious. Most of his victims struggled and kicked at this point in the proceedings. They knew what was coming.

'The Chevalier is dead, Sir. What do you want me to do?'

'Keep your voice down, for a start.' De Bale glanced over at the crowd. These people wanted blood. Huguenot blood. If they didn't get it, they would turn on him and the executioner and tear them limb from limb. 'Draw him anyway.'

'I'm sorry, Sir?'

'You heard me. Draw him anyway. And contrive that he twitches, man. Shriek through your nose if you have to. Ventriloquise. Make a big play with the entrails. The crowd have to think that they see him suffer.'

The two young squires were moving forward to unbuckle the Chevalier's armour.

De Bale waved them back. 'The Maître will do it. Return to your homes. Both of you. You have done your duty by your master. He is ours now.'

The squires backed away, white-faced.

'Just take off the gorget, plackart and breastplate, Maître. Leave the greaves, cuisses, helm and gauntlets in place. The horses will do the rest.'

The executioner busied himself about his business. 'We're ready, Sir.'

De Bale nodded and the *bourreau* made his first incision.

2

Michel de Nostredame's House, Salon-de-Provence, 17 June 1566

'De Bale is coming, Master.'

'I know.'

'How could you know? It is not possible. The news was only brought in by carrier pigeon ten minutes ago.'

The old man shrugged, and eased his oedema-ravaged leg until it lay more comfortably on the footstool. 'Where is he now?'

'He is in Orléans. In three weeks he will be here.'

'Only three weeks?'

The manservant moved closer. He began to wring his hands. 'What shall you do, Master? The Corpus Maleficus are questioning all those whose family were once of the Jewish faith. Marranos. Conversos. Also gypsies. Moors. Huguenots. Anyone not by birth a Catholic. Even the Queen cannot protect you down here.'

The old man waved a disparaging hand. 'It hardly matters any more. I shall be dead before the monster arrives.'

'No, Master. Surely not.'

'And you, Ficelle? Would it suit you to be away from here when the Corpus come calling?'

'I shall stay at your side, Master.'

The old man smiled. 'You will better serve me by doing as I ask. I need you to undertake a journey for

3

me. A long journey, fraught with obstacles. Shall you do as I ask?'

The manservant lowered his head. 'Whatever you ask me I will do.'

The old man watched him for a few moments, seemingly weighing him up. 'If you fail in this, Ficelle, the consequences will be more terrible than any de Bale – or the Devil he so unwittingly serves – could contrive.' He hesitated, his hand resting on his grotesquely inflated leg. 'I have had a vision. Of such clarity that it dwarfs the work to which I have until now dedicated my life. I have held back fifty-eight of my quatrains from publication for reasons which I shall not vouchsafe – they concern only me. Six of these quatrains have a secret purpose – I shall explain to you how to use them. No one must see you. No one must suspect. The remaining fifty-two quatrains must be hidden in a specific place that only you and I can know. I have sealed them inside this bamboo capsule.' The old man reached down beside his chair and withdrew the packed and tamped tube. 'You will place this capsule where I tell you, and in exactly the manner I stipulate. You will not deviate from this. You will carry out my instructions to the letter. Is that understood?'

'Yes, Master.'

The old man lay back in his chair, exhausted by the intensity of what he was trying to communicate. 'When you return here, after my death, you will go to see my friend and the trustee of my estate, Palamède Marc. You will tell him about your errand and assure him of its success. He will then give you a sum of money. A sum of money that will secure you and your family's future for generations to come. Do you understand me?'

'Yes, Master.'

'Will you trust to my judgement in this matter, and follow my instructions to the letter?'

4

'I will.'

'Then you will be blessed, Ficelle. By a people you will never meet, and by a history neither you nor I can remotely envisage.'

'But you know the future, Master. You are the greatest seer of all time. Even the Queen has honoured you. All France knows of your gifts.'

'I know nothing, Ficelle. I am like this bamboo tube. Doomed to transmit things but never to understand them. All I can do is pray that there are others, coming after me, who will manage things better.'

PART ONE

1

Quartier St-Denis, Paris,
Present Day

Achor Bale took no real pleasure in killing. That had long since left him. He watched the gypsy almost fondly, as one might watch a chance acquaintance getting off an airplane.

The man had been late of course. One only had to look at him to see the vanity bleeding from each pore. The 1950s moustache à la Zorro. The shiny leather jacket bought for fifty euros at the Clignancourt flea market. The scarlet see-through socks. The yellow shirt with the Prince of Wales plumes and the outsized pointed collar. The fake gold medallion with the image of Sainte Sara. The man was a dandy without taste – as recognisable to one of his own as a dog is to another dog.

'Do you have the manuscript with you?'

'What do you think I am? A fool?'

Well, hardly that, thought Bale. A fool is rarely self-conscious. This man wears his venality like a badge of office. Bale noted the dilated pupils. The sheen of sweat on the handsome, razor-sharp features. The drumming of the fingers on the table. The tapping of the feet. A drug addict, then. Strange, for a gypsy. That must be why he needed the money so badly. 'Are you Manouche or Rom? Gitan, perhaps?'

'What do you care?'

'Given your moustache, I'd say Manouche. One of Django Reinhardt's descendants, maybe?'

'My name is Samana. Babel Samana.'

'Your gypsy name?'

'That is secret.'

'My name is Bale. No secret there.'

The gypsy's fingers increased their beat upon the table. His eyes were everywhere now – flitting across the other drinkers, testing the doors, plumbing the dimensions of the ceiling.

'How much do you want for it?' Cut straight to the chase. That was the way with a man like this. Bale watched the gypsy's tongue dart out to moisten the thin, artificially virilised mouth.

'I want half a million euros.'

'Just so.' Bale felt a profound calmness descending upon him. Good. The gypsy really did have something to sell. The whole thing wasn't just a come-on. 'For such a sum of money, we'd need to inspect the manuscript before purchase. Ascertain its viability.'

'And memorise it! Yes. I've heard of such things. This much I know. Once the contents are out into the open it's worthless. Its value lies in its secrecy.'

'You're so right. I'm very glad you take that position.'

'I've got someone else interested. Don't think you're the only fish in the sea.'

Bale's eyes closed down on themselves. Ah. He would have to kill the gypsy after all. Torment and kill. He was aware of the telltale twitching above his right eye. 'Shall we go and see the manuscript now?'

'I'm talking to the other man first. Perhaps you'll even bid each other up.'

Bale shrugged. 'Where are you meeting him?'

'I'm not saying.'

9

'How do you wish to play this then?'

'You stay here. I go and talk to the other man. See if he's serious. Then I come back.'

'And if he's not? The price goes down?'

'Of course not. Half a million.'

'I'll stay here then.'

'You do that.'

The gypsy lurched to his feet. He was breathing heavily now, the sweat dampening his shirt at the neck and sternum. When he turned around Bale noticed the imprint of the chair on the cheap leather jacket.

'If you follow me, I'll know. Don't think I won't.'

Bale took off his sunglasses and laid them on the table. He looked up, smiling. He had long understood the effect his freakishly clotted eyes had on susceptible people. 'I won't follow you.'

The gypsy's mouth went slack with shock. He gazed in horror at Bale's face. This man had the *ia chalou* – the evil eye. Babel's mother had warned him of such people. Once you saw them – once they fixed you with the stare of the basilisk – you were doomed. Somewhere, deep inside his unconscious mind, Babel Samana was acknowledging his mistake – acknowledging that he had let the wrong man into his life.

'You'll stay here?'

'Never fear. I'll be waiting for you.'

~

Babel began running as soon as he was out of the café. He would lose himself in the crowds. Forget the whole thing. What had he been thinking of? He didn't even *have* the manuscript. Just a vague idea of where it was. When the three *ursitory* had settled on Babel's pillow as a child to decide his fate, why had they chosen drugs as his weakness? Why not drink? Or women? Now O Beng had got into him and sent him this cockatrice as a punishment.

Babel slowed to a walk. No sign of the *gadje*. Had he been imagining things? Imagining the man's malevolence? The effect of those terrible eyes? Maybe he had been hallucinating? It wouldn't be the first time he had given himself the heebie-jeebies with badly cut drugs.

He checked the time on a parking meter. Okay. The second man might still be waiting for him. Perhaps he would prove more benevolent?

Across the road, two prostitutes began a heated argument about their respective pitches. It was Saturday afternoon. Pimp day in St-Denis. Babel caught his reflection in a shop window. He gave himself a shaky smile. If only he could swing this deal he might even run a few girls himself. And a Mercedes. He would buy himself a cream Mercedes with red leather seats, can holders and automatic air conditioning. And get his nails manicured at one of those shops where blond *payo* girls in white pinafores gaze longingly at you across the table.

Chez Minette was only a two-minute walk away. The least he could do would be to poke his head inside the door and check out the other man. Sting him for a down-payment – a proof of interest.

Then, groaning under a mound of cash and gifts, he would go back to the camp and placate his *hexi* of a sister.

11

Adam Sabir had long since decided that he was on a wild goose chase. Samana was fifty minutes late. It was only his fascination with the seedy milieu of the bar that kept him in situ. As he watched, the barman began winding down the street-entrance shutters.

'What's this? Are you closing?'

'Closing? No. I'm sealing everybody in. It's Saturday. All the pimps come into town on the train. Cause trouble in the streets. Three weeks ago I lost my front windows. If you want to get out you must leave by the back door.'

Sabir raised an eyebrow. Well. This was certainly a novel way to maintain your customer base. He reached forward and drained his third cup of coffee. He could already feel the caffeine nettling at his pulse. Ten minutes. He would give Samana another ten minutes. Then, although he was still technically on holiday, he would go to the cinema and watch John Huston's *Night of the Iguana* – spend the rest of the afternoon with Ava Gardner and Deborah Kerr. Add another chapter to his no doubt unsaleable book on the hundred best films of all time.

'*Une pression, s'il vous plaît. Rien ne presse.*'

The barman waved a hand in acknowledgement and continued winding. At the last possible moment a lithe figure slid under the descending shutters and straightened up, using a table for support.

'*Ho! Tu veux quoi, toi?*'

Babel ignored the barman and stared wildly about the room. His shirt was drenched beneath his jacket and sweat was cascading off the angular lines of his chin. With single-minded intensity he concentrated his attention on each table in turn, his eyes screwed up against the bright interior glare.

Sabir held up a copy of his book on Nostradamus, as they had agreed, with his photograph on prominent display. So. The gypsy had arrived at last. Now for the let-down. 'I'm over here, Monsieur Samana. Come and join me.'

Babel tripped over a chair in his eagerness to get to Sabir. He steadied himself, limping, his face twisted towards the entrance to the bar. But he was safe for the time being. The shutters were fully down now. He was sealed off from the lying *gadje* with the crazy eyes. The *gadje* who had sworn to him that he wouldn't follow. The *gadje* who had then trailed him all the way to Chez Minette, not even bothering to hide himself in the crowd. Babel was still in with a chance.

Sabir stood up, a quizzical expression on his face. 'What's the matter? You look as though you've seen a ghost.' Close to, all the savagery that he had detected in the gypsy's stare had transformed itself into a vacant mask of terror.

'You're the writer?'

'Yes. See? That's me. On the inside back cover.'

Babel reached across to the next table and grabbed an empty beer glass. He smashed it down on to the surface between them and ground his hand in the broken shards. Then he reached across and took Sabir's hand in his bloodied paw. 'I'm sorry for this.' Before Sabir had time to react, the gypsy had forced his hand down on to the broken glass.

'Jesus! You little bastard . . .' Sabir tried to snatch his hand back.

The gypsy clutched hold of Sabir's hand and pressed

it against his own, until the two hands were joined in a bloody scum. Then he smashed Sabir's bleeding palm against his forehead, leaving a splattered imprint. 'Now. Listen! Listen to me.'

Sabir wrenched his hand from the gypsy's grasp. The barman emerged from behind his bar brandishing a foreshortened billiard cue.

'Two words. Remember them. Samois. Chris.' Babel backed away from the approaching barman, his bloodied palm held up as if in benediction. 'Samois. Chris. You remember?' He threw a chair at the barman, using the distraction to orientate himself in relation to the rear exit. 'Samois. Chris.' He pointed at Sabir, his eyes wild with fear. 'Don't forget.'

3

Babel knew that he was running for his life. Nothing had ever felt as certain as this before. As complete. The pain in his hand was a violent, throbbing ache. His lungs were on fire, each breath tearing through him as if it were studded with nails.

Bale watched him from fifty metres back. He had time. The gypsy had nowhere to go. No one he could speak to. The Sûreté would take one look at him and put him in a straitjacket – the police weren't overly charitable to gypsies in Paris, especially gypsies covered in blood. What had happened in that bar? Who had he seen? Well, it wouldn't take him long to find out.

He spotted the white Peugeot van almost immediately. The driver was asking directions of a window cleaner. The window cleaner was pointing back towards St-Denis and scrunching his shoulders in Gallic incomprehension.

Bale threw the driver to one side and climbed into the cab. The engine was still running. Bale slid the van into gear and accelerated away. He didn't bother to check in the rear-view mirror.

~

Babel had lost sight of the *gadje*. He turned and looked behind him, jogging backwards. Passers-by avoided him, put off by his bloodied face and hands. Babel stopped. He stood in the street, sucking in air like a cornered stag.

The white Peugeot van mounted the kerb and smashed into Babel's right thigh, crushing the bone. Babel ricocheted off the bonnet and fell heavily on to the pavement. Almost immediately he felt himself being lifted – strong hands on his jacket and the seat of his trousers. A door was opened and he was thrown into the van. He could hear a terrible, high-pitched keening and belatedly realised that it was coming from himself. He looked up just as the *gadje* brought the heel of his hand up beneath his chin.

4

Babel awoke to an excruciating pain in his legs and shoulders. He raised his head to look around, but saw nothing. It was only then that he realised that his eyes were bandaged and that he was tied, upright, to some sort of metal frame from which he hung forward, his legs and arms in cruciform position, his body in an involuntary semicircle, as though he were thrusting out his hips in the course of some particularly explicit dance. He was naked.

Bale gave Babel's penis another tug. 'So. Have I got your attention at last? Good. Listen to me, Samana. There are two things you must know. One. You are definitely going to die – you cannot possibly talk your way out of this or buy your life from me with information. Two. The manner of your death depends entirely on you. If you please me, I will cut your throat. You won't feel anything. And the way I do it, you will bleed to death in under a minute. If you displease me, I will hurt you – far more than I am hurting you now. To prove to you that I intend to kill you – and that there is no way back from the position in which you find yourself – I am going to slice your penis off. Then I shall cauterise the wound with a hot iron so that you don't bleed to death before your time.'

'Don't! Don't do it! I will tell you anything you want to know. Anything.'

Bale stood with his knife held flat against the outstretched skin of Babel's member. 'Anything? Your penis, against the information that I seek?' Bale shrugged his shoulders. 'I don't understand. You know that you will never use it again. I have made this quite clear. Why should you wish to retain it? Don't tell me that you are still labouring under the delusion that there is hope?'

A filament of saliva drooled from the edge of Babel's mouth. 'What do you want me to tell you?'

'First. The name of the bar.'

'Chez Minette.'

'Good. That is correct. I saw you enter there myself. Who did you see?'

'An American. A writer. Adam Sabir.'

'Why?'

'To sell him the manuscript. I wanted money.'

'Did you show him the manuscript?'

Babel gave a fractured laugh. 'I don't even have it. I've never seen it. I don't even know if it exists.'

'Oh dear.' Bale let go of Babel's penis and began stroking his face. 'You are a handsome man. The ladies like you. A man's greatest weakness always lies in his vanity.' Bale criss-crossed his knife blade over Babel's right cheek. 'Not so pretty now. From one side, you'll still do. From the other – Armageddon. Look. I can put my finger right through this hole.'

Babel started screaming.

'Stop. Or I shall mark the other side.'

Babel stopped screaming. Air fluttered through the torn flaps of his cheek.

'You advertised the manuscript. Two interested parties answered. I am one. Sabir the other. What did you intend to sell to us for half a million euros? Hot air?'

'I was lying. I know where it can be found. I will take you to it.'

'And where is that?'

'It's written down.'

'Recite it to me.'

17

Babel shook his head. 'I can't.'

'Turn the other cheek.'

'No! No! I can't. I can't read . . .'

'How do you know it's written down then?'

'Because I've been told.'

'Who has this writing? Where can it be found?' Bale cocked his head to one side. 'Is a member of your family hiding it? Or somebody else?' There was a pause. 'Yes. I thought so. I can see it on your face. It's a member of your family, isn't it? I want to know who. And where.' Bale grabbed hold of Babel's penis. 'Give me a name.'

Babel hung his head. Blood and saliva dripped out of the hole made by Bale's knife. What had he done? What had his fear and bewilderment made him reveal? Now the *gadje* would go and find Yola. Torture her too. His dead parents would curse him for not protecting his sister. His name would become unclean – *mahrimé*. He would be buried in an unmarked grave. And all because his vanity was stronger than his fear of death.

Had Sabir understood those two words he had told him in the bar? Would his instincts about the man prove right?

Babel knew that he had reached the end of the road. A lifetime spent building castles in the air meant that he understood his own weaknesses all too well. Another thirty seconds and his soul would be consigned to hell. He would have only one chance to do what he intended to do. One chance only.

Using the full hanging weight of his head, Babel threw his chin up to the left, as far as it could stretch, and then wrenched it back downwards in a vicious semicircle to the right.

Bale took an involuntary step backwards. Then he reached across and grabbed a handful of the gypsy's hair. The head lolled loose, as if sprung from its moorings.

'Nah!' Bale let the head drop forward. 'Impossible.'

Bale walked a few steps away, contemplated the corpse for a second and then approached again. He bent forwards and filleted the gypsy's ear with his knife. Then he slid off the blindfold and thumbed back the man's eyelids. The eyes were dull – no spark of life.

Bale cleaned his knife on the blindfold and walked away, shaking his head.

5

–

Captain Joris Calque of the Police Nationale ran the unlit cigarette beneath his nose, then reluctantly replaced it in its gunmetal case. He slid the case into his jacket pocket. 'At least this cadaver's good and fresh. I'm surprised blood isn't still dripping from its ear.' Calque stubbed his thumb against Babel's chest, withdrew it, then craned forwards to monitor for any colour changes. 'Hardly any lividity. This man hasn't been dead for more than an hour. How did we get to him so fast, Macron?'

'Stolen van, Sir. Parked outside. The van owner called it in and a *pandore* on the beat ran across it forty minutes later. I wish all street crime was as easy to detect.'

Calque stripped off his protective gloves. 'I don't understand. Our murderer kidnaps the gypsy from the street, in full public view, and in a stolen van. Then he drives straight here, strings the gypsy up on a bed frame that he has conveniently nailed to the wall before the event, tortures him a little, breaks his neck, and then leaves the van parked out in the street like a signpost. Does that make any sense to you?'

'We also have a blood mismatch.'

'What do you mean?'

'Here. On the victim's hand. These cuts are older than the other wounds. And there is alien blood mixed in with the victim's own. It shows up clearly on the portable spectrometer.'

'Ah. So now, not satisfied with the van signpost, the killer leaves us a blood signpost too.' Calque shrugged. 'The man is either an imbecile or a genius.'

6

—

The pharmacist finished bandaging Sabir's hand. 'It must have been cheap glass – you're lucky not to need any stitches. You're not a pianist, by any chance?'

'No. A writer.'

'Oh. No skills involved, then.'

Sabir burst out laughing. 'You could say that. I've written one book about Nostradamus. And now I write film reviews for a chain of regional newspapers. But that's about it. The sum total of a misspent life.'

The pharmacist snatched a hand to her mouth. 'I'm so sorry. I didn't mean what you think I meant. Of course writers are skilful. I meant digital skills. The sort in which one needs to use one's fingers.'

'It's all right.' Sabir stood up and eased on his jacket. 'We hacks are used to being insulted. We are resolutely bottom of the pecking order. Unless we write bestsellers, that is, or contrive to become celebrities, when we magically spring to the top. Then, when we can't follow up, we sink back down to the bottom again. It's a heady profession, don't you agree?' He disguised his bitterness behind a broad smile. 'How much do I owe you?'

'Fifty euros. If you're sure you can afford it, that is.'

'Ah. *Touché!*' Sabir took out his wallet and riffled through it for notes. Part of him was still struggling to understand the gypsy's actions. Why would a man attack a total stranger? One he was hoping would buy something valuable off him? It made no earthly sense. Something was preventing him from going to the police, however, despite the encouragement of the barman and the three or four customers who had witnessed the attack. There was more to this than met the eye. And who or what were Samois and Chris? He handed the pharmacist her money. 'Does the word Samois mean anything to you?'

'Samois?' The pharmacist shook her head. 'Apart from the place, you mean?'

'The place? What place?'

'Samois-sur-Seine. It's about sixty kilometres south-east of here. Just above Fontainebleau. All the jazz people know it. The gypsies hold a festival there every summer in honour of Django Reinhardt. You know. The Manouche guitarist.'

'Manouche?'

'It's a gypsy tribe. Linked to the Sinti. They come from Germany and northern France. Everybody knows that.'

Sabir gave a mock bow. 'But you forget, Madame. I'm not everybody. I'm only a writer.'

Bale didn't like barmen. They were an obnoxious species, living off the weakness of others. Still. In the interests of information-gathering he was prepared to make allowances. He slipped the stolen ID back inside his pocket. 'So the gypsy attacked him with a glass?'

'Yes. I've never seen anything like it. He just came in, leaking sweat, and made a beeline for the American. Smashed up a glass and ground his hand in it.'

'The American's?'

'No. That was the odd thing. The gypsy ground his own hand in it. Only then did he attack the American.'

'With the glass?'

'No. No. He took the American's hand and did the same thing with it as he'd done with his own. Then he forced the American's hand on to his forehead. Blood all over the place.'

'And that was it?'

'Yes.'

'He didn't say anything?'

'Well, he was shouting all the time. "Remember these words. Remember them."'

'What words?'

'Ah. Well. There you have me. It sounded like Sam, *moi*, *et* Chris. Perhaps they're brothers?'

Bale suppressed a triumphant smile. He nodded his head sagely. 'Brothers. Yes.'

The barman tossed his hands up melodramatically. 'But I've just talked to one of your officers. Told him everything I know. Do you people want me to change your nappies for you as well?'

'And what did this officer look like?'

'Like you all look.' The barman shrugged. 'You know.'

Captain Calque glanced over his shoulder at Lieutenant Macron. 'Like him?'

'No. Nothing like him.'

'Like me, then?'

'No. Not like you.'

Calque sighed. 'Like George Clooney? Woody Allen? Johnny Halliday? Or did he wear a wig, perhaps?'

'No. No. He didn't wear a wig.'

'What else did you tell this invisible man?'

'Now there's no need to be sarcastic. I'm doing my duty as a citizen. I tried to protect the American . . .'

'With what?'

'Well . . . My billiard cue.'

'Where do you keep this offensive weapon?'

'Where do I keep it? Where do you think I keep it? Behind the bar, of course. This is St-Denis, not the Sacré-Coeur.'

'Show me.'

'Look. I didn't hit anybody with it. I only waved it at the gypsy.'

'Did the gypsy wave back?'

'Ah. *Merde*.' The barman slit open a pack of Gitanes

with the bar ice-pick. 'I suppose you'll have me up for smoking in a public place next? You people.' He blew a cloud of smoke across the counter.

Calque relieved the barman of one of his cigarettes. He tapped the cigarette on the back of the packet and ran it languorously beneath his nose.

'Aren't you going to light that?'

'No.'

'*Putain.* Don't tell me you've given up?'

'I have a heart condition. Each cigarette takes a day off my life.'

'Worth it though.'

Calque sighed. 'You're right. Give me a light.'

The barman offered Calque the tip of his cigarette. 'Look. I've remembered now. About your officer.'

'What have you remembered?'

'There was something strange about him. Very strange.'

'And what was that?'

'Well. You won't believe me if I tell you.'

Calque raised an eyebrow. 'Try me.'

The barman shrugged. 'He had no whites to his eyes.'

9

—

'The man's name is Sabir. S.A.B.I.R. Adam Sabir. An American. No. I have no more information for you at this time. Look him up on your computer. That should be quite enough. Believe me.'

Achor Bale put down the telephone. He allowed himself a brief smile. That would sort Sabir. By the time the French police were through with questioning him, he would be long gone. Chaos was always a good idea. Chaos and anarchy. Foment those, and you forced the established forces of law and order on to the back foot.

Police and public administrators were trained to think in a linear fashion – in terms of rules and regulations. In computer terms, hyper was the opposite of linear. Well then. Bale prided himself on his ability to think in a hyper fashion – skipping and jumping around wherever he fancied. He would do whatever he wanted to do, whenever he wanted to do it.

He reached across for a map of France and spread it neatly out on to the table in front of him.

10

—

The first Adam Sabir knew of the Sûreté's interest in him was when he switched on the television set in his rented flat on the Ile St-Louis and saw his own face, full-size, staring back at him from the plasma screen.

As a writer and occasional journalist, Sabir needed to keep up with the news. Stories lurked there. Ideas simmered. The state of the world was reflected in the state of his potential market, and this concerned him. In recent years he had got into the habit of living to a very comfortable standard indeed, thanks to a freak one-off bestseller called *The Private Life of Nostradamus*.

The original content had been just about nil – the title a stroke of genius. Now he desperately needed a follow-up or the money tap would turn off, the luxury lifestyle dry up, and his public melt away.

Samana's advertisement in that ludicrous free rag of a newspaper, two days before, had captured his attention, therefore, because it was so incongruous and so entirely unexpected:

> Money needed. I have something to sell. Notre Dame's [sic] lost verses. All written down. Cash sale to first buyer. Genuine.

Sabir had laughed out loud when he first saw the ad – it had so obviously been dictated by an illiterate. But how would an illiterate know about Nostradamus's lost quatrains?

It was common knowledge that the sixteenth-century seer had written 1,000 indexed four-line verses, published during his lifetime, and anticipating, with an almost preternatural accuracy, the future course of world events. Less well known, however, was the fact that fifty-eight of the quatrains had been held back at the very last moment, never to see the light of day. If an individual could find the location of those verses, they would become an instant millionaire – the potential sales were stratospheric.

Sabir knew that his publisher would have no compunction in anteing up whatever sum was needed to cement such a sale. The story of the find alone would bring in hundreds of thousands of dollars in newspaper revenue, and would guarantee front-page coverage all over the world. And what wouldn't people give, in this uncertain age, to read the verses and understand their revelations? The mind boggled.

Until the events of today, Sabir had happily fantasised a scenario in which his original manuscript, like the *Harry Potter* books before him, would be locked up in the literary equivalent of a Fort Knox, only to be revealed to the impatiently slavering hordes on publication day. He was already in Paris. What would it cost him to check the story out? What did he have to lose?

Following the brutal torture and murder of an unknown male, police are seeking the American writer Adam Sabir, who is wanted for questioning in connection with the crime. Sabir is believed to be visiting Paris, but should under no circumstances be approached by members of the public, as he may be dangerous. The quality of the crime is of so serious a nature that the Police Nationale are making it their priority to identify the murderer, who, it is strongly believed, may be preparing to strike again.

'Oh Jesus.' Sabir stood in the centre of his living room and stared at the television set as if it might suddenly decide to break free from its moorings and crawl across the floor towards him. An old publicity photo of himself was taking up the full extent of the screen, exaggerating every feature of his face until he, too, could almost believe that it depicted a wanted criminal.

A death-mask 'Do You Know this Man?' photograph of Samana followed, its cheek and ear lacerated, its eyes dully opened, as if its owner were sitting in judgement on the millions of couch-potato voyeurs taking fleeting comfort from the fact that it was someone else, and not they, depicted over there on the screen.

'It's not possible. My blood's all over him.'

Sabir sat down in an armchair, his mouth hanging open, the throbbing in his hand uncannily echoing the throbbing of the linking electronic music that was even now accompanying the closing headlines of the evening news.

11
—

It took him ten frenetic minutes to gather all his belongings together – passport, money, maps, clothes, and credit cards. At the very last moment he rifled through the desk in case there was anything in there he might use.

He was borrowing the flat from his English agent, John Tone, who was on holiday in the Caribbean. The car was his agent's, too, and therefore unidentifiable – its very anonymity might at least suffice to get him out of Paris. To buy him time to think.

He hastily pocketed an old British driving licence in Tone's name and some spare euros he found in an empty film canister. No photograph on the driving licence. Might be useful. He took an electricity bill and the car papers, too.

If the police apprehended him he would simply plead ignorance – he was starting on a research trip to St-Rémy-de-Provence, Nostradamus's birthplace. He hadn't listened to the radio or watched the TV – didn't know the police were hunting for him.

With luck he could make it as far as the Swiss

border – bluster his way through. They didn't always check passports there. And Switzerland was still outside the European Union. If he could make it as far as the US Embassy in Bern he would be safe. If the Swiss extradited him to anywhere, it would be to the US, not to Paris.

For Sabir had heard tales about the French police from some of his journalist colleagues. Once you got into their hands, your number was up. It could take months or even years for your case to make its way through the bureaucratic nightmare of the French jurisdictional system.

He stopped at the first hole-in-the-wall he could find and left the car engine running. He'd simply have to take the chance and get some cash. He stuffed the first card through the slit and began to pray. So far so good. He'd try for a thousand euros. Then, if the second card failed him, he could at least pay the motorway tolls in untraceable cash and get himself something to eat.

Across the street, a youth in a hoodie was watching him. Christ Jesus. This was hardly the time to get mugged. And with the keys left in a brand-new Audi station wagon, with the engine running.

He pocketed the cash and tried the second card. The youth was moving towards him now, looking about him in that particular way young criminals had. Fifty metres. Thirty. Sabir punched in the numbers.

The machine ate the card. They were closing him down.

Sabir darted back towards the car. The youth had started running and was about five metres off.

Sabir threw himself inside the car, and only then remembered that it was British made, with the steering wheel placed on the right. He plunged across the central divider and wasted three precious seconds searching around for the unfamiliar central locking system.

The youth had his hand on the door.

Sabir crunched the automatic shift into reverse and the car lurched backwards, throwing the teenager temporarily off balance. Sabir continued backwards up the street, one foot twisted behind him on to the passenger seat, his free hand clutching the steering wheel.

Ironically he found himself thinking not about the mugger – a definite first, in his experience – but about the fact that, thanks to his forcibly abandoned bank card, the police would now have his fingerprints, and a precise location of his whereabouts, at exactly 10.42 p.m., on a clear and starlit Saturday night, in central Paris.

12

Twenty minutes out of Paris, and five minutes shy of the Evry autoroute junction, Sabir's attention was caught by a road sign – thirty kilometres to Fontainebleau. And Fontainebleau was only ten short kilometres downriver from Samois. The pharmacist had told him so. They'd even had a brief, mildly flirtatious discussion about Henri II, Catherine de Medici, and Napoleon, who had apparently used the place to bid farewell to his Old Guard before leaving for exile on Elba.

Better to forget the autoroute and head for Samois. Didn't they have number-plate recognition on the autoroutes? Hadn't he heard that somewhere? What if they had already traced him to Tone's flat? It wouldn't be long before they connected him with Tone's Audi, too. And then they'd have him cold.

If he could only get the quatrains from this Chris person, he might at least be able to persuade the police that he was, indeed, a bona fide writer, and not a psycho on the prowl. And why should the gypsy's death have had anything to do with the verses anyway? Such people were always engaging in feuds, weren't they? It was probably only an argument over money or a woman and he, Sabir, had simply got in the way of it. When you looked at it like that, the whole thing took on a far more benevolent aspect.

Anyway, he had an alibi. The pharmacist would remember him, surely? He'd told her all about the gypsy's behaviour. It simply didn't make sense for him to have tortured and killed the gypsy with his hand torn to shreds like that. The police would see that, wouldn't they? Or would they think he'd followed the gypsy and taken revenge on him after the bar fight?

Sabir shook his head. One thing was for certain. He needed rest. If he carried on like this he would begin to hallucinate.

Forcing himself to stop thinking and to start acting, Sabir slewed the car across the road and down a wood-land track, just two kilometres short of the village of Samois itself.

'He's slipped the net.'

'What do you mean? How do you know that?'

Calque raised an eyebrow. Macron was certainly coming on – no doubt about that. But imagination? Still, what could one expect from a two-metre-tall Marseillais? 'We've checked all the hotels, guest houses and letting agencies. When he arrived here he had no reason to conceal his name. He didn't know he was going to kill the gypsy. This is an American with a French mother, remember. He speaks our language perfectly. Or at least that's what the fool claims on his website. Either he's gone to ground in a friend's house, or he's bolted. My guess is that he's bolted. In my experience it's a rare friend who's prepared to harbour a torturer.'

'And the man who telephoned in his name?'

'Find Sabir and we'll find him.'

'So we stake out Samois? Look for this Chris person?'

Calque smiled. 'Give the girlie a doll.'

The first thing Sabir saw was a solitary deerhound crossing the ride in front of him, lost from the previous day's exercise. Below him, dissected by trees, the River Seine sparkled in the early morning sun.

He climbed out of the car and stretched his legs. Five hours' sleep. Not bad in the circumstances. Last night he'd felt nervous and on edge. Now he felt calmer – less panic-stricken about his predicament. It had been a wise move to take the turning to Samois, and even wiser to pull over into the forest to sleep. Perhaps the French police wouldn't run him to ground so easily after all? Still. Wouldn't do to take unnecessary risks.

Fifty metres down the track, with the car windows open, he picked up woodsmoke and the unmistakable odour of fried pork fat. At first he was tempted to ignore it and continue on his way, but hunger prevailed. Whatever happened, he had to eat. And why not here? No cameras. No cops.

He instantly convinced himself that it would make perfect sense to offer to buy his breakfast direct from whoever happened to be doing the cooking. The mystery campers might even be able to point him towards Chris.

Abandoning the car, Sabir cut through the woods on foot, following his nose. He could feel his stomach expanding towards the smell of the bacon. Crazy to think that he was on the run from the police. Perhaps, being campers, these people wouldn't have had access to a television or a newspaper?

Sabir stood for some time on the edge of the clearing, watching. It was a gypsy camp. Well. He'd lucked into it, really. He should have realised that no one in their right mind would have been camping out in a northern manorial forest in early May. August was the time for camping – otherwise, if you were French, you stayed in a hotel with your family and dined in comfort.

One of the women saw him and called out to her husband. A bunch of children came running towards him and then stopped, in a gaggle. Two other men broke off from what they were doing and started in his direction. Sabir raised a hand in greeting.

The hand was pulled violently from behind him and forced to the rear of his neck. He felt himself being driven down to his knees.

Just before he lost consciousness he noticed the television mast on one of the caravans.

15

'You do it, Yola. It's your right.'

The woman was standing in front of him. An older man placed a knife in her hand and shooed her forward. Sabir tried to say something but he found that his mouth was taped shut.

'That's it. Cut off his balls.' 'No. Do his eyes first.' A chorus of elderly women were encouraging her from their position outside the caravan doorway. Sabir looked around. Apart from the woman with the knife, he was surrounded entirely by men. He tried to move his arms but they were bound tightly behind his back. His ankles were knotted together and a decorated pillow had been placed between his knees.

One of the men upended him and manhandled his trousers over his hips. 'There. Now you can see the target.'

'Stick it up his arse while you're at it.' The old women were pushing forward to get a better view.

Sabir began shaking his head in a futile effort to free the tape from his mouth.

The woman began inching forward, the knife held out in front of her.

'Go on. Do it. Remember what he did to Babel.'

Sabir began a sort of ululation from inside his taped mouth. He fixed his eyes on the woman in fiendish concentration, as if he could somehow will her not to follow through with what she intended.

Another man grabbed Sabir's scrotum and stretched it away from his body, leaving only a thin membrane of skin to be cut. A single blow of the knife would be enough.

Sabir watched the woman. Instinct told him that she was his only chance. If his concentration broke and he looked away, he knew that he was done for. Without fully understanding his own motivation, he winked at her.

The wink hit her like a slap. She reached forward and ripped the tape off Sabir's mouth. 'Why did you do that? Why did you mutilate my brother? What had he done to you?'

Sabir dragged a great gulp of air through his swollen lips. 'Chris. Chris. He told me to ask for Chris.'

The woman stepped backwards. The man holding Sabir's testicles let go of them and leaned across him, his head cocked to one side like a bird dog. 'What's that you say?'

'Your brother smashed a glass. He pressed his hand into it. Then mine. Then he ground our two hands together and placed the imprint of mine on his forehead. He then told me to go to Samois and ask for Chris. I wasn't the one that killed him. But I realise now that he was being followed. Please believe me. Why should I come here otherwise?'

'But the police. They are looking for you. We saw on the television. We recognised your face.'

'My blood was on his hand.'

The man threw Sabir to one side. For a moment Sabir was convinced that they were going to slit his throat. Then he could feel them unbandaging his hand – inspecting the cuts. Hear them talking to each other in a language he could not understand.

'Stand up. Put your trousers on.'

They were cutting the ropes behind his back.

One of the men prodded him. 'Tell me. Who is Chris?'

Sabir shrugged. 'One of you, I suppose.'

Some of the older men laughed.

The man with the knife winked at him, in unconscious echo of the wink that had saved Sabir's testicles two short minutes before. 'Don't worry. You'll meet him soon. With or without your balls. The choice is yours.'

16

At least they're feeding me, thought Sabir. It's harder to kill a man you've broken bread with. Surely.

He spooned up the last of the stew, then reached down with his manacled hands for his coffee. 'The meat. It was good.'

The old woman nodded. She wiped her hands on her voluminous skirts but Sabir noticed that she did not eat. 'Clean. Yes. Very clean.'

'Clean?'

'The spines. Hedgehogs are the cleanest beasts. They are not *mahrimé*. Not like . . .' She spat over her shoulder. 'Dogs.'

'Ah. You eat dogs?' Sabir was already having problems with the thought of hedgehogs. He could feel the onset of nausea threatening.

'No. No.' The woman burst into uproarious laughter. 'Dogs. Hah hah.' She signalled to one of her friends. 'Heh. The *gadje* thinks we eat dogs.'

A man came running into the clearing. He was instantly surrounded by young children. He spoke to a few of them and they peeled off to warn the camp.

Sabir watched intently as boxes and other objects were swiftly secreted beneath and inside the caravans. Two men broke off from what they were doing and came towards him.

'What is it? What's happening?'

They picked him up between them and carried him, splay-legged, towards a wood-box.

'Jesus Christ. You're not going to put me in there?

I'm claustrophobic. Seriously. I promise. I'm not good in narrow places. Please. Put me in one of the caravans.'

The men tumbled him inside the wood-box. One of them drew a stained handkerchief from his pocket and thrust it into Sabir's mouth. Then they eased his head beneath the surface of the box and slammed shut the lid.

17

Captain Calque surveyed the disparate group in front of him. He was going to have trouble with this lot. He just knew it. Knew it in his bones. Gypsies always shut up shop when talking to the police – even when it was one of their own who had been the victim of a crime, as in this case. Still they persisted in wanting to take the law into their own hands.

He nodded to Macron. Macron held up the photograph of Sabir.

'Have any of you seen this man?'

Nothing. Not even a nod of recognition.

'Do any of you know who this man is?'

'A killer.'

Calque shut his eyes. Oh well. At least someone had actually spoken to him. Addressed a comment to him. 'Not necessarily. The more we find out, the more it seems that there may be a second party involved in this crime. A party whom we have not yet succeeded in identifying.'

'When are you going to release my brother's body so that we can bury him?'

The men were making way for a young woman – she manoeuvred herself through the closed ranks of women and children and moved to the forefront of the group.

'Your brother?'

'Babel Samana.'

Calque nodded to Macron, who began writing vigorously in a small black notebook. 'And your name?'

'Yola. Yola Samana.'

'And your parents?'

'They are dead.'

'Any other relatives?'

Yola shrugged, and indicated the surrounding sea of faces.

'Everyone?'

She nodded.

'So what was he doing in Paris?'

She shrugged again.

'Anyone know?'

There was a group shrug.

Calque was briefly tempted to burst out laughing – but the fact that the assembly would probably lynch him if he were to do so, prevented him from giving in to the emotion. 'So can anyone tell me anything at all about Samana? Who he was seeing – apart from this man Sabir, of course. Or why he was visiting St-Denis?'

Silence.

Calque waited. Thirty years of experience had taught him when, and when not, to press an issue.

'When are you giving him back?'

Calque summoned up a fake sigh. 'I can't tell you that exactly. We may need his body for further forensic tests.'

The young woman turned to one of the older male gypsies. 'We must bury him within three days.'

The gypsy hitched his chin at Calque. 'Can we have him?'

'I told you. No. Not yet.'

'Can we have some of his hair then?'

'What?'

'If you give us some of his hair, we can bury him. Along with his possessions. It has to be done within three days. Then you can do what you like with the body.'

'You can't be serious.'

'Will you do as we ask?'

'Give you some of his hair?'

'Yes.'

Calque could feel Macron's eyes boring into the back of his head. 'Yes. We can give you some of his hair. Send one of your people to this address . . .' Calque handed the gypsy a card. 'Tomorrow. Then you can formally identify him, and cut the hair at the same time.'

'I will go.' It was the young woman – Samana's sister.

'Very well.' Calque stood uncertainly in the centre of the clearing. The place was so completely alien to him and to his understanding of what constituted a normal society, that he might as well have been standing in a rainforest discussing ethics with a group of Amerindian tribesman.

'You'll call me if the American, Sabir, tries to make contact with you in any way? My number is written on the card.'

He glanced around at the assembled group.

'I'll take that as a yes, then.'

18

Sabir was close to delirium when they lifted him out of the wood-box. Later, when he tried to reassemble the emotions he had felt upon being forced into the box, he found that his mind had blocked them out entirely. For self-protection, he assumed.

For he hadn't been lying when he said he was claustrophobic. Years before, as a child, some schoolmates had played a prank on him which had involved locking him inside the trunk of a professor's car. He had blacked out then, too. The professor had found him, half dead, three hours later. Made one hell of a stink about it. The story had appeared in all the local newspapers.

Sabir had claimed not to remember who had perpetrated the prank, but almost a decade on he had had his revenge. As a journalist himself he had become possessed of considerable powers of innuendo and he had used these to the full. But the revenge hadn't cured him of his claustrophobia – if anything, in recent years, it had got even worse.

Now he could feel himself sickening. His hand was throbbing and he suspected that he may have picked up an infection during the course of the night. The cuts had reopened, and as he'd had nothing to clean them with before reapplying the bandage, he could only presume that they had attracted a few unwanted bacteria along the way – the incarceration in the wood-box must simply have compounded the issue.

His head lolled backwards. He tried to raise a hand but couldn't – in fact, his entire body seemed beyond his control. He felt himself being carried into a shady place, then up a few stairs and into a room in which light drifted on to his face through coloured panes of glass. His last memories were of a pair of dark brown eyes staring intently into his, as if their owner were trying to plumb the very depths of his soul.

~

He awoke to a deadening headache. The air was stifling, and he found difficulty in breathing, as if his lungs had been three-quarters filled with foam rubber whilst he was sleeping. He looked down at his hand. It had been neatly rebandaged. He tried to raise it but only managed one desultory twitch before allowing it to collapse helplessly back on to the bed.

He realised that he was inside a caravan. Daylight was streaming in through the coloured glass windows beside him. He attempted to raise his head to see out of the single white pane but the effort was beyond him. He collapsed back on to the pillow. He'd never felt so completely out of contact with his body before – it was as if he and his limbs had become disjointed in some way, and the key to their retrieval had been lost.

Well. At least he wasn't dead. Or in a police hospital. One had to look on the bright side.

~

When next he awoke it was night-time. Just before opening his eyes, he became aware of a presence beside him. He pretended to be asleep, and allowed his head to loll to one side. Then he cracked his eyelids and tried to pick up whoever was sitting there in the darkness without her being aware of his look. For it was a woman – of that he was certain. There was the heavy

42

scent of patchouli and some other, more elusive smell, that reminded him vaguely of dough. Perhaps this person had been kneading bread?

He allowed his eyes to open wider. Samana's sister was perched on the chair at his bedside. She was hunched forward, as if in prayer. But there was the glint of a knife in her lap.

'I am wondering whether to kill you.'

Sabir swallowed. He tried to appear calm but he was still having trouble inhaling, and his breath now came out in small, uncomfortable puffs, like a woman in childbirth. 'Are you going to? I wish you'd get on with it then. I'm certainly not able to defend myself – like that time you had me tied up and were going to castrate me. You're just as safe now. I can't even raise my hand to ward you off.'

'Just like my brother.'

'I didn't kill your brother. How many times do I have to tell you? I met him once. He attacked me. God knows why. Then he told me to come here.'

'Why did you wink at me like that?'

'It was the only way I could think of to communicate my innocence to you.'

'But it angered me. I nearly killed you then.'

'I had to risk that. There was no other way.'

She sat back, considering.

'Is it you that's been looking after me?'

'Yes.'

'Funny way to behave to someone you intend to kill.'

'I didn't say I intended to kill you. I said I was thinking about it.'

'What would you do with me? With my body?'

'The men would joint you, like a pig. Then we'd burn you.'

There was an uncomfortable silence. Sabir fell to

wondering how he had managed to get himself into a position like this. And for what? 'How long have I been here?'

'Three days.'

'Jesus.' He reached down and lifted his bad hand with his good. 'What was wrong with me? *Is* wrong with me?'

'Blood poisoning. I treated you with herbs and kaolin poultices. The infection had moved to your lungs. But you'll live.'

'Are you quite sure of that?' Sabir immediately sensed that his effort at sarcasm had entirely passed her by.

'I spoke to the pharmacist.'

'The who?'

'The woman who treated your cuts. The name of where she worked was in the newspaper. I went to Paris to collect some of my brother's hair. Now we are going to bury him.'

'What did the woman say?'

'That you are telling the truth.'

'So who do you think killed your brother.'

'You. Or another man.'

'Still me?'

'The other man, perhaps. But you were part of it.'

'So why don't you kill me now and have done with it? Joint me like a suckling pig?'

'Don't be in such a hurry.' She slipped the knife back underneath her dress. 'You will see.'

19

Later that same night they helped Sabir out of the caravan and into the clearing. A couple of the men had constructed a litter and they lifted him on to it and carried him out into the forest and along a moonlit track.

Samana's sister walked beside him as if she owned him, or had some other vested interest in his presence. Which I suppose she does, thought Sabir to himself. I'm her insurance policy against having to think.

A squirrel ran across the track in front of them and the women began to chatter excitedly amongst themselves.

'What's that all about?'

'A squirrel is a lucky omen.'

'What's a bad one?'

She shot a look at him, then decided that he was not being flippant. 'An owl.' She lowered her voice. 'A snake. The worst is a rat.'

'Why's that?' He found that he was lowering his voice too.

'They are *mahrimé*. Polluted. It is better not to mention them.'

'Ah.'

By this time they had reached another clearing, furnished with candles and flowers.

'So we're burying your brother?'

'Yes.'

'But you haven't got his body? Just his hair?'

'Shh. We no longer talk about him. Or mention his name.'

'What?'

'The close family does not talk of its dead. Only other people do that. For the next month his name will not be mentioned amongst us.'

An old man came up to Yola and presented her with a tray, on which was a wad of banknotes, a comb, a scarf, a small mirror, a shaving kit, a knife, a pack of cards and a syringe. Another man brought food, wrapped up in a waxed paper parcel. Another brought wine, water and green coffee beans.

Two men were digging a small hole near to an oak tree. Yola made the trip to the hole three times, laying one item neatly over another. Some children came up behind her and scattered kernels of corn over the heap. Then the men filled in the grave.

It was at this point that the women began wailing. The back hairs on Sabir's head rose atavistically.

Yola fell to her knees beside her brother's grave and began beating her breast with earth. Some women near her collapsed in jerking convulsions, their eyes turned up into their heads.

Four men, carrying a heavy stone between them, entered the clearing. The stone was placed on top of Samana's grave. Other men then brought his clothes and his remaining possessions. These were heaped on to the stone and set alight.

The wails and lamentations of the women intensified. Some of the men were drinking liquor from small glass bottles. Yola had torn off her blouse. She was striping her breasts and stomach with the earth and wine of her brother's funeral libation.

Sabir felt miraculously disconnected from the realities of the twenty-first century. The scene in the clearing had taken on all the attributes of a demented bacchanal, and the light from the candles and the fires lit up the undersides of the trees, reflecting back off the transported faces below as if in a painting by Ensor.

The man who had presented Sabir's testicles to the knife came over and offered him a drink from a pottery cup. 'Go on. That'll keep the *mulés* away.'

'The *mulés*?'

The man shrugged. 'They're all around the clearing. Evil spirits. Trying to get in. Trying to take . . .' He hesitated. 'You know.'

Sabir swallowed the drink. He could feel the heat of the spirit burning away at his throat. Without knowing why, he found himself nodding. 'I know.'

20

Achor Bale watched the funeral ceremony from the secure position he had established for himself inside the shelter of a small stand of trees. He was wearing a well-worn camouflage suit, a Legionnaire's cloth fatigue hat, and a stippled veil. From even as close as five feet away, he was indistinguishable from the undergrowth surrounding him.

For the first time in three days he was entirely sure of the girl. Before that he hadn't been able to approach close enough to the main camp to achieve a just perspective. Even when the girl had left the camp, he had been unable, to his own entire satisfaction, to pinpoint her. Now she had comprehensively outed herself, thanks to her conspicuous mourning for her lunatic brother's immortal soul.

Bale allowed his mind to wander back to the room

in which Samana had died. In all his extensive years of experience both inside and outside the Foreign Legion, Bale had never seen a man achieve the seemingly impossible task of killing himself whilst under total restraint. That old chestnut of swallowing the tongue presented insurmountable physical difficulties, and no man, as far as he was aware, could *think* himself to death. But to use gravity like that, and with such utter conviction? That took balls. So why would he do it? What had Samana been protecting?

He refocused the night glasses on the girl's face. Wife? No. He thought not. Sister? Possibly. But it was impossible to tell in this light, with the contortions she was engineering on her facial features.

He swung the glasses on to Sabir. Now there was a man who knew how to make himself indispensable. At first, when he had established Sabir's presence as a certainty in the camp, Bale had been tempted to make another of his mischievous telephone calls to the police. Remove the man permanently from the scene without any unnecessary recourse to further violence. But Sabir was so unaware of himself, and therefore such an easy man to follow, that it seemed something of a waste.

The girl, he knew, would be a far harder prospect. She belonged to a defined and close-knit society, which did not easily venture abroad. Lumber her with a well-meaning Sabir and the whole process became intrinsically simpler.

He would watch and wait, therefore. His moment – as it always did – would come.

21

'Can you walk?'

'Yes. I think I can manage.'

'You must come with me, then.'

Sabir allowed Samana's sister to ease him to his feet. He noticed that, although she was prepared to touch him with her hands, she made great play at avoiding any contact with his clothes.

'Why do you do that?'

'Do what?'

'Veer away from me whenever I stumble – as if you're afraid I might be diseased.'

'I don't want to pollute you.'

'Pollute *me*?'

She nodded her head. 'Gypsy women don't touch men who are not their husbands, brothers, or sons.'

'Why ever not?'

'Because there are times when we are *mahrimé*. Until I become a mother – and also at certain times of the month – I am unclean. I would dirty you.'

Shaking his head, Sabir allowed her to usher him towards the caravan entrance. 'Is that why you always walk behind me, too?'

She nodded.

By this time Sabir was almost grateful for the perverse and mysterious attentions of the camp, for they had not only secured him from the notice of the French police and cured him of an illness which, on the run, may well have resulted in his death from septic shock – but they had also comprehensively upended his notions of sensible, rational behaviour. Everybody needed a stint in a gypsy camp, Sabir told himself wryly, to shake them out of their bourgeois complacency.

He had resigned himself, in consequence, to only eventually learning what they required from him, when and where it suited them to enlighten him. And he sensed, as he supported himself down the rootstock balustrade outside the caravan, that this moment had finally come.

～

Yola indicated that Sabir should accompany her towards a group of men seated on stools near the periphery of the camp. An enormously fat man with an outsized head, long black hair, copious moustaches, gold-capped front teeth and a ring on every finger, sat, in a much larger chair than everybody else's, at the head of the convocation. He was wearing a generously cut, traditionally styled double-breasted suit, made notable only by an outlandish sequence of purple and green stripes laced into the fabric and by double-width zoot-suit lapels.

'Who the heck's that?'

'The Bulibasha. He is our leader. Today he is to be Kristinori.'

'Yola, for Christ's sake . . .'

She stopped, still positioned just behind him and to the right. 'The Chris you were searching for? That my brother spoke to you about? This is it.'

'What? That's Chris? The fat guy? The Chief?'

'No. We hold a Kriss when something important must be decided. Notice is given, and everyone attends from many kilometres around. Someone is elected Kristinori, or judge of the Kriss. In important cases, it is the Bulibasha who takes this role. Then there are two other judges – one for the side of the accuser, and one for the person who is accused – chosen from amongst the *phuro* and the *phuro-dai*. The elders.'

'And this is an important case?'

'Important? It is life or death for you.'

22

Sabir found himself ushered, with a certain amount of formal politeness, on to a bench set into the earth in front of, and below, the Bulibasha. Yola settled on the ground behind him, her legs drawn up beneath her. Sabir assumed that she had been allocated this spot in order to translate the proceedings to him, for she was the only woman in the assembly.

The main body of women and children were congregated behind and to the right of the Bulibasha, in the position Yola always took in relation to him. Sabir noticed, too, that the women were all wearing their best clothes, and that the older, married women were sporting headscarves and prodigious amounts of gold jewellery. Unusually, they were made up with heavy kohl around the eyes, and their hair, beneath their scarves, no longer hung free, but was instead put up in ringlets and elaborate braids. Some had henna on their hands, and a few of the grandmothers were smoking.

The Bulibasha held up a hand for silence, but everybody continued talking. It seemed that the debate about Sabir was already well under way.

Impatiently, the Bulibasha indicated that the man who had stretched Sabir's testicles for the knife should come forward.

'That is my cousin. He is going to speak against you.'

'Oh.'

'He likes you. It is not personal. But he must do this for the family.'

'I suppose they're going to joint me like a pig if this thing goes against me?' Sabir tried to sound as though he was joking, but his voice cracked halfway through and gave him away.

'They will kill you, yes.'

'And the upside?'

'What is that?'

'What happens if things go my way?' Sabir was sweating badly now.

'Then you will become my brother. You will be responsible for me. For my virginity. For my marriage. You will take my brother's place in everything.'

'I don't understand.'

Yola sighed impatiently. She lowered her voice to a harsh whisper. 'The only reason you are still alive today is that my brother made you his *phral*. His blood brother. He also told you to come back here amongst us and ask for a Kriss. You did this. We then had no choice but to honour his dying wish. For what a dying man asks for, he must get. And my brother knew that he would die when he did this thing to you.'

'How can you possibly know that?'

'He hated *payos* – Frenchmen – more even than he detested *gadjes*. He would never have asked one to be a brother to him except in the most extreme of circumstances.'

'But I'm not a *payo*. Okay, my mother's French, but

my father's American and I was born and brought up in the United States.'

'But you speak perfect French. My brother would have judged you on that.'

Sabir shook his head in bewilderment.

Yola's cousin was now addressing the assembly. But even with his fluent command of French, Sabir was having difficulty making out what was being said.

'What language is that?'

'Sinto.'

'Great. Could you please tell me what he is saying?'

'That you killed my brother. That you have come amongst us to steal something that belongs to our family. That you are an evil man, and that God visited this recent illness on you to prove that you are not telling the truth about what happened to Babel. He also says that it is because of you that the police have come amongst us, and that you are a disciple of the Devil.'

'And you say he *likes* me?'

Yola nodded. 'Alexi thinks you are telling the truth. He looked into your eyes when you thought that you were about to die, and he saw your soul. It seemed white to him, not black.'

'Then why is he saying all this stuff about me?'

'You should be pleased. He is exaggerating terribly. Many of us here feel that you did not kill my brother. They will hope that the Bulibasha gets angry with what is being said, and pronounces you innocent.'

'And do you think I killed your brother?'

'I will only know this when the Bulibasha gives his verdict.'

23

Sabir tried to look away from what was happening in front of him, but couldn't. Yola's cousin Alexi was giving a masterclass in applied histrionics. If this was someone secretly on his side, then Sabir decided that he would rather sup with the Devil and have done with it.

Alexi was on his knees in front of the assembled judges, weeping and tearing at his hair. His face and body were covered with dirt, and his shirt was torn open, revealing three gold necklaces and a crucifix.

Sabir glanced at the Bulibasha's face for any signs that he was becoming impatient with Alexi's dramatics, but, to all intents and purposes, he seemed to be drinking the stuff in. One of the younger children, whom Sabir assumed must be one of the Bulibasha's daughters, had even crept on to his capacious lap and was bouncing up and down in her excitement.

'Do I get to say my piece?'

'No.'

'What do you mean?'

'Someone else will talk for you.'

'Who, for Christ's sake? Everybody here seems to want me killed.'

'Me. I will speak for you.'

'Why would you do that?'

'I have told you. It was my brother's dying wish.'

Sabir realised that Yola didn't want to be drawn any further. 'What's happening now?'

'The Bulibasha is asking whether my brother's family would be happy if you paid them gold for his life.'

'And what are they saying?'

'No. They want to cut your throat.'

Sabir allowed his mind to wander briefly into a fantasy of escape. With everybody concentrating on Alexi, he might at least manage a five-yard head start before they brought him down at the edge of the camp. Action, not reaction – wasn't that how they trained soldiers to respond to an ambush?

Alexi got up off the ground, shook himself, and walked past Sabir, grinning. He even winked.

'He seems to think he put that over rather well.'

'Do not joke. The Bulibasha is talking to the other judges. Asking their opinion. At this stage it is important how he begins to think.' She stood up. 'Now I shall speak for you.'

'You're not going to do all that breast-beating stuff?'

'I don't know what I shall do. It will come to me.'

Sabir dropped his head on to his knees. Part of him still refused to believe that anyone was taking this seriously. Perhaps it was all some gigantic joke perpetrated on him by a tontine of disgruntled readers?

He looked up when he heard Yola's voice. She was dressed in a green silk blouse buttoned to one side across her chest, and her heavy red cotton dress reached down to just above her ankles, interleaved with numerous petticoats. She wore no jewellery as an unmarried woman, and her uncovered hair was bunched in ringlets over her ears, with ribbons alongside, and sewn into, the chignon at the back of her head. Sabir underwent a strange emotion as he watched her – as if he was indeed related to her in her some way, and this intense recognition was in some sense relevant in a manner beyond his understanding.

She turned to him and pointed. Then she pointed down to her hand. She was asking the Bulibasha something and the Bulibasha was answering.

Sabir glanced around at the two surrounding groups. The women were all intent on the Bulibasha's words, but some of the men in Alexi's group were watching him intently, although seemingly without malevolence – almost as though he were a puzzle they were being forced to confront against their wills, something curious that had been imposed on them from the outside, and which they were nevertheless forced to factor in to whatever equation was ruling their lives.

Two of the men helped raise the Bulibasha to his feet. One of them passed him a bottle and he drank from it, and then sprinkled some of the liquid in an arc out in front of him.

Yola came back to Sabir's side and helped him rise to his feet.

'Don't tell me. It's verdict time.'

She paid him no mind, but stood, a little back from him, watching the Bulibasha.

'You. *Payo*. You say you did not kill Babel?'

'That is correct.'

'And yet the police are hunting for you. How can they be wrong?'

'They found my blood on Babel, for reasons that I have already explained to you. The man who tortured and killed him must have told them about me, for Babel knew my name. I am innocent of any crime against him and his family.'

He turned to Alexi. 'You believe this man killed your cousin?'

'Until another man confesses to the crime, yes. Kill him and the blood score will be settled.'

'But Yola has no brother now. Her father and mother are dead. She says that this man is Babel's *phral*. That he will take Babel's place. She is unmarried. It is important that she has a brother to protect her. To ensure that no one shames her.'

'That is true.'

'Do you all agree to abide by the Kristinori's rule?'

There was a communal affirmative from around the camp.

'Then we will leave it to the knife to decide in this vendetta.'

21

'Jesus. They don't want me to fight somebody?'

'No.'

'Then what the hell do they want?'

'The Bulibasha has been very wise. He has decided that the knife will decide in this case. A wooden board will be set-up. You will lay the hand that you killed Babel with on to it. Alexi will represent my family. He will take a knife and throw it at your hand. If the blade, or any other part of the knife, strikes your hand, it will mean that O Del says you are guilty. Then you will be killed. If the knife misses you, you are innocent. You will then become my brother.'

'O Del?'

'That is our name for God.'

~

Sabir stood near the Bulibasha and watched as two of

the men erected the board that was going to decide his life or death. You couldn't make it up, he thought to himself. No one in their right minds would believe this. Not in the twenty-first century.

Yola handed him a glass of herb tea.

'What's this for?'

'To give you courage.'

'What's in it?'

'A secret.'

Sabir sipped the tea. 'Look. This guy Alexi. Your cousin. Is he any good with knives?'

'Oh yes. He can hit anything he aims at. He is very good.'

'Christ, Yola. What are you trying to do to me? Do you want me to be killed?'

'I don't want anything. O Del will decide on your guilt. If you are innocent, he will spoil Alexi's aim, and you will go free. Then you will become my brother.'

'And you really believe that they will kill me if the knife strikes my hand?'

'Without a doubt they will kill you. It must be that way. The Bulibasha would never allow you to go free after a Kriss has decided that you are guilty. That would go against our custom – our *mageripen* code. It would be a scandal. His name would become *mahrimé*, and he would be forced to go in front of the Baro-Sero to explain himself.'

'The Baro-Sero?'

'The chief of all the gypsies.'

'And where does he hang out?'

'In Poland, I think. Or perhaps it is Romania.'

'Oh Christ.'

~

'What happens if he misses my hand and gets *me*?' Sabir was standing in front of the board. Two of the gypsies were attaching his hand to the board with a thin leather strap which passed through two holes in the wood, above and below his wrist.

'That means O Del has taken the decision away from us, and has punished you Himself.'

'I knew it.' Sabir shook his head. 'Can I at least stand at an angle?'

'No. You must stand straight on, like a man. You must pretend that you don't care what is happening. If you are innocent, you have nothing to fear. Gypsies like men who behave like men.'

'I can't tell you how encouraging that is.'

'No. You must listen to me. It is important.' She stood in front of him, her eyes locked on to his. 'If you survive this, you will become my brother. I will take your name until I take my husband's. You will have a *kirvo* and a *kirvi* from amongst the elders, who will be your godparents. You will become one of us. For this, you must behave like us. If you behave like a *payo*, no one will respect you and I will never find a husband. Never be a mother. What you do now – how you behave – will show to my family how you will be for me. Whether the *ursitory* allowed my brother to choose wisely, or like a fool.'

~

Alexi upended the bottle into Sabir's mouth, then finished it himself. 'I like you, *payo*. I hope the knife misses. I really do.'

Achor Bale grinned. He lay in a sand scrape he had dug for himself, on a small rise about fifty feet above the clearing. The scrape was well concealed from marauding children by a gorse bush, and Bale was covered by a camouflage blanket interleaved with bracken, twigs and other small branches.

He adjusted the electronic zoom on his binoculars and focused them on Sabir's face. The man was rigid with fear. That was good. If Sabir was to survive, this fear of his would stand Bale in good stead in his search for the manuscript. He could use it. Such a man was manipulable.

The girl, on the other hand, was more of a problem. She came from a defined culture, with defined mores. Just like her brother. There would be parameters. Lines she would not cross. She would die before telling him of certain things she considered more important than her life. He would have to approach her in other ways. Through her virginity. Through her desire to be a mother. Bale knew that the Manouche gypsies defined a woman solely through her ability to have children. Take this away and the woman had no centre. No meaning. It was something he would bear in mind.

Now the girl's cousin was walking away from Sabir, the knife in his hand. Bale adjusted the binoculars again. Not a throwing knife. That was bad. The weight would be difficult to gauge. No balance. Too much drift.

Ten yards. Fifteen. Bale sucked at his teeth. Fifteen yards. Forty-five feet. A crazy distance. It would be hard even for him to hit a defined target at such a divide. But perhaps the gypsy was better than he suspected. The man had a smile on his face, as if he felt confident about his abilities.

Bale swung the binoculars back towards Sabir. Well. At least the American was putting on a good front for a change. He was standing straight up and facing the knife-thrower. The girl was standing over to the side, watching him. They were all watching him.

Bale saw the gypsy draw back his hand for the throw.

It was a heavy knife. It would need some power to take it that distance.

Alexi swung forward, driving the knife in a long, looping arc towards Sabir. There was a communal gasp from the onlookers. Bale's tongue darted out from between his teeth in concentration.

The knife struck the board just above Sabir's hand. Had it touched? The blade was curved. There couldn't be much in it.

The Bulibasha and a few of his minions were moving at a leisurely pace towards the board to inspect the position of the knife. All the gypsies were converging on the Bulibasha. Would they kill Sabir straight off? Make it a communal effort?

The Bulibasha pulled out the knife. He flourished it three times around his head, then reached towards Sabir's arm and cut through the leather straps. Then he threw the knife away from him disdainfully.

'Oh, what a lucky boy,' said Bale under his breath. 'Oh what a lucky, lucky boy.'

25

—

'The police are watching you.'

Sabir raised his head from the pillow. It was Alexi. It was obvious, however, that if Sabir expected any mention of – or even an apology for – that morning's proceedings, he would have to wait a very long time indeed.

'What do you mean, watching me?'

'Come.'

Sabir rose and followed Alexi out of the caravan. Two children, a boy and a girl, were waiting outside, their faces tense with suppressed excitement.

'These are your cousins, Bera and Koiné. They have something to show you.'

'My cousins?'

'You are our brother now. These are your cousins.'

Sabir wondered for a moment whether Alexi was having him on. By the time he had gathered his wits together and had realised that no sarcasm was intended, it was too late to offer to shake hands with his new family, for the children had gone.

Alexi had already started walking towards the periphery of the camp. Sabir hurried to catch up with him.

'How do you know it's the police?'

'Who else would be watching you?'

'Who else indeed?'

Alexi stopped in his tracks. Sabir watched as his face gradually changed expression.

'Look, Alexi. Why would the police bother to keep me under observation? If they knew I was here they would simply come in and pick me up. I am wanted for murder, don't forget. I can't see the Sûreté playing a waiting game with me.'

They had reached the ridge behind the camp. The children were pointing towards a gorse bush.

Alexi ducked down and wriggled his way underneath the bush. 'Now. Can you see me?'

'No.'

'You come and do it.'

Alexi made way for Sabir, who eased himself beneath the thorns. Straight away he encountered an indentation which allowed him to slide down underneath the bush, and emerge, head forwards, the other side.

Sabir instantly saw what Alexi was getting at. The entire camp was within his line of vision but it was a virtual impossibility for anyone inside the camp to see him in turn. He backed awkwardly out of the den.

'The children. They were playing *panschbara*. That's when you draw a grid in the sand with a stick and then throw a bicycle chain into it. Bera threw the chain too far. When he ducked down to collect it, he found this place. You can see that it is freshly made – not a blade of grass to be seen.'

'You understand now why I don't think it's the police.' Sabir found himself trying to weigh Alexi up. Estimate his intelligence. Judge whether he might be of use in what lay ahead.

Alexi nodded. 'Yes. Why would they wait? You are right. They want you too badly for that.'

'I must talk to Yola. I think she has some explaining to do.'

26

—

'Babel was a drug addict. Crack cocaine. Some of his Parisian friends thought it would be amusing to make an addict of a gypsy. Our people rarely touch drugs. We have other vices.'

'I don't see what that has to do . . .'

Yola placed her fist against her chest. 'Listen to me.

Babel also played cards. Poker. High stakes. Gypsies are crazy for card games. He couldn't leave them alone. Any money he got, he would go straight to Clignancourt and gamble it away with the Arabs. I don't know how much he lost. But he didn't look good, these last weeks. We thought he was sure to end up in jail, or badly beaten up. When we heard about his death, it seemed at first that the gambling must have been the cause. That he owed money, and that the *maghrébins* had gone too far in punishing him. Then we heard about you.' She transformed her fist into an out-turned palm.

'Did he really have anything to sell? When he wrote that ad?'

Yola bit her lip. Sabir could tell that she was struggling internally with a problem only she could resolve.

'I'm your brother now. Or so I'm told. Which means that I will act in your interests from now on. It also means that I promise not to take advantage of anything you tell me.'

Yola returned his gaze. But her eyes were nervous, darting here and there across his face – not settling on any particular feature.

Sabir suddenly realised what her brother's betrayal and death might really mean to her. Through no fault of her own, Yola now found herself locked into a relationship with a total stranger – a relationship formalised by the laws and customs of her own people so that she might not, of her own volition, easily end it. What if this new brother of hers was a crook? A sexual predator? A confidence trickster? She would have little recourse to any but partial justice.

'Come with me into my mother's caravan. Alexi will accompany us. I have a story to tell you both.'

—

27

Yola indicated that Sabir and Alexi should sit on the bed above her. She took her place on the floor, her legs drawn up, her back against a brightly painted chest.

'Listen. Many, many families ago, one of my mothers made friends with a *gadje* girl from the neighbouring town. At this time we came from the south, near Salon-de-Provence . . .'

'*One* of your mothers?'

'The mother of her mother's mother, but many times over.' Alexi scowled at Sabir as though he were being forced to explain milking to a dairymaid.

'Just how long ago would this have been?'

'As I said. Many families.'

Sabir was fast realising that he was not going to get anywhere by being too literal. He would simply have to suspend the rational, pedantic side of his nature, and go with the swing. 'I'm sorry. Continue.'

'This girl's name was Madeleine.'

'Madeleine?'

'Yes. This was at the time of the Catholic purges, when gypsies had the privileges we used to enjoy – of free movement and help from the *châtelain* – taken away from us.'

'Catholic purges?' Sabir struck himself a glancing blow on the temple. 'I'm sorry. But I can't seem to get my head around this. Are we talking about the Second World War here? Or the French Revolution? The Catholic Inquisition, maybe? Or something a little more recent?'

'The Inquisition. Yes. That is what my mother called it.'

'The Inquisition? But that happened five hundred years ago.'

'Five hundred years ago. Many families. Yes.'

'Are you serious about this? You're telling me a story that occurred five hundred years ago?'

'Why is that strange? We have many stories. Gypsies don't write things down – they tell. And these tales are passed down. My mother told me, just as her mother told her, and just as I shall tell my daughter. For this is a woman's tale. I am only telling you this because you are my brother, and because I think my brother's death was caused by his curiosity in this matter. As his *phral*, you must now avenge him.'

'*I* must avenge him?'

'Did you not understand? Alexi and the other men will help you. But you must find the man who killed your *phral* and kill him in turn. It is for this reason that I am telling you of our secret. Our mother would have wanted it.'

'But I can't go around killing people.'

'Not even to protect me?'

'I don't understand. This is all going too fast.'

'I have something this man wants. This man who killed Babel. And now he knows I have it, because you brought him here. Alexi has told me of the hiding place on the hill. While I am here, in the camp, I am safe. The men are protecting me. They are on the lookout. But one day he will get through and take me. Then he will do to me what he tried to do to Babel. You are my brother. You must stop him.'

Alexi was nodding, too, as if what Yola said was perfectly normal – a perfectly rational way of behaving.

'But what is it? What do you have that this man wants?'

Without answering, Yola rocked forwards on to her knees. She opened a small drawer concealed beneath the bed and drew out a broad red leather woman's belt. With a seamstress's deft touch she began to unpick the stitching from the belt with a small penknife.

28

Sabir held the manuscript on his knee. 'This is it?'

'Yes. This is what Madeleine gave one of my mothers.'

'You're sure this girl was called Madeleine?'

'Yes. She said her father had requested her to give it to the wife of the chief of the gypsies. That if the papers fell into the wrong hands it might possibly mean the destruction of our race. But that we should not physically destroy the papers but hide them, as they were subject to the Will of God and held other secrets that may one day become important too. That her father had left this and some other papers to her in his Testament. In a sealed box.'

'But this *is* the Testament. This is a copy of Michel Nostradamus's Will. Look here. It is dated the 17th of June 1566. Fifteen days before his death. And with a codicil dated the 30th of June, just two days before. Yola, do you know who Nostradamus was?'

'A prophet. Yes.'

'No. Not exactly a prophet – Nostradamus would have rejected that name. He was a scryer, rather. A seer. A man who – and only with God's permission, of course – could sometimes see into the future and anticipate future events. The most famous and the most successful seer in history. I've spent a long time studying him. It's why I allowed myself to be tempted by your brother's advertisement.'

'Then you will be able to tell me why this man wants what you have in your hand. What secrets the paper contains. Why he will kill for it. For I cannot possibly understand it.'

Sabir threw up his hands. 'I don't think it does contain any secrets. It's already well known about, and in the public domain – you can even find it on the internet, for Christ's sake. I know of at least two other original copies in private hands – it's worth a little money, sure, but hardly enough to kill for. It's just a Will like any other.' He frowned. 'But one thing in it does bear upon what you are telling me. Nostradamus did have a daughter called Madeleine. She was fifteen when he died. Listen to this. It is part of the codicil – that's a piece of writing added after the actual Will has been written and witnessed, but equally binding on any heirs.

'Et aussy a légué et lègue à Damoyselle Magdeleine de Nostradamus sa fille légitime et naturelle, outre ce que luy a esté légué par sondt testament, savoir est deux coffres de bois noyer estant dans Vestude dudt codicillant, ensemble les habillements, bagues, et joyaux que lade Damoyselle Magdeleine aura dans lesdts coffres, sans que nul puisse voir ny regarder ce que sera dans yceux; ains dudt légat l'en a fait maistresse incontinent après le décès dudt collicitant; lequel légat lade Damoyselle pourra prendre de son autorité, sans qu'elle soit tenue de les prendre par main d'autruy ny consentement d'aucuns . . .'

'And he also bequeaths and has bequeathed to Mademoiselle Madeleine Nostradamus, his legitimate and natural daughter, in addition to that which he bequeathed her in his Will, two coffers made of walnut wood which are at present in the testator's study, together with the clothes, rings, and jewels she shall find in those coffers, on the strict understanding that no one save her may look at or see those things which he has placed inside the coffers; thus, according to this legacy, she has been made mistress of the coffers and their contents after the death of the legator; let this testamentary commission represent all the authority the said Mademoiselle may need so that no one may impede her physically, nor withhold their consent morally, to her taking charge of the legacy forthwith . . .'

'I don't understand.'

'It's simple. You see, in his original Will, of which this forms part, Nostradamus left his eldest daughter, Madeleine, 600 crowns, to be paid to her on the day that she married, with 500 crown-pistolets each to be paid to his two youngest daughters, Anne and Diana, on a similar occasion, also as dowries. Then he suddenly changes his mind, two days before his death and decides to leave Madeleine a little something extra.' Sabir tapped the paper in front of him. 'But he wants no one else to see what he is leaving her, so he has it sealed inside two coffers, just as it says here. But to allay any jealous suspicions that he is leaving her extra money, he constructs a list of what she might hope to find there. Jewels, clothes, rings, and whatnot. But that doesn't make any sense, does it? If he's leaving her family heirlooms, why hide them? She's his eldest daughter – according to medieval custom, she's entitled to them. And if they once belonged to his mother, everybody would know about them already, wouldn't they? No. He is leaving her something else. Something secret.' Sabir shook his head. 'You've not told me everything, have you? Your brother understood enough about what Nostradamus had indirectly left your ancestors to mention "lost verses" in his ad. "All written down". Those were his words. So where are they written down?'

'My brother was a fool. It pains me to say it, but he was not in his senses. The drugs changed him.'

'Yola, you're not being straight with me.'

Alexi reached down and prodded her with his finger. 'Go on. You must tell him, *luludji*. He is head of your family now. You owe him a duty. Remember what the Bulibasha said.'

Sabir sensed that Yola could still not find it in herself to trust him. 'Would it help if I gave myself up to the police? If I play it right, I might even be able to convince them to switch their attentions from me to the man who really killed your brother. That way you'd be safe.'

Yola pretended to spit. 'You really think they would do that? Once they have you in their hands they will let you dig your own grave with the key to your cell, and then they will shit inside the hole. When you give yourself up, they will throw us to the winds, just as they would like to do now. Babel was a gypsy. The *payos* don't care about him. They never have. Look what they did to us in the *gherman* war. Before it even began, they hurried to intern us. At Montreuil and Bellay. Like cattle. Then they allowed the *ghermans* to slaughter one finger in three of our people in France. One madman makes many madmen, and many madmen makes madness. That's what our people say.' She clapped her hands together above her head. 'There is no gypsy – none – Manouche, Rom, Gitan, Piemontesi, Sinti, Kalderash, Valsikané – still living, who did not have part of his family massacred. In my mother's time, every gypsy more than thirteen years old was forced to carry a *carnet anthropométrique d'identité*. And do you know what they put on this card? Height, breadth, skin pigmentation, age, and the length of the nose and right ear. They treated us like animals being stamped, registered, and sent to the slaughterhouse. Two photos. The prints from five separate fingers. All to be checked when we arrived or left from any commune. They called us Bohémiens and Romanichels – insulting names to us. This only stopped in 1969. And you wonder why three-quarters of us, like my brother, can neither read nor write?'

Sabir felt as if he'd been run over by a herd of stampeding buffaloes. The bitterness in Yola's voice was uncomfortably raw – unnervingly real. 'But you can. You can read. And Alexi.'

Alexi shook his head. 'I left school at six. I didn't like it. Who needs to read? I can talk, can't I?'

Yola stood up. 'You say these two coffers were made of walnut wood?'

'Yes.'

'And that you are now my *phral*? That you willingly accept this responsibility?'

'Yes.'

She pointed to the brightly painted chest behind her. 'Well, here is one of the coffers. Prove it to me.'

29

'It's the car, all right.' Captain Calque let the tarpaulin fall back over the number-plate.

'Shall we have it taken in?' Macron was already unsheathing his cellphone.

Calque winced. 'Macron. Macron. Macron. Think of it this way. The gypsies have either killed Sabir, in which case bits of him are probably scattered throughout seven *départements* by now, slowly investing the local flora and fauna. Or, more likely, he has been able to convince them of his innocence and that is the reason why they are hiding his car for him, and have not already repainted it and sold it on to the Russians. We would do better, would we not – as spying on the main camp does not seem to be a practical option – to stake it out, and wait for him to return and claim it. Or do you still think we should call for the breakers to come with their winches, their sirens, and their loudhailers, and have it, as you say, "taken in?"'

'No, Sir.'

'Tell me, lad. What part of Marseille are you from?'

Macron sighed. 'La Canebière.'

'I thought that was a road.'

'It is a road, Sir. But it is also a place.'

'Do you want to go back there?'

'No, Sir.'

'Then get on to Paris and order a tracking device. When you have the tracking device, conceal it somewhere inside the car. Then test it at five hundred metres, a thousand metres, and fifteen hundred metres. And Macron?'

'Yes, Sir?'

Calque shook his head. 'Nothing.'

30

Achor Bale was profoundly, systematically, indisputably, bored. He had had enough of surveillance, spying, lying in thickets and skulking under gorse bushes. For a few days it had been amusing, watching the gypsies going about their daily business. Dissecting the stupidity of a culture that had refused to keep pace with the rest of the twenty-first century. Watching the absurd behaviour of these ant-like creatures as they argued, cheated, fondled, shouted, swindled, and duped each other in a failed attempt to make up for the dud hand that society had dealt them.

What did the fools expect, when the Catholic Church still blamed them for forging the nails which pierced Jesus's hands and feet? According to Bale's reading of the story, two blacksmiths, pre-Crucifixion, had refused to do the Romans' dirty work for them, and had been killed for their trouble. The third smith the Romans approached had been a gypsy. This gypsy had just finished forging three large nails. 'Here's twenty denarii,' the drunken legionnaires had told him. 'Five each for the first three, and five more for the fourth that you will make for us while we wait.'

The gypsy agreed to complete the work while the legionnaires enjoyed a few more tumblers of wine. But the moment he started forging the fourth nail, the ghosts of the two murdered smiths appeared in the clearing and warned him not, under any circumstances, to work for the Romans, as they were intending to crucify a just man. The soldiers, terrified by the apparition, bolted, without waiting for their fourth nail.

But the story didn't end there. For this gypsy was a sedulous man, and figuring that he had already been well paid for his work, he set to once more, ignoring the warnings of the two dead smiths. When he eventually completed the fourth nail, and while it was still red hot, he plunged it into a bath of cooling water – but no matter how many times he did this, or from what depth he drew the water, the nail still remained close to molten. Appalled by the implications of what he had done, the gypsy gathered up his belongings and made off.

For three days and three nights he ran, until he arrived in a whited city where nobody knew him. Here he set to work for a rich man. But the first time he laid hammer to iron, a terrible cry escaped from his lips. For there, on the anvil, lay the red-hot nail – the missing fourth nail of Christ's Crucifixion. And each time he set to work – either in a different manner or in a different place – the same thing happened, until nowhere in the world was safe from the accusing vision of the red-hot nail.

And that, at least according to Romany lore, explains why gypsies are doomed to wander the earth for ever, searching for a safe place in which to set-up their forges.

'Idiots,' said Bale, under his breath. 'They should have killed the Romans and blamed it on the families of the dead smiths.'

He had already identified the two men guarding the camp. One of them was slumped under a tree, smoking, and the other was asleep. What were these people thinking of? He would have to chivvy them up. Once

Sabir and the girl were forced out on to the road, they would be that much easier to pick off.

Smiling to himself, Bale unzipped the flat leather case he had been carrying in the poacher's pocket of his waxed Barbour coat and eased out the Ruger Redhawk. The double-action revolver was made from satinised stainless steel, with a rosewood grip. It sported a seven-and-a half-inch barrel, a six-round, Magnum-filled magazine, and telescopic sights, zeroed-in for eighty feet. Thirteen inches in length, it was Bale's favourite hunting gun, with enough power to stop an elk. Recently, at the firing range in Paris, he had achieved a consistent series of three-inch groupings at ninety-six feet. Now that he had live bait to fire at, he wondered if it were possible to remain quite so accurate?

His first slug hit two inches below the heel of the sleeping gypsy. The man jerked awake, his body inadvertently taking the form of a set square. Bale aimed his second slug at the exact place the man's head had been resting two seconds before.

Then he turned his attention to the second gypsy. His first slug took out the man's cigarette tin, and the second, part of a tree branch just above his head.

By this time the two men were running back towards the camp, screaming. Bale missed the television aerial with his first bullet but broke it in two with his second. As he was shooting, Bale was also keeping a weather eye on the door of the caravan through which Sabir, the girl and the knife-wielding man had disappeared some twenty minutes earlier. But no one emerged.

'Well that's it. Just one magazine today.'

Bale reloaded the Ruger and slipped it back inside its case, and the case back into the poacher's pocket sewn into the seat of his coat.

Then he headed down the hill towards his car.

31

'Is that a car approaching?' Alexi had his head cocked to one side. 'Or did the Devil sneeze?' He stood up, a quizzical expression on his face, and made as if to go outside.

'No. Wait.' Sabir held up a warning hand.

There was a second loud report from the far side of the camp. Then a third. Then a fourth.

'Yola, get down on the floor. You too, Alexi. Those are gunshots.' He screwed up his face, evaluating the echo. 'From this distance it sounds like a hunting rifle. Which means a stray bullet could puncture these walls with ease.'

A fifth shot ricocheted off the caravan roof.

Sabir eased himself towards the window. In the camp, people were running in every direction, screaming, or calling for their loved ones.

A sixth shot rang out, and something thumped on to the roof, then skittered loudly down the outside of the caravan.

'That was the television aerial. I think this guy's got a sense of humour. He's not shooting to kill, anyhow.'

'Adam. Please get down.' It was the first time Yola had used his name.

Sabir turned towards her, smiling. 'It's all right. He's only trying to smoke us out. We're safe if we stay inside. I've been expecting something like this to happen ever since Alexi showed me his hiding place. Now that he can't spy on us any more, it's logical that he should want to drive us out in the open, where he can pick us off at his leisure. But we'll only go when we're good and ready.'

'Go? Why should we go?'

'Because otherwise he'll end up by killing somebody.' Sabir pulled the chest towards him. 'Remember what he did to Babel? This guy isn't a moralist. He wants what he thinks we have in this chest. If he finds we have nothing, he will become very angry indeed. In fact I don't think he would believe us.'

'Why weren't you scared when the firing started?'

'Because I spent five years as a volunteer with the 182nd Infantry Regiment of the Massachusetts Army National Guard.' Sabir put on a hick country-boy accent. 'I'm very proud to tell you, ma'am, that the 182nd were first mustered just seventy years after Nostradamus's death. I'm a Stockbridge Massachusetts boy myself – born and bred.'

Yola looked bewildered, as if Sabir's sudden descent into levity suggested an unexpected side to his nature that she had hitherto ignored. 'You were a soldier?'

'No. A reservist. I was never on active duty. But we trained pretty hard and pretty realistically. And I've been hunting, and using weapons all my life.'

'I am going outside to see what happened.'

'Yes. I reckon it's safe now. I'm going to stay here and take another look at this coffer. You don't have the other one, by any chance?'

'No. Only this. Someone painted it over because they thought it looked too dull.'

'I guessed that much.' Sabir started tapping around the exterior of the box. 'You ever check this out for a false bottom or a secret compartment?'

'A false bottom?'

'I thought not.'

32

'I'm getting two readings.'

'You're what?'

'I'm getting two separate readings from the tracking device. It's as if there's a shadow on the screen.'

'Didn't you test it as I told you?'

Macron swallowed audibly. Calque already thought him an idiot. Now he'd be convinced of it. 'Yes. It tested fine. I even tried it at two kilometres and it was clear as a bell. We lose GPS, of course, if he goes into a tunnel, or parks in an underground car park, but that's the price we pay for having a live feed.'

'What are you talking about, Macron?'

'I'm saying that if we ever lose him, it might take us a little while to restore contact.'

Calque unclipped his seat belt and began to ease his shoulders, as if, with each kilometre they were travelling away from Paris, he was being relieved of a great weight.

'You should really keep that on, Sir. If we have an accident, the airbag won't function properly without it.' The minute he'd uttered these words, Macron realised that he'd made yet another unforced error in the litany of unforced errors which peppered his ever deteriorating relationship with his boss.

For once, though, Calque didn't rise to the occasion and administer his usual stinging rebuke. Instead, he raised his chin in a speculative manner and stared out of the window, completely ignoring Macron's blunder. 'Did it ever occur to you, Macron, that there may be two tracking devices?'

'Two, Sir? But I only placed one.' Macron had begun fantasising about the happy life he could have had working as an assistant in his father's bakery in Marseille, rather than as dogsbody to a grumpy police captain on the verge of retirement.

'I'm talking about our friend. The one who likes making telephone calls.'

Macron immediately revised what he had been about to say. Nobody could accuse him of not learning on the job. 'Then he'll be picking up the ghosting, too, Sir. He'll know we planted a device, and that we're running parallel to him.'

'Well done, boy. Good thinking.' Calque sighed. 'But I suspect that that thought won't bother him overmuch. It should bother us, though. I'm slowly getting a picture here that isn't very pretty. I can't prove anything, of course. In fact I don't even know if this man with no whites to his eyes really exists, or if we are simply summoning up a demon for ourselves and should concentrate our attentions on Sabir. But we must start treading more carefully from now on.'

'A demon, Sir?'

'Just a figure of speech.'

33

—

'Where are we going?'

'To where it says on the base of the coffer.'

Alexi leaned forward from the rear seat and clapped

Sabir on the shoulder. 'That's telling her. Hey, *luludji*? What do you think of your *phral* now? Maybe he'll leave you lots of money when this crazy man kills him? You got lots of money, Adam?'

'Not on me.'

'But you got money? In America, maybe? Can you get us a green card?'

'I can give you a black eye.'

'Hey? You hear that? That's funny. I ask him for a green card and he offers me a black eye. This guy must be a Berber.'

'Is anyone following us?'

'No. No. I looked. And I keep on looking. We're clear.'

'I don't understand it.'

'Maybe he didn't find the car. The boys hid it well. You owe me for that, *gadje*. They were going to break it up and sell off the pieces, but I told them you would pay them for protecting it.'

'Pay them?'

'Yeah. You got to leave them money too, when you die.' Alexi suddenly sat up higher. 'Hey, *gadje*. Pull over behind that car. The one parked down the track.'

'Why?'

'Just do it.'

Sabir pulled the Audi across the hard shoulder and down the track.

Alexi got out and began stalking around, his head cocked sideways. 'It's okay. There's no one here. They're off walking.'

'You're not going to steal it?'

Alexi made a disgusted face. He squatted down and began unscrewing the car's number-plate.

~

'He's stopped.'

'You mustn't follow suit. Keep on driving. Go past him. But if you see another car pulled over, mark it. We'll call in back-up.'

'Why don't you just pick up Sabir and have done with it?'

'Because the gypsies aren't stupid, whatever you might think of them. If they haven't killed Sabir, it's for a reason.' Calque flicked a glance down the side track. 'Did you see what he was doing down there?'

'They. There were three of them.' Macron cleared his throat uncertainly. 'If I were them, I'd be switching number-plates. Just in case.'

Calque smiled. 'Macron. You never cease to amaze me.'

~

'What do you hope to gain by that? The minute they come back to the car they'll see you've switched their plates.'

'No.' Alexi smiled. 'People don't look. They don't see things. It'll be days before he notices anything. He'll probably only realise we've switched the plates after the police pounce down on him waving their machine guns – or when he loses his car in a supermarket parking.'

Sabir shrugged. 'You sound as if you've done this sort of thing before.'

'What do you mean? I'm like a priest.'

Yola bestirred herself for the first time. 'I can understand my brother knowing about the first paper. My mother doted on him. She would have told him anything. Given him anything. But how did my brother know what was on the base of the coffer? He couldn't read.'

'Then he found someone in the camp who could.

81

Because he used part of the same wording in his ad.'

Yola glanced at Alexi. 'Who would he find?'

Alexi shrugged. 'Luca can read. He would do anything for Babel. Or for a handful of euros. He's sly, too. It would be just like him to plan all this, and then set Babel up to act in his place.'

Yola hissed, 'That Luca. If I find he did this, I will put a hex on him.'

'A hex?' Sabir glanced back at Yola. 'What do you mean, a hex?'

Alexi laughed. 'She's *hexi*, this girl. A witch. Her mother was a witch. And her grandmother too. That's why no one will marry her. They think that if they give her a beating she will poison them. Or give them the evil eye.'

'She'd be right.'

'What do you mean? A man's got to beat a woman sometimes. Otherwise, how can he keep her in order? She'd be like one of your *payo* women. With balls the size of hand grenades. No, Adam. If, by a miracle, Yola ever finds herself a husband, you've got to talk to him. Tell him how to manage her. Keep her pregnant. That's the best thing. If she's got children to look after, she can't nag him.'

Yola flicked at her front teeth with her thumb, as if she were getting rid of a piece of unwanted gristle. 'And what about you, Alexi? Why aren't you married? I'll tell you why. Because your penis is split in half. One bit goes west, towards the *payos*, and the other bit stays in your hand.'

Sabir shook his head in bewilderment. Both of them were smiling, as if they derived comfort from the badinage. Sabir secretly suspected that it reinforced, rather than truncated, their communality. He suddenly felt jealous, as if he, too, wanted to belong to such a light-hearted community. 'When you've both stopped arguing, shall I tell you what was written – or rather burned – on to the base of the coffer?'

They both turned to him as if he had offered, out of the blue, to read them a bedtime story.

'It's in medieval French. Like the Will. It's a riddle.'

'A riddle? You mean like this one? "I have a sister who runs without legs and who whistles without a mouth. Who is she?"'

Sabir was getting used to the gypsy way with a non sequitur. At first, the sudden loss of a train of thought had disturbed his sense of order and he had fought to get back on track. Now he smiled and yielded himself up to it. 'Okay. I give up.'

Yola hammered the seat behind him. 'It's the wind, idiot. What did you think it was?' She and Alexi erupted into gales of laughter.

Sabir smiled. 'Now do you want to hear what I found? Then we'll see if you're as good solving riddles as you are at setting them.'

'Yes. Tell us.'

'Well, the original French goes like this:

"*Hébergé par les trois mariés*
Celle d'Egypte la dernière fit
La vierge noire au camaro duro
Tient le secret de mes vers à ses pieds"

'When I first read it, I took it to mean the following:

"*Sheltered by the three married people*
The Egyptian woman was the last one
The Black Virgin on her hard bed
Holds the secret of my verses at her feet"

'But that makes no sense.'

'You're darned right it makes no sense. And it's not in Nostradamus's usual style, either. It doesn't rhyme, for

83

a start. But then it doesn't pretend to be a prophecy. It's clearly meant to be a guide, or map, towards something of greater importance.'

'Who are the three married people?'

'I've not the faintest idea.'

'Well, what about the Black Virgin, then?'

'That's a lot clearer. And it's where the key, in my opinion, lies. *Camaro duro* doesn't really mean "hard bed", you see. It's one of those phrases one supposes must signify something, but it's actually meaningless. Yes, *cama* is bed in Spanish and *duro* means hard. But the mention of the Black Virgin gave me the true key. It's an anagram.'

'A what?'

'An anagram. That means when one or two words disguise another word, which can be made out of all the letters. Hidden inside the words *camaro duro* we have a clear anagram for Rocamadour. That's a famous place of pilgrimage in the Lot valley. Some say it's even the true beginning of the Santiago de Compostela pilgrimage. And there's a famous Black Virgin there, which women have gone to for many generations to pray for success in having children. Some even say that she is half man, half woman – half Mary and half Roland. For the paladin Roland's phallic sword, Durendal, resides to this day in a vulva-shaped cleft high up in the rock near the Virgin's shrine. She was certainly there in Nostradamus's time. In fact I don't think she's moved anywhere in eight centuries.'

'Is that where we're going, then?'

Sabir looked at his two companions. 'I don't think we have much choice in the matter.'

34

Yola set two of the cups of coffee into their holders, and gave the third to Sabir. 'You mustn't be seen. These garages have cameras. We shouldn't stop in such places again.'

Sabir watched Alexi winding his way through the shop towards the rest room. 'Why is he here, Yola?'

'He wants to kidnap me. But he doesn't have the courage. And now he is scared that you might do so when he isn't around. That's why he's here.'

'Me? Kidnap you?'

Yola sighed. 'In Manouche families, a man and a woman run off together when they want to get married. It is called a "kidnapping". If a man "kidnaps" you, it is the equivalent of marriage because the girl will no longer be – I don't know how to say this – intact.'

'You're joking.'

'Why should I joke? I'm telling you the truth.'

'But I'm your brother.'

'Not by blood, stupid.'

'What? That means I could marry you?'

'With the Bulibasha's permission, as my father is dead. But if you did that, Alexi would get seriously angry. And then he might choose to really hit you with the knife.'

'What do you mean "might choose to really hit me"? He missed me cleanly.'

'Only because he wanted to. Alexi is the best knife-thrower in the camp. He does it at circuses and fairgrounds. Everybody knows that. That's why the Bulibasha chose the knife judgement. They all realised

Alexi thought you were innocent of Babel's death. Otherwise he would have split your hand in two.'

'Do you mean all that theatre was just a put-on? That everybody knew all the time that Alexi was going to miss me?'

'Yes.'

'But what if he'd hit me by mistake?'

'Then we'd have had to kill you.'

'Oh great. That makes sense. Yeah. I see it all clearly now.'

'You mustn't be angry, Adam. This way, everybody accepts you. If we'd done it another way, you would have had problems later.'

'Well that's all right then.'

~

Calque watched the two of them through his binoculars. 'I recognise the girl. It's Samana's sister. And Sabir, of course. But who's the swarthy one using the *pissoire*?'

'Another cousin, probably. These people are sick with cousins. Scratch one and cousins fall off them like ticks.'

'Don't you like gypsies, Macron?'

'They're layabouts. No southerner likes gypsies. They steal, trick, and use people for their own purposes.'

'*Putain*. Most people do that in one way or another.'

'Not like them. They despise us.'

'We haven't made life easy for them.'

'Why should we?'

Calque pretended to nod. 'Why indeed?' He would have to watch Macron more carefully, though, in future. In his experience, if a man had one outspoken prejudice, he would be doubly as likely to harbour other, more secret ones, which would only emerge in a crisis. 'They're moving. Look. Give them half a minute and then follow on behind.'

'Are you sure this is regular, Sir? I mean, leaving a murderer to go about his business on the public highway? You saw what he did to Samana.'

'Have you forgotten about our other friend so quickly?'

'Of course not. But we've nothing against him but your instinct. We have Sabir's actual blood on Samana's hand. We can place him at the murder scene.'

'No we can't. But we can place him at the bar where the blooding took place. And we have him travelling, seemingly of his own free will, with Samana's sister. What do you think? That she's suffering from Stockholm syndrome?'

'Stockholm syndrome?'

Calque frowned. 'Sometimes, Macron, I forget that you are quite so young. A Swedish criminologist, Nils Bejerot, coined the term in 1973 after a bank robbery in the Norrmalmstorg district of Stockholm went wrong, and a number of hostages were taken. Over the course of six days, some of the hostages began to sympathise more with their captors than with the police. The same thing happened to the newspaper heiress Patty Hearst.'

'Ah.'

'Do you think that Sabir has somehow managed to mesmerise an entire gypsy camp and turn them into his willing accomplices?'

Macron sucked at his teeth. 'I wouldn't put anything at all past such people.'

35

'Do you still feel capable of handling this situation alone?'

Achor Bale was briefly tempted to throw the handset out of the car window. Instead, he gave the woman in the vehicle overtaking him a sarcastic smile, in response to her disapproving look about his use of a cellphone whilst driving.

'Of course, Madame. Everything is copacetic, as the Americans say. I have Sabir under surveillance. I've identified the police car following them. The poor fools have even switched number-plates in an effort to throw off any pursuit.'

The woman's husband was now leaning forward and gesticulating for him to put down his phone.

Peugeot drivers, thought Bale. In England, they would drive Rovers. In America, Chevrolets or Cadillacs. He pretended to lose concentration and allowed his car to drift a little towards the Peugeot.

The husband's eyes opened wider. He reached across his wife and honked the horn.

Bale glanced into his rear-view mirror. Alone on the road. Might be amusing. Might even buy him a little extra time. 'So do you want me to continue or not, Madame? Just say the word.'

'I want you to continue.'

'Very well.' Bale snapped the telephone shut. He accelerated forward and cut viciously in front of the Peugeot. Then he slowed down.

The man hooted again.

Bale pulled slowly to a stop.

The Peugeot stopped behind him and the man got out.

Bale watched him in the rear-view mirror. He hunched down a little in his seat. Might as well milk this a little. Enjoy the process.

'What do you think you are doing? You very nearly caused an accident.'

Bale shrugged. 'Look. I'm incredibly sorry. My wife is expecting a baby. I'm due at the hospital. I just needed to check up on how to get there.'

'A baby, you say?' The man glanced quickly back at his wife. He began visibly to relax. 'Look. I'm sorry to make such a fuss. But it's happening all the time, you know. You really should get yourself a hands-off set. Then you can talk in the car as much as you want without being a danger to other road users.'

'You're right. I know it.' Bale watched a Citroën drift past them and curl around the corner. He glanced down at the tracking radar. A kilometre already. He'd have to make this fast. 'Sorry again.'

The man nodded and started back for his car. He shrugged his shoulders at his wife and then raised his hands placatingly when she scowled at him.

Bale slipped the car into reverse and stamped on the accelerator. There was the hysterical screech of rubber and then the tyres held their traction and the car lurched backwards.

The man turned towards Bale, his mouth agape.

'Oy ya yoi ya yoi.' Bale swung open his car door and leapt out. He glanced wildly up and down the road. The woman was screaming. Her husband was entirely hidden between and beneath the two cars, and was making no sound.

Bale grabbed the woman's hair through the open

front window of the Peugeot and began to drag her out. One of her shoes caught between the automatic shift and the stowaway compartment dividing the two front seats. Bale yanked even harder and something gave. He dragged the woman around to the nearside rear door, which still had a winding mechanism.

He half wound down the window and pushed the woman's head into the gap, facing into the car. Then he wound up the window as tightly as he could and slammed the car door shut.

~

'What have we here?' Calque reached towards the dashboard and raised himself partly out of his seat. 'You'd better slow down.'

'But what about . . .'

'Slow down.'

Macron cut his speed

Calque squinted at the scene ahead of them. 'Call an ambulance. Fast. And the *police judiciaire*.'

'But we're going to lose them.'

'Get the first-aid kit. And clip on the flasher.'

'But that'll identify us.'

Calque had the door open before the vehicle had fully stopped. He ran stiffly to where the man was lying and knelt down beside him. 'Right, Macron. You can tell the paras that he's still breathing. Barely. But they'll need a brace. He may have damaged his neck.' He moved towards the woman. 'Madame. Stay still. Don't struggle.'

The woman moaned.

'Please. Stay still. You've broken your foot.' Calque tried to unwind the window but the mechanism was damaged. The woman's face had already turned purple.

It was clear that she was having difficulty breathing. 'Macron. Bring the hammer. Fast. We're going to have to break the glass.'

'What hammer?'

'The fire extinguisher, then.' Calque took off his jacket and wrapped it around the woman's head. 'It's all right, Madame. Don't struggle. We need to break the glass.'

All tension suddenly went out of the woman's body and she slumped heavily against the car.

'Quick. She's stopped breathing.'

'What do you want me to do?'

'Smash the window with the extinguisher.'

Macron drew back the fire extinguisher and lashed at the window. The extinguisher bounced off the security glass.

'Give it to me.' Calque grabbed the extinguisher. He smashed the butt against the window glass. 'Now give me your jacket.' He wrapped the jacket around his hand and punched through the shattered glass. He eased the woman to the ground and laid her head on the jacket. Hunching forwards, he struck her sharply over the heart. He felt with two fingers below her left breast, and then began depressing her sternum. 'Macron. When I tell you, give her two spaced breaths.'

Macron crouched down by the woman's head.

'You called the ambulance?'

'Yes, Sir.'

'Good lad. We'll keep this up until they get here. Has she still got a pulse?'

'Yes, Sir. It's fluttering a little, but it's there.'

Between double-handed strokes, Calque looked into Macron's eyes. 'Now do you believe me? About the second man?'

'I always believed you, Sir. But do you really think he did this?'

'Two breaths.'

Macron bent forward and gave the woman the kiss of life.

Calque restarted his two-handed strokes. 'I don't simply believe it, boy. I know it.'

36

Yola spat the last of her pumpkin seed husks on to the floor of the car. 'Look. Wild asparagus.'

'What?'

'Wild asparagus. We have to stop.'

'You can't be serious.'

Yola gave Sabir a sharp tap on the shoulder. 'Is somebody timing us? Are we being chased? Is there a deadline for this thing?'

'Well, of course not . . .'

'So stop.'

Sabir looked to Alexi for support. 'You don't think we should stop, do you?'

'Of course we should stop. How often do you see wild asparagus growing beside the road? Yola must have her *cueillette*.'

'Her what?' Aware that he was being outvoted, Sabir swung the car around and headed back towards the asparagus clump.

'Wherever they go, gypsy women conduct what they call a *cueillette*. That means they never pass by free food – herbs, salad, eggs, grapes, walnuts, Reines Claudes

– without stopping to collect it.'

'What the hell are Reines Claudes?'

'Green plums.'

'Oh. You mean greengages?'

'Reines Claudes. Yes.'

Sabir glanced back up the road behind them. A Citroën breasted the corner and thundered guilelessly past. 'I'm taking us to where we can't be seen. Just in case a police car comes by.'

'No one will recognise us, Adam. They're looking for one man, not two men and a woman. And in a car with different plates.'

'Still.'

Yola hammered the seat-back in front of her. 'Look. I can see some more. Over there by the river.' She rustled about in her rucksack and came up with two knotted plastic bags. 'You two go and collect the asparagus by the road. I'll collect the other stuff. I can see dandelions, nettles and marguerites too. You boys are lucky. We're going to have a feast tonight.'

37

Achor Bale had bought himself forty minutes' grace. Forty minutes in which to extract all the information he needed. Forty minutes for the police to deal with the scene he had left behind him, liaise with the ambulance service and placate the local back-up.

He slammed his foot on to the accelerator and watched the tracking markers converge. Then he sucked in his breath and slowed down.

Something had changed. Sabir wasn't moving forward any more. As Bale watched, the marker began slowly retracing its steps towards him. He hesitated, one hand poised over the steering wheel. Now the marker was stationary. It was flashing less than five hundred metres ahead of him.

Bale pulled off the road twenty metres before the apex of the corner. He hesitated before abandoning his car, but then decided that he had neither the time, nor a suitable location, in which to hide it. He'd just have to risk the police driving by and making the somewhat unlikely connection between him and a stationary vehicle.

He hurried over the breast of the hill and down through a small wood. Why had they stopped so soon after the last halt? A picnic? An accident? It could be anything.

The best thing would be if he could get them all together. Then he could concentrate on one whilst the others were forced to watch. That way nearly always worked. Guilt, thought Bale, was the major weakness of the Western world. When people didn't feel guilt, they built empires. When they began to feel guilt, they lost them. Look at the British.

He saw the girl first, squatting alone near the riverbank. Was she taking a leak? Was that what this was all about? He searched for the men but they were out of sight. Then he saw that she was dissecting clumps of vegetation and stuffing the residue into a series of plastic bags. Jesus Christ. These people weren't to be believed.

He checked around for the men one final time, and then cut down towards the girl. This was simply too good to be true. They must have known he was coming. Laid it all on in some way.

He hesitated for a moment, when he was about fifteen feet from the girl. She made a pretty picture, squatting there in her long gypsy dress by the river. A perfect picture of innocence. Bale was reminded of something from the long-distant past but he couldn't quite identify the scene. The sudden lapse disturbed him, like an unexpected current of cold air travelling through a tear in a pair of trousers.

He ran the last few yards, confident that the girl hadn't heard his approach. At the last possible moment she began to turn around but he was already on top of her, pinning her arms to the ground with his knees. He had expected her to scream, and had taken the precaution of pinching shut her nose – it was a method which nearly always worked with women, and was far better than risking one's hand over a panic-stricken person's mouth – but the girl was strangely silent. It was almost as if she had been expecting him.

'If you cry out, I shall break your neck. Just like I did to your brother. Do you understand me?'

She nodded.

He couldn't see her face properly, as he had her pinioned down from the back, with her body underneath him and her arms stretched out in a cruciform position. He rectified this by angling her head to one side.

'I'm going to say this once and once only. In ten seconds time I am going to knock you out with my fist. While you are unconscious I am going to raise your skirt, take off your underpants, and conduct an exploration inside you with my knife. When I encounter your fallopian tubes I am going to cut them. You will bleed badly but it won't kill you. The men will probably find you before that happens. But you will never be a mother. Do you understand me? That will be gone. For ever.'

He heard rather than saw her evacuating her bladder.

Her eyes turned up in themselves and started fluttering.

'Stop that. Wake up.' He pinched her cheek as hard as he could. Her eyes began to refocus. 'Now listen. What did you find? Where are you going? Tell me these things and I will leave you alone. Your ten seconds have started.'

Yola began to moan.

'Eight. Seven. Six.'

'We're going to Rocamadour.'

'Why?'

'To the Black Virgin. Something is hidden at her feet.'

'What?'

'We don't know. All it said on the bottom of the coffer was that the secret of the verses is at her feet.'

'The bottom of what coffer?'

'My mother's coffer. The one my mother gave me. The one that belonged to the daughter of Nostradamus.'

'Is that it?'

'That's everything. I swear to you.'

Bale took some of the weight off her arms. He glanced back up the valley. No sign of the men. Kill her? No point really. She was as good as dead already.

He dragged her to the edge of the riverbank and tumbled her in.

38

'I hope to hell this is worth all the trouble we're going to.'

'What? What are you talking about? The verses?'

'No. The wild asparagus.'

Alexi circled his fingers. 'You can bet it will be. Yola cooks good. All we need now is a rabbit.'

'And how do you propose to catch that?'

'You can run it over. I'll tell you if I see one by the roadside. But don't squash it – you've got to time it just right so that you hit its head with the outside of the wheel. The flesh won't taste as good as one that God Himself kills, but it'll be the next best thing.'

Sabir nodded wearily. What had he expected Alexi to say? That they'd go into the next town and buy a shotgun? 'Can you see Yola? We'd better be going.'

Alexi straightened up. 'No. She went down by the river. I'll go and call her.'

Sabir trudged back towards the car, shaking his head. It was an odd thing to admit but he was slowly beginning to enjoy himself. He wasn't a great deal older than Alexi but there had been times in the past few years when he'd realised that he was starting to lose his zest for life – his sense of the absurd. Now, with the loose artillery of Alexi and Yola acting in counterpoint to the still lurking threat of the police, he suddenly felt all the excitement of the unknown bubbling up again in his stomach.

'Adam!' The shout came from just beyond a small stand of trees down near the river.

Sabir dropped the asparagus and started to run.

The first thing he saw was Alexi floundering in the river. 'Quickly, Adam. I can't swim. She's in the water.'

'Where?'

'Just below you. Her face is down but she's still alive. I saw her arm move.'

Sabir crested the bank and executed a clumsy leap into the slow-moving river. He reached Yola with his first surge and levered her up into his arms.

She raised a hand as if to ward him off, but her eyes were dead when they looked up at him, and there was no real force left in the movement. Sabir clutched her to his chest, and allowed the force of the river to sweep them back towards the bank.

'I think she's had a fit of some sort. Run up to the car and get a blanket.'

Alexi floundered out of the water. He gave a single, anxious glance backwards and then pounded up the hill towards the car.

Sabir laid Yola down on to the sand. She was breathing normally, but her face was sheet-white and her lips had already turned an unhealthy blue.

'What is it? What happened?'

She began shaking, as if, with her retrieval from the water, some other non-mechanical process had been triggered.

Sabir glanced up to check on Alexi's progress. 'Look, I'm sorry. Alexi's bringing a dry blanket. I'm going to have to get you out of these clothes.' He had expected – even hoped for – an argument. But there was no response. He began undoing Yola's blouse.

'You shouldn't do that.' Alexi had reached Sabir's side. He proffered the blanket. 'She wouldn't like it.'

'She's cold as ice, Alexi. And she's in shock. If wc leave her in these clothes she'll catch pneumonia. We need to wrap her up in this blanket and then get her back to the car. I can start driving with the air conditioning set to full heat. She'll warm up quickly then.'

Alexi hesitated.

'I'm serious. If you don't want to embarrass her, turn away.' He eased off her blouse, and then worked the skirt down over her hips. He was surprised to notice that she wore no underwear of any sort.

'God, she's beautiful.' Alexi was staring down at her. He was still clutching the blanket.

'Give me that.'

'Oh. Okay.'

Sabir wrapped Yola in the blanket. 'Now take her legs. Let's get her up to the car before she freezes to death.'

39

'Don't you think it's time to call in back-up?'

'We're forty-five minutes behind them. What sort of back-up do you think we need, Macron? A jet fighter?'

'What if the eye-man strikes again?'

'The eye-man?' Calque smiled, amused by Macron's unexpectedly creative imagination. 'He won't.'

'How can you be so sure?'

'Because he's achieved his purpose. He's bought himself a few hours' leeway. He knows that by the time we've restored . . .' Calque hesitated, searching for the right word.

'GPS trilateration?'

'GPS trilateration . . . exactly . . . and caught up with the car, he'll have what he wants.'

'And what's that?'

'Search me. I'm after the man, not his motive. I leave all that sort of rot to the judicial courts.' Calque made a pillow of his jacket and placed it between his head and the window. 'But I know one thing for certain. I wouldn't want to be in Sabir's or the girl's shoes during the next sixty minutes.'

~

'Is she coming round?'

'She's got her eyes open.'

'Right. I'll stop the car but leave the engine running for heat. We can put the back seats down and stretch her out more comfortably.'

Alexi glanced across at Sabir. 'What do you think happened? I've never seen her like this.'

'She must have been picking asparagus near the water's edge and fallen in. She probably struck her head – that's a hefty bruise she's got on her cheek. Anyway, she's definitely in shock. The water was incredibly cold. She wouldn't have been expecting it.' He frowned. 'Is she epileptic, by any chance? Or diabetic?'

'What?'

'Nothing. Forget it.'

Once they'd arranged the back seats and settled Yola comfortably, the two men stripped down.

'Look, Alexi, I'll drive while you dry the clothes on the heater. Do Yola's first. I'll put the thing on blow. We'll swelter, but I can't think of any other way to do it. If the police catch three naked people in a moving vehicle, it'll take them weeks to figure out what we were doing.' He reached for the automatic shift.

100

'I told him.' It was Yola's voice.

The two men turned towards her.

'I told him everything.' She was sitting up now, the blanket puddled around her waist. 'I told him we are going to Rocamadour. And about the Black Virgin. I told him where the verses are hidden.'

'What do you mean, told him? Told who?'

Yola noticed her nakedness and slowly drew the blanket up to cover her breasts. She appeared to be thinking and acting in slow motion. 'The man. He jumped on me. He smelt strangely. Like those green insects you crush and they smell of almonds.'

'Yola. What are you talking about? What man?'

She took a deep breath. 'The man who killed Babel. He told me. He said he would break my neck just like he broke Babel's.'

'Oh Christ.'

Alexi levered himself up in his seat. 'What did he do to you?' His voice was shaking.

Yola shook her head. 'He did nothing. He didn't have to. His threats were enough to get him everything he wanted.'

Alexi closed his eyes. He snorted. His jaw began to work behind his tightly pursed mouth as if he were conducting an angry internal dialogue with himself.

'Did you see him, Yola? Did you see his face?'

'No. He was on top of me. From the back. He had my arms pinned down with his knees. I couldn't turn my head.'

'You were right to tell him. He's mad. He would have killed you.' Sabir turned back to the steering wheel. He slipped the car into drive and began accelerating wildly up the road.

Alexi opened his eyes. 'What are you doing?'

'What am I doing? I'll tell you what I'm doing. We

know where the bastard's going now, thanks to Yola. So I'm going to get to Rocamadour ahead of him. And then I'm going to kill him.'

'Are you crazy, Adam?'

'I'm Yola's *phral*, aren't I? You all told me I had to protect her. To take revenge for Babel's death. Well now I'm going to do it.'

40

Achor Bale watched the blip diminish and then finally disappear off the edge of his screen. He leaned forward and switched off the tracking device. It had been a very satisfactory day's work, when all was said and done. He had taken the initiative and it had paid off handsomely. It was a good lesson. Never leave the enemy to his own devices. Irritate him. Force him into sudden decisions that are open to error. That way you will achieve your end satisfyingly and with commendable speed.

He checked the map on the seat next to him. It would take him a good three hours to get to Rocamadour. Best to leave it until the crypt was shut, and the staff had gone to their dinner. No one would expect a break-in at the Sanctuary – that would be an absurd idea. Perhaps he should crawl up the steps on his knees, like England's King Henry II – a descendant, or so they said, of Satan's daughter Melusine – after the priests had persuaded him to do reluctant penance both for the murder of Thomas à Becket and for his dead son's sacrilegious plundering of the shrine? Ask for dispensation. Secure himself a *nihil obstat*.

Mind you, he hadn't actually killed anybody recently. Unless the girl had drowned, of course. Or the woman in the car had asphyxiated herself. Her husband had definitely still been twitching when last he looked, and Samana had been indisputably responsible for his own death.

All in all, then, Bale's conscience was clear. He could steal the Black Virgin with impunity.

41

—

'We've found them again. They're heading towards Limoges.'

'Excellent. Tell the pinheads to give us a new reading every half an hour – that way we'll have a chance to make up for lost time and get them back on our screen.'

'Where do you think they're going, Sir?'

'To the seaside?'

Macron didn't know whether to laugh or to cry. He was becoming more and more convinced that he was teamed up with an unregenerate madman – someone who bent all the rules on principle, simply to suit his own agenda. The two of them should have been back in Paris by now, happily confining themselves to a 35-hour week and leaving the continued investigation of the murder to their colleagues in the south. Macron could have been working at his squash and improving on his six-pack at the police gym. Instead, they were subsisting on prepacked meals and coffee, with the occasional catnap in the back seat of the car. He could feel himself going physically downhill. It didn't matter to Calque, of course – he was a wreck already.

'The weekend's approaching, Sir.'

'And?'

'And nothing. It was just an observation.'

'Well, confine your observations to the case in hand. You're a public servant, Macron, not a lifeguard.'

~

Yola emerged, fully clothed, from behind the bushes.

Sabir shrugged his shoulders and made a face. 'I'm sorry we had to undress you. Alexi was against it, but I insisted. I apologise.'

'You did what you had to. Did Alexi see me?'

'I'm afraid so.'

'Well, now he'll know what he's been missing.'

Sabir burst out laughing. He was astonished at how resilient Yola was being. He had half expected her to react hysterically – to lurch into a depression, or melancholia, triggered by delayed shock from the attack. But he had underestimated her. Her life had scarcely been a bed of roses up to that point, and her expectations about the depths to which people would stoop in terms of their behaviour were probably a good deal more realistic than his own. 'He's angry. That's why he's gone off. I think he feels responsible for the attack on you.'

'You must let him steal the Virgin.'

'I'm sorry?'

'Alexi. He is a good stealer. It is something he does well.'

'Oh. I see.'

104

'Have you never stolen anything?'

'Well, no. Not recently.'

'I thought so.' She weighed something up in her head. 'A gypsy can steal every seven years. Something big, I mean.'

'How did you figure that one out?'

'Because an old gypsy woman saw Christ carrying the Cross on the way to the Calvary hill.'

'And?'

'And she didn't have any idea who Christ was. But when she saw His face, she felt pity for Him and decided to steal the nails with which they were to crucify Him. She stole one, but before she could steal the second, she was caught. The soldiers took her and beat her. She cried out to the soldiers to spare her because she had stolen nothing for seven years. A disciple heard her and said, 'Woman, you are blessed. The Saviour permits you and yours to steal once every seven years, now and for ever.' And that's why there were only three nails at the Crucifixion. And why Jesus Christ's feet were crossed and not spread apart, as they should have been.'

'You don't believe all that hokum, do you?'

'Of course I believe it.'

'And that's why gypsies steal?'

'We have the right. When Alexi steals the Black Virgin, he won't be doing anything wrong.'

'I'm very relieved to hear it. But what about me? What if I find the man who attacked you, and kill him? Where do I stand?'

'He has shed our family's blood. His should be shed in turn.'

'As simple as that?'

'It's never simple, Adam. To kill a man.'

42

Sabir hesitated by the car door. 'Have either of you ever taken a driving test?'

'A driving test? No. Of course not. But I can drive.'

'Can you drive, Yola?'

'No.'

'Okay, then. We know where we are. Alexi, you take the wheel. I've got to map us out a different route to the shrine. Babel's murderer obviously knows our car – he must have found it and followed us all the way from the camp. Now that he thinks he's finally got rid of us, we don't want to tip him off again by blundering past him in the overtaking lane, do we?' He spread the map out in front of him. 'Yes. It looks like we can bypass Limoges and get to Rocamadour via Tulle.'

'This car hasn't got proper gears.'

'Just stick it in drive, Alexi and press on the gas pedal.'

'Which one's drive?'

'The fourth one down. The letter looks like a horse stirrup, but sideways on.'

Alexi did as he was told. 'Hey. That's not bad. It changes gear by itself. This is better than a Mercedes.'

Sabir could feel Yola's eyes fixed on him from the back seat. He turned towards her. 'Are you okay? There is such a thing as delayed shock, you know. Even for tough nuts like you.'

She shrugged. 'I'm okay.' Then her expression clouded. 'Adam. Do you believe in hell?'

'Hell?' He made a face. 'I suppose so.'

'We don't.' She shook her head. 'Gypsies don't even think the Devil, O Beng, is really such a bad man. We believe that everyone will come to Paradise one day. Even him.'

'So?'

'I think this man is bad, Adam. Really bad. Look what he did to Babel. It's not human to do that.'

'So what are you telling me? That you're changing your mind about hell and the Devil?'

'No. Not that. But I didn't tell you everything he said to me. I want you and Alexi to understand exactly who you are dealing with.'

'We're dealing with a murdering maniac.'

'No. He's not that. I've been thinking about this. He's cleverer than that. He knows exactly where to strike. How to damage you the most and get what he wants.'

'I don't get it. What are you trying to tell me?'

'He said he would knock me out. That while I was unconscious, he would damage me inside with his knife so I could no longer have babies. No longer be a mother.'

'Jesus Christ.'

'Listen, Adam. He knows about us. About gypsy ways. Perhaps he's even part-gypsy himself. He knew that if he just attacked me and tried to hurt me, I might not have told him what he wanted to know. I might have lied. When he said what he said to me, I was so convinced that he would really do it that I wet myself. He could have done anything to me then and I wouldn't have fought him. And with Babel. The same thing. Babel was vain. It was his main weakness. He was like a woman. He spent hours looking at himself and prettying himself before the mirror. This man marked his face. Nowhere else. Just his face. I saw him in the mortuary.'

'I don't get you.'

'He works on people's weaknesses. He's an evil man, Adam. Really evil. He doesn't simply murder. He's a destroyer of souls.'

'All the more reason to rid the world of him then.'

Yola usually had an answer for everything. This time she merely turned her head towards the window and held her peace.

43

'They don't seem to provide tyre irons any more in cars.' Sabir rummaged further in the rear storage compartment. 'I can't exactly hit him with the jack. Or the warning triangle.'

'I'll cut you a thorn stick.'

'A what?'

'From a holly bush. I can see one over there. It's the strongest wood. Even before it's been dried. If you walk somewhere with a stick, no one will ever question you. That way, you always have a weapon.'

'You're a real case. You know that, Alexi?'

They were parked on the battlements above the Rocamadour shrine. Below them were gardens, set into the sheer rock of the cliffs, intersected with winding paths and viewpoints. A few tourists were strolling around in a desultory way, wasting time before dinner.

'Look at those searchlights. We need to get in before dusk. When they turn those things on, this whole hillside will light up like a Christmas tree.'

'Do you think we've beaten him to it?'

'We'll only know when you break into the shrine.'

Alexi sniffed. 'But I won't break into the shrine.'

'What do you mean? You aren't bottling out on me, are you?'

'Bottling . . .? I don't understand.'

'Turning chicken.'

Alexi laughed and shook his head. 'Adam. It's a simple enough rule. Breaking into somewhere is very difficult – but breaking out is easy.'

'Oh. I see.' Sabir hesitated. 'At least I think I do.'

'So where will you be?'

'I'll hide outside, then and watch. If he comes along, I'll whop him one with your holly stick.' He waited for the stunned reaction, but it didn't come. 'No. It's all right. I'm only joking. I haven't gone mad.'

Alexi looked nonplussed. 'But what will you really do?'

Sabir sighed. He realised that he was still a very long way indeed from understanding the gypsy mentality. 'I'll just stay hidden outside, as we agreed. That way I can warn you by wolf-whistling when I see him. When you get to the Virgin, bring her back to Yola in the car, and then come down and join me again. Between the two of us we should be able to bushwhack him somewhere inside the shrine, where it's safer, and where there aren't any people around to get in the way.'

'You don't think she'll be angry with us?'

'Who? Yola? Why?'

'No. I mean the Virgin.'

'Christ, Alexi. You're not having second thoughts on me, are you?'

'No. No. I will take it. But I will pray to her first. Ask her to forgive me.'

'You do that. Now cut me that stick.'

44

Alexi woke up just as the evening caretaker was bolting the outside doors of the Basilica. He had secreted himself, forty minutes earlier, behind the altar of the St-Sauveur Basilica, which someone had conveniently covered with a long-fringed blue and white linen cloth. Then he had almost immediately fallen asleep.

For ten panic-stricken seconds he wasn't quite sure where he was. Then he rolled himself deftly out from under the altar cloth and stood up, prior to a stretch. It was at this point that he realised that someone else was in the church with him.

He crouched back behind the altar and felt for his knife. It took him a snap five seconds to remember that he had thrown it on to the back seat of the car, after cutting Sabir's stick. Not for the first time, Alexi found himself cursing his congenital inattention to detail.

He eased himself around the side of the altar, opening his eyes as wide as he could to gather in the last of the evening light inside the church. The stranger was hunched forward in one of the choir-stall chairs, about fifteen metres from where he was crouching. Had he been asleep as well? Or was he praying?

As he watched, the man stood up and moved towards the inner door of the shrine – it soon became clear by the manner of his progress that he had been listening and waiting for the watchman too. He raised the latch with his hand, swung the door silently open and stepped inside.

Alexi looked wildly towards the Basilica doors. Sabir was outside them, and as effectively out of reach as if someone had sealed him behind the gate of a bank vault. What should he do? What would Sabir want him to do?

He took off his shoes. Then he eased himself out from behind the altar and padded towards the shrine. He inched his head around the door.

The man had switched on a torch and was investigating the massive glazed brass plinth on which the Virgin was displayed. As Alexi watched, he began levering at the base of the cabinet. When he found that he couldn't open the front, he turned sharply around and looked back towards the Basilica.

Alexi froze against the outside wall.

The man's footsteps started back in his direction.

Alexi tiptoed as far as the altar and hid himself in the same place he had used before. If the man had heard him, he was done for anyway. He might as well die on sanctified ground.

There was the sudden shriek of a chair leg being dragged across a stone floor. Alexi popped his head out from cover. The man was pulling two choir-stall chairs behind him. It was obvious that he intended to make a ladder for himself so that he could more easily reach the Virgin.

Using the sound of the chairs as cover, Alexi followed the stranger back into the crypt. This time, though, he took advantage of the man's inattention to approach much closer to the display cabinet. He lay down between two pews close to the front of the main aisle, affording himself both the opportunity to see what was happening and sufficient cover from the solid oak pew-front between them should the man decide he needed to return to the Basilica for a third chair.

As Alexi watched, the man set one chair on top of the other, and then tested them for sureness. He tut-tutted loudly, and then muttered something to himself under his breath.

Alexi watched as the man fixed the torch into the back of his trousers and began to climb up the makeshift ladder. So this was it. This would be his one chance. If he botched it, he was dead. He would wait until the man was teetering on the apex of the chairs, and then overset him.

At the crucial moment, the man reached up for one of the brass candle sconces below the Virgin's plinth and swung himself effortlessly on to the display cabinet itself.

Alexi, who had not anticipated the sudden move sideways, found himself caught halfway between the pew and the cabinet. The man turned and stared at him full on. Then he smiled.

Without thinking, Alexi picked up one of the heavy brass candlesticks that flanked the cabinet, and swung it at the man with all his might.

The candlestick struck Achor Bale just above the right ear. He let go of the side of the cabinet and tumbled eight feet backwards on to the granite floor. Alexi had already armed himself with the second candlestick but he soon saw that it wasn't necessary. The stranger was out cold.

Alexi separated the two chairs. Grunting, he manhandled Bale on to the chair nearest the cabinet. He felt around in Bale's pockets and withdrew a wallet stuffed with banknotes and a small automatic pistol. '*Putain!*'

He pocketed the wallet and the pistol and looked wildly around the Sanctuary. He noticed some damask curtains, held back with cord. He stripped the cord from the curtains and tied Bale's arms and body to the chair-back. Then he used the remaining chair to clamber up the display cabinet and secure the Virgin.

45

Sabir heard the crash clearly from his hiding place across the small square in front of the Sanctuary. He had been listening with all his attention ever since he had first heard the distant sound of barking chair-legs from deep inside the Basilica. The crash, however, had come from much closer to where the Virgin was situated.

He broke cover and made straight for the heavy crypt door. It was tightly sealed. He backed away from the building and glanced up at the windows. They were all too high for him to reach.

'Alexi!' He tried to make his voice carry through the Sanctuary walls, but not further than the courtyard itself. It was a tall order – the courtyard acted as a perfect echo chamber. He waited a few more moments to see if the door would open, then, grimacing, he tried again, but louder. 'Alexi! Are you in there? Answer me.'

'Hey you! What are you doing here?' The elderly *gardien* was hurrying towards him, a worried expression on his face. 'This area is entirely closed off to tourists after nine o'clock in the evening.'

Sabir offered up a brief prayer of thanks that he had left his holly stick behind him in his urge to get across to the shrine. 'Look, I'm terribly sorry. But I was passing by and I heard a terrible crash from inside the shrine. I think someone's in there. Can you open up?'

The watchman hurried forward, relief at Sabir's non-aggressive tone now mingling with his anxiety. 'A crash, you say? Are you sure?'

'It sounded like someone was throwing chairs about.

Do you think you've got vandals?'

'Vandals?' The man's face took on a curious livid quality, as if he had suddenly been vouchsafed a foretaste of hell. 'But how could you have been passing by? I shut the outside gates ten minutes ago.'

Sabir suspected that the *gardien* was probably encountering the first real crisis of his career. 'Look. I'll be honest with you. I dozed off. Over there on the stone bench. It was stupid, I know. I'd just woken up when I heard the crash. You'd better take a look. I'll back you up. It may be a false alarm, of course. You're responsible to the church authorities, aren't you?'

The man hesitated, temporarily confused by Sabir's plethora of different messages. Fear for his position finally won out over his suspicions, however, and he began to feel around in his pocket for the keys. 'You're sure you heard a crash?'

'Clear as a bell. It came from just inside the Sanctuary.'

At that exact moment, as if to order, there was another, louder crash, followed by a strangled cry. Then silence.

The watchman's mouth fell open and his eyes widened. Hands shaking, he inserted the key into the massive oak door.

46

Achor Bale opened his eyes. Blood was trickling down his face and the runnels at the side of his mouth – he darted out his tongue and mopped some up. The coppery taste acted as a welcome stimulant.

He eased his neck against his shoulder and then scissored his jaws open and shut like a horse. Nothing broken. No real harm done. He glanced downwards.

The gypsy had tied him to the chair. Well. That was only to be expected. He ought to have checked over every inch of the Sanctuary first. Not assumed that his intervention with the girl had been enough to drive them off. He had never expected her to survive the river. *Tant pis*. He should have killed her outright when he had the chance – but why risk leaving traces when nature can do the job for you? The call had been a good one – the end result was just one of those things. The three of them had been incredibly quick off the mark. He must revise his opinion of Sabir. Not underestimate him again.

Bale let his chin fall back on to his chest, as if he were still unconscious. His eyes were wide open, though, and taking in all the gypsy's movements.

Now the man was clambering down the side of the display cabinet, the Black Madonna in his hands. With no hesitation whatsoever, the gypsy then upended the statue and stared intently at its base. As Bale watched, Alexi set the Madonna carefully on the floor and prostrated himself in front of it. Then he alternately kissed and laid his forehead on her feet, the baby Jesus, and on the Madonna's hand.

Bale rolled his eyes. No wonder these people were still persecuted by all and sundry. He felt like persecuting them himself.

The gypsy stood up and glanced across at him. Here it comes, thought Bale. I wonder how he'll do it? Knife probably. He couldn't really see the gypsy using the pistol. Too modern. Too complicated. He probably wouldn't be able to figure out the trigger mechanism.

Bale kept his head resolutely on his chest. I'm dead, he said to himself. I'm not breathing. The fall killed me. Come over here and check me out, *diddikai*. How can you resist? Just think what fun you'll have boasting about your exploits to the girl. Impressing the *gadje*. Playing the big man amongst your tribe.

Alexi started across the floor towards him. He stopped briefly to pick up one of the fallen brass candlesticks.

So that's how you're going to do it, eh? Beat me to death while I'm tied up? Nice. But first you'll have to check if I'm still alive. Even you wouldn't stoop to beating up a dead man. Or would you?

Alexi stopped in front of Bale's chair. He reached out and eased Bale's head away from his chest. Then he spat in Bale's face.

Bale threw himself and the chair backwards, kicking viciously upwards with both feet as he did so. Alexi screamed. He dropped the candlestick and fell, first to his knees, and then, groaning, he curled himself up in a ball on the ground.

Bale was on his feet now, hunched forwards, but with the chair still attached to his back, like a snail. He hopped towards Alexi's writhing body and threw himself backwards, corkscrew fashion, chair foremost, on to Alexi's head.

Then he rolled away, one eye on the main door of the church, the other on Alexi.

Twisting his body sideways, Bale managed to roll most of his weight on to his knees. Then he lurched upright and allowed the weight of the chair to carry him backwards against a stone pillar. He felt the chair begin to splinter. He repeated the exercise twice more, and the chair disintegrated behind him.

Alexi was twitching. One hand was reaching out across the stone floor towards the fallen candlestick.

Bale shrugged off the remaining ropes from around his shoulders and started towards him.

47

Sabir pushed past the *gardien* and into the Sanctuary antechamber. It was dark in there – almost too dark to see.

The *gardien* threw some hidden switches, and the place was transformed by a series of floodlights hidden in the roof joists. Broken pieces of wood and discarded rope lay scattered in an arc across the flagstones. Alexi lay to one side, a few feet away from the Black Madonna, his face covered in blood. A man was crouching over him, feeling through his pockets.

Sabir and the *gardien* froze. As they watched, one of Alexi's hands emerged from beneath his body, clutching a pistol. The man lurched backwards. Alexi pointed the pistol straight out in front of himself, just as if he were in the process of shooting at the man – but nothing happened. No sound emerged.

The man retreated towards the Basilica, his eyes fixed on Alexi and the pistol. At the very last moment he glanced towards Sabir and smiled. He drew a finger lightly across his throat.

Alexi let the pistol clatter to the floor. When Sabir looked again at where the man had been, he was gone.

'Can he get out that way?'

The *gardien* nodded. 'There is an exit. Yes. It's how he must have come in.'

Sabir dropped down beside Alexi – his brain was seething with possible exit strategies for themselves now. He put one hand dramatically over Alexi's heart. 'This man is badly injured. We need an ambulance.'

The *gardien* clutched at his throat. 'A mobile phone doesn't work in here. It's too near the mountainside. There's no reception. I'll need to phone from the office.' He didn't move.

'Look. I've got the pistol. I'll keep this man covered, and make sure the Virgin comes to no harm. Go and phone for the police and an ambulance. It's urgent.'

The old man seemed about to answer back.

'Otherwise I'll go and phone, and you stay here. Here's the pistol.' He held it out, butt first.

'No. No, Monsieur. They wouldn't know who you are. You stay here. I'll go.' The *gardien*'s voice was shaking and he looked on the verge of collapse.

'Be careful on the stairs.'

'Yes. Yes. I will. I'm all right. I'm all right now.'

Sabir turned his attention to Alexi. 'Can you hear me?'

'He landed on me with the chair. Some of my teeth are smashed.' Alexi's voice was blurred, as if he were talking from somewhere deep inside a sealed container. 'I think my jaw is maybe broken too. And some ribs.'

'And the rest of you?'

'I'm all right. I'll be able to walk.'

'Okay. We've got about five minutes' grace in which to make our way out of here and back up to the car. Here. Take this.' He handed Alexi the pistol.

'It's useless. It doesn't work.'

'Take it anyway. And try to pull yourself together a little while I wrap up the Virgin.'

'Check on the base first.'

'What do you mean?'

'There's writing there. I couldn't read it but it's burned in. Just like on that coffer of Yola's. It's the first place I looked.'

Sabir hefted the Black Madonna. It was a good deal lighter than he had at first supposed. Around two feet tall, it was carved out of dark stained wood and garlanded with two crowns, one on the Virgin's head and one on that of Jesus – in addition, the Virgin wore a golden necklet. Her body was partially encased in a sort of fabric, which was coming apart across her left breast, revealing paler wood beneath. She was seated on a chair, and the baby Christ was seated on her lap. His face was not that of a child, however, but that of a wise older man.

'You're right. I'm going to trace it.'

'Why not take it with us?'

'It'll be safer here than out on the road with us. And we don't want a second police force on our tail. If nothing's stolen, there's a fair chance they'll drop the whole thing after a few days, with nobody but the old man to question. We've got what we came for. I figure this is just another fragment of a larger map that will eventually lead us to the verses.' He laid a piece of paper across the base of the Madonna, and began tracing across it with the stump of a pencil.

'I can't stand up. I think he did more damage than I thought.'

'Wait for me. I'll be with you in a minute.'

Alexi made an attempt at a laugh. 'Don't worry, Adam. I'm not going anywhere.'

—

48

Sabir stopped to catch his breath. Alexi was leaning against him with all his weight. Below them they could hear the distant sound of approaching police sirens. 'I still haven't fully recovered from my blood poisoning. I'm as weak as a kitten. I don't think I can get you up there alone.'

'How much further do we have to go?'

'I can see the car now. I can't risk calling Yola, though. Someone might hear.'

'Why don't you leave me here and go to fetch her? Both of you could carry me the last bit of the way.'

'Are you sure you're all right?'

'I think I've just swallowed one of my teeth. If I don't choke on it, I'll be all right.'

Sabir left Alexi leaning against the protective fence at the edge of the path. He hurried up the hill.

Yola was standing by the car, a worried expression on her face. 'I didn't know what to do. I heard the sirens. I wasn't sure if they were for you or for someone else.'

'Alexi is injured. We're going to have to carry him up the steepest part of the hill between us. Are you up to it?'

'Is he badly hurt?'

'He's lost a few teeth. He may have a broken jaw. Possibly some cracked ribs. Someone landed on him with a chair.'

'Someone?'

'Yes. That someone.'

'Is the man dead? Did you kill him?'

'Alexi tried to kill him. But the pistol jammed.'

Yola took Alexi's feet, with Sabir taking the main weight of his body.

'We're going to have to make this fast. The minute that old *gardien* talks to the police and tells them that there was a pistol involved in the break-in, we're for it. They'll seal off the entire valley and send in the paramilitaries. And as I remember from the map, there are only three ways out of here. And they're as good as covering the two main ones already.'

49

‒

'I'm pretty certain nobody's been following us.' Sabir squinted ahead, trying to make out the road signs.

They were beyond the main danger area now, on the Route National 20, with considerably more traffic on the road to disguise their passage. The relief in the car was palpable, as if, through luck and sheer good timing, they had succeeded in avoiding a particularly nasty accident.

'How is he?'

Yola shrugged. 'I don't think his jaw is broken. Some

of his ribs are definitely cracked, though. Now he'll have the perfect excuse for being idle.'

Alexi looked as though he were about to sass her back, but then he unexpectedly changed tack and punched at his trouser pocket. 'Ha! Do you believe this? I had it right in here.'

'What?'

'The wallet.' Alexi shook his head disconsolately. 'That bloody thief bastard stole back his own wallet. And it was stuffed with cash. I could have lived like a king. Even bought myself some gold teeth.'

Sabir laughed. 'Don't knock it, Alexi. The fact that he was worried we might find out his identity probably saved your life. If he hadn't gone searching for his wallet, he would have had ample time to kill you before we came in.'

Alexi's attention had moved on. He raised his head from the seat and flashed his remaining teeth at Yola. 'Hey, nurse. I heard what you said about being idle. It's not just my ribs, you know. He kicked me in the balls, too.'

Yola extended the gap between them on the rear seat. 'You can deal with those yourself. I don't want to go anywhere near them.'

'You hear that, *gadje*? This woman is frigid. No wonder no one has ever offered to kidnap her.'

Yola drew up her knees as if in self-defence. 'Don't flatter yourself. Now that you've been damaged in the balls, you'll make a useless kidnapper to someone too. You'll probably be impotent. They'll be forced to go elsewhere if they want their eyes taken out. Or use a cucumber.'

'That's not true!' Alexi reached forwards, grunting, and tapped Sabir on the shoulder. 'That's not true, is it, Adam? That if you get kicked in the balls you'll go impotent?'

122

'How should I know? It could be, I suppose. You'll know in a few days, either way.' Sabir turned to Yola. 'Yola, what did you mean by "if they want their eyes taken out"?'

Yola dropped her gaze. She glanced out of the car window. Silence descended on the three of them.

'Oh, yeah. I get it. Sorry.' Sabir cleared his throat. 'Look, I want to say something to the two of you. Something important.'

'We haven't eaten yet.'

'What?'

'Never say something important when you are hungry or in pain. The hunger and pain speak instead of you, and what you say is of no value.'

Sabir let out a sigh – he knew when he was beaten. 'I'll stop at a restaurant, then.'

'A restaurant?'

'Yes. And we'd better set about finding a hotel.'

Yola started laughing. Alexi began to join in, but stopped very quickly when he realised how much it cost him in rib and jaw pain.

'No, Adam. We'll sleep in the car tonight, as it's too late to arrive anywhere without causing questions to be asked. Then tomorrow, first thing in the morning, we'll drive to Gourdon.'

'Why would we want to go there?'

'There's a permanent campsite. We can get food. Somewhere proper to sleep. I have cousins there.'

'More cousins!'

'Don't scoff, Adam. Now that you are my *phral*, they will be your cousins too.'

123

50

Captain Joris Calque did not approve of television at breakfast. In fact he didn't approve of television per se. But the *patronne* of the *chambre d'hôte* in which he and Macron now found themselves appeared to think it was what was expected. She even stood behind them at the table, commenting on all the local news.

'I suppose, being policemen, that you are always on the lookout for new crimes?'

Macron inconspicuously raised his eyes to heaven. Calque concentrated even more intently on his banana fritters with apple mousse.

'Nothing is sacred any more. Not even the Church.'

Calque realised that he would have to say something, or be considered rude. 'What? Has someone stolen a church?'

'No, Monsieur. Far worse than that.'

'Good God!'

Macron nearly achieved the nose trick with his scrambled egg. He covered it up with a coughing fit, which necessitated Madame fussing around him for a couple of minutes, dispensing coffee and hearty slaps on the back.

'No. Not a church, Inspector.'

'Captain.'

'Captain. As I said. Something far worse than that. The Virgin herself.'

'Someone stole the Virgin?'

'No. There was heavenly intervention. The thieves were stopped in their tracks and punished. They must have been after the jewels in her and the baby Jesus's crown. Nothing is sacred any more, Inspector. Nothing.'

'And what Virgin was this, Madame?'

'But it's just been on the television.'

'I was eating, Madame. One cannot eat and look at the same time. It is unhealthy.'

'It was the Virgin at Rocamadour, Inspector. The Black Madonna herself.'

'And when did this attempted theft occur?'

'Last night. After they had locked the Sanctuary. They even used a pistol. Fortunately the *gardien* wrestled it from one of the men – like Jacob wrestling with the angel. And then the Virgin made her miraculous intervention and drove the robbers off.'

'Her miraculous intervention?' Macron had stopped with the fork halfway to his mouth. 'Against a pistol? At Rocamadour? But, Captain . . .'

Calque glanced meaningfully across the table at him. 'You are right, Madame. Nothing is sacred any more. Nothing.'

51

'And this man pretended that he was a member of the public? He pretended to help you?' Calque was trying to estimate the *gardien*'s age, but he finally gave up at around seventy-two.

'Oh yes, Monsieur. It was he who brought my attention to the disturbance in the Sanctuary in the first place.'

'But now you think that he was part of the gang?'

'Certainly, Monsieur. I am sure of it. I left him behind covering the other man with the pistol. I needed to phone, you see, but the only problem is that the mobile phones the church authorities give us don't work here underneath the cliff. They are useless. We have to go back to the office and use the old landline whenever we want to call out. They do it on purpose, in my opinion, to stop us from misusing the service.' He crossed himself in penance for his uncharitable thoughts. 'But then all these modern contraptions don't really work. Take my grandson's computer, for instance . . .'

'Why didn't they take the Black Madonna with them, if they were part of the same gang? They had ample time before either you, or the police, returned to the scene.'

'The younger boy was injured, Monsieur. He had blood all over his face. I believe he fell while trying to steal the Virgin.' He crossed himself again. 'Perhaps the older man could not carry both him and the Virgin?'

'Yes. Yes. You may be right. Where is the Virgin now?'

'Back in her case.'

'May we see her?'

The old man hesitated. 'It will mean returning to the storeroom to fetch the ladder and . . .'

'My junior, Lieutenant Macron, will arrange all that. You won't have to put yourself to any additional trouble on our behalf. That, I promise you.'

'Well, all right then. But please take care. It is a miracle she was not damaged in the fracas of last night.'

'You behaved very well. It is entirely to your credit that the Virgin has been restored.'

The *gardien* hitched his shoulders. 'You think so? You really think so?'

'I am entirely convinced of the fact.'

126

'Look, Macron. Come over here and tell me what you make of this.' Calque was staring at the base of the Virgin. He allowed his thumb to travel over the deeply incised letters that had been chiselled into the wood.

Macron took the Virgin from his hands. 'Well, the carving was certainly done a long time ago. You can tell that by the way the wood has darkened. Quite unlike these other marks on her breast.'

'Those were probably done in the Revolution.'

'What do you mean?'

'Neither the Protestants, during the Wars of Religion, nor our revolutionary ancestors, approved of graven images. In most of the churches of France they destroyed statues of Christ, the Virgin and the Holy Saints. They tried that here too. Legend has it that they tore off the silver which originally covered the Virgin, and then were so astonished by the dignity of what was revealed beneath, that they left her alone.'

'You don't believe in all that rot, do you?'

Calque took back the Virgin. 'It's not a matter of belief. It's a matter of listening. History keeps its secrets on open display, Macron. Only someone with eyes to see and ears to hear can disentangle their real essence from the flotsam and jetsam that float alongside them.'

'I don't understand what you are talking about.'

Calque sighed. 'Let's take this as an example. It's a statue of the Virgin and Child, wouldn't you say?'

'Of course it is.'

'And we know that this particular Virgin protects sailors. You see that bell up there? When it suddenly tolls of its own accord, it means a sailor has been miraculously saved from the sea by the Virgin's intervention. Or that a

127

storm will come, and a miracle occur.'

'That's just the wind, surely. Wind usually comes before a storm.'

Calque smiled. He spread some paper over the base of the statue, and began to trace over the letters with his pen. 'Well, Isis, the Egyptian goddess, wife and sister of Osiris and sister of Set, was also believed to save sailors from the sea. And we know that she was frequently depicted seated on a throne, with her son, Horus the Child, on her lap. Horus is the god of light, of the sun, of the day, of life, and of good, and his nemesis, Set, who was Isis's sworn enemy, was the god of the night, of evil, of darkness, and of death. Set had tricked Osiris, chief of the gods, into trying out a beautifully crafted coffin, and had sealed him inside it and sent him down the Nile, where a tree grew around him. Later, he cut Osiris's body into fourteen pieces. But Isis found the coffin and its contents and reassembled them, with Thoth, the mediator's, help, and Osiris then came back to life just long enough to impregnate her with Horus, their son.'

'I don't understand . . .'

'Macron, the Black Virgin is Isis. The Christ figure is Horus. All that happened was that the Christians usurped the ancient Egyptian gods and transformed them into something more palatable to a modern sensibility.'

'Modern?'

'Osiris was resurrected, you see. He came back from the dead. And he had a son. Who pitted himself against the forces of evil. Doesn't that sound familiar to you?'

'I suppose so.'

'Both Jesus and Horus were born in a stable. And their births are both celebrated on the 25th of December.'

Macron's eyes had begun to glaze.

Calque shrugged. 'Well. Anyway. Here is what Sabir

and your eye-man were looking for.' He held up the sheet of paper.

'It's in gobbledegook.'

'No it's not. It's written in reverse. All we need to do is to find a mirror, and we should be able to disentangle it.'

'How do you know they were looking for it?'

'Logic, Macron. Look. They broke in here for a purpose. That purpose was to steal the Virgin. But the eye-man was also here. They succeeded in driving him away, though, leaving Sabir, the gypsy and the *gardien* alone in the Sanctuary. But the old man is bewildered by it all, and is too old to take charge, so he obeys Sabir and trots off back to the office to phone. The two of them could easily have managed to take the Virgin with them then. She's only around seventy centimetres tall, and hardly weighs anything. But they don't. They leave her behind. And why do they do that? Because they already have what they came for. Bring me that torch.'

'But it's evidence. There may be fingerprints on it.'

'Just bring me the torch, Macron.' Calque turned the paper over. 'Now we'll shine it against the writing.'

'Ah. That's clever. No need of a mirror.'

'Take this down in your notebook:

"*Il sera ennemi et pire qu'ayeulx
Il naistra en fer, de serpente mammelle
Le rat monstre gardera son secret
Il sera mi homme et mi femelle*"'

'What does it mean?'

'Don't you understand your own language?'

'Well, of course I do.'

'Then you decipher it.'

'Well, the first line reads "He will be an enemy and worse . . ."' Macron hesitated.

129

'". . . than anyone before him."'

'"He will be born in iron . . ."'

'". . . of hell," Macron. *Enfer* means hell. Ignore the fact that it's been split in two. People aren't born of iron.'

'". . . of hell," then, "with the nipple of a serpent . . ."'

'". . . he will suckle from a serpent's breast."'

Macron sighed. He exhaled loudly, as if he had just hefted a set of massive weights in the gym. '"The monstrous rat will hide his secret . . ."'

'Go on.'

'"He will be half man and half woman."'

'Excellent. But the last line may also be read as "He will be neither man nor woman."'

'How do you work that one out?'

'Because of the clue given in line one. The use of the word '*ennemi*'. It implies that when *mi* reappears, the *em* should be changed to *en*.'

'You're joking?'

'Have you never done crosswords?'

'They didn't have crosswords in medieval France.'

'They had better than crosswords. They had the Kabbalah. It was normal practice to disguise or codify one word by using another. Just as the author has done in line three, with *rat monstre*. It's an anagram. We know that because the two words are followed by the word *secret*, which acts as the pointer. Just like in crosswords. Again.'

'How do you know all these things?'

'It's a little thing called a classical education. Linked to another little thing called common sense. It's something they obviously failed to teach you people down in that *bidonville* of a school of yours in Marseille.'

Macron allowed the insult to wash over him. For once

in his life he found himself more interested in the case than in himself. 'Who do you think wrote this stuff? And why are these maniacs after it?'

'Do you want my honest opinion?'

'Yes.'

'The Devil.'

Macron's mouth dropped open. 'You're not serious?'

Calque folded up the sheet of paper and put it in his pocket. 'Of course I'm not serious. The Devil doesn't bother to write people billets-doux, Macron. Hell always comes by Express Delivery.'

52
—

Yola sat up higher in her seat. 'Look. There's going to be a wedding.' She turned and stared critically at the two men. 'I shall have to wash and mend your clothes. You can't appear in public like that. And you'll need jackets and ties.'

'My clothes are fine as they are, thank you.' Sabir turned to Yola. 'And how the hell did you work that one out about the wedding? We haven't even arrived in the camp yet.'

Alexi let out a snort. He lay sprawled across the back seat, with his bandaged head propped comfortably against the window. 'Are all you *gadjes* blind? We've already passed four caravans on the way here. Where do you think they're going?'

'To a funeral? To another of your Krisses?'

'Did you notice the faces of the women?'

'No.'

'Well, if you used your eyes for once – like a gypsy – you would have seen that the women were excited, not sad.' He ran his finger around the inside of his mouth, testing the new geography. 'Have you got fifty euros on you?'

Sabir switched his attention back to the road. 'That will scarcely be enough to buy you a new set of gold teeth.'

Alexi grimaced. 'Have you got them?'

'Yes.'

'Well give them to me. I'm going to have to pay someone to watch the car.'

'What are you talking about, Alexi?'

'Just what I said before. If you don't pay someone to watch it, someone else will strip it clean. They're thieves, these people.'

'What do you mean, "these people"? They're your people, Alexi.'

'I know that. That's why I know they're thieves.'

～

Sabir and Alexi had been allocated the corner of one of Alexi's cousins' caravans. Alexi was recuperating on the single cot, with Sabir seated below him, on the floor.

'Show me the pistol, Alexi. I want to see why it misfired.'

'It didn't misfire. It just didn't fire at all. I would have had him. Straight through the nose.'

'You know about safety catches?'

'Of course I know about safety catches. What do you think I am? An idiot?'

132

'And you know about cocking?'

'Cocking? What's cocking?'

'Ah.' Sabir sighed. 'Before you can shoot an automatic pistol, you have to pull back this catch here, and cock it. It's called locking and loading in the military.'

'*Putain*. I thought it worked like a revolver.'

'Only revolvers work like revolvers, Alexi. Here. Try it.'

'Hey. It's easy.'

'Stop pointing it at me.'

'It's all right, Adam. I'm not going to shoot you. I don't hate *gadjes* that bad.'

'I'm very relieved to hear it.' Sabir frowned. 'So tell me, Alexi. Where's Yola gone?'

'To be with the women.'

'What do you mean?'

'I mean that we won't see her so much for a while. Not like when we're on the road.'

Sabir shook his head. 'I don't get this gypsy split between men and women, Alexi. And what's all this about impurities and polluting people? What did she call it? *Mah* . . . something or other.'

'*Mahrimé*.'

'That's it.'

'It's normal. There are things that pollute, and things that don't pollute.'

'Like hedgehogs.'

'Yes. Hedgehogs are clean. So are horses. They don't lick their own genitals. Dogs and cats are filthy.'

'And women?'

'They don't do that either. What do you think? That they're contortionists?'

Sabir slapped the sole of Alexi's foot. 'I'm serious. I really want to know.'

'It's complicated. Women can pollute when they're

bleeding. When that happens, a woman can't hold someone else's baby, for instance. Or touch a man. Or cook. Or walk over a broom. Or do anything, really. That's why a woman must never be above a man. In a bunk, say. Or in a house. He would be polluted.'

'Jesus.'

'I tell you, Adam. In my father's time it used to be worse. Gypsy men could not travel on the Paris Metro, in case, by accident, a gypsy woman would be on the pavement above them. Food had to be placed outside the house, in case a woman walked on the floor above it. Or touched it with her dress.'

'You can't be serious.'

'I'm very serious. And why do you think Yola asked me to be in the room with you when she showed you the coffer?'

'Because she wanted to involve you?'

'No. Because it is not right for an unmarried woman to be alone in a room with a bed in it, in company with a man who is not her brother or her father. Also you were a *gadje*, and that made you *mahrimé*.'

'So that's why the old woman back at the camp wouldn't eat with me?'

'You've got it. She would have polluted you.'

'She would have polluted *me*? But I thought *I* would have polluted her?'

Alexi made a face. 'No. I was wrong. You haven't got it.'

'And then all this stuff with women wearing long dresses. And yet Yola doesn't seem to mind baring her breasts in public. I'm thinking of during the funeral.'

'Breasts are for feeding children.'

'Well I know that . . .'

'But a woman shouldn't show her knees. That's not good. It's up to her not to inflame her father-in-law's

134

passions. Or those of men other than her husband. Knees can do that.'

'But what about all the women here in France? You see them in the street all the time. Hell, they bare just about everything.'

'But they are *payos*. Or *gadje*. They don't count.'

'Oh. I see.'

'Now you are one of us, Adam, you matter. Not as much as a real gypsy, maybe. But you matter.'

'Thank you for that. I'm very relieved.'

'Maybe we even get you a wife some day. Someone ugly. Whom no one else wants.'

'Fuck you, Alexi.'

53

—

'There's going to be a wedding.'

'A wedding?' Calque looked up from the library book he was working on.

'Yes. I talked to the chief of the Gourdon gendarmerie just as you suggested. There have been caravans arriving for three days now. They've even drafted in two extra officers in case of disturbances. Drunks. Trouble with the townspeople. That sort of thing.'

'Any movement of our trio?'

'None. I suspect they're going to be here for the duration. Especially if one of them is injured. Their car is parked at the periphery of the camp. Frankly, they must be mad. A brand-new Audi in that place? It's like waving a pair of used panties in front of a pubescent boy.'

'Your metaphor lacks both grace and merit, Macron.'

'I'm sorry, Sir.' Macron searched around for something neutral to say. Some harmless way of diffusing his anger at the situation Calque was placing them in. 'What are you doing, Sir?'

'I'm trying to decode this anagram. At first I thought *rat monstre* was simply an anagram for *monastère*. That it meant that the secret of whatever it is these people are searching for will be kept in a monastery.'

'But there aren't enough letters for that. Look. There are too many tees and not enough ees.'

'I know that.' Calque scowled at him. 'I've realised that. However, I was making the perfectly reasonable assumption that the author of this verse may have been using an antiquated spelling – *monastter*, for instance. Or *montaster*.'

'But it's not that?'

'No. Now I'm looking through this book for other sites in France which have Black Virgins. Perhaps we'll get to it that way.'

'But why does it have to be in France?'

'What are you talking about, Macron?'

'Why does the place in which this secret is hidden have to be in France? Why not in Spain?'

'Explain yourself.'

'My mother is very Catholic, Sir. Particularly so, I should say. When I was a child, she would frequently take us the few hundred kilometres down the coast to Barcelona. By train. On the Estérel. It was her idea of a day out.'

'Get to the point, Macron. I haven't got time to listen to stories of your happy childhood holidays just now.'

'No, Sir. I'm coming to the point. Near Barcelona,

not far from Terrassa, lies one of Spain's holiest shrines. It's called Montserrat. I don't remember if there's a Black Virgin there, but it's one of the spiritual homes of the Jesuits. St Ignatius de Loyola hung up his armour there after he decided to become a monk. My mother is particularly fond of the Jesuits, you see.'

Calque rocked back in his chair. 'Macron. For once in your life you've succeeded in surprising me. Perhaps we'll make a detective of you yet.' He began leafing through the book. 'Yes. Here we are. Montserrat. And it's spelled with two tees. Brilliant. And there is a Black Virgin there. Listen to this:

'The worship of La Virgen de Montserrat, otherwise known as La Morenita, or the Dark One, dates back to 888, when she was found hidden high on the Sierra de Montserrat by a group of shepherds, under the protection of a flock of angels. Carved by St Luke himself, the statue was believed to have been brought from Jerusalem to Montserrat by St Peter, where it had lain undisturbed for hundreds of years. Soon after her discovery, the Bishop of Manresa tried to move the statue, but she remained firmly in place. The Count of Barcelona became her first protector and his son dedicated a shrine to her in 932, an endowment sanctified by King Lothaire of France in 982. Montserrat is now a centre for both pilgrimage and for the promulgation of Catalan nationalism. Married couples visit from all over Spain in order to have their union blessed by the Virgin, for, as the saying goes, "No es ben casat qui no dun la done a Montserrat." "A man is not properly married until he has taken his bride to Montserrat." It is also alleged that the present shrine once housed an altar to Venus, goddess of beauty, mother of love, Queen of laughter, the mistress of the graces and pleasure, and the patroness of courtesans.'

Calque clapped his hands together. 'Venus, Macron.

Now we're getting somewhere. Do you remember how the verse went? "He will be neither man nor woman." '

'What's that got to do with Venus?'

Calque sighed. 'Venus was also called Cypria, after her main place of worship on the island of Cyprus. There was a famous statue there, in which Cypria was portrayed with a beard and carrying a sceptre. However, and here is the link with the verse, the male-seeming Cypria had the body of a woman, and was dressed in female clothes. Catullus, when he saw the statue, even called her the *duplex Amathusia*. She is a hermaphrodite, in other words, just like her son.'

'A what?'

'A hermaphrodite. Half man, half woman. Neither one thing, nor the other.'

'And what's that got to do with the Black Virgin?'

'Two things. One: it confirms your reading of Montserrat – excellent work, Macron. Two: when paired with the writing carved on its base, it further reinforces the connection between the Black Virgin of Montserrat and that of Rocamadour.'

'How do you figure that one out?'

'Do you remember the faces of the Virgin of Rocamadour and her son? Look. Here is a picture.'

'I don't see anything. It's just a statue.'

'Macron. Use your eyes. The two faces are similar. Interchangeable. They could both be male, or both be female.'

'I'm completely lost. I really don't see what this has to do with our murder.'

'Frankly, neither do I. But I agree with you about the wedding. I think the gypsies will stay here for the duration and lick their wounds. Sabir is another matter, of course. And where he goes, the eye-man will surely follow. So we are going to be ahead of the game for once.

We are going on a field trip.'

'A field trip? To where?'

'To renew acquaintance with your childhood haunts, Macron. We are going to Spain. To Montserrat. To visit a lady.'

54

Achor Bale watched the new young security guard work his dog in and out of every corner of the St-Sauveur Basilica. You had to hand it to the Rocamadour church authorities. They hadn't been slow off the mark in the recruitment stakes. Still. Must be soul-destroying work. What were the chances of a miscreant coming back to the scene of his crime the very evening after an attempted robbery? A million to one against? More than that, probably. Bale eased himself closer to the edge of the organ loft. Another minute and the man would be directly beneath him.

It had been child's play to switch the tracker back on and follow Sabir and the two gypsies as far as Gourdon. In fact Bale had been sorely tempted to ambush them that first night, while they were sleeping in the car. But they had chosen a particularly inconvenient spot, slap bang in the middle of a bustling market town, on the outskirts of the Bouriane – the sort of place that had security cameras, and eager-beaver policemen on the lookout for drunks and pugnacious young farmers.

Bale's decision had been duly validated when he had

heard on the radio that the robbers had left the Virgin behind them. What was that all about? Why hadn't they stolen her? They had his pistol. And the *gardien* was midway between senescence and the grave. No. He had definitely seen the gypsy squinting at the base of the Virgin before indulging in all that religious mumbo-jumbo of his – which meant that there was something written there, just as the girl had implied at the riverbank. Something that Bale desperately needed to see.

Now the security guard was zigzagging up and down between the pews, urging his dog forwards with a sequence of short whistles. You'd think someone was filming him, the zeal he was showing for his new job. Any normal human being would have stopped for a cigarette long ago. This one would have to be put well out of the way. The dog, too, of course.

Bale threw the candle-holder high over the man's head, counted to three and launched himself out of the loft. The man had made himself an easy mark, just as he'd known. Hearing the noise of the candle-holder, he'd instantly turned away from his perusal of the organ and flashed his torch at the fallen object.

Bale's feet caught him on the back of the neck. The man jerked forward, landing with the full weight of Bale's projectile body driving him on to the flagstones. It had been an eight-foot drop for Bale. The security guard might as well have launched himself off a foot ladder with a rope tied around his neck.

Bale heard the vertebral crunch immediately he landed, and turned his attention directly to the dog. The dead man still had his hand looped through the braided leather leash. The Alsatian instinctively backed away, crouching prior to his leap forward. Bale grabbed the leash and swung, like a baseball player striking out for a home run. The Alsatian took off, propelled both by its own forward impetus and the centrifugal throw-out of Bale's swing. Bale let go of the leash at the perfect moment. The principle of the fulcrum worked to its full effect, sending the dog star-fishing across the church like an athlete's hammer shot. The animal struck the stone wall of the church, fell to the floor and began howling. Bale ran across and stamped on its head.

He stood for a moment, listening, with his mouth and eyes wide open like a cat. Then, satisfied that no one had overheard him, he set off for the Sanctuary.

55

Sabir resettled the blanket over his groin. There were times – and this was one of them – when he wished that Yola could wean herself off the habit of bursting into people's rooms unannounced. Earlier that afternoon she had taken their clothes to the communal washtub, leaving both of the men wrapped in blankets, like shipwreck victims, and forced to contemplate indefinite, unwanted siestas. Now Sabir found himself frantically searching around for something innocuous to say in order to defuse his embarrassment.

'All right. I've thought of another riddle for you. This one is a real stinker. Ready? "What is greater than God? More evil than the Devil? The poor already have it. The rich want it. And if you eat it, you die."'

Yola scarcely looked up from what she was doing. 'Nothing, of course.'

141

Sabir slumped back against the wall. 'Oh Christ. How did you get the answer so quickly? It took me well over an hour when my cousin's boy tried it out on me.'

'But it's obvious, Adam. I got it in the first line. When you asked what is greater than God. Nothing is greater than God. The rest falls into place when you realise that.'

'Yeah, well, I got that bit too. But I didn't stop to think that it might be the answer. I just got irritated and outraged that anyone could imagine that there was something greater than God.'

'You're a man, Adam. Men are born angry. That's why they have to laugh at everything. Or strike out at things. Or act like children. If they didn't, they'd go mad.'

'Thank you. Thank you for that one. Now I know where I get my sense of humour.'

Yola had conjured up an entire change of clothing for herself. She was sporting a red-flowered blouse, buttoned to the collar, and a hip-hugging green skirt with a flared rim, reaching to just below the knee. The skirt was cinched in at the waist with a broad leather belt studded with small mirrors, and she was wearing Cuban-heeled shoes with ankle straps. Her hair was partially up, just as it had been at the Kriss.

'Why don't you ever wear jewellery? Like some of the other women?'

'Because I'm a virgin and still unmarried.' Yola cast a loaded glance at Alexi, who somehow contrived to ignore it. 'It wouldn't be seemly to compete with the bride and her married female relatives.' She fussed around laying out two sets of clothes on the bed, near Alexi's feet. 'Your own clothes are still drying. I'll bring them in when they're ready. But here are two suits and two ties I borrowed. Also some shirts. They should fit you. Tomorrow, at the wedding, you must also have some paper money ready to give to the bride. You'll need to pin it on to her dress with this.' She handed each man a safety pin.

'Eh, Adam . . .'

'Don't tell me, Alexi. You need to borrow some money.'

'It's not only me. Yola needs some too. But she's too proud to ask.'

Yola flapped her hand in irritation. Her gaze was focused on Sabir. 'What were you going to tell us in the car? When I stopped you?'

'I don't understand . . .'

'You said you had something important to say. Well. We've eaten. We've rested. Now you can speak.'

It had to come, thought Sabir. I should have learned by now – Yola never leaves a thing alone until she's worried the juice out of it. 'I think you both ought to stay here. For the time being, at least.'

'What do you mean?'

'Alexi's injured. He needs to recuperate. And you, Yola . . . Well, you had a terrible shock.' He reached across the table for his wallet. 'I've figured out the rhyme on the foot of the Black Virgin, you see.' He pulled out a crumpled piece of paper and flattened it against his knee. 'I think it refers to Montserrat. That's a place in Spain. In the hills above Barcelona. At least that seems to be the gist of it.'

'You think we're wasting our time, don't you? That's why you don't want us along? You think this man will appear again and harm us if we continue along this path. But worse this time, maybe?'

'I think we're on a dangerous wild goose chase, yes. Look. Nostradamus, or your ancestors, or whoever carved these things on the Virgin's feet – they could have carved stuff on half a hundred Virgins around the country. Things

143

were much looser then than they are now. People made pilgrimages all over the place. It doesn't take a genius to work out that eighty per cent of the Virgins that existed then are probably gone – victims of a dozen different religious wars. Not to mention the Revolution, the First and Second World Wars and the war with Prussia. Your people were nomadic, Yola. Far more so than they are now. They spent their time avoiding armies, not going in search of them. It's odds on that if we find writing on the Montserrat Virgin's feet, it'll just lead us somewhere else. And then somewhere else again. That the verses, or whatever it is we are searching for, are long gone.'

'Then why did the man follow us? What does he want?'

'I think he's crazy. He's got some notion in his head that there's money tied up in this thing, and he simply can't leave it alone.'

'You don't believe that.'

Sabir shook his head. 'No.'

'So why are you saying this? Don't you like us any more?'

Sabir felt momentarily at a loss, as if he had been blind-sided by a child. 'Of course I like you. These last few days . . . well . . . they've felt like years. Like we've always been together. I don't know how to explain it.'

'Because we've met before? Is that what you are saying?'

'Met before? No. I wasn't . . .'

'Alexi has told you I am *hexi*. This means I know things sometimes. Sense things. That happened with you. I instantly sensed that you meant the right thing by me. That you hadn't killed Babel. I fought against it, but my instinct told me I was right. Alexi felt it too.' She cast a surreptitious glance back towards the bed. 'He's not *hexi*, though. He's just a stupid gypsy.'

144

Alexi made a rude sign at her but his heart wasn't in it. He was watching her intently. Listening to her words.

'We gypsies feel things stronger than *payos* and *gadjes*. We listen to the voices inside us. Sometimes it sends us wrong. Like it did with Babel. But most times it's right.'

'And where's it sending you now?'

'With you.'

'Yola. This man is evil. Look what he did to you. To Babel. He would have killed Alexi, too, if we'd given him the time.'

'You were going to leave without us. To sneak out at night. Like a thief. Weren't you?'

'Of course I wasn't.' Sabir could feel the lie reflected on his face. Even his mouth went loose in the telling of it, muffling his words.

'Listen to me. You're Babel's *phral*. He exchanged his blood with you. Which means that we are related, all three of us, by blood as well as by law. So we're going to this wedding. Together. We're going to be happy and joyful and remind ourselves of what living on this earth really means. Then, when the morning after the wedding comes, you'll stand in front of us and tell us whether you want us to go with you or not. I owe a duty to you now. You are my brother. The head of my family. If you tell me not to come, I shall obey. But you will scar my heart if you leave me behind. And Alexi loves you like a brother. He will weep and be sad to know you do not trust him.'

Alexi put on a mournful face, only half mitigated by the holes left by his missing teeth.

'All right, Alexi. You don't need to lay it on with a trowel.' Sabir stood up. 'Now that you've decided what it is we need to do, Yola, could you please tell me if there is anywhere to wash and shave around here?'

'Come outside. I will show you.'

Sabir caught Yola's warning look just as he was about to include Alexi in his intended exodus. Clutching the blanket about him like a Roman toga, he followed her out of the hut.

She stood, hands on her hips, looking out over the camp. 'You see that man? The blond one who is watching us from the steps of the new caravan?'

'Yes.'

'He wants to kidnap me.'

'Yola . . .'

'His name is Gavril. He hates Alexi because Alexi's father was a chief and gave a ruling against his family that resulted in an exile.'

'An exile?'

'That is when a person is banished from the tribe. Gavril is angry, also, that he is blond and an only child. People say that he was abducted from a *gadje* woman. That his mother couldn't have children of her own and so her husband did this terrible thing. So he is doubly angry.'

'And yet he wants to kidnap you?'

'He is not really interested in me. He just pesters me to go behind the hedge with him because he knows it angers Alexi. I was hoping he would not be here. But he is. He will be happy that Alexi has been injured. Happy that he has lost some teeth and cannot afford to replace them.'

Sabir could feel the tectonic plates of his former certainties shifting and resettling themselves into a subtly different configuration. He was getting used to the feeling now. Almost liking it. 'And what do you want me to do about him?'

'I want you to watch out for Alexi. Stay with him. Don't let him drink too much. In our weddings, men and women are separated, for the most part, and I will not be able to protect him from himself. This man, Gavril, means badly by us. You are Alexi's cousin. Once you've been introduced to the head man here, and formally invited to the wedding, people will stop staring at you, and you will be able to blend in more. No one will dare to denounce you. Now you stick out like an albino.'

'Yola. Can I ask you a question?'

'Yes.'

'Why does everything have to be so damned complicated around you?'

56
—

Captain Bartolomeo Villada i Lluçanes, of the Policia Local de Catalunya, offered Calque a Turkish cigarette from the amber cigarette box he kept in a specially carved indentation on his desk.

'Do I look like a smoker?'

'Yes.'

'You're right. I am. But my doctor has warned me to give up.'

'Does your doctor smoke?'

'Yes.'

'Does your undertaker smoke?'

'Probably.'

'Well then.'

Calque took the cigarette, lit it and inhaled. 'Why is

it that something which kills you can also make you feel the most alive?'

Villada sighed. 'It is what is called by the philosophers a paradox. When God made us, he decided that literalism would be the bane of the world. He therefore invented the paradox to counteract it.'

'But how do we counteract the paradox?'

'By taking it literally. See. You are smoking. And yet you understand the paradox of your position.'

Calque smiled. 'Will you do as I ask, then? Will you take this risk with your men? I would fully understand if you decided against it.'

'You really believe that Sabir will abandon his friends and come alone? And that the man you call the eye-man will follow him?'

'They both need to know what is on the base of La Morenita. Just as I do. Can you arrange it?'

'A visit to La Morenita will be arranged. In the interests of cross-border cooperation, needless to say.' Villada gave an ironical inclination of the head. 'As for the other thing . . .' He tapped his lighter on the desk, swivelling it from back to front between his fingers. 'I shall stake out the Sanctuary, as you suggest. For three nights only. The Virgen de Montserrat has much significance for Catalunya. My mother would never forgive me if I allowed her to be violated.'

57

Sabir didn't feel entirely comfortable in his borrowed
suit. The lapels were nearly a foot wide and the jacket
fitted him like a morning coat – in fact, it made him look
like Cab Calloway in *Stormy Weather*. The shirt, too,
left something to be desired; he had never been fond
of sunflowers and waterwheels, particularly in terms of
creative design. The tie was of the fluorescent kipper
variety and clashed abominably with his shirt, which
itself clashed with the maroon stripes which some joker
of a tailor had allowed to be interleaved throughout the
suiting material. At least the shoes were his own.

'You look fantastic. Like a gypsy. If you didn't have
that *payo* mug of yours, I'd want you for a brother.'

'How do you keep a straight face when you say things
like that, Alexi?'

'My jaw is broken. That is how.'

Despite all Yola's protestations to the contrary, Sabir
still felt that he stuck out like an albino. Everyone was
watching him. Wherever he went, whatever he did,
gazes slid off him and then back on again as soon as his
attention was diverted towards somewhere else. 'Are you
sure they're not going to turn me in? I'm probably still
appearing nightly on TV. There's probably a reward.'

'Everybody here knows of the Kriss. They know you
are Yola's *phral*. That the Bulibasha at Samois is your
kirvo. If anyone denounced you, they would have to
answer to him. They would be exiled. Like that arsehole
Gavril's uncle.'

Gavril was watching them from the periphery of the

camp. When he saw that Alexi had noticed him, he raised one finger and plunged it inside a ring made out of the thumb and index finger of his other hand. Then he stuck it in his mouth and rolled his eyes.

'A friend of yours?'

'He's after Yola. He wants to kill me.'

'The two things don't necessarily tally.'

'What are you talking about?'

'I mean if he kills you, Yola won't marry him.'

'Oh yes. She probably would. Women forget. After a while he'd convince her that he was in the right. She'd get hot in her stomach and let him kidnap her. She's already old not to be married. What's happening tonight is bad. She will see this wedding and start thinking even more unwell of me. Then Gavril will look better to her.'

'She's old not to be married because she's keeping herself for you, Alexi. Or hadn't you noticed that? Why the hell don't you just kidnap her and have done with it?'

'Would you let me?'

Sabir aimed a playful slap at Alexi's head. 'Of course I'd let you. She's obviously in love with you. Just as you are with her. That's why you argue all the time.'

'We argue because she wants to dominate me. She wants to wear the trousers. I don't want a woman who nags me. Whenever I go away, she'll get angry. And then she'll punish me. Yola is *hexi*. She'll put spells on me. This way, I'm free. I don't have to explain myself to anyone. I can fuck *payo* women, just like she said.'

'But what if someone else took her? Someone like Gavril?'

'I'd kill him.'

Sabir groaned and turned his attention back to the bridal party, which was fast approaching the centre of the camp. 'You'd better tell me what's happening.'

'But it's just like any other wedding.'

'I don't think so, somehow.'

'Well. Okay then. You see those two over there? That's the father of the bride and the father of the groom. They will have to convince the Bulibasha that they have agreed on a bride-price. Then the gold must be handed over and counted. Then the Bulibasha will offer the couple bread and salt. He'll tell them, "When the bread and salt no longer taste good to you, then you will no longer be husband and wife." '

'What's the old woman doing, waving the handkerchief?'

'She is trying to convince the father of the groom that the bride is still a virgin.'

'You're kidding?'

'Would I kid you, Adam? Virginity is very important here. Why do you think Yola is always going on about being a virgin? That makes her more valuable. You could sell her for a lot of gold if you could find a man willing to take her on.'

'Like Gavril?'

'His cellar is empty.'

Sabir realised that he would get no further along that route. 'So why the handkerchief?'

'It's called a *mocador*. A *pañuelo*, sometimes. That old woman you see holding it – well, she's checked with her finger that the bride is really a virgin. Then she stains the *mocador* in three places with blood from the girl. After that has been done, the Bulibasha pours *rakia* on the handkerchief. This will move the blood into the shape of a flower. Only virgin's blood will do this thing – pig's blood wouldn't behave in that way. Now look. She's tying the handkerchief on a stick. This means that the father of the groom has accepted that the girl is a virgin. Now the old woman will carry the stick around the camp so that everyone else can see that Lemma has not had her eyes closed by another man.'

'What's the bridegroom called?'

'Radu. He's my cousin.'

'Who isn't?'

~

Sabir caught sight of Yola on the other side of the square. He waved a hand at her, but she lowered her head and ignored him. He idly wondered what new faux pas he'd just committed.

Over by the wedding party, the Bulibasha raised a vase and brought it down with all his force on the bridegroom's head. The vase splintered into a thousand pieces. There was a communal gasp from the assembled crowd.

'What the hell was all that about?'

'The more pieces the vase breaks into, the happier the couple will be. This couple will be very happy.'

'Are they married now?'

'Not yet. First the bride has to eat something made with herbs taken from above a grave. Then she must have her hands painted with henna – the longer the henna stays on, the longer her husband will love her. Then she must carry a child over the threshold of her caravan, for if she doesn't produce a child within a year, Radu can throw her out.'

'Oh, that's great. That's very enlightened.'

'It doesn't often happen, Adam. Only when the couple fight. Then it is a good excuse for both parties to end an unhappy state.'

'And that's it?'

'No. In a few minutes, we will carry the bride and groom around the camp on our shoulders. The women will sing the traditional *yeli yeli* wedding song. Then the bride will go and change into her other costume. Then we will all dance.'

'You can dance with Yola, then.'

'Oh no. Men dance with men and women with women. There's no mixing.'

'You don't say. You know something, Alexi? Nothing about you people surprises me any more. I just figure out what I expect to happen, turn it around on its head, and then I know I've got it right.'

58
—

It had taken Achor Bale three hours to foot-slog his way over the hills behind the Montserrat Sanctuary, and he was starting to wonder whether he wasn't taking caution to ridiculous extremes.

Nobody knew his car. Nobody was following him. Nobody was waiting for him. The chances of a French policeman making a connection between the Rocamadour murder and the death of the gypsy in Paris were thin in the extreme. And then to extrapolate from there to Montserrat? Still, something was niggling at him.

He had turned on the tracker twenty miles from Manresa, but he had known that the chances of picking up Sabir were pretty slim. Frankly, he didn't much care if he never encountered the man again. Bale was not one to harbour grudges. If he made an error, he rectified it – it was as simple as that. Back at Rocamadour he had made an error in not giving the Sanctuary the once over. He had underestimated Sabir and the gypsy, and he had paid the price – or rather the new watchman had paid the price.

This time he would not be so cavalier. Barring the train, which was too limiting, there was only one effective way into Montserrat, which was by road. Having left his car suitably concealed on the far side of the ridge, therefore, he would come in over the mountains, on the understanding that if the police had, by some miracle, been forewarned of his arrival, they would be monitoring the two obvious incoming routes, and not those people exiting in the opposite direction by train, or hijacked vehicle, early in the morning.

One aspect of the fiasco at Rocamadour still irritated him, however. Bale had never lost a gun before – neither during his years on active service with the Legion, nor as a result of the many activities he had engaged in for the Corpus Maleficus after that period. And particularly not a gun that he had been given, in person, by the late Monsieur, his adoptive father.

He had been inordinately fond of the little .380 calibre Remington 51 self-loader. All of eighty years old, and one of the very last units off the factory production line, it had been small and easy to conceal. Hand-milled to reduce glare, it had a particularly effective delayed blow-back, which saw the slide and the breech-block travelling in tandem for a short distance after each shot, powering the slide back over the recoil spring, during which time the breech-block was fleetingly braced in its tracks before continuing on to rejoin it. In this manner the spent cartridge was ejected and the action re-cocked in one and the same process, with a fresh round being chambered on the return stroke. Brilliant. Bale liked mechanical things that worked as they were meant to.

Regret, though, was for losers. The return of the pistol could wait. Now that he had secured his very own copy of the Rocamadour verse he could put all thoughts of failure aside and get on with the job in hand. The most important new factor was that he didn't need to follow people around any more, or brutalise them for their secrets. This suited Bale admirably. For he wasn't by nature a vindictive or a brutal man. To his way of thinking, he was simply doing his duty in terms of the Corpus Maleficus. For if he and his ilk didn't act when they needed to, Satan, the Great Pimp, and his *hetaera*, the Great Whore, would take dominion over the earth, and the reign of God would be ended. 'He that leadeth into captivity shall go into captivity: he that killeth with the sword must be killed with the sword. Here is the patience and the faith of the saints.'

It was for this reason that God had granted adherents of the Corpus Maleficus free rein to unloose anarchy, when and where they wished, on to an imminently threatened world. Only by diluting total evil and turning it into its partial, controllable variant, could Satan be stopped. This was the ultimate purpose of the three Antichrists foretold in the Book of Revelation, just as Madame, his adoptive mother, had described to him in her original exposition of his mission. Napoleon and Adolf Hitler, the two previous Antichrists – together with the Great One still to come – were beings specifically designed by God in order to prevent the world from turning to the Devil. They acted as the Devil's objective correlative – placating him, as it were, and ensuring that he was kept in a state of bemused satisfaction.

This was why Bale and the rest of the adepts of the Corpus Maleficus had been given the task of protecting the Antichrists, and, if at all possible, sabotaging the so-called Second Coming – which might more correctly be termed the Second Great Placebo. It was this Second Coming that would galvanise the Devil from his interregnum, triggering the Final Conflict. For this purpose adepts were needed who were, in themselves, close to perfection. 'These are they which were not defiled with women; for they are virgins. These are they which follow the Lamb whithersoever he goeth . . . And in their mouth was found no guile: for they are without fault before the throne of God.'

It was a simple charge, and one which Achor Bale had embraced throughout his life with evangelical zeal. 'And I saw as it were a sea of glass mingled with fire: and them that had gotten the victory over the beast, and over his image, and over his mark, *and* over the number of his name, stand on the sea of glass, having the harps of God.'

Bale was proud of the initiative he had used in following up Sabir. Proud that he had spent the better part of his life fulfilling a solemn duty of care.

'We are not anti-anything, we are anti-everything.' Wasn't that how Madame, his mother, had explained it to him? 'It's impossible to publicise us because no one would believe you. Nothing is written down. Nothing transcribed. They build – we destroy. It is as simple as that. For order can only emerge from flux.'

59

'Did you know that Novalis believed that after the Fall of Man, Paradise was broken up and scattered in fragments all over the earth?' Calque eased himself into a more comfortable position. 'And that this is why pieces of it are now so hard to find?'

Macron rolled his eyes, counting on the rapidly encroaching dusk to mask his irritation. He was becoming used to Calque's labyrinthine thought patterns, but he still found the whole process curiously unsettling. Did Calque do it on purpose to make him feel inferior? And if so, why? 'Who was Novalis?'

Calque sighed. 'Novalis was the pen name of Georg Philipp Friedrich Freiherr von Hardenberg. In pre-Republican Germany, a Freiherr was the rough equivalent of a Baron. Novalis was a friend of Schiller and a contemporary of Goethe. A poet. A mystic. What have you. He also mined salt. Novalis believed in a *Liebesreligion* – a Religion of Love. Life and death as intertwined concepts, with an intermediary necessary between God and Man. But this intermediary does not have to be Jesus. It can be anyone. The Virgin Mary. The Saints. The dead beloved. Even a child.'

'Why are you telling me this, Sir?' Macron could feel the words clogging up his throat like biscuit dust. 'You know I'm no intellectual. Not like you.'

'To pass the time, Macron. To pass the time. And to try and make sense out of the apparent nonsense we found on La Morenita's foot.'

'Oh.'

Calque grunted, as though someone had unexpectedly prodded him beneath the ribs. 'It was that Catalan police captain. Villada. An extremely well-educated man, like all Spaniards. He got me thinking about all this with something he said about literality and paradox.'

Macron closed his eyes. He wanted to sleep. In a bed. With a goose-down duvet, and his fiancée curled up next to him with her bottom tightly spooned against his groin. He didn't want to be here in Spain on the basis of a five-hundred-year-old message from a dead lunatic, staking out a valueless wooden statue with two erect phalluses sprouting alongside it, in the company of an embittered police captain who would clearly rather be spending his workdays in a university research library. This was the second night in a row they had spent out in the open. The Catalan police were already beginning to look at them askance.

There was a buzzing in his pocket. Macron started and then caught himself. Had Calque realised that he had been dozing? Or was he so bound up with his calculations and his myths and his philosophising that he wouldn't even notice if the eye-man came up behind him and slit his gizzard?

He glanced down at the illuminated screen of his cellphone. Something moved inside him as he read the message – some fatalistic djinn that lurked in his gut and emerged in times of danger and uncertainty to berate him for his lack of imagination and his endless, ruinous doubts. 'It's Lamastre. They picked up the eye-man's tracker four hours ago. Twenty kilometres from here. Up near Manresa. He must have been checking for Sabir.'

'Four hours ago? You can't be serious?'

'Someone clearly went off duty without reporting forward.'

'Someone will clearly find himself back on the beat

next payday. I want you to get me his name, Macron. Then I'm going to run his guts through a sausage machine and feed him to himself for breakfast.'

'There's something else, Captain.'

'What? What else can there be?'

'There's been a murder. Back at Rocamadour. Last night. No one told them, apparently. So they didn't make the connection. Then they weren't sure how best to contact you, as you refuse to carry a cellphone while on active duty. It was the replacement security guard. Broken neck. Whoever got him got his dog, too. Threw it against a wall and stamped on its head. That's a whole new technique, in my experience.'

Calque screwed shut his eyes. 'Is the Virgin gone?'

'No. Apparently not. He must have been after the same thing we were. And Sabir. And the gypsy.' Macron was briefly tempted to crack a joke about the sudden popularity of virgins but decided against it. He glanced up from the phone. 'Do you think the eye-man's been and gone from here already? He would have had time, if he drove straight on here after doing the security man. It's autoroute all the way down. He could easily have averaged a hundred and sixty.'

'Impossible. There are ten armed men scattered around these buildings and in the shallows of the foothills. The eye-man hasn't flown in by microlight, and he damned certainly hasn't secreted himself inside the Sanctuary. No. His only rational way in is by the main road, now that the train has stopped running for the night. I am going down to warn Villada.'

'But, Sir. This is a stakeout. No one must move from their positions. I can text the Captain. Forward Lamastre's message to him as an attachment.'

'I need to talk to him personally, not write him a bloody letter. Wait here, Macron. And keep your eyes peeled. Use the night scope if you have to. And if you suspect that the eye-man is armed, kill him.'

60

Achor Bale fell to his knees behind a rock. Something was moving in front of him. He squinted through the dusk but was unable to make out sufficient detail to satisfy himself. Easing the Redhawk into his hand, he began to inch his way further down the hillside. Whatever was moving was making a meal of it. Small stones clattered down ahead of him, and there was even a grunt as whatever it was encountered an unexpected obstacle. Not a wild goat, then, but a man. The smell of sweat and stale cigarette smoke wafted towards him on the lightly heated breeze.

Bale was just ten yards away from Macron when he finally caught sight of movement. Macron was using the night glasses to follow his superior's tortured attempts at a soundless progress down the hillside. Bale levelled the silenced pistol on the back of Macron's head. Then, dissatisfied with his view of the front sight, he felt around in his pocket for a small piece of white paper. He balled up the paper in his mouth, covered it in saliva, then wadded it, papier-mâché like, over the red-tipped aiming nipple, so that it stood just proud of the silencer. He lined the sight up once again with Macron's head, then let out a long, disappointed sigh. It was quite simply too dark for accuracy.

He sheathed the Redhawk and felt around for his leather sap. With this in hand, he began to belly his way over the rocks towards Macron, using the distant clatter Calque was still making as cover.

At the last possible moment Macron sensed something and reared up from his position, but Bale's first blow caught him flat on the side of the head. Macron scythed to the ground, his arms pressed tightly against his flanks. Bale crept forward and squinted into Macron's face. So. It wasn't Sabir. And it wasn't the gypsy. Lucky, now, that he hadn't used the pistol.

Grinning, Bale felt around in Macron's pockets until he found his cellphone. He lit up the screen and checked for messages. Then, with an angry grunt, he ground the phone into the earth with his foot. Only a policeman would encrypt his text messages and, once encrypted, make them accessible only with a password – it was like wearing a belt *and* braces.

He dug around further in Macron's pockets. Money. Identity papers. A picture of a mixed race girl in a white dress sporting an overbite that her parents were obviously either too tight or too poor to have rectified. Lieutenant Paul Macron. An address in Créteil. Bale pocketed the wad of material.

Reaching down, he took off Macron's shoes and tossed them behind him into the brush. Then, taking first one foot in his hand and then the other, like a mother cat scruffing her kittens, he struck Macron a further sharp blow with the sap against each instep.

Satisfied with his work, he picked up the night glasses and monitored the surrounding hillside. He was just in time to catch sight of Calque's spectrally pale head disappearing behind a bluff six hundred metres below him.

So what was happening? How much did the police

already know about him? He had obviously underestimated them as well, for they too must have had access
to the message hidden on the Virgin's base, thanks to
Sabir's quick thinking in not making off with her when
he had the chance.

Bale rather regretted knocking out Macron now.
A missed opportunity. To question a man in absolute
silence, and on a staked-out hillside – that would have
been a definite first in his experience. How could he have
achieved it? Only one way to find out.

Bale eased himself out of the hide and set off towards
the bluff. It was obvious that these idiotic policemen
were only looking for him down in the valley – it would
have taken far too much imagination for them to imagine
him traversing a barren and, to all intents and purposes,
impassable mountainside. This meant that he would be
able to approach them from behind.

Every fifty metres or so he stopped and listened with
his mouth open and both hands cupped behind his ears.
When he was about two hundred metres from the bluff
he hesitated. More cigarette smoke. Was it the same man
coming back? Or was one of the paramilitaries sneaking
a quick drag?

He eased himself away from the bluff and down
towards the final escarpment overlooking the Sanctuary
square. Yes. He could make out a man's head highlighted
against the almost luminous backdrop of the stone
cladding.

Bale snaked his way down towards the man's hideout.
He had had an idea. A good idea. And he intended to
test it out.

61

Calque dropped into the front seat of the control car beside Villada. Villada briefly acknowledged him with his eyes, and then continued his scanning of the railway line and surrounding buildings.

When he was satisfied that nothing was moving, he put down his night glasses and turned towards Calque. 'I thought you were staking out the hillside?'

'I left Macron doing that.' He squatted down in the car-well and lit a cigarette, cupping it between his two hands. 'Want one?'

Villada shook his head.

'The eye-man. He's here.'

Villada raise an eyebrow.

'Our people botched it. He used his tracker four hours ago, up near Manresa. He also killed a man back at Rocamadour. Last night. A security guard. Got his dog, too. This man is no lightweight, Villada. I'd even go so far as to say he was trained in assassination. Both the gypsy, in Paris, and the security guard at Rocamadour had their necks broken. And that diversionary scene he set up on the N20. With the man and the woman. That was masterfully done.'

'You almost sound as if you admire him.'

'No. I hate his guts. But he's efficient. Like a machine. I only wish I knew what he was really after.'

Villada flashed him a smile. 'Perhaps he's after you?' He reached down for the radio transceiver, as if to defuse the import of his words. 'Dorada to Mallorquin. Dorada to Mallorquin. Do you receive me?'

The transceiver crackled and shot out a brief burst of static. Then a measured voice came through. 'Mallorquin to Dorada. Receiving.'

'The mark is close by. There's a chance he may be coming in over the Sierra. Adjust your position if you have to. And shoot to kill. He murdered a French security guard last night. And that wasn't his first. I don't want any of our men to be next on his list.'

Calque reached across and took Villada's arm. 'What do you mean, coming in over the Sierra?'

'It's simple. If your people noted him four hours ago in Manresa and we haven't picked up any sign of him since, I will give you odds of fifty to one that he's coming in across the ridge. It's what I'd do in his place. If he finds no one waiting for him, then he just sneaks in and hijacks the Virgin, hops on a train or steals a car, and he's out again. If he finds we're here, he simply hikes back over the Sierra and we're none the wiser.'

'But I've left Macron out there. Like a sitting duck.'

'Don't worry. I'll send one of my men back for him.'

'I'd appreciate that, Captain Villada. Thank you. Thank you very much.'

62

—

Bale was on his belly, about twenty yards from the camouflaged paramilitary, when the man suddenly turned round and began to monitor the hillside behind him through his binoculars.

So. His plan to waylay the policeman, question him, and steal his clothes, was a non-starter. *Tant pis*. It was obvious, too, that he would no longer be able to break into the Sanctuary and check out the base of La Morenita. Wherever you found one of these concealed clowns lurking about, there were always more nearby. They operated in packs, like meerkats. The idiots obviously thought there was safety in numbers.

Bale felt around for his pistol. He couldn't just wait there until dawn – he'd have to take action. The policeman was now outlined neatly against the luminous expanse of the Sanctuary square behind him. He would kill the man, then lose himself near the buildings. The police would figure that he'd headed back into the hills and focus their manpower in that direction. By morning, the place would be abuzz with helicopters.

But then they would almost certainly find his car. Lift it for DNA and prints. They'd have him cold. Get him on to their computers. Start up a record on him. Bale shivered superstitiously.

The paramilitary stood up, hesitated a little, and then started up the hill towards Bale. What the hell was happening? Had he been seen? Impossible. The man would have let rip with his Star Z-84 sub-machine gun. Bale smiled. He had always wanted a Star. A useful little gun: 600 rounds a minute; 9mm Luger Parabellum; 200-metre effective range. The Star would provide some compensation at least for the loss of his Remington.

Bale lay still, with his face turned to the ground. His hands – the only other part of him that might show up in the incipient moonlight – were tucked safely away underneath him, cradling the pistol.

The man was coming straight at him. He'd be looking ahead, though. Not expecting anything at ground level.

Bale took a deep breath and held it. He could hear

the man breathing. Smell the man's sweat and the waft of garlic left over from his dinner. Bale fought back the temptation to raise his head and check out exactly where the man was.

The man's foot slid off a stone and brushed Bale's elbow. Then the paramilitary was past him and heading up towards Macron.

Bale swivelled around on his hip. In one surge he was behind the man, the Redhawk held against his throat. 'Drop. To your knees. No sound.'

Bale noted the sharp intake of breath. The tensing of the man's shoulders. It was no-go. The man intended to respond.

He thrashed the man across the temple with the barrel of the Redhawk, and then again across the base of the neck. Pointless killing him. He didn't want to alienate the Spanish any more than was strictly necessary. This way they'd just resent the French for having put them in such an invidious, humiliating position. If he killed one of them, they'd sic Interpol on him, and harass him until the day he died.

He liberated the Star, and then rifled the man's pockets for anything else of use. Handcuffs. Identity papers. He was briefly tempted to take the man's helmet transceiver but then decided that the rest of the paramilitary chameleons might be able to trace him on the back of it.

Should he revisit Lieutenant Macron? Give him another tap on the head?

No. No point. He had maybe half an hour's start across the mountains before they cottoned on to what had happened. With luck, that would be enough. There was no way they could track him effectively in the dark – and by dawn he would be long gone. Back to Gourdon to renew acquaintance with friend Sabir.

63

'I think you've had enough to drink, Alexi. You're going to feel like hell tomorrow.'

'My teeth and my ribs are hurting now. The *rakia* is good for them. It is antiseptic.' He slurred the word so badly that it sounded like 'athletic'.

Sabir looked around for Yola but she was nowhere to be seen. The wedding celebration was on its final legs, with musicians gradually dropping out either through exhaustion or inebriation, whichever came first.

'Give me the gun. I want to shoot it.'

'That wouldn't be a good idea, Alexi.'

'Give me the gun!' Alexi grabbed Sabir by the shoulders and shook him. 'I want to be John Wayne.' He threw his hand out in a great arc to encompass the camp and the surrounding caravans. 'I am John Wayne! You hear me? I am going to shoot out your lights!'

Nobody took any notice of him. Throughout the evening, at surprisingly frequent intervals, men had stood up, in a fever of alcohol, and declared themselves. One had even claimed to be Jesus Christ. His wife had hurried him off to catcalls and jeering from as yet less inebriated souls. Sabir supposed this must be what the novelist Patrick Hamilton had meant when he defined the four stages of drunkenness as plain drunk, fighting drunk, blind drunk and dead drunk. Alexi was at the fighting drunk stage and clearly had a long way still to go.

'Hey! John Wayne!'

Alexi swung around dramatically, his hands falling to

his hips and to an imaginary pair of six-shooters. 'Who asks for me?'

Sabir had already identified Gavril. Well here goes, he thought to himself. Whoever said life isn't predictable?

'Yola tells me you lost your balls. That the same guy who kicked out your teeth also bit your balls off.'

Alexi weaved a little, his face contorted in concentration. 'What did you say?'

Gavril wandered closer but his eyes were elsewhere, as if part of him felt detached from whatever it was he was machinating. 'I didn't say anything. Yola said it. I don't know anything about your balls. In fact I've always known you didn't have any. It's a family problem. None of the Dufontaines have balls.'

'Alexi. Leave it.' Sabir put one hand on Alexi's shoulder. 'He's lying. He's trying to wind you up.'

Alexi shrugged him off. 'Yola never said that. She never said my balls didn't work. She knows nothing about my balls.'

'Alexi . . .'

'Then who else told me?' Gavril threw out his arms in triumph.

Alexi glanced around, as if he expected Yola suddenly to appear from around the corner of one of the caravans and confirm what Gavril was saying. He had a peeved expression on his face, and one side of his mouth was hanging down, as if he'd suffered a minor stroke alongside his crushing by the chair.

'You won't find her here. I just left her.' Gavril sniffed his fingers melodramatically.

Alexi lurched across the clearing towards Gavril. Sabir reached out one arm and swung him around, just as you would do a child. Alexi was so taken aback that he lost his footing and landed heavily on his rump.

Sabir stepped between him and Gavril. 'Leave it off.

He's drunk. If you have a problem, you can sort it out another time. This is a wedding, not a Kriss.'

Gavril hesitated, his hand hovering over one pocket.

Sabir could see that Gavril had worked himself up into thinking that he could deal with Alexi once and for all – and that Sabir's presence between him and Alexi was not something that he had made any allowances for. Sabir felt the cold weight of the Remington in his pocket. If Gavril came at him, he would pull out the pistol and shoot a warning round at his feet. End the thing there. He certainly didn't fancy taking a knife-thrust through the liver at this early stage in his life story.

'Why are you talking for him, *payo*? Hasn't he got the balls to talk for himself?' Gavril's voice had begun to lose its urgency.

Alexi was lying face down on the ground with his eyes shut, and was obviously way beyond talking to anybody. He had clearly moved from fighting drunk all the way through to dead drunk without bothering to visit blind drunk in between.

Sabir pressed home his advantage. 'As I said – you can both sort this out another time. A wedding is certainly not the place to do it.'

Gavril clicked his teeth and gave a backwards thrust of the head. 'All right, *gadje*. You tell that prick Dufontaine this from me. When he comes to the festival of Les Trois Maries, I shall be waiting for him. Sainte Sara can decide between us.'

Sabir felt as if the earth was gently rocking beneath his feet. 'The festival of Les Trois Maries? Is that what you just said?'

Gavril laughed. 'I forget. You are an interloper. Not one of us.'

Sabir ignored the implied insult – his eyes were fixed

on Gavril's face, willing him to answer. 'Where is that held? And when?'

Gavril turned as if to go, then changed his mind at the last moment. It was clear that he was relishing the sudden turnaround in the dynamics of the conversation. 'Ask anyone, *payo*. They will tell you. The festival of Sara-e-Kali is held every year at Les Saintes-Maries-de-la-Mer in the Camargue. Four days from now. On the 24th of May. What do you think we are all doing here at this piss-pot of a wedding? We are making our way south. All French gypsies go there. Even that eunuch lying next to you.'

Alexi gave a twitch, as if he had registered the insult somewhere deep inside his unconscious mind. But the alcohol proved too powerful a soporific and he began to snore.

64

'Why John Wayne?'

'What do you mean?'

'Why John Wayne? Last night. At the wedding.'

Alexi shook his head in a vain attempt to clear it. 'It was a movie. *Hondo*. I saw it on my grandfather's television. I wanted to be John Wayne when I saw that movie.'

Sabir laughed. 'Strange, Alexi. I never had you down as a film buff.'

'Not any films. I only like cowboys. Randolph Scott.

Clint Eastwood. Lee Van Cleef. And John Wayne.' His eyes shone. 'My grandfather, he preferred Terence Hill and Bud Spencer, but to me they weren't real cowboys. Just Italian gypsies pretending to be cowboys. John Wayne was the real stuff. I wanted to be him so bad it gave me heartburn.' They both fell silent. Then Alexi glanced up. 'Gavril. He said things, didn't he?'

'Some.'

'Lies. Lies about Yola.'

'I'm glad you realise they were lies.'

'Of course they're lies. She wouldn't tell him that about me. About that guy kicking me in the balls when he was still tied up.'

'No. She wouldn't.'

'Then how would he know? How did he get this information?'

Sabir closed his eyes in a 'God give me patience' sort of a way. 'Ask her yourself. I can see her coming through the window.'

'Vila Gana.'

'What's that?'

'Nothing.'

'Does *vila* mean vile? Is that it?'

'No. It means a witch. And Gana is Queen of the witches.'

'Alexi . . .'

Alexi threw off his blanket dramatically. 'Who else do you think told Gavril? Who else knew? You saw that *diddikai* sniffing his fingers, didn't you?'

'He was winding you up, you idiot.'

'She's broken the *leis prala*. She's not *lacha* any more. She's not a *lale romni*. I shall never marry her.'

'Alexi, I can't understand half of what you're saying.'

'I'm saying she's broken the law of brotherhood. She's immoral. She's not a good woman.'

171

'Jesus Christ, man. You can't be serious.'

The door opened. Yola tilted her head around the frame. 'Why are you two arguing? I could hear you from the other side of the camp.'

Alexi fell silent. He contrived a look on his face that was both peevish, angry, and prepared for chastisement at one and the same time.

Yola remained on the threshold, looking in. 'You've argued with Gavril, haven't you? You've had a fight?'

'That's what you'd like, isn't it? For us to fight? Then you would feel wanted.'

Sabir started towards the door. 'I think I'd better leave you both to it. Something tells me we're not a long way shy of a quorum here.'

Yola held up her hand. 'No. You stay. Otherwise I must go. It wouldn't be right for me to be here only with Alexi.'

Alexi slapped the bed in mock invitation. 'What do you mean it wouldn't be right? You spent time alone with Gavril. You let *him* touch you.'

'How can you say that? Of course I didn't let him touch me.'

'You told him the man in the church bit off my balls. After he punched out my teeth. You think that's right? To tell someone that? To make a fool out of me? That bastard will spread it all around the camp. I'll be a laughing stock.'

Yola fell silent. Her face flushed pale underneath her sun-darkened skin.

'Why aren't you wearing your *dikló*, like a proper married woman? Are you telling me Gavril didn't kidnap you last night? That the *spiuni gherman* didn't take you behind the hedge and turn you on your side?'

Sabir had never yet seen Yola cry. Now large tears welled up in her eyes and overran her face, unchecked.

172

She dropped her head and stared fixedly at the ground.

'*Sacais sos ne dicobélan calochin ne bridaquélan.* Is that it?'

Yola sat down on the caravan step, with her back to Alexi. One of her girlfriends approached the door of the caravan but Yola shooed her off.

Sabir couldn't understand why she didn't respond. Didn't refute Alexi's allegations. 'What did you just say to her, Alexi?'

'I said "Eyes that can't see, break no heart". Yola knows what I mean.' He turned his head away and stared fixedly at the wall.

Sabir looked from one to the other of them. Not for the first time he wondered what sort of a madhouse he had stumbled into. 'Yola?'

'What? What is it you want?'

'What exactly did you say to Gavril?'

Yola spat on the ground, then teased the spittle with the point of her shoe. 'I didn't say anything to him. I haven't spoken to him. Except to trade insults.'

'Well, I don't understand . . .'

'You don't understand anything, do you?'

'Well, no. I suppose I don't.'

'Alexi.'

Alexi glanced up hopefully when he heard Yola addressing him. It was obvious that he was fighting a losing battle with whatever it was that was eating away at him.

'I'm sorry.'

'Sorry for letting Gavril take out your eyes?'

'No. Sorry for telling Bazena about what happened to your balls. I thought it was funny. I shouldn't have told her. She is hot for Gavril. He must have made her tell him. It was wrong of me not to think how it might harm you.'

'You told Bazena?'

'Yes.'

'And you didn't speak to Gavril?'

'No.'

Alexi swore under his breath. 'I'm sorry I questioned your *lacha*.'

'You didn't. Damo couldn't understand what you were saying. So there was no questioning.'

Sabir squinted at her. 'Who the heck's Damo?'

'You are.'

'I'm Damo?'

'That's your gypsy name.'

'Would you mind explaining that? I haven't been renamed since my last baptism.'

'It's the gypsy word for Adam. We are all descended from him.'

'So's just about everybody, I guess.' Sabir pretended to weigh up his new name. Secretly, he was delighted at the change in tone of the conversation. 'What's your word for Eve?'

'Yehwah. But she's not our mother.'

'Oh.'

'Our mother was Adam's first wife.'

'You mean Lilith? The witch who preyed on women and children? The woman who became the serpent?'

'Yes. She is our mother. Her vagina was a scorpion. Her head was that of a lioness. At her breasts she suckled a pig and a dog. And she rode on a donkey.' She half turned, measuring Alexi's response to her words. 'Her daughter, Alu, was originally a man but he changed into a woman – it is from her that some gypsies have the second sight. Through her line, Lemec, the son of Cain, had a son by his wife Hada. This was Jabal, father of all those who live in a tent and are nomadic. We are also related to Jubal, father of all musicians, for

Tsilla, Jubal's son, became the second wife of Lemec.'

Sabir was about to say something – to make some pungent comment about the infuriating way gypsies played around with logic – but then he noticed Alexi's face and it suddenly dawned on him why Yola had started on her discourse in the first place. She had been way ahead of him.

Alexi was transfixed by her story. All anger had clearly left him. His eyes were dreamy, as if he had just received a massage with a swansdown glove.

Perhaps, thought Sabir, it was all true and Yola really was a witch after all?

65

That morning Sabir walked from the encampment into the outskirts of Gourdon. He was wearing a greasy baseball cap he had liberated from a cupboard in the caravan and a red-and-black stitched leather jacket with lightning stripes, a plethora of unnecessary zips and about a yard and a half of dangling chains. If anybody recognises me now, he thought to himself, I really am done for – my credibility is shot for ever.

Still. This was his first time alone and in a public place since the camp at Samois, and he felt awkward and nervous. Like an impostor.

Carefully skirting the main streets – in which the market was in full swing and law-abiding people were taking their breakfast in cafés, like regular citizens – Sabir was suddenly struck by how detached he had become to the so-called real world. His reality was back in the gypsy camp, with the dusty children, and the dogs, and the cooking pots, and the long dresses of the women. The town seemed almost colourless by comparison. Up itself. Anally retentive.

He bought himself a croissant at a mobile stand and stood eating it on the town ramparts, looking back over the market, enjoying his rare taste of solitude. What madness had he let himself in for? In little more than a week his life had changed tack in its entirety, and he was now certain, in his heart of hearts, that he would never be able to return to his old ways. He belonged to neither one world nor the other now. What was the gypsy expression? *Apatride*. With no nationality. It was their word for gypsyhood.

He spun abruptly around to face the man standing behind him. Did he have time to reach for his pistol? The presence of innocent bystanders in the square decided him against it.

'Monsieur Sabir?'

'Who's asking?'

'Capitaine Calque. Police Nationale. I've been following you since you left the camp. In fact you've been under continuous observation ever since your arrival from Rocamadour, three days ago.'

'Oh Jesus.'

'Are you armed?'

Sabir nodded. 'Armed, yes. But not dangerous.'

'May I see the pistol?'

Sabir gingerly opened his pocket, stuck two fingers in, and retrieved the pistol by the barrel. He could almost feel the sniper scopes converging on the roof of his skull.

'May I inspect it?'

'Hell, yes. Be my guest. Keep it if you want.'

Calque smiled. 'We are alone here, Monsieur Sabir. You may hold me up, if you wish. You do not have to give me the pistol.'

Sabir ducked his head in wonder. 'You're either lying through your teeth, Captain, or you're taking one heck of a risk.' He offered Calque the pistol, butt first, as if it were a piece of rotting fish.

'Thank you.' Calque took the pistol. 'A risk, yes. But I think we've just proved something quite important.' He hefted the automatic in his hand. 'A Remington 51. Nice little pistol. They stopped making these in the late 1920s. Did you know that? This is almost a museum piece.'

'You don't say?'

'It's not yours, I take it?'

'You know very well that I took it off that guy in the Rocamadour Sanctuary.'

'May I take the serial number? It might prove interesting.'

'How about the DNA? Isn't that what you people swear by these days?'

'It's too late for DNA. The pistol has been prejudiced. I simply need the serial number.'

Sabir exhaled in a long, ragged outpouring of breath. 'Yes. Please. Take the serial number. Take the gun. Take me.'

'I told you. I'm alone.'

'But I'm a killer. You people had my face splashed all over the TV and newspapers. I'm a threat to public safety.'

'I don't think so.' Calque put on his reading glasses and took down the serial number in a small black notebook. Then he offered the pistol back to Sabir.

'You can't be serious?'

'I'm very serious, Monsieur Sabir. You will need to be armed for what I am about to ask you to do.'

66

Sabir squatted down beside Yola and Alexi. It was more than obvious that they were on speaking terms again. Yola was roasting some green coffee beans and wild chicory root over an open fire in preparation for Alexi's breakfast.

Sabir handed her the bag of croissants. 'I've just had a run-in with the police.'

Alexi laughed. 'Did you steal those croissants, Damo? Don't tell me you got caught first time out?'

'No, Alexi. I'm serious. A captain of the Police Nationale just picked me up. He knew exactly who I was.'

'*Malos mengues!*' Alexi slapped himself on the forehead with his flattened palm. He reared up, prepared for flight. 'Are they already in the camp?'

'Sit down, you fool. Do you think I'd still be here if they really intended to take me?'

Alexi hesitated. Then he dropped back on to the tree stump he had been using as a seat. 'You're crazy, Damo. I nearly threw up. I thought I was going straight to prison. It's not funny to joke that way.'

'I wasn't joking. You remember that guy who came to talk to you in the camp at Samois? With his assistant? About Babel? While I was in the wood-box?'

'The wood-box. Yes.'

'It was the same guy. I recognised his voice. It was the last thing I heard before I blacked out.'

'But why did he let you go? They still think it was you that murdered Babel, don't they?'

'No. Calque doesn't. That's his name, by the way. Calque. He was the police officer Yola saw in Paris.'

Yola nodded. 'Yes, Damo. I remember him well. He seemed a fair man – at least for a *payo*. He accompanied me down to the place where they keep the dead to make sure that they allowed me to cut Babel's hair myself. That they didn't give me somebody else's hair. Otherwise Babel wouldn't have been properly buried. He understood this, when I told him. At least he pretended to.'

'Well, Calque and some of his Spanish cronies have just had a run-in with the maniac who kicked Alexi in the balls. Only guess where it happened? Montserrat. The bastard went back to Rocamadour after we'd left and worked the riddle out for himself. He's been on our tail ever since Samois, apparently. Tracking our car.'

'Tracking our car? That is impossible. I've been watching.'

'No, Alexi. Not by sight. With an electronic bug. Which means he can follow us at a distance of, say, a kilometre, and never be seen. That's how he got to Yola so fast.'

'*Putain*. We'd better take it out of there.'

'Calque wants us to keep it in.'

Alexi screwed his face up in concentration as he tried to disentangle the different elements Sabir was giving him. He looked down at Yola. She was filtering the coffee and chicory through a sieve as though nothing had happened. 'What do you think, *luludji*?'

Yola smiled. 'I think we should listen to Damo. I think he has something more to tell us.'

Sabir took the cup Yola offered him. He sat down beside her on the log. 'Calque wants us to act as bait.'

'What is bait?'

'As a lure. For the man who killed Babel. So that the police can trap him. I have told him that I am willing to

179

do this, in order to clear my name. But that you must both be allowed to decide for yourselves.'

Alexi drew his hand across his throat. 'I am not working with the police. This I will not do.'

Yola shook her head. 'If we are not with you, the man will know something is wrong. He will be suspicious. Then the police will lose him. Is this not so?'

Sabir glanced at Alexi. 'He nearly crippled Calque's assistant back at Montserrat. He also cold-cocked one of the Spanish paramilitaries out on the Sierra. And he killed a security guard back at Rocamadour two days ago. Which serves us damned well right for not checking out the newspapers or the radio during the wedding. Back on the road, before he attacked Yola, he ran over and injured an innocent bystander and half throttled his wife, merely in order to create a diversion. The French police want him, and they want him bad. This is a big operation now. And we're to be a major part of it.'

'What does he want, Damo?' Yola had forgotten herself for long enough to be seen drinking coffee with the two men in public. One of the older married women walked by and frowned at her, but she took no notice.

'The verses. Nobody knows why.'

'And where are they? Do we know?'

Sabir took a sheet of paper out of his pocket. 'Look. Calque just gave me this. He got it off the base of La Morenita at Montserrat:

"L'antechrist, tertius
Le revenant, secundus
Primus, la foi
Si li boumian sian catouli"

'*Primus, secundus, tertius, quartus, quintus, sextus, septimus, octavus, nonus, decimus.* Those are the ordinal numbers in Latin, corresponding to first, second, third, fourth, fifth, and so on. So the Antichrist is the third one. The ghost, or the one who comes back, is the second one. Faith, is the first one. And the last bit I don't understand at all.'

'It means "if the gypsies are still Catholic." '

Sabir turned towards Yola. 'How the hell do you know that?'

'Because it's in Romani.'

Sabir sat back and weighed up the pair sitting in front of him. He already felt a powerful sense of kinship with them, and he was gradually becoming aware of what a wrench he would feel at losing them, or at having his relationship with them curtailed in any way. They had become strangely familiar to him, like real, rather than simply notional, members of his family. With a burgeoning sense of amazement at his own humanity, Sabir realised that he needed them – probably more than they needed him. 'I kept something back from Calque. Some information. I'm still not sure I did the right thing, though. But I wanted us to retain an edge. Something neither side knew about.'

'What information was that?'

'I kept the first quatrain from him. The one that was carved on the base of your coffer. The one that reads:

"Hébergé par les trois mariés
Celle d'Egypte la dernière fit
La vierge noire au camaro duro
Tient le secret de mes vers à ses pieds"

'I've been thinking about it a lot, recently, and I think it holds the key.'

'But you already translated it. It gave us the clue to Rocamadour.'

'But I translated it wrongly. I missed some of the clues. Specifically in the first – and traditionally most

181

important – line. I had it down as "*Sheltered by the three married people*", and stupidly, because it seemed to make no sense, I paid no real attention to it after that. If I'm brutally honest, I allowed myself to be distracted by the neat little anagram in line three, and my own cleverness in teasing it out and interpreting it. Intellectual vanity has done for far wiser people than me, and Nostradamus knew this. He may even have rigged the whole thing to send idiots like me off half-cocked – as a sort of riddle, or something, to see if we were bright enough to warrant taking seriously. Five hundred years ago such a mistake would have cost me weeks of useless travelling. Luck and modern progress have cut that down to only a few days. It was something that Gavril said to me last night that made me change my mind about it.'

'Gavril. That *pantrillon*. What can he have said that would enlighten anybody?'

'He said that you and he would sort out your disagreement at the feet of Sainte Sara, Alexi. At the festival of Les Trois Maries. At Saintes-Maries-de-la-Mer, in the Camargue.'

'So what? I'm looking forward to it. It'll give me an opportunity to free him up a little space for a few extra gold teeth himself.'

'No. It's not that.' Sabir shook his head impatiently. 'Les Trois Maries. The Three Marys. Don't you see it? That acute accent I wrote down in the quatrain – the one over *maries*, which turned it into *mariés* – that was simply Nostradamus's way of covering the meaning with soot. We didn't read it right. And it skewed the real meaning of the quatrain. The only thing I still don't understand is who the mysterious Egyptian woman is.'

Yola rocked forwards. 'But that's simple. She is Sainte Sara. She, too, is a Black Virgin. To the Rom she is the most famous Black Virgin of all.'

'What are you talking about, Yola?'

'Sainte Sara is our patron saint. The patron saint of all the gypsies. The Catholic Church does not recognise her as a true saint, of course, but to gypsies she matters far more than the other two real saints – Marie Jacobé, the sister of the Virgin Mary, and Marie Salomé, the mother of the apostle James the Greater, and also of John.'

'So what's the Egyptian connection, then?'

'Sainte Sara is called by us Sara l'Egyptienne. People who think they know things say that all gypsies originally come from India. But we know better. Some of us came from Egypt. When the Egyptians tried to cross the Red Sea, after the flight of Moses, only two escaped. These two were the founders of the gypsy race. One of their descendants was Sara-e-kali – Sara-the-black. She was an Egyptian Queen. She came to Saintes-Maries-de-la-Mer when it was a centre for worship of the Egyptian sun god – it was called Oppidum-Râ in those days. Sara became its Queen. When the three Maries – Marie Jacobé, Marie Salomé and Marie Magdalene, together with Martha, Maximinius, Sidonius, and Lazarus the Resurrected – were cast adrift from Palestine in a boat without oars, sails, or food, they landed at Oppidum-Râ, driven there by the wind of God. Queen Sara went down to the shore to see who they were, and to decide on their fate.'

'Why didn't you tell me this before, Yola?'

'You misled me. You said they were three married people. But Sara was a virgin. Her *lacha* was untarnished. She was unmarried.'

Sabir raised his eyes heavenwards. 'So what happened when Sara went down to check them out?'

'At first she taunted them.' Yola made a hesitant face. 'This must have been meant as a test, I think. Then one of the Maries climbed out of the boat and stood on the water, like Jesus did at Bethsaida. She asked Sara to do the same. Sara walked into the sea and was swallowed up by the waves. But the second Marie cast her cloak upon the waters, and Sara climbed up on it and was saved. Then Sara welcomed them to her town. Helped them to build a Christian community there, after they had converted her. Marie Jacobé and Marie Salomé stayed on at Les Saintes-Maries until they died. Their bones are still there.'

Sabir sat back. 'So everything was already contained in that first verse. The rest was simply waffle. Just as I said.'

'No. I don't think so.' Yola shook her head. 'I think it was also a test. To check that the gypsies were still Catholic – *si li boumian sian catouli*. That we were still worthy to receive the verses. Like a sort of pilgrimage you have to make before you can learn an important secret.'

'A rite of passage, you mean? Like the search for the Holy Grail?'

'I don't understand what you are saying. But yes. If, by that, you mean a test to make sure one is worthy to learn something, it would surely add up to the same thing, wouldn't it?'

'Yola.' Sabir took her head in both his hands and squeezed. 'You never cease to amaze me.'

67

Macron was angry. Deep, seat-of-the-pants, mouth-foamingly, slaveringly, angry. The side of his head had swelled up, giving him an unsightly black eye, and his jaw felt as though someone had run a pile-driver across it. He had a blinding headache and his feet, where the eye-man had tenderised them with his sap, made him feel as if every step he took was taken barefoot, over a bed of oval pebbles, in a sandbox.

He watched Calque approaching via the café tables, twisting and turning his hips just as if he'd heard somewhere – and believed – that all fat men must, by default, be excellent dancers. 'Where have you been?'

'Where have I been?' Calque raised an eyebrow at Macron's tone.

Macron backtracked swiftly, with as much dignity as he was able to muster. 'I'm sorry, Sir. My head is hurting. I'm feeling a little grumpy. That didn't come out right.'

'I agree with you. In fact I agree with you so much that I think you should be in a hospital, not sitting here in a café drooling coffee out of a grotesquely swollen mouth. Look at you. Your own mother wouldn't recognise you.'

Macron grimaced. 'I'm all right, I tell you. The Spanish medico told me I don't have concussion. And my feet are just bruised. These crutches take some of the pressure off when I walk.'

'And you want to be in for the kill? Is that it? To get your revenge. Stumping along behind the eye-man on a pair of crutches?'

'Of course not. I'm detached. A professional. You know that.'

'Do I?'

'Are you going to throw me off the case? Send me home? Is that what you're trying to say to me?'

'No. I'm not going to do that. And shall I tell you why?'

Macron nodded. He wasn't sure what he was about to hear, but he sensed that it might be unpleasant.

'It was my fault the eye-man got you. I shouldn't have left you alone on the hill. Shouldn't have abandoned my position. You might have been killed. In my book, that allows you one favour, and one favour only. Do you want to stay on the case?'

'Yes, Sir.'

'Then I'll tell you where I've just been.'

68
—

Sabir rubbed his face with his hands, just as though he were smoothing in a squirt or two of suntan lotion. 'There's just one snag to all this.'

'And what's that?'

'Not only will the French police not know exactly where we are going, thanks to my partially holding out on Calque, but they will still be out to get me – with everything they have in their arsenal – for Babel and the nightwatchman's murder. With you both along as accessories after the fact.'

'You can't be serious?'

'Oh yes I can. Deadly serious. Captain Calque told me that he is doing this entirely off his own initiative.'

'And you believe him?'

'Yes I do. He could have taken me into custody this morning and thrown away the key. Claimed all the kudos for himself. I was perfectly prepared to surrender to him without a struggle. I'm no cop killer. I told him so myself. He even held the Remington in his hand and then gave it back to me.'

Alexi whistled.

'The authorities could have spent months pinning that maniac's actions on to me, by which time the man they call the eye-man would have been long gone – probably with the verses in tow, and ready for sale on the open market. And who could prove where he found them? Nobody. Because they've got no DNA evidence – the death of an unknown gypsy doesn't rate a full police procedural over here, apparently. And anyway, they would already have had me in custody, so why bother with the rest? The ideal suspect. Whose blood is conveniently splattered all over the crime scene. Open and shut, no?'

'Then why is Calque doing this? They will send him to the guillotine, surely – or exile him to Elba, like Napoleon – if things go wrong.'

'Hardly that. He's simply doing it because he wants the eye-man, and he wants him badly. It was his fault his assistant got nailed. And he holds himself responsible for the nightwatchman's death, too. He reckons he should have figured that the eye-man would come back to sort over unfinished business. But he says he got so carried away with his own and his assistant's brilliance in working out the Montserrat code, that he couldn't see the light for the trees. A bit like me, really.'

'Are you sure it's not a trap? So they can get both

of you? I mean, perhaps they think you are working together?'

Sabir groaned. 'What the hell. I don't know. All I know is that he could have taken me in this morning, and he didn't. That's one heck of a bona fide in my book.'

'So what do we do?'

Sabir lurched backwards in mock surprise. 'What do we do? We head for the Camargue, that's what we do. Via Millau. That much I have agreed with Calque. Then we lose ourselves for a few days amongst ten thousand of your closest relatives. Always bearing in mind, of course, that the eye-man can track our car wherever and whenever he wants to – and that we are still murder suspects, with the French police hot on our trail, handcuffs and machine guns at the ready.'

'*Jesu Cristu!* And then?'

'And then, in six days' time, at the absolute height of the festival of the Three Maries, we steal out of hiding and filch the statue of Sainte Sara from in front of a church crammed to the rafters with frantically worshipping acolytes. Without tangling with the eye-man. And without getting ourselves strung up, or hacked to pieces, by a crazed mob of vengeful zealots in the process.' Sabir grinned. 'How do you like them apples, Alexi?'

PART TWO

1

Achor Bale felt a deep calm descend on him as he watched the tracker pick out the location of Sabir's car and follow it, pulsing gently.

And yes. There was the ghost of the police tracker too. So they were still on the job. Too much to hope that they had marked Sabir down for the attack in Montserrat. But there was a fair-to-middling chance that they had him tagged for the nightwatchman killing. Strange, though, that they still refused to pick him up – they must be after the verses as well. Both he and the police, it seemed, were playing a waiting game.

Bale smiled, and fumbled around on the passenger seat for Macron's identity card. He held it up in front of him and spoke directly to the photograph. 'How are your feet, Paul? A little tender?' He would meet Macron again – he was convinced of that. There was unfinished business there. How dare the French police pursue him into Spain? He would have to teach them a lesson.

For the moment, though, he would concentrate all his energies on Sabir. The man was heading south – and not towards Montserrat. Now why was that? He could hardly have heard about the attack there. And he had the exact same information concerning the verses that Bale had – the gist of the quatrain burned on to the base of the coffer, and the additional verse from Rocamadour. Had the little gypsy girl at the river held something back from him when she had described the coffer-verse's contents? No. He hardly thought so. You could always tell when somebody was so scared they couldn't even control their bladder any more – it was impossible to counterfeit a fear as strong as that. It was like a springbok being taken by a lion – all the springbok's physical mechanisms would close down once the lion had him around the neck, so that he'd be dead of shock even before his windpipe was crushed between the lion's teeth.

That was the way Monsieur, his late father, had trained Bale to behave – to go forward unthinkingly, and with total conviction. To decide in your head the optimum outcome of your actions, and to remain true to that outcome regardless of any diversionary tactics on the part of your opponent. Chess functioned in much the same way, and Bale was good at chess. It was all about the will to win.

To cap it all, his most recent phone call to Madame, his mother, had been of an entirely satisfactory nature. He had omitted to describe the fiasco in Montserrat, of course, and had simply explained to her that the people he was following had been held up by a wedding – these were gypsies, after all, and not rocket scientists. They were the sorts of people who would stop to pick wild asparagus by the roadside whilst on the run from the police. Sublime.

Madame, in consequence, had professed herself entirely satisfied with his conduct, and had told him that, of all her many children, he was the one she held most dear to her heart. The one she most counted on to do her bidding.

As Bale drove south, he could feel the shades of Monsieur, his late father, smiling benevolently on him from beyond the grave.

2

'I know where we must go to hide.'

Sabir turned towards Yola. 'And where's that?'

'There is a house. Deep in the Camargue. Near the Marais de la Sigoulette. For many years it has been at the centre of a battle for succession on the part of five brothers, who all inherited from their father – strictly according to the letter of Napoleonic law, needless to say – and then could not agree on what to do with their shared property. None of them will speak to the others. So no one pays for the upkeep of the property, or to have it guarded. My father won the use of this house about fifteen years ago in a bet, and it has become our territory since then. Our *patrin*.'

'He won the use of it from the brothers? You're joking?'

'No. From some other gypsies who had also found it. It's quite illegal to the *gadje* way of thinking, of course, and nobody else knows about the deal – but with us the thing is set in stone. It's simply accepted. We sometimes stay there when we go to the festival. There is no road in, only a rutted track. Around there, the *gardiens* use only their horses for transport.'

'The *gardiens*?'

'They are the guardians of the Camargue bulls. You see them on horseback, riding their white horses, sometimes carrying lances. They know every corner of the Camargue marshes. They are our friends. When Sara-e-kali is carried down to the sea, it is the Nacioun Gardiano who guard her for us.'

'So they know about this house too?'

'No. No one knows we use it but us. From the outside it does not seem inhabited. We have a way in through the cellar, though, so that it still seems as if the house is unlived in even when we are using it.'

'What do we do with the car?'

'We should leave it somewhere a long way away from the Camargue.'

'But then the eye-man would lose touch with us. We have an agreement with Calque, remember?'

'Then we leave it in Arles for the time being. We can hitch a ride into the Camargue with other gypsies. They will take us when they see us. We make a *shpera* sign on the road, and they will stop. Then we get off a few kilometres from the house and walk in, carrying our food with us – for anything else we need I can go out and do the *manghèl*.'

'Do the what?'

'Beg from farmhouses.' Alexi looked up from his driving. He was becoming used to explaining things about the gypsy world to Sabir. His face even took on a particular expression – somewhere between that of a commercially driven television pundit and a newly enlightened spirit guide. 'Ever since she was a *chey*, Yola, like all gypsy girls, has had to learn how to persuade local farmers to share their excess food. Yola is an artist at the *manghèl*. People feel privileged to give her things.'

Sabir laughed. 'That I can well believe. She's certainly managed to persuade me to do a whole raft of things I would never have dreamed of doing if I'd had even a fraction of my wits about me. Speaking of which, what do we do when we are inside the house, and you've plundered the local countryside for food?'

'Once inside, we hide up until the festival. Kidnap Sara. Conceal her. Then we go back to the car and drive

193

away. We call Calque. The police will do the rest.'

The smile froze on Sabir's face. 'Sounds awful easy, the way you tell it.'

3

'I think I've got him.'

'Drop back then.'

'But I should keep him in sight.'

'No, Macron. He will see us and spook. We'll have one chance at this and one only. I've arranged an invisible roadblock just before Millau, where the road narrows through a canyon. We let him drive through it. Half a kilometre further on there's another – this time obvious – roadblock. We let Sabir and the gypsies pass. Then we seal it off. If the eye-man tries to double back, we'll have him like a rat in a trap. Even he won't be able to scramble up sheer cliff.'

'What about the verses?'

'Fuck the verses. I want the eye-man. Off the streets. For good.'

Secretly, Macron had already begun to think that his boss was losing it. First, the mess-up at Rocamadour, which had resulted in the unnecessary death of the nightwatchman – Macron had long since convinced himself that were he to have been running the investigation, such a thing would never have happened. Then the criminal stupidity of Calque abandoning his post back at Montserrat, which had resulted in Macron taking the rap – it was he, after all, and not Calque, whom the eye-man had beaten up. And now this.

Macron was convinced that they could take the eye-man themselves. Follow him at a safe distance. Isolate and identify his vehicle. Position unmarked vehicles front and back of him. Then sweep him up. There was no earthly need for static roadblocks – they were always more trouble than they were worth. If you weren't careful, you'd end up on a high-speed chase though a rock-strewn field of sunflowers. Then three weeks filling in forms explaining the damage to police vehicles. The sort of bureaucracy, he, Macron, excoriated.

'He's driving a white Volvo SUV. It has to be him. I'm approaching a little closer. I need to make sure. Call in the number-plate.'

'Don't go any closer. He'll pick us up.'

'He's not a superman, Sir. He's got no idea we know he's tracking Sabir.'

Calque sighed. It had been deeply stupid of him to grant the single favour to Macron. But that's what guilt did for you. It made you soft. The man was clearly a bigot. With every day they remained on the road together, his bigotry became more pronounced. First it was the gypsies. Then it was the Jews. Now it was his fiancée's family. They were *métis*. Mixed race. Macron accepted that in his girlfriend, apparently, but couldn't abide it in her family.

Calque privately supposed the man must vote for the Front National – but he, personally, was of a generation which considered it impolite to question another man about his political affiliations. So he would never know. Or perhaps Macron was a communist? In Calque's opinion, the Communist Party were even worse racists than the Front National. Both of the parties switched their votes back and forth to each other when they found it expedient. 'That's close enough, I tell you. You forget how he outsmarted us all on the Sierra de Montserrat. Villada thought it impossible for a single man to make it off the hill before he was surrounded and swept up by the police cordon. The bastard must be able to move like a cat. He must have been outside the line before the Spanish even began their operation.'

'He's speeding up.'

'Let him. We have thirty more kilometres to go before we can slip the noose around his neck. I have a helicopter on standby at Rodez airport. CRS at Montpellier. He can't escape.'

Calque looked as though he were competent, thought Macron – *sounded* as though he were competent – but it was all bullshit. The man was a dilettante. Why pass up an opportunity to nail the eye-man now in favour of a pie-in-the-sky plan that would probably cover the lot of them in even further ignominy? One more mistake, and he, Paul Eric Macron, might as well write off any chances he ever had of further promotion, and vote himself straight back on to the beat as a sort of eternal *pandore*.

Macron eased his foot down on the throttle. They were on winding country lanes. The eye-man would be concentrating all his attention ahead. It wouldn't occur to him to check the road half a kilometre behind. Macron inconspicuously popped the button on the holster he had slid in under his seat that morning.

'I said slow down.'

'Yes, Sir.'

Calque brought the binoculars back up to his eyes. The road was so winding that looking through them for more than a few seconds at a time made him feel nauseous. Yes. Macron was right. The Volvo SUV had to be the car. For twenty kilometres now it had been the only vehicle between them and Sabir. He felt a dryness in his mouth – a fluttering in the pit of his stomach – that he usually felt only in the presence of his ruinous-to-maintain ex-wife.

When they breasted the next corner, Bale was standing eighty metres away in the centre of the road. He was holding the Star Z-84 sub-machine that he had liberated from the Catalan paramilitary at *porte armes* position.

Bale smiled, braced the Z-84 against his right shoulder, and squeezed the trigger.

4

—

Macron threw the wheel violently to the left – it was an instinctive reaction, without any basis whatsoever in driver training or in ambush coordination. The unmarked police car began to tip. He threw the wheel in the opposite direction to counterbalance it. The police car continued on its original path, but this time in a series of violent somersaults.

Bale glanced down at the weapon in his hand. Incredible. It worked even better than he had hoped.

The police car settled on its side, accompanied by a tinkling and a groaning of metal. Glass, plastic, and strips of aluminium littered a fifty-metre swathe of the road. A thick oil slick was forming beneath and beyond the car, like a blood haemorrhage.

Bale glanced quickly up and down the road. Then he crouched down and swept up the discarded shell cases and put them in his pocket. He had aimed the gun high on purpose, with its trajectory towards an open field. It amused him to think that the two policemen – if they had survived the crash – would have no way of proving that he had actually been there at all.

With one further, almost idle, glance behind him, he climbed back into the Volvo and continued on his way.

5

—

'What's to stop the eye-man from simply attacking us and making us tell him where the verses are?'

'Because we don't know where the verses are. At least not as far as he's concerned.'

Alexi made a puzzled face. He glanced questioningly at Yola, but she was sound asleep on the back seat.

'Think about it, Alexi. He only knows what Yola told him. No more. And she wasn't able to tell him about the Three Maries because she didn't know about them herself.'

'But . . .'

'In addition, he's only got the quatrain from the base of the Black Virgin of Rocamadour to go on. Which sent him to Montserrat. But in Montserrat he failed to get hold of the quatrain hidden at La Morenita's feet – the quatrain which cements the gypsy connection. And neither does he know about my meeting with Calque, or that Calque gave me the text of the Montserrat quatrain as a token of good faith. So he's got to stick with us.

He's got to assume we are on our way to somewhere specific in order to pick up another part of the message. Why should he mess with us, then? He doesn't know we know we're being followed. And he's probably so bloody cocksure after eluding the Spanish police at Montserrat that he thinks he'll be able to take on the whole of the Police Nationale single-handed if they should be dumb enough, or angry enough, to mess with him again.'

'How do you know that?'

'Simple psychology. And the single look I got at his face in the Rocamadour Sanctuary. This is a guy who's used to getting what he wants. And why does he get it? Because he acts. Instinctively. And with not one iota of conscience. Look at his record. He goes straight for the jugular every time.'

'Why don't we ambush him then? Use his own tactics against him? Why wait for him to come to us?'

Sabir sat back in his seat.

'The police will fuck it up, Damo. They always do. It was my cousin he killed. And Yola's brother. We swore to avenge him. You agreed to that. We have this man on a string – he follows wherever we go. Why not tug at the string a little? Draw him in? We'd be doing Calque a favour.'

'You think that, do you?'

'Yes. I think it.' Alexi grinned, sarcasm oozing from every pore. 'I like the police. You know I do. They've always been fair to us gypsies, wouldn't you say? Treated us respectfully and with dignity? Given us courtesy and equal rights with the rest of the French population? Why shouldn't we help them for a change? Return the compliment?'

'You haven't forgotten what happened last time?'

'We're better prepared this time. And if the worst comes to the worst the police can always act as our back-up. It'll be like John Wayne in *Stagecoach*.'

Sabir gave him an old-fashioned look.

'Yeah. I know. I know. We're not playing a game of cowboys and Indians. But I think we ought to use this guy's own tactics against him. It nearly worked last time . . .'

'. . . apart from your balls and your teeth. . .'

'. . . apart from my balls and my teeth. Yes. But it will work this time. If we plan it right, that is. And if we don't lose our nerve.'

6

—

Calque eased himself out through the broken front window of the police car. He lay for a while, spreadeagled on the ground, looking up at the sky. Macron had been right. The airbag did work with the seat belt. In fact it worked so well that it had broken his nose. He put up a hand and fumbled at the new shape, but didn't quite have the courage to yank it back into place. 'Macron?'

'I can't move, Sir. And I can smell petrol.'

The car had settled at the exact apex of the corner. Calque had an absurd vision of prising open the boot, taking out the warning triangles, and then limping back to set them up so that no one would inadvertently run into the back of them. Health and safety directives insisted that he should also wear a reflective vest when he did this. For a brief moment he was actually tempted to laugh.

Instead, he struggled to his knees and craned down to peer under the wreck. 'Can you reach the keys?'

'Yes.'

'Well switch off the engine then.'

'It happens automatically when the airbags inflate. But I've turned the thing off anyway to make sure.'

'Good lad. Can you reach your cellphone?'

'No. My left hand is caught between the seat and the door. And the airbag is between my right hand and my pocket.'

Calque sighed. 'All right. I'm standing up now. I'll get to you in a moment.' Calque rocked on his feet. All the blood moved to his body's periphery, and for a moment he thought he would fall down in a dead faint.

'Are you all right, Sir?'

'My nose is broken. I'm feeling a bit weak. I'm coming now.' Calque sat down in the road. Very slowly he lay back down and closed his eyes. From somewhere behind him there came the sudden, distant scream of over-heated brakes.

7

'How did he get the sub-machine gun?'

'From the Spanish paramilitary, of course. Villada never got around to telling me that bit.'

Calque was sitting beside Macron in the Accident and Emergency department of Rodez Hospital. Both of them were bandaged and taped. Calque had one arm in a sling. His nose had been reset, and he could feel the residual effects of the local anaesthetic niggling away at his front teeth.

'I can still drive, Sir. If you can get us a fresh car, I'd like to take another shot at the eye-man.'

'Did you say *another* shot? I can't remember the first one.'

'It was only a manner of speaking.'

'Well it was a stupid manner of speaking.' Calque laid his head back on to the seat cushion. 'The roadblock boys don't even believe the eye-man was there because there are no bullet holes anywhere in the car. I've told them the bastard obviously cleaned up after himself, but still they amuse themselves thinking that we smashed up the car by mistake and are trying to cover our tracks.'

'You mean he did it on purpose? He's trying to make us into a laughing stock?'

'He's laughing at us. Yes.' Calque ran a cigarette beneath his nose and prepared to light it. A nurse shook her head and motioned him outside with her finger. Calque sighed. 'They want to take the case away from me. Give it to the DCSP.'

'But they can't do that.'

'They can. And they will. Unless I give them a convincing reason otherwise.'

'Your seniority, Sir.'

'Yes. That's convincing. I can feel every day of it in my back, in my arms, in my upper thighs, and in my feet. I think there's a place halfway up my right calf which still feels young and vigorous though. Maybe I should show them that?'

'But we've seen him. We've seen his face.'

'At eighty metres. From a moving car. Behind a sub-machine gun.'

'But they don't know that.'

Calque sat forward. 'Are you suggesting I lie to them, Macron? Exaggerate the extent of my knowledge? Merely in order to keep a case that has threatened, on a number of occasions now, to finish us off?'

'Yes, Sir.'

Bunching his fingers like a crane clamp, Calque gently palpated his newly straightened nose. 'You may have a point, my boy. You may have a point.'

8

'I need access to the internet.'

'The what?'

'To a computer. I need an internet café.'

'Are you mad, Damo? The police are still looking for you. Someone will probably read the news on the computer next to you, see your photo, call in your details, and watch happily as they come to pick you up. Then, if they film the whole scene of your capture on their webcams, they can post it straight away and make their names. They will be instant millionaires. Better than the lottery.'

'I thought you couldn't read, Alexi? How come you know so much about computers?'

'He plays games.'

Sabir turned round and stared at Yola. 'I'm sorry?'

She yawned. 'He goes to internet cafés and he plays games.'

'But he's a grown-up.'

'Still.'

Alexi couldn't see Yola's face as he was driving but he managed to dart a few concerned glances into the rear-view mirror. 'What's wrong with playing games?'

'Nothing. If you're fifteen.'

Yola and Sabir were trying to hide their enjoyment behind faked straight faces. Alexi was the perfect subject for teasing because he took everything which referred to himself at absolute face value, whereas, when it referred to other people, he was considerably more selective.

Alexi had obviously succeeded in reading their minds for once, for he immediately changed tack to a more serious subject. 'Tell me why you need the internet, Damo?'

'To find a new Black Virgin. We need to pinpoint a place, well away from the Camargue, to which we can lure the eye-man. And which he will believe in. For this we need a Black Virgin.'

Yola shook her head. 'I don't think you should do this.'

'But you were all for it. Back at Samois. And when we went to Rocamadour.'

'I have a sense about this man. You should leave him to the police. As you agreed with the Captain. I have a very bad feeling.'

'Leave him to the police? Those fools?' Alexi rocked himself back and forwards against the steering wheel. 'And then you both laugh at me for playing games? It is you who are the games players, not me.' Alexi paused dramatically, waiting for a response. When it didn't come, he forged ahead, undaunted. 'I say let Damo go and find his Black Virgin. Then we lead the eye-man there. This time we make a plan that is foolproof. We will be waiting for him. He comes in – we shoot him.

Then Damo beats him to a pulp with his stick. We bury him somewhere. The police can look for him for the next ten years – that will keep a few of them out of our hair, won't it?'

Yola threw up her arms. 'Alexi, when O Del gave out brains, He only had a certain amount to go round. He tried to be fair, of course, but it was difficult for Him, because your mother nagged Him so much that He forgot all about what He was doing and took away what little brains you had by mistake. And now look.'

'Who did He give them to? My brains I mean? Damo, I suppose? Or Gavril? Is that what you are saying?'

'No. I think He made a really big mistake. I think He gave them to the eye-man.'

9

—

'I've got it.' Sabir slid into the passenger seat of the Audi, clutching a piece of paper. 'Espalion. It's only fifty kilometres from here as the crow flies. And it's perfectly reasonable that we should choose a roundabout route to get there – the police are still after us, as well as the eye-man.' He allowed his gaze to travel over their two faces. 'I don't see why he shouldn't swallow it, do you?'

'Why Espalion?'

'Because it's got what we need. It's in the opposite direction to Saintes-Maries, for a start. And it's got its very own Black Virgin, called La Négrette. Okay, she's missing a child – but you can't have everything. She's situated in a small chapel alongside a hospital, which means that the chapel will almost certainly have no watchman – unlike Rocamadour – as patients and their relatives will require access at all times of the day and night. It's got miracles, too – La Négrette is prone to fits of weeping, apparently, and whenever she is painted she always returns to her original colour. She was found during the Crusades and brought back to the Château de Calmont d'Olt by the Sieur de Calmont. It says here that La Négrette was threatened during the Revolution, when the castle was sacked, but some good soul saved her. So it's completely believable that she was around in Nostradamus's time. The Pont-Vieux at Espalion is even a World Heritage Site. On the pilgrim route to Santiago de Compostela, just like Rocamadour. It's perfect.'

'So how do we trap the eye-man?'

'The minute we stop at Espalion, my bet is that he'll suspect what we're after. And he'll almost certainly try to get there ahead of us. He's never more than about a kilometre behind us anyway, according to Calque, so we've got maybe two or three minutes to set up a trap. That's not enough, obviously. So Yola and I need to find a taxi now. Pronto. I've hatched a little plan.'

10

Sabir got out of the taxi. He had twenty minutes before Alexi was due to arrive in the Audi, with the eye-man close behind. Twenty minutes to find a fail-safe spot from which to trigger an ambush.

He had dropped Yola off five minutes before. She was waiting near a telephone booth in the town centre. If she didn't hear from them within half an hour, she was to call Calque and tell him what was going down. It wasn't an elegant plan, but with three against one, Sabir felt that it afforded them the infinitesimal edge they needed in order to turn the tables.

But it all came down to him. He had the Remington. He was a fair shot. But he knew that he wouldn't survive a straight face-off with the eye-man. It wasn't a matter of skill – he knew that much – but of will. He wasn't a killer. The eye-man was. It was as simple as that. So he had to cripple the eye-man – put him out of business – before he was able to respond.

Sabir's gaze travelled over the hospital grounds. Would the eye-man come straight in by car? Or would he leave the car and come in on foot, as he'd done at Montserrat? Sabir could feel the sweat breaking out all over his face.

No. He would have to go into the chapel. Wait for the eye-man there.

He suddenly had an intense feeling of claustrophobia. What was he doing? How had he got himself into this absurd position? He must be crazy.

He ran into the chapel, nearly overturning an elderly

lady and her son who had just been in to pray.

There was a service going on. The priest was preparing for Mass. Christ Jesus.

Sabir backed out, looking wildly behind him at the car park. Twelve minutes. Sabir began jogging down the road in the direction of town. It was impossible. They couldn't start a shoot-out in a chapel chock-full with celebrants and partakers of the Host.

Perhaps Alexi would be early? Sabir slowed down to an amble. Fat chance. And a fat success of an ambush he'd managed. When O Del gave out brains, it wasn't only Alexi who had found himself short-changed.

Sabir sat down on a bollard at the side of the road. At least Alexi had enough room to turn round here. At least he'd thought of that.

He took out the Remington and placed it on his lap.

Then he waited.

11

'They're conducting Mass. The place is packed. It'd be a bloodbath.'

'So it's off? We don't do it?'

'We've got three minutes to turn round and pick Yola up. Then I suggest we get the hell out of here. Once outside town we dump the fucking tracker and head for Les Saintes-Maries. And to heck with Calque and the eyeman.'

Alexi slewed the Audi round and headed back towards

town. 'Where did you leave Yola?'

'She's sitting in the Café Centrale. Next door to a phone booth. I took the number. I was going to phone her if everything went well.'

Alexi glanced at Sabir and then quickly forward. 'What if we meet the eye-man coming in? He knows our car.'

'We'll have to chance it. We can't leave Yola staked out in the centre of town like mouse bait.'

'What if he sees *her*, then?'

Sabir felt himself go cold. 'Stop by that phone-box over there. I'm going to call her. Now.'

~

Achor Bale threw the list on to the passenger seat. Espalion. A Black Virgin called La Négrette. Near the hospital. This was it, then.

He'd received the list of all the Black Virgin sites south of the Lyon/Massif Central meridian only two days ago, via his cellphone. Courtesy of Madame, his mother's, private secretary. She had made up the list for him just in case, using research material from Monsieur, his father's, library. At the time he'd thought she was being over-cautious – interfering, even. Now he knew she'd done the right thing.

He squeezed down on the accelerator. It would be good to get this thing over and done with. It had all taken too long. Left him too much in the frame. The longer you remained out in the field, the more likely you were to make a mistake. The Legion had taught him that. Look what happened at Dien Bien Phu against the Vietminh.

Bale hit the periphery of Espalion at seventy miles an hour, his eyes searching to right and to left, looking for red 'H' signs.

He slowed down towards the centre of town. Pointless drawing attention to himself. He'd have time. The three stooges didn't even realise he was still following them.

He pulled up near the Café Centrale to ask for directions.

The girl. She was sitting there.

So they'd left her. Gone to do the dirty work themselves. Come back later. Pick her up when it was safe. Gentlemen.

Bale climbed out of the car. As he did so, the phone rang in the nearby booth.

The girl glanced across him at the booth. Then back towards him. Their eyes met. Bale's face broke into a welcoming smile, as if he had just encountered a long-lost friend.

Yola stood up, knocking back her chair. A waiter started instinctively towards her.

Bale turned casually around and made his way back to his car.

When he turned to look, the girl was already running for her life.

12
—

Bale pulled gently away from the kerb, as if he had changed his mind about having a cup of coffee, or had left his wallet at home. He didn't want anyone remembering him. He glanced back to his left. The girl was sprinting down the road, with the waiter in hot pursuit. Silly bitch.

She hadn't paid her bill.

He drew up beside the waiter and gently tapped his horn. 'Sorry. My fault. We're in a hurry.' He waved a twenty-euro note out of the window. 'Hope this covers the tip.'

The waiter looked at him in astonishment. Bale smiled. His clotted eyes always affected people that way. Mesmerised them, even.

As a child, his condition had fascinated a wide variety of doctors – papers had even been written about him. One doctor had told him that before his case was brought to their attention, eyes without whites ('no-whites', the doctor had called them, in which only the proximal interommatidial cells were pigmented) had only ever been noted in *Gammarus chevreuxi Sexton* – a sand shrimp. He was an entirely new genetic type, therefore. A true Mendelian recessive. If he ever had children, he could found a dynasty.

Bale put on his sunglasses, amused at the waiter's discomfiture. 'Drugs, don't you know. The young these days. Not fit to be let off the leash. If she owes more, tell me.'

'No. That's all right. That's fine.'

Bale shrugged. 'The truth is that she needs to go back to the clinic. Hates the thought of it. Always does this to me.' He waved at the waiter as he accelerated away. The last thing Bale wanted was a new police presence dogging his every footstep. It had already cost him far too much effort getting rid of the last bunch. This way, the waiter would explain what had happened to his customers, and everyone would be satisfied. By the time they made it home, the story would have grown wings, and a dozen different endings.

Yola looked wildly back over her shoulder. She slowed down. What was he doing? He was talking to the waiter. Stupid – so stupid – to run off without paying. She tried to catch her breath but her heart seemed temporarily out of her control.

What if he wasn't the man? Why had she run like that? There had been something about him. Something about the way he had smiled at her. As if she had known him before, almost. A familiarity.

She halted at the corner of the street and watched his interaction with the waiter. He would drive away. He had nothing to do with her. She had panicked for nothing. And the phone had been ringing. Perhaps Damo had wanted her to call the police? Perhaps he had wanted to tell her that they had killed the eye-man?

The eye-man? She remembered the man's eyes now. Remembered how they had pierced through her back at the café.

She moaned softly to herself and began to run again. Behind her the Volvo started to gain speed.

13
—

At first Yola ran without thinking – away – simply away – from the white car. At one point, however, she had the presence of mind to slip down a narrow alley where she knew that the big Volvo could not follow her. The momentary decline of tension calmed her and allowed her mind to dominate her emotions for the first time in the three minutes since she had recognised her assailant.

The Volvo appeared again near the exit of the alley and began to dog her at a slower, more uneven pace – impulsively speeding up and then slowing down when she least expected it. She suddenly realised that he was herding her – herding her like a cow – towards the periphery of the town.

And Damo had telephoned. It had to be him. Which meant that he and Alexi might be coming back to collect her.

She looked back over her right shoulder, towards the town centre. They would be coming in on the hospital road. Her only chance would be to meet them. If the eye-man carried on like this, she would eventually tire and then he could pick her up with ease.

She saw a man exit from a shop – reach down and adjust his socks – stride across for his bicycle, which was tethered to a plane tree. Should she call him? No. She instinctively understood that the eye-man would have no qualms at all about killing him. There was something fatalistic about the way he was following her – as if the whole thing were preordained. She would involve no one – no one who was outside the present hermetic loop.

With her hand on her heart, she ran back towards the centre of town, angling her direction so that she would bisect the incoming road – the road on which Alexi and Damo might be travelling. How long since they had telephoned? Five minutes? Seven? She was panting like a horse, her lungs unused to the dry town air.

The Volvo picked up speed again, as if he was really coming for her this time – as if he intended to knock her down.

She ran into a newsagent's shop – then immediately

ran out again – fearful of being trapped. If only a police car would drive by. Or a bus. Anything.

She ducked down another alley. Behind her the Volvo accelerated away, anticipating her exit.

She doubled back and continued on towards the main road. If he turned back now – turned back before he reached the exit of the alley – she was done for.

Now she really ran, her breath escaping from her lips in shrieks of effort. She remembered his hands on her. His words. The terminal effect of his words. She had known there was no escape. Known that he would do exactly what he said he would do by the river. If he got hold of her now, he would knock her out to silence her. He could do anything to her. She would never know.

She burst on to the main highway, looking to right and left for signs of the Audi. The road was empty.

Should she turn back towards town? Back towards the café? Or head towards the hospital?

She took the hospital road. She was limping now, and quite unable to run.

When Bale's Volvo breasted the corner of the road, she stumbled and fell to her knees.

It was midday. Everybody was having lunch. She was alone.

14

—

'It's Yola. She's been knocked down.' Sabir slewed the car across the road and towards the kerb.

'Damo. Look.' Alexi reached across and took his arm.

Sabir glanced up. A white Volvo SUV with tinted window-glass breasted the corner at a leisurely pace and then stopped, on the wrong side of the road, about fifty metres from the girl. The door opened and a man got out.

'It's him. It's the eye-man.'

Sabir stepped out of the Audi.

Yola stumbled to her feet and stood, gently weaving, her eyes fixed on the Volvo.

'Alexi. Go and fetch her.' Sabir took the Remington out of his pocket. He didn't point it at the eye-man – that would have been absurd, given the distance between them – but held it flat against the side of his trousers, as if he had meant to slip it back inside his pocket but had temporarily forgotten that he was holding a gun. 'Now take her back to the car with you.'

The eye-man didn't move. He merely stood watching their movements like a neutral observer at a formal exchange of prisoners.

'Are you both inside?' Sabir didn't dare take his eyes off his eerily unmoving opponent.

'Is that my pistol?' The man's voice was measured – controlled – as if he were conducting a prearranged negotiation between hostile factions.

Sabir began to feel light-headed – almost hypnotised. He held up the pistol and looked at it.

'I'll give you a ten-minute start if you leave it behind you on the road.'

Sabir shook his head. He felt dazed. In an alternative reality. 'You can't be serious.'

'I'm deadly serious. If you agree to leave the gun behind you, I shall move away from my car and walk back towards the centre of town. I'll return in ten

215

minutes. You can go off in any direction you want. As long as it's not towards the hospital, of course.'

Alexi pushed himself across the front seat. He whispered urgently to Sabir, 'He doesn't realise that we know about his tracker. He's sure he can pick us up again without any problem if we've already taken La Négrette. But he's counting on us not having done that. There are only four roads out of this town. He'll see which direction we are going in and he'll follow. We need those ten minutes. Leave him the gun. We'll ditch the tracker, as you said.'

Sabir raised his voice. 'But then we'll have no way of defending ourselves.'

Alexi whispered through gritted teeth, 'Damo, leave him the fucking gun. We'll get another one down in the . . .' He stopped, as though he thought that Bale might be able to read his lips, or miraculously hear his words from a distance of over fifty metres. '. . . where we're going.'

Bale reached behind himself and drew the Ruger from its sheath. He raised the pistol and held it in both hands, aimed at Sabir. 'I can take out your knee. Then you won't be able to drive. Or I can take out your front tyre. Same effect. This pistol is accurate to eighty-five yards. Yours is accurate to maybe ten.'

Sabir stepped back behind the protection of the car door.

'It'll punch through that, no problem. But it's in no one's vested interest to cause a ruckus out here. Leave the gun. Leave my way clear to the hospital. And you can go.'

'Put your gun away. Inside the car.'

Bale moved over to the Volvo. He tossed the Redhawk on to the front seat.

'Now step away.'

Bale took three steps out into the road. A blue Citroën camionette drove past them, its passengers busy talking – paying them no heed.

Sabir concealed the Remington behind his back and made as if he was getting back inside the Audi.

'Do we have an agreement, Mister Sabir?'

'Yes.'

'Then you'll leave the pistol by the kerbside, in the gutter. I'm walking away now.' He triggered the Volvo's automatic door locks. 'If you don't do as you say, I will hunt you down, regardless of what I find in the hospital chapel, and make sure you suffer for a very long time indeed before you die.'

'I'll leave the pistol. Don't worry.'

'And the Black Virgin?'

'She's still at the hospital. We haven't had time to collect her. You know that.'

Bale smiled. 'The girl. You can tell her she's very brave. You can also tell her I'm sorry I frightened her down at the river.'

'She can hear you. I'm sure she'll be touched by your sentiments.'

Bale shrugged and turned as if to go. Then he stopped. 'The pistol. It was Monsieur, my father's, you know. Please place it gently.'

15

'Do you think he's mad?' Alexi had just switched their number-plates for the third time – as usual, he favoured picnic places and scenic stops with broad vistas, which he could easily evaluate for incoming owners.

'No.'

'Why not?' He slid back on to the front seat, tucking the screwdriver into the glove compartment. 'He could have taken us easy. He had that monster of a pistol. All he needed to do was to run at us, shooting.'

'What? Like *Butch Cassidy and the Sundance Kid*?'

'Now you're kidding me, Damo. But seriously. We couldn't have made it away in time.'

'But he doesn't want *us*.'

'What do you mean?'

'We're simply a means to an end, Alexi. A means to get to the verses. Start a shoot-out on the outskirts of town and he lowers his chances of getting there before the cops. The whole place is sealed off. As you said, there are only four roads out of here – it would be child's play for the police to close down all the exits. Then send in a helicopter. Like netting rabbits with a ferret.'

'Now I know what it feels like to be a rabbit. And all my life I thought I was a ferret.'

'You are a ferret, Alexi. A brave ferret.' Yola sat up on the back seat. 'Thank you for saving me.'

Alexi blushed. He made a face, hunched his shoulders, started to grin and then slapped the dashboard. 'I did, didn't I? He could have shot me. But still I ran out into the street and got you. You saw that, Damo?'

'I saw it.'

'I got you, didn't I, Yola?'

'Yes. You got me.'

Alexi sat on the front seat, grinning to himself. 'Maybe I kidnap you when we're in Saintes-Maries. Maybe I ask Sainte Sara to bless our future children.'

Yola sat up a little higher. 'Is that a proposal of marriage?'

Alexi looked resolutely forward – an El Cid, riding back into Valencia at the head of his army. 'I only said maybe. Don't get your hopes up too crazy.' He pounded Sabir on the shoulder. 'Eh, Damo? Start as you mean to go on, heh? That's the way with women.'

Sabir and Yola's gaze met in the rear-view mirror. She rolled her eyes in resignation. He hunched his shoulders and tipped his head in sympathetic response. She replied with a secret smile.

16

—

'They've got rid of the tracker.'

'What? The eye-man's tracker?'

'No. Ours. I think it's the only one they found. I think they *think* it's the eye-man's tracker. Is that what you told them? That there's only one?'

Calque sighed. Life was not going exactly as planned. Still. Whenever did it? He had married young, with all his ideals intact. The marriage had been a disaster from the start. His wife had proved to be a scold and he had proved to be a moral coward. A disastrous combination. Twenty-five years of misery had ensued, to such an extent that even these last ten years of court cases, punitive alimony and penury had sometimes appeared as a godsend. All he had left was his police work and a disenchanted daughter who got her husband to return his phone calls. 'Can we still trace Sabir's car through the eye-man's tracker?'

'No. Because we don't have the correct code.'

'Can we get it?'

'They're working on it. There are only about a hundred million possible combinations.'

'How long?'

'A day. Maybe two.'

'Too long. How about the serial number of the pistol?'

'It was first registered back in the 1930s. But nothing before 1980 has been computerised yet. So all the pre-war records – at least the ones that weren't commandeered by the Nazis – are kept out at Bobigny, in a warehouse. A researcher has to check through them all by hand. Same problem as the tracker code, then. But with fifty per cent less chance of success.'

'Then we need to return to the gypsy camp at Gourdon. Pick up their trail from there.'

'How do you work that one out?'

'Our trio were there three days. Someone will have talked to someone. It always happens.'

'But you know how these people are. Why do you think they will suddenly talk to you now?'

'I don't. But it's as good a way as any of passing the time until your pinhead friends manage to get us back on to these people's – as you insist on calling them – tail.'

17

Achor Bale took a bite of his sandwich, then refocused the binoculars on the gypsy camp, chewing speculatively. He was up in the church tower, allegedly rubbing brasses and copying memorials. The priest was what the English might have called a 'good egg' and had seen no particular objection to Bale spending the day up there with his charcoal and his etching paper – the hundred-euro donation towards church funds had probably helped, though.

So far, however, Bale had seen no one he recognised from the Samois camp. That would have constituted his first line of attack. The second line depended on incongruities. Find someone or something that didn't fit in and make an approach through them. Things that didn't conform to established norms always represented weaknesses. And weaknesses represented opportunities.

So far he had identified a married girl with no children, an old woman whom nobody spoke to or touched, and a blond man who looked as if he had stumbled off the set of a movie about Vikings – either that, or straight from the parade ground of the SS training camp at Paderborn, circa 1938. The guy looked like no gypsy Bale had ever encountered. But still they seemed to accept him as one of themselves. Curious. It would certainly bear investigating.

Bale felt no particular rancour about the blind alley of the statue at Espalion. It was a fair cop, as they say. The three of them had played him for a sucker and he had fallen for it. It had been an outstanding set-up and he had been forced to re-evaluate his view of them yet again. Particularly the girl, who had truly led him on – to such an extent that he had been entirely convinced of her terror of him. She had played the wooden horse to perfection and he must never underestimate her again.

Tant pis. He had Monsieur, his father's, Remington back – before it occurred to anyone to try and trace it – and he had cleared his back-trail of policemen. So his time had not been entirely wasted.

But he was forced to admit that Sabir's choice of Espalion had been nothing short of inspired. Everything about it had been right. In consequence, he was sure that the real clue to the location of the verses must be in the exact opposite direction to the one in which the trio had allegedly been travelling. That's what book-learning intellectuals like Sabir always did – think things out in unnecessary detail. Which gave the true Black Virgin a home somewhere down in the south of France. That narrowed the field considerably. Which made Bale's enforced return north – towards Gourdon – even more irritating. But it had to be.

He had lost the trio on his tracker almost from the start. Personally, he reckoned that Sabir had headed down the D920 towards Rodez and had then veered east, on the D28, to Laissac. From there he could easily have contrived his way down to Montpellier and the meeting of the three autoroutes. Perhaps they were still intending to head for Montserrat after all? That would make a kind of sense. In which case they'd be in for an awful shock. If he understood the mentality of the Spanish police correctly, they'd have the place staked out for a good six months yet, with everybody – officers and men – on copious amounts of overtime, and making the most of any opportunity to be seen wandering around in shiny leather jackets and riding breeches, lugging sub-machine guns. Latins were the same the world over. They loved the show far more than the substance.

The blond man was making his way out of camp towards the centre of town. Very well. He would try him first. He would be easier to get to than either the girl or the old woman.

Bale finished his sandwich, collected up his brass-rubbing kit and binoculars, and started down the steps.

18
—

Calque watched Gavril picking his way amongst the street-market stalls. This was the tenth gypsy whose movements he and Macron had monitored that morning. Being blond, though, Gavril blended into the background far more effectively than the others of his immediate tribe. But there was still something 'other' about him – some simmering anarchic streak that warned people that he wouldn't necessarily conform to their mores, or agree with their opinions.

The locals, Calque noticed, gave him a wide berth once they had succeeded in clocking him. Was it the gaudy shirt, in definite need of a wash? The cheap mock-alligator shoes? Or the ridiculous belt with the branding-iron buckle? The man walked as if he were carrying a seven-inch knife on his hip. But he wasn't. That much was obvious. But he might have one somewhere else about his person. 'Pick him up, Macron. He's the one we want.'

Macron moved in. He was still a patchwork of Band-Aids, hidden bandages, Mercurochrome and surgical gauze – not to mention tender on his feet. But Macron, being Macron, somehow contrived to hide these disadvantages beneath his own particular form of swagger. Calque shook his head in mild despair as he watched his subordinate home in on the gypsy.

'Police Nationale.' Macron flashed his badge. 'You will please accompany us.'

For a moment it seemed as if Gavril were about to run, but Macron clamped his upper arm in the catch-all grip they were taught at cadet school. Gavril sighed – as if this were not the first time this had happened to him – and went along quietly.

When he saw Calque he hesitated for a moment, thrown by the arm sling and the nose bandage. 'Who won? You or the horse?'

'The horse.' Calque nodded to Macron, who eased Gavril against a wall, legs splayed, and patted him down for concealed weapons.

'Only this, Sir.' It was an Opinel penknife.

Calque knew that he wouldn't be able to make any long-term legal running with a simple penknife. 'How long is the blade?'

'Oh, about twelve centimetres.'

'Two centimetres longer than the legal allowance?'

'Looks that way. Yes, Sir.'

Gavril snorted. 'I thought this sort of harassment had stopped? I thought you'd been told to treat us like everybody else? I don't see you shaking down all the good citizens over there.'

'We need to ask you some questions. If you answer them adequately, you can go. Along with your penknife and your no doubt unsullied record. If you don't, we take you in.'

'Oh, so this is how you get gypsies to talk these days?'

'Exactly. Would you have spoken to us otherwise? In the camp, say? Would you have preferred that?'

Gavril shuddered, as if someone had walked over his grave.

No audience, thought Calque – this man would definitely need an audience in order to cut up rough. For a moment Calque felt almost sorry for him. 'Firstly, your name.'

There was the briefest of hesitations – then capitulation. 'Gavril La Roupie.'

Macron burst out laughing. 'You're joking. La Roupie? You're really called La Roupie? That means rubbish where I come from. Are you sure it's not Les Roupettes? That's what we call balls down in Marseille.'

Calque ignored him. He kept his eyes fixed on the gypsy, watching for any change in facial expression. 'Do you have your identity card with you?'

Gavril shook his head.

'Strike two,' said Macron, jovially.

'I'll make this simple. We want to know where Adam Sabir and his two companions have gone. He is wanted for murder, you know. And they are wanted as accomplices.'

Gavril's face closed down.

Calque immediately sensed that the mention of murder had been a mistake. It had thrown La Roupic too much on the defensive. He tried to back-pedal. 'Understand this. We don't think you're involved in any way. We simply need information. This man is a killer.'

Gavril shrugged. But the potential conduit had obviously closed. 'I'd give it if I could. The people you mention mean nothing to me. All I know is that they left here two days ago, and haven't been seen or heard of since.'

'He's lying,' said Macron.

'I'm not lying.' Gavril turned to face Macron. 'Why would I lie? You can make life very difficult for me. I know that. I'd help you if I could. Believe me.'

'Give him back his penknife.'

'But, Sir . . .'

'Give him back his penknife, Macron. And one of my cards. If he calls us with information which directly results in an arrest, he will get a reward. Did you hear that, La Roupie?'

They both watched as Gavril jostled his way back through the crowd of early morning shoppers.

'Why did you do that, Sir? We could have sweated him some more.'

'Because I made another mistake, Macron, in my long litany of recent mistakes. I mentioned the word "murder". That's taboo for gypsies. It means years of prison. It means trouble. Didn't you see him close up like a Belon oyster? I should have come at him another way.' Calque squared his shoulders. 'Come on. Let's find ourselves another one. I obviously need the practice.'

19

'What did you tell the two *Ripoux*?' Bale pressed the point of his knife against the back of Gavril's thigh.

'Oh Christ? What's this now?'

Bale stuck the blade a quarter of an inch through Gavril's flesh.

'Aiee! What are you doing?'

'My hand slipped. Every time you don't answer one of my questions, it's going to slip further. Failure to answer three questions and I'm through to the femoral artery. You'll bleed to death in under five minutes.'

'Oh *putain*!'

'I repeat. What did you tell the two *Ripoux*?'

'I told them nothing.'

'It's slipped again.'

'Aaahhh.'

'Keep your voice down, or I'll stick my knife up your arsehole. Do you hear me?'

'Jesus. Jesus Christ.'

'Let me rephrase my question. Where have Sabir and his two sea lice gone to?'

'Down to the Camargue. To the festival. Sainte Sara.'

'And when is this festival?'

'In three days' time.'

'And why have they gone there?'

'All gypsies go there. Sainte Sara is our patron saint. We go to get her blessing.'

'How do you get a blessing from a saint?'

'Her statue. We go up to her statue and get it to bless

us. We touch it. We try to kiss it.'

'What sort of statue are we talking about?'

'Jesus Christ. Just a statue. Please take the knife out of my leg.'

Bale twisted the knife. 'Is this statue black, by any chance?'

Gavril began to keen. 'Black? Black? Of course it's black.'

Bale snatched the knife from Gavril's leg and stepped backwards.

Gavril doubled up, clutching his thigh in both hands, as if it were a rugby ball.

Bale rabbit-punched him on the back of the neck before he had a chance to look upwards.

20

'We can't wait until the festival, Alexi. We have to check out the statue before it starts. I don't trust that maniac not to put two and two together and make it six. If he asks the right questions, any gypsy will tell him about Sainte Sara and the festival. It'd be like waving a red flag in front of a bull.'

'But they'll have it guarded. They know people want to come in and touch her, so they cordon her off. Post security guards there until the festival. Then she's brought out and swung over the penitents. Everybody leaps up and tries to grab her. Men hold up their children. But she's never out of someone's sight. It's not going to be like at Rocamadour. This is different. If we could only wait until the festival is over. She's left alone then. Anyone can go in and see her.'

'We can't wait. You know that.'

'Why does he want these verses, Damo? Why is he prepared to kill for them?'

'One thing I can tell you. It's not simply about money.'

'How do you know that?'

'You saw him, didn't you? He was prepared to give up all his advantage over us simply in order to get his father's gun back. Do you think that's normal behaviour? For someone out to make himself a fortune? With the verses in his hands, he could buy himself a thousand guns. Publishers all over the world would climb over themselves in a bidding war to get their hands on something like that. That's why I interested myself in the verses originally – venal financial gain. I'm not ashamed to admit it. Now I think there's something more to them – some secret which the eye-man either thinks they will reveal, or which he fears. Nostradamus obviously discovered something – something of profound significance both to the world and to you gypsies. He had already predicted exactly when he was going to die. So he decided to protect his discovery. Not to publish but to hide. He believed in God – he believed that his gifts were specifically God-given. And in my opinion he believed that God would provide the correct outlet and the correct time frame for his revelations to be made public.'

'I think you're crazy, Damo. I think there's nothing there. I think we're chasing a *mulo*.'

'But you saw the carvings on the coffer? And under the Black Virgin? You can see the pattern for yourself.'

'I'd like to believe you. I really would. But I can't

even read, Damo. Sometimes my mind gets so mixed up thinking of these things that I want to pull it out like string and untangle it.'

Sabir smiled. 'What do you think, Yola?'

'I think you're right, Damo. I think there's something about these verses we don't understand yet. Some reason the eye-man is prepared to kill for them.'

'Maybe he even wants to destroy them? Have you thought of that one?'

Yola's eyes widened. 'Why? Why would anyone want to do that?'

Sabir shook his head. 'That's the hundred-thousand-dollar question. If I could answer that one, we'd be home free.'

21

There were some amongst his friends who believed that Gavril had always been angry. That some *mulo* had entered his body at birth and, like a surgeon worrying at a tumour, had kept on at him ever since. That this was the reason he turned out looking like a *gadje*. That maybe he hadn't been kidnapped at birth after all, but had simply been cursed, way back in another life, and that his looks were a result of that. He was worse than simply *apatride*. He was a freak even to his own community.

Bazena, anyway, believed this. But she was hot in her belly for him, and so was way beyond sense in the matter.

Today Gavril seemed angrier than ever. Bazena glanced at the old woman who was acting as her temporary *duenna*, and then back at Gavril's hair. He was lying on the ground, his trousers around his ankles, and she was stitching the wound in his leg. It didn't look like a dog bite to her – more like a knife-wound. And the livid bruise on his neck certainly hadn't been made escaping over any fence. What did he do – fall backwards? But who was she to argue with him. She wondered for a moment what their children would look like? Whether they would take after her, and be gypsies, or whether they would take after Gavril, and be cursed? The thought made her go weak at the knees.

'When are your people leaving for Les Saintes-Maries?'

Bazena slipped in the last stitch. 'Later. In maybe an hour.'

'I shall go with you.'

Bazena sat up straighter. Even the old *duenna* began to take notice.

'I shall travel up front. With your father and your brother. Here.' He poked around inside his pocket and came up with a crumpled twenty-euro note. 'Tell them this is for the diesel. For my part of the diesel.'

Bazena looked across at the old *duenna*. Was Truffeni thinking what she was thinking? That Gavril was making it clear that he intended to kidnap her, when they were at Les Saintes-Maries, and ask for Sainte Sara's blessing on their marriage?

She tied the stitches off and rubbed over his leg with burdock.

'Aiee. That hurts.'

'I need to do it. It's antiseptic. It will clean the wound. Protect you from infection.'

Gavril rolled over and pulled up his trousers. Both

231

Bazena and the old woman averted their eyes.

'Are you sure you're not *mahrimé*? You haven't polluted me?'

Bazena shook her head. The old woman cackled, and made a rude sign with her fingers.

Yes, thought Bazena. She, too, thinks he wants me. She, too, thinks he has lost interest in Yola.

'Good.' He stood up, the anger still flaring in his eyes. 'I'll see you then. At your father's caravan. In an hour.'

22

'It's impossible. We're on a hiding to nothing.'

Macron made a face. 'I told you these people were useless. I told you these people were untrustworthy.'

Calque drew himself up. 'I think we've discovered just the opposite. They are obviously trustworthy, as they have refused to give their own people away. And as for useless – well. Enough said.'

Macron was sitting on a stone wall, with his back hunched against a corner of the church. 'My feet . . . Jesus Christ they hurt. In fact everything hurts. If I ever catch that bastard, I'm going to deglaze him with a blowtorch.'

Calque took the unlit cigarette out of his mouth. 'An odd manner of expression for a policeman. I assume you are just letting off steam, Macron, and don't really mean what you are saying?'

'Just letting off steam. Yes, Sir.'

'I'm very relieved to hear it.' Calque detected an echo of cynicism in his own voice, and it distressed him. He made a conscious effort at lightening his tone. 'How are your pinheads getting on with disentangling the tracker code?'

'They're getting there. Tomorrow morning at the latest.'

'What did we do before computers, Macron? I confess, I've quite forgotten. Real police work, perhaps? No. That cannot possibly be so.'

Macron closed his eyes. Calque was on the same old bandwagon as ever – would he never change? Fucking iconoclast. 'Without computers we wouldn't have got this far.'

'Oh, I think we would.' More pomposity. Sometimes Calque made himself ill with it. He sniffed at the air like a bloodhound anticipating a day's hunting. 'I smell *coq au vin*. No. There's more. I smell *coq au vin* and *pommes dauphinoises*.'

Macron burst out laughing. Despite his profound irritation with the man, Calque could always be counted on to make a person laugh. It was as if he held the secret within himself of suddenly being able to tap into a hidden conduit of mutuality – of mutual Frenchness – like Fernandel, for instance, or Charles de Gaulle. 'Now that's what I call police work. Shall we investigate further, Sir?' He opened his eyes, still not completely certain of Calque's mood. Was the Captain still down on him, or was he cutting him some slack at long last?

Calque flicked his cigarette into a nearby bin. 'Lead the way, Lieutenant. Food, as the philosophers say, must always precede duty.'

23

'It's perfect.' Sabir looked around the interior of the Maset de la Marais. 'The brothers are crazy to have abandoned a place like this. Look over there.'

Alexi craned his neck to where Sabir was pointing.

'That's an original Provençal cupboard. And look at that.'

'What?'

'The bergère suite. Over there. In the corner. It must be at least a hundred and fifty years old.'

'You mean these things are worth money? They're not just old junk?'

Sabir suddenly remembered who he was talking to. 'Alexi, you leave them alone, huh? These people are our hosts. Even though they may not know it. Okay? We owe them the courtesy of letting their stuff alone.'

'Sure. Sure. I'm not going to touch anything.' Alexi didn't sound convinced. 'But what do you *think* they're worth? Just at a guess?'

'Alexi?'

'Sure. Sure. It was only a question.' He shrugged. 'I suppose they would interest one of those antique dealer guys in Arles? If they knew they were here, that is.'

'Alexi.'

'Okay. Okay.'

Sabir smiled. What did the pundits say? You can take a horse to water, but you can't make it drink. 'How far is it to Les Saintes-Maries?'

Alexi's eyes were still straying towards the furniture. 'You know something, Damo? With you finding stuff for me, and me selling it, we could make a hell of a good living. You could even buy yourself a wife, maybe, after a year or two. And not so ugly as the first one I offered you.'

'Les Saintes-Maries, Alexi. How far?'

Alexi sighed. 'Ten kilometres as the crow flies. Maybe fifteen by car.'

'That's a heck of a long way. Is there nowhere nearer that would be safe to stay in? That would give us easier access?'

'Not unless you want every policeman within sixty square kilometres to know exactly where you are.'

'Point taken.'

'You could always steal a horse, though.'

'What are you talking about?'

'On the next farm. They've got dozens of horses scattered about. Over maybe a couple of hundred hectares. They can't possibly know where they all are at any one time. We simply borrow three. There's harness and saddles in the *buanderie* to ride them with. Then we keep them in the barn when we're not using them. Nobody would know. We can ride cross-country into Les Sainte-Maries whenever we want, and leave them with some gypsies just outside town. That way the *gardiens* don't recognise their own horses and get pissed off at us.'

'Are you serious? You want us to become horse thieves?'

'I'm always serious, Damo. Don't you know that yet?'

～

'Look what I've got.' Yola set down a wooden crate stuffed with farm produce. 'Cabbages, a cauliflower,

235

some courgettes . . . I've even got a marrow. Now all we need is some fish. Can you sneak over to the Baisses de Tages and catch us something, Alexi? Or steal some *tellines* from the cages?'

'I haven't got time for any of that nonsense. Damo and I are going to ride over to Les Saintes-Maries and check out the Sanctuary. See if we can figure out any way to come at the statue of Sainte Sara before the eye-man gets here.'

'Ride? But we haven't got a car any more. We left it in Arles.'

'We don't need a car. We're going to steal some horses.'

Yola stood watching Alexi – weighing him up. 'I'm coming with you then.'

'That's not a good idea. You'd just slow us up.'

'I'm coming with you.'

Sabir stared from one to the other of his two ad hoc relations. As usual, where the two of them were concerned, there always seemed to be some hidden tension in the air that he wasn't picking up. 'Why do you want to come, Yola? It could be dangerous. There will be police everywhere. You've already had two run-ins with this man – you don't need a third.'

Yola sighed. 'Look at him, Damo. Look at his guilty face. Don't you realise why he's so keen to go into town?'

'Well, we need to prepare . . .'

'No. He wants to drink. Then, when he's had enough to make himself ill, he'll start looking around for Gavril.'

'Gavril? Jesus, I forgot about him.'

'But he hasn't forgotten about you or Alexi. You can count on that.'

236

24

'We're on a wild goose chase, Sir. The pistol was last registered in 1933. And the man to whom it was registered has probably been dead for years. There may have been six changes of address in the interim. Or six changes of owner. The researcher tells me that when the war ended, nobody really caught up with their paperwork again until the 1960s. Why waste our time on it?'

'Have your pinheads cracked the tracker code yet?'

'No, Sir. No one has told me anything along those lines.'

'Do you have any other leads you are not telling me about?'

Macron groaned. 'No, Sir.'

'Read me out the address.'

'Le Domaine de Seyème, Cap Camarat.'

'Cap Camarat? That's near St-Tropez, isn't it?'

'Pretty much.'

'Your neck of the woods, then?'

'Yes, Sir.' Macron did not relish the prospect of returning, with Calque in tow, to somewhere quite so near home.

'Who was it registered to?'

'You're not going to believe this name.'

'Try me.'

'It says here it's registered to Louis de Bale, Chevalier, Comte d'Hyères, Marquis de Seyème, Pair de France.'

'A Pair de France? You're joking?'

'What's a Pair de France?'

Calque shook his head. 'Your knowledge of your own history is execrable, Macron. Have you no interest whatsoever in the past?'

'Not in the aristocracy, no. I thought we got rid of all that in the Revolution?'

'Only temporarily. They were reinstated by Napoleon, got rid of again in the Revolution of 1848, and then brought back by decree in 1852 – and as far as I know they've been around ever since. Established titles are even protected by law – which means by you and me, Macron – however much your Republican soul may resent doing it.'

'So what's a Pair de France when it's at home, then?'

Calque sighed. 'The Pairie Ancienne is the oldest and most exclusive collective title of nobility in France. In 1216 there were nine Pairs. A further three were created twelve years later, in 1228, to mimic the twelve paladins of Charlemagne. You've heard of Charlemagne, surely? Bishops, dukes and counts, mostly, deputed to serve the King during his coronation. One peer would anoint him, another would carry the royal mantle, another his ring, another his sword, and so on . . . I thought I knew them all, but this man's names and titles are unfamiliar to me.'

'Perhaps he's a fake? Assuming he's not dead, of course, which he undoubtedly is, as we're talking upwards of seventy-five years here since he first registered the pistol.' Macron gave Calque a withering look.

'You can't fake things like that.'

'Why ever not?'

'Because you can't. You can fake small titles – people do it all the time. Even ex-Presidents. And then they end up in the *Livre de Fausse Nobilité Française*. But big titles like that? No. Impossible.'

'What? These people even have a book of fake peerages?'

238

'More than that. The whole thing is like a mirror, really.' Calque weighed Macron up, as if he feared that he might be about to cast pearls before swine. 'For instance, there's a fundamental difference between Napoleonic titles and those which preceded them, like the one we've got here. Napoleon, being a bloody-minded so-and-so, gave some of his favourites the same, or already existing, names and titles – to humiliate the original owners, probably, and keep them in their place. But the effects proved unexpectedly long term. For even now, if you place a Napoleonic noble higher up the table than an Ancient noble with the same name, the Ancient noble, and all his family will simply turn over their plates and refuse to eat.'

'What? Just sit there?'

'Yes. And that is the sort of family we're probably dealing with here.'

'You're kidding me?'

'It would be seen as a calculated insult, Macron. Just like someone saying that the schools of Marseille produce only cretins. Such a statement would be palpably untrue and, in consequence, subject to castigation – except in certain extreme cases, of course, when it is found to be perfectly correct.'

25

For three hours Gavril had paced the streets of Les Saintes-Maries searching for any sign of Alexi, Sabir or

Yola. During that time he had bearded every gypsy, every *gardien*, every street musician, ostler, panhandler and palm reader that came into his ken, but he was still no further along.

He knew the town intimately, his parents having joined in the annual pilgrimage right up until his father's death, three years earlier. Since that time, however, his mother had dug in her heels and now refused to travel more than thirty kilometres in any direction from their home campsite near Reims. As a result of her intransigence, Gavril, too, had drifted out of the pilgrimage habit. He had been lying, therefore, when he had declared to Sabir that of course he was heading south with the rest of his clan. But some *mulo* had prodded him, none the less, into challenging Alexi to meet him at Sainte Sara's shrine. Some unconscious – even superstitious – force, whose exact origin he was unaware of.

What it finally came down to was this. If he could just get rid of Alexi – take Yola from him and marry her himself – his gypsyhood would be proven. No one could deny him his place inside the community. For Yola's family were gypsy nobility. He would be marrying into a bloodline that stretched all the way back to the great Exodus and beyond. Maybe even as far as Egypt itself. Once he had sons and daughters of such a lineage, no one could reasonably question his rights or his antecedents. The stupid, hurtful story of his father kidnapping him from a *gadje* woman would be laid to rest for ever. He might even become Bulibasha himself one day, given luck, money, and a little measured diplomacy. He would grow his hair long. Dye it red if he chose to. Piss in all their faces.

It was the two *gadje* policemen who had been the first to plant the larger idea in his mind, with their calling cards, and their hints, and their miserable insinuations.

As a direct consequence of their intervention, he had made up his mind to kill Alexi, then betray Sabir to the authorities for the promised reward. No one could blame him for defending himself against a criminal, surely? Then he would be free to revenge himself on that other *gadje* bastard who had so humiliated him and carved up his leg.

For that guy, too, had proved to be a fool – like all *gadjes*. Hadn't he given away exactly what he was after, with all his questions and his threats? Something to do with the statue of Sara-e-Kali itself? Gavril kicked himself for having wasted so much time parading around town and asking dumb questions. The man and Sabir were obviously linked – both, after all, had shown an unlikely interest in the festival. They must be after the same thing, therefore. Perhaps they wanted to steal the statue and hold it to ransom? Make all the gypsies in the world pay to have it back? Gavril shook his head in wonder at *gadje* stupidity. Gypsies would never pay for anything. Didn't these people know that?

Now all he had to do was to wait at the Sanctuary door and let them come to him. The festival, after all, was a mere forty-eight hours away. That gave him ample time to put his plan into action. And when he needed to rest, there was always Bazena. It would be child's play to persuade her to stand in for him. The silly bitch still imagined he wanted her. Well, it would be very convenient indeed to have her on tap. So he would cosy her along a little – feed her a sliver or two of hope.

First thing on his wish-list was to get her begging outside the church – that way no one could go past into the Sanctuary without her noticing. And she would be making money for him at the same time. A double whammy.

Yes. Gavril had it all worked out. He was finally

coming into his own – he could feel it. Now, after all these years, he would make the bastards pay. Pay for a lifetime of grief and petty humiliations because of his blond hair.

With the idea still burning in his head, Gavril hurried back through the town towards Bazena's father's caravan.

26

—

Achor Bale watched Gavril's antics with something close to bemusement. He had been following the idiot ever since figuratively firing him out of the gun at Gourdon – but the last three hours had finally and categorically persuaded him that he had never in his life trailed a man so sublimely unconscious of everything that was going on around him. Talk about a one-track mind. This gypsy merely had to think of a thing and, from then onwards, he would concentrate on it to the exclusion of all else – his thought processes almost clanked each time they fell into place. He was like a racehorse fitted with blinkers.

The man had been ridiculously easy to trail from Gourdon, after the leg-skewering. Now, in the tourist-infested streets of Les Saintes-Maries, the thing took on a simplicity quite out of kilter with the potential end results. Bale spent a happy fifteen minutes watching Gavril browbeating a young woman into agreeing with some new plan or other he had hatched. Then a further twelve as she settled herself on a patch of cleared ground in a corner of the square nearest to the entrance to the church. The girl almost immediately began begging – not from the gypsies, you understand, but from the tourists.

You devious little bastard, thought Bale. That's the way. Get other people to do your dirty work for you. Now I suppose you're going off to catch your forty winks?

Ignoring Gavril, Bale settled himself down in a nearby café, put on a wide-brimmed hat and sunglasses as a sop to the local police force, and began watching the girl.

27

'*Putain!* Look at this place. It must be worth a fucking fortune.'

Calque winced, but said nothing.

Macron hobbled out of the car. He stared out at the mass of Cap Camarat ahead of them, and then at the wide crescent of clear blue water leading to the Cap de St-Tropez on their left. 'It's just the sort of place Brigitte Bardot would live in.'

'Hardly,' said Calque.

'Well I think it is.'

A middle-aged woman in a tweed and cashmere twinset walked towards them from the house.

Calque gave a small inclination of the head. 'Madame La Marquise?'

The woman smiled. 'No. I am her private secretary. My name is Madame Mastigou. And Madame's correct title is Madame la Comtesse. The Marquisate is considered the lesser title by the family.'

Macron flashed his teeth in a delighted grin behind Calque's back. That would teach the snotty bastard. Serve him right to be such a snob. He always had to know everything about everything. And still he messed up.

'Have you both been in a car accident? I notice your assistant is limping. And you, if I may say so, Captain, look as though you've come straight from the wars.'

Calque gave a rueful acknowledgement of his arm sling and of the tape still criss-crossing his newly shaped nose. 'That is just what happened, Madame. We were in pursuit of a criminal. A very vicious criminal. Which is why we are here today.'

'You don't expect to find him in the house, surely?'

'No, Madame. We are investigating a pistol known to have been in his possession. This is why we wish to talk to your employer. The pistol may well have belonged to her father. We need to trace its itinerary over the past seventy-five years.'

'Seventy-five years?'

'Since its first registration in the early 1930s. Yes.'

'It was registered in the 1930s?'

'Yes. The early 1930s.'

'Then it would have belonged to Madame la Comtesse's husband. He is dead.'

'I see.' Calque could sense rather than see Macron rolling his eyes behind him. 'Madame la Comtesse is a very elderly lady, then?'

'Hardly, Monsieur. She was forty years younger than Monsieur le Comte when they married in the 1970s.'

'Ah.'

'But please. Come with me. Madame la Comtesse is expecting you.'

Calque followed Madame Mastigou towards the house, with Macron limping along behind. As they reached the front door, a hovering footman reached across and opened it.

'This can't be happening,' whispered Macron. 'This is a filmset. Or some sort of joke. People don't live like this any more.'

Calque pretended not to hear him. He allowed the footman to steady him up the front steps with only the lightest of touches on his uninjured arm. Secretly, he was rather grateful for the support, for he had been disguising from Macron just how fragile he really felt for fear of losing ground. Macron was a product of the *bidonvilles* – a street fighter – always on the lookout for weakness. Calque knew that his only real advantage lay in his brain, and in the depth of his knowledge about the world and its history. Lose that edge, and he was dead meat.

'Madame la Comtesse is waiting for you in the library.'

Calque followed the footman's outstretched arm. The secretary, or whatever she was, was already announcing them.

Here we go, he thought. Another wild goose chase. I should take the sport up professionally. At this rate, when we get back to Paris – and with Macron's gleeful input around the office – I shall become the laughing stock of the entire 2ème arrondissement.

28

'Look. It's Bazena.' Alexi was about to throw up his arm, but Sabir stopped him.

The two of them stepped back, in tandem, behind the screen separating two outside shopfronts.

'What's she doing?'

Alexi craned around the screen. 'I don't believe this.'

'Believe what?'

'She's begging.' He turned to Sabir. 'I'm serious. If her father or her brother saw her, they'd take a horsewhip to her.'

'Why? I see gypsies begging all the time.'

'Not gypsies like Bazena. Not from families like hers. Her father is a very proud man. You wouldn't want to get on the wrong side of him. Even I would think twice.' He spat on his hands superstitiously.

'Then what's she doing it for?'

Alexi closed his eyes. 'Hold it. Let me think.'

Sabir darted his head around the corner of the screen and checked out the square.

Alexi grabbed him by the shirt. 'I've got it! It has to be something to do with Gavril. Perhaps he's got her looking out for us?'

'Why doesn't he look out for us himself?'

'Because he's a lazy sonofabitch.'

'I see. You're not prejudiced, by any chance?'

Alexi cursed under his breath. 'What do we do, Damo? We can't go into the Sanctuary with Bazena there. She'll run off and tell Gavril, and he'll blunder in and mess everything up.'

'We'll get Yola to talk to her.'

'What good will that do?'

'Yola will think of something to say. She always does.'

Alexi nodded, as if the comment seemed self-evident to him. 'Okay then. Stay here. I will find her.'

~

Alexi found his cousin seated with a gaggle of her girlfriends, exactly as prearranged, outside the town hall, on the Place des Gitans. 'Yola. We've got a problem.'

'You've seen the eye-man?'

'No. But nearly as bad. Gavril has staked out the church – he's got Bazena begging near the doorway.'

'Bazena? Begging? But her father will kill her.'

'I know that. I already told Damo.'

'So what are you going to do?'

'I'm not going to do anything. You are.'

'Me?'

'Yes. You are going to talk to her. Damo says you always know what to say.'

'He says that, does he?'

'Yes.'

One of the other girls started to giggle.

Yola tugged at the girl's breasts. 'Be quite, Yeleni. I've got to think.'

It surprised Alexi that the girls hearkened to Yola, and didn't simply answer her back, as they customarily did to anyone her age who was still of spinster rank. Normally, the fact that she was so late unmarried would have diminished her status in the female community – for some of these young women had already given birth, or were pregnant for the second or third time. But he had to admit that Yola had a particular air about her which

247

commanded attention. It would certainly reflect well on him, were he to marry her.

Still. The thought of Yola keeping an eye on all his doings filled him with a prescient dread. Alexi acknowledged that he was weak-willed when it came to women. It was next to impossible for him to pass up any opportunity whatsoever to sweet-talk *gadje* girls. Yola was right. And that was all very well as things went. But once they were married, she was not the sort of woman to turn a blind eye to such proceedings. She'd probably castrate him while he was asleep.

'Alexi, what are you thinking about?'

'Me? Oh, nothing. Nothing at all.'

'Then go and tell Damo that I shall clear the way for us to go to the Sanctuary. But not to be surprised at how I do it.'

'Okay.' Alexi was still thinking about what it would be like to be poisoned or castrated. He didn't know which he would prefer. Both seemed inevitable if he married Yola.

'Did you hear me?'

'Sure. Sure I heard you.'

'And if you see Gavril, and he doesn't see you, avoid him.'

29

—

'Captain Calque? Please sit down. And you, too, Lieutenant.'

Calque collapsed gratefully on to one of the three large sofas set around the fireplace. Then he levered himself back up while the Countess sat down.

Macron, who had at first been tempted to perch on the arm of one of the sofas and dangle the soles of his painful feet in the air, thought better of it, and joined him.

'Would you both like some coffee?'

'That's quite all right.'

'I shall order some for myself then. I always have coffee at this hour.'

Calque looked like a man who had forgotten to buy his lottery ticket and whose numbers had just flashed up on the television screen.

'Are you sure you won't join me?'

'Well. Now that you mention it.'

'Excellent. Milouins, a pot of coffee for three, please. And bring some madeleines.'

'Yes, Madame.' The footman backed out of the room.

Macron made another incredulous face but Calque refused to meet his eyes.

'This is our summer house, Captain. In the nineteenth century it used to be our winter house, but everything changes, does it not? Now people seek out the sun. The hotter the better, no?'

Calque felt like blowing out his cheeks, but didn't. He felt like a cigarette, but suspected that he might simply set off a hidden smoke alarm – or trigger a ruckus about ashtrays – if he gave in to his craving. He resolved to forgo both, and not subject himself to any more stress than was strictly necessary. 'I wanted to ask you something, Madame. Purely as a matter of record. About your husband's titles.'

'My son's titles.'

'Ah. Yes. Your son's titles. Simple curiosity. Your son is a Pair de France, is he not?'

'Yes. That is correct.'

'But I understood there to be only twelve Pairs de France. Please correct me if I am wrong.' He held up his fingers. 'The Archbishop of Reims, who traditionally conducted the Royal crowning. The Bishops of Laon, Langres, Beauvais, Châlons and Noyons, who, respectively, anointed the King, and bore his sceptre, his mantle, his ring, and his belt. And then there were the Dukes of Normandy, Burgundy, and Aquitaine (also known as Guyenne). The Duke of Burgundy bore the crown and fastened the belt. Normandy held the first square banner, with Guyenne holding the second. Finally there were the Counts: Champagne, Flanders and Toulouse. Toulouse carried the spurs, Flanders the sword, and Champagne the Royal Standard. Am I not correct?'

'Extraordinarily so. One would think that you had just this minute looked these names up in a book and memorised them.'

Calque flushed. He could feel the blood churning through his damaged nose.

'No, Madame. Captain Calque really does know his stuff.'

Calque gave Macron an incredulous stare. Good God. Were we talking class solidarity here? That had to be the answer. There could be no other possible reason for Macron to defend him so sedulously, and in so public a manner. Calque inclined his head in genuine appreciation. He must remember to make more of an effort with Macron. Encourage him more. Calque even felt the vestige of a slight affection clouding his habitual irritation at Macron's youthful brashness. 'And so we come to your husband's family, Madame. Forgive me.

But I still don't understand. This would surely make them the thirteenth Pair? But no record of such a Pair exists, as far as I am aware. What would your husband's ancestor have carried during the Coronation?'

'He wouldn't have carried anything, Captain. He would have protected.'

'Protected? Protected from whom?'

The Countess smiled. 'From the Devil, of course.'

30

—

Yola felt that she'd timed her two interventions just about perfectly. First she'd sent Yeleni to wake Gavril and tell him that Bazena needed to speak to him. Urgently.

Then she'd allowed five minutes to go by before hurrying to tell Badu, Bazena's father, that his daughter had just been seen begging outside the church. The five minutes were to allow for the fact that Badu and Stefan, Bazena's brother, would undoubtedly hit the ground running the moment they heard the news. Now Yola was running herself, unwilling to miss the unravelling of her plot.

Alexi saw her coming. 'Look. It's Yola. And over there, Gavril. Oh shit. Badu and Stefan.'

To Sabir it seemed as if the scene had been loosely modelled on the car chase from the original *Pink Panther* film – the one in which the old man, bewildered by the plethora of police cars and two horsepower Citroëns circling the square in front of him, finally brings out his armchair, plumps it down in a prime location, and watches the outcome in comfort.

Gavril, entirely unaware of Badu and Stefan, was hurrying towards Bazena. She, caught in flagrante, with a cloth laid out in front of her covered in coins, had just noticed her father and brother. She stood up and called out to Gavril. Gavril stopped. Bazena motioned him violently away. Badu and Stefan saw the movement, turned, and recognised Gavril. Gavril, instead of standing his ground and simply pleading ignorance, decided to do a bunk. Badu and Stefan split up – a move that they had obviously practised on numerous occasions before – and came at Gavril from opposing halves of the square. Bazena started screaming and pulling at her hair.

Within a span of ninety seconds from the start of Yola's plan, maybe fifty gypsies, of all sexes and ages, had converged, as if from nowhere, on the centre of the square. Gavril was backing up in front of Badu and Stefan, who had their knives out. People were flooding out from inside the Sanctuary to see what all the commotion was about. Two policemen on motorcycles were approaching from another part of town but gypsies were already impeding them and making sure their view of the fight was spoilt. Bazena had thrown herself around her father's neck and was hanging on for dear life, while her brother was circling Gavril, who also had his knife out but was still busy fiddling with the metal locking ring.

'This is it. This is my moment.' Alexi darted away amongst the crowd before Sabir could question his intentions.

'Alexi! For Christ's sake! Keep out of it!'

But it was too late to stop him. Alexi was already sprinting around the periphery of the crowd in the direction of the church.

31

Alexi had been a master thief all his life – and master thieves know how to use happenstance. To benefit from the moment.

He was certain that the watchman would eventually be tempted out of the Sanctuary. How could he not be, when the entire congregation of the church had exited in a drove before him, spurred on by curiosity about what might be happening above them in the square?

Alexi could imagine the sequence of thoughts that would be passing through the security guard's head. His duty, surely, lay outside? Sainte Sara could look after herself for a few moments, could she not? There was no formal threat against her that he knew of. Nobody had warned him to take especial care. What harm would it do to break up the morning's monotony with a breath of fresh air and a riot?

He had just secreted himself on the right-hand side of the main door when the watchman burst through at the tail of the crowd, his face alight with anticipation. Alexi darted in behind him and straight down to the Sanctuary. He had been coming to this place all his life. He knew its geography like the back of his hand.

Sainte Sara was standing in a corner of the deserted crypt, surrounded by votive offerings, photographs, candles, knickknacks, poems, plaques, blackboards with people's names inscribed, and flowers – many, many flowers. She was dressed in at least twenty layers of donated clothing, interleaved with capes, ribbons and hand-stitched veils, with only her mahogany-brown face, dwarfed by its silver crown, peeping through the stifling density of the fabric surrounding her.

Crossing himself superstitiously, and casting a 'please forgive me' glance at the nearest crucifix, Alexi upended Sara-e-kali, and ran his hand across her base. Nothing. It was as smooth as alabaster.

With a desperate glance at the entrance to the crypt, Alexi muttered a prayer, took out his penknife, and began scraping.

~

Achor Bale had watched the rapid unfolding of events in the square in front of him with keen interest. First the hasty appearance of the blond idiot – then the two angry gypsies, bearing down on the begging girlfriend. Then the begging girlfriend crying out and drawing everyone's attention to the blond boyfriend, who would otherwise have undoubtedly noticed what was happening before anyone had a chance to see him, and been able to make himself scarce before the shit really hit the fan. Which it was doing now.

The two motorcycle cops were still trying to force their way through the crowd. The blond boyfriend was facing off against the younger of the two men and, if Bale wasn't mistaken, he was waving around an Opinel penknife – which would undoubtedly break the first time it encountered anything more substantial than a wishbone. The older man – the father, probably – was busy fending off his hysterical daughter, but it was clear that he would soon succeed in struggling free, upon which the two of them would fillet the blond long before the police had a dog's dinner's chance of getting close.

Bale glanced around the square. The whole thing seemed somehow contrived to him. Riots almost never happened organically – of their own accord. People orchestrated them. At least in his experience. He'd even stage-managed one or two himself during his time with the Legion – not under the Legion's particular aegis, needless to say, but merely as a means of forcing their involvement in a situation which, without them, might simply have resolved itself with no recourse to violence.

He remembered one riot in Chad with particular affection – it was during the Legion's deployment there during the 1980s. Forty dead – dozens more injured. Word from the Corpus was that he had come perilously close to starting a civil war. How Monsieur, his father, would have been pleased.

Legio Patria Nostra – Bale felt almost nostalgic. He had learned a great many useful things in the Legion's 'combat village' in Fraselli, Corsica – and also in Rwanda, Djibouti, Lebanon, Cameroon and Bosnia. Things he might have to put into practice now.

He stood up to get a better view. When that failed, he climbed on to the café table, using his hat as a sunshield. No one noticed him – all eyes were on the square.

He glanced over towards the entrance to the Sanctuary just in time to see Alexi, who had been lurking behind the main door, dart in behind the emerging watchman.

Excellent. Bale was having his work done for him again. He looked around the square for Sabir but couldn't mark him. Best head down to the crypt entrance. Wait for the gypsy to come back out. In the maelstrom that was the Place de l'Eglise, no one would be in the least bit surprised to find a second corpse with a knife-wound in its chest.

32

Calque was having difficulty with the Countess. It had begun when she had nosed out his resistance to her assertion that her husband's family were responsible for protecting the Angevin, Capetian, and Valois Kings from diabolical intercedence.

'Why is this not written down? Why have I never heard of a thirteenth Pair de France?'

Macron looked on in incredulity. What was Calque doing? He was here to investigate a pistol, not a bloodline.

'But it is written down, Captain Calque. It is simply that the documents are not available to scholars. What do you think? That all history happened exactly as historians have described it? Do you really suppose that there are not noble families all over Europe who are keeping private correspondence and documents away from prying eyes? That there are not secret societies, still secret today, about whose existence no one is yet aware?'

'Do you know of any such societies, Madame?'

'Of course not. But they certainly exist. You may count on it. And with more power, perhaps, than might be supposed.' A strange look came over the Countess's face. She reached down and rang her bell. Without a word, Milouins entered the room and began clearing up the coffee things.

Calque realised that the interview was on its final legs. 'The pistol, Madame. The one registered in your husband's name. Who possesses it now?'

'My husband lost it before the war. I distinctly remember him telling me. It was stolen by a gamekeeper who had become temporarily disenchanted with his position. The Count notified the police – I am sure the records still exist. They conducted an informal inquiry but the pistol was never recovered. It was of little import. My husband had many pistols. His collection was of note, I believe. I do not interest myself in firearms, however.'

'Of course not, Madame.' Calque knew when he was beaten. The chances of there being records still in existence of an informal inquiry about a missing firearm during the 1930s were infinitesimal. 'But you married your husband, as I understand it, during the 1970s? How would you possibly know about events that took place in the 1930s?'

Macron's mouth dropped open.

'My husband, Captain, always told me everything.' The Countess stood up.

Macron levered himself to his feet. He enjoyed watching Calque fail in his first attempt at lift-off from the sofa. The old man must be feeling the accident, he thought to himself. Perhaps he's a bit more fragile than he lets on? He's certainly acting bloody strangely.

The Countess gave her bell a double ring. The footman came back in. She nodded towards Calque and the footman hurried to help him.

'I'm sorry, Madame. Lieutenant Macron and I were involved in a vehicle collision. In pursuit of a miscreant. I am still a little stiff.'

A collision? In pursuit of a miscreant? What the hell was Calque playing at? Macron started towards the door. Then he stopped. The old man wasn't as stiff as all that. He was putting it on.

'Your son, Madame? Might he not have something to

257

add to the story? Perhaps his father spoke to him about the pistol?'

'My son, Captain? I have nine sons. And four daughters. Which of them would you like to talk to?'

Calque stopped in his tracks. He weaved a little, as if he were on his last legs. 'Thirteen children? I'm astonished, Madame. How can that be possible?'

'It is called adoption, Captain. My husband's family have funded a nunnery for the past nine centuries. As part of its charitable work. My husband was badly injured during the war. From that moment on it became impossible that he should ever procure an heir for himself. It is why he married so late. But I persuaded him to rethink his position on the succession. We are wealthy. The nunnery has an orphanage. We took as many as we could. Adoption is a well-established custom in French and Italian noble families in the case of *force majeure*. Infinitely preferable to the name dying out.'

'The present Count, then? May I know his name?'

'Count Rocha. Rocha de Bale.'

'May I talk to him?'

'He is lost to us, Captain. For reasons best known to himself he joined the Foreign Legion. As you know, Legionnaires are forced to register under new names. We never knew what that was. I have not seen him for many years.'

'But the Legion takes only foreigners, Madame. Not Frenchmen. Apart from in the officer class. Was your son an officer, then?'

'My son was a fool, Captain. At the age at which he enlisted he would have been capable of any folly. He speaks six languages. It is not beyond the realms of possibility that he passed himself off as a foreigner.'

'As you say, Madame. As you say.' Calque nodded his appreciation to the footman. 'We certainly seem to have struck a dead end in our investigation.'

The Countess appeared not to have heard him. 'I can assure you that my son knows nothing of his father's pistol. He was born thirty years after the events you describe. We adopted him as a twelve-year-old. On account of my husband's advanced age.'

Calque was never slow in seizing an opportunity. He pressed his luck. 'Could you not transfer the title to your second son? Safeguard the heritage like that?'

'That possibility died with my husband. The entailment is inalienable.'

Calque and Macron found themselves smoothly transferred into the hands of the capable Madame Mastigou. In a bare thirty fluidly managed seconds, they were back in their car and heading down the drive towards Ramatuelle.

Macron flicked his chin at the retreating house. 'What the heck was that all about?'

'What the heck was what all about?'

'That charade back there. For twenty minutes I even forgot the pain in my feet. You were so convincing, I almost fell for your act myself. I nearly volunteered to help you down the stairs.'

'Charade?' said Calque. 'What charade? I don't know what you are talking about, Macron.'

Macron flashed him a look.

Calque was grinning.

Before Macron could press him further, the phone buzzed. Macron pulled over into a lay-by and answered.

'Yes. Yes. I've got that. Yes.'

Calque raised an eyebrow.

'They've cracked the eye-man's tracker code, Sir. Sabir's car is in a long-term car park in Arles.'

'That's of very little use to us.'

259

'There's more.'

'I'm listening.'

'A knifing. In Les Saintes-Maries-de-la-Mer. In front of the church.'

'So what?'

'A check I did. Following our investigations in Gourdon. I flagged up all the names of the people we interviewed. Told our office to inform me of any incidents whatsoever involving gypsies. To cross-correlate the names, in other words.'

'Yes, Macron? You've already impressed me. Now give me the pay-off.'

Macron restarted the engine. Best not to smile, he told himself. Best not to show any emotion whatsoever. 'The police are searching for a certain Gavril La Roupie in relation to the crime.'

33

Gavril had forgotten about Badu and Stefan. In his single-minded excitement at working out the plot to kidnap Sainte Sara, he had quite overlooked the fact that Bazena boasted two of the most vicious male relatives this side of the Montagne Saint-Victoire. Stories about them were legion. Father and son always acted together, one drawing attention away from the other. Their bar fights were legendary. It was rumoured that they had seen off more victims between them than the first atomic bomb.

It had been the drive down to Les Saintes-Maries that had done the damage. Both men had been in an unnaturally avuncular frame of mind. The festival was their highlight of the year – ample opportunities abounded for the settling of old scores and the creating of new ones. Gavril was so close to them, and so obvious, that he didn't count. They were used to him. And it wouldn't have occurred to them that he could ever be so stupid as to force Bazena on to the streets. So they had drawn him into their vicious little world, and made him, ever so briefly, an accomplice before the fact.

Now Stefan was coming at him and all he had to defend himself was a bloody Opinel penknife. When Badu finally succeeded in disentangling himself from his daughter, Gavril knew that he was for it. They would carve out his lights.

Gavril threw the penknife with all his might at Stefan, and then legged it through the crowd. There was a roar behind him but he paid it no mind. He had to get away. He could decide how best to conduct damage limitation exercises later. This was a matter of life and death.

He zigzagged through the assembled gypsies like a madman – like an American footballer running interference through an enemy team's defences. Instinctively, Gavril used the five bells in the open see-through tower of the church as his visual guide, meaning to sprint down towards the docks and steal himself a boat. With only three possible roads out of town, and both incoming and outgoing motor traffic moving at a snail's pace in the run-up to the festival, it was the only sensible way to go.

Then, on the junction of the Rue Espelly and the Avenue Van Gogh, and just in front of the Bull Arena, he saw Alexi. And behind him, Bale.

34

Alexi had been just about to return the statue of Sainte Sara to its plinth in disgust. This had all been a grotesque waste of time. How did Sabir expect things that had happened hundreds of years before to carry over into the modern-day era? It was madness.

For his part, Alexi found it almost impossible to imagine himself twenty years back in time, let alone five hundred. The jottings that Sabir had so confidently decoded seemed to him nothing but the ramblings of a madman. It served people right if they insisted on writing everything down and communicating that way. Why didn't they simply talk to each other? If everyone just talked, the world would make considerably more sense. Things would be immediate. Just as they were in Alexi's world. He woke up every morning and thought about the way he felt now. Not about the past. Or the future. But now.

He nearly missed the cork of resin. Over the centuries it had weathered to a similar walnut sheen to the rest of Sainte Sara's painted plinth. But its consistency was different. When he gouged at it with his penknife, it came up in spirals, like wood-shavings, rather than as powder. He levered away at it until it popped out. He felt inside the hole with his finger. Yes. There was something else there.

He stuck his penknife inside the hole and twisted. A gob of fabric came out. Alexi spread it across his hand and looked at it. Nothing. Just a motheaten bit of linen with worm holes in it.

He peered into the hole, but couldn't see anything.

Intrigued, he tapped the statue sharply on the ground. Then again. A bamboo tube fell out. Bamboo? Inside a statue?

Alexi was about to snap the bamboo in two when he heard the sound of footsteps coming down the broad stone stairway to the crypt.

Swiftly, he tidied away the marks of his passage and returned the statue to its place. Then he prostrated himself on the ground before it.

He could hear the footsteps approaching him. *Malos mengues!* What if it was the eye-man? He'd be a sitting duck.

'What are you doing here?'

Alexi levered himself up and blinked. It was the watchman. 'What do you think I'm doing? I'm praying. This place is a church, isn't it?'

'No need to get shirty about it.' It was obvious that the watchman had had run-ins with gypsies before, and wished to avoid a recurrence. Particularly after what he had just seen in the square.

'Where is everybody?'

'You mean you didn't hear?'

'Hear what? I was praying.'

The watchman shrugged. 'Two of your people. Arguing over a woman. One threw a knife at the other. Caught him in the eye. Blood everywhere. They tell me the eye was hanging out on a string down the man's cheek. Disgusting. Still. Serves people right for fighting on a holy occasion. They should have been down here, like you.'

'Thrown knives don't pop eyes out on to cheeks. You're making this up.'

'No. No. I saw the blood. People were screaming. One of the policemen had the eye on a pad and was trying to put it back in.'

'Mary Mother of God.' Alexi wondered whether it was Gavril who had lost his eye. That would queer his pitch. Slow him up a little. Perhaps he wouldn't be quite so keen to laugh at other people's deformities now that he was missing an organ of his own? 'Can I kiss the Virgin's feet?' Alexi had seen some resin shavings still on the floor – a quick puff of air would lose them beneath Sainte Sara's skirts.

The watchman looked around. The crypt was deserted. People's attention was still obviously focused on what was happening up in the square. 'Okay. But make it quick.'

35

Bale had moved in on Alexi almost immediately the gypsy had left the church. But the gypsy was hyper-alert. Like a greyhound after a race. Whatever he'd been doing in there had psyched him up, and his adrenalin was pumping.

Bale had half expected the gypsy to turn immediately back into the square, to check out what was happening, and to find Sabir. But the gypsy had hurried down through the Place Lamartine towards the sea instead. Why? Had he found something in there?

Bale decided to shadow Alexi out of town. It was always a good idea to get well clear of the most populated areas. The location of the killing would matter as little as the end result, as far as the police were concerned.

It would still be merely another gypsy knifing. But this way he would have ample time to rifle through Alexi's pockets and find whatever it was he'd filched or copied down from inside the crypt. He quickened his pace, therefore, and sacrificed invisibility, counting on the crowd to protect him.

It was then that Alexi saw him. Bale knew he'd been seen because the gypsy missed his footing in shock and fell briefly down on to one knee. Alexi was no Johnny-Head-in-the-Air, like Gavril.

Bale started running. It was now or never. He couldn't let the man get away. The gypsy was clutching something tightly to his chest – the loss of the use of one of his arms was actively hampering his speed. So whatever it was, was important to him. Therefore it was important to Bale.

Now he was heading for the Arena. Good. Once he was out on the Esplanade it would be far easier to see him. Far easier to mark him out from the crowd.

People turned to stare as the two men pounded past them.

Bale was fit. He had to be. Ever since the Legion he'd realised that fitness equated with health. Your body listened to you. Fitness freed it from the oppression of gravity. Find the right balance and you could very nearly fly.

Alexi was light on his feet but nobody could call him fit. In fact he had never consciously exercised in his life. He merely lived an unconsciously healthy life, in natural harmony with his instincts, which drove him more towards feeling healthy than to feeling unwell. Gypsy men traditionally died young, usually as a result of smoking, genes and alcohol. In Alexi's case he had never taken to smoking. His genes he could do nothing about. But alcohol had always been a weakness, and he was still feeling the after-effects of both the wedding blow-out and being fallen upon from a considerable height by a man in a chair. The same man who was now following him.

He could sense himself starting to flag. Five hundred metres to go until he reached the horses. Please God they had left the saddles on. If he knew Bouboul's family, no one would have even bothered to touch the horses after he, Yola, and Sabir had arrived in town from the Maset de la Marais, two hours before, and left them in Bouboul's care. The horses offered him his only chance of escape. He had had the opportunity to check out all three and he knew that the mare with the four black socks was by far the best. If the eye-man didn't catch him before he reached Bouboul's, he would still be in with a chance. He could even ride bareback if the worst came to the worst.

One thing Alexi was supremely good at was coping horses. He had done it ever since he was a child.

Now all he had to do was to reach the beach and pray.

─

Gavril could feel the anger of outrage building up in him as he followed Bale and Alexi. It was their fault that this succession of tragedies had happened to him. Without falling foul of Alexi he would never have met the *gadje*. And without the *gadje* spearing him in the leg with his knife he would never have had the run-in with the police. And, in consequence, he would never have heard of the reward. Or had it been the other way around? Sometimes Gavril's mind ran away with him and he lost track of things.

Either way, he would still have come to Les Saintes-Maries, it is true, but he would have been in control of events, and not have allowed events to control him. He could have confronted Alexi at his leisure, when the fool was good and drunk. Gavril was a master of low shots – of playing to the gallery. What he didn't like were sudden changes to established patterns.

Perhaps he could still pull the pig from the fire? If he allowed the *gadje* to deal with Alexi, the man would lose concentration. It would cause him to be vulnerable. With both of them in hand, Gavril would really have something to sell to the policemen. A simple phone-call would do it. Then, after they paid him the reward, he could negotiate with the policemen so that Badu and Stefan would be warned off messing with him. All gypsies were scared witless of prison. It would be the one thing capable of controlling them.

Maybe he could still marry Yola? Yes. This way his plans needn't be changed after all. All could be well again.

Hurrying after the two men, he idly wondered how much money Bazena had been able to inveigle from the tourists before her interfering father had managed to put a stop to it.

36
—

Sabir looked vainly around for Alexi. What had the idiot done? Last seen, he had been heading off towards the church. But Sabir had checked out the crypt and found him nowhere. And this crypt wasn't like the one at

Rocamadour. Here, there was nowhere to hide – unless he'd somehow managed to secrete himself beneath Sainte Sara's multi-layered skirts.

He returned to the town hall as arranged. 'Have you found him?'

Yola shook her head.

'Well what do we do then?'

'Maybe he's gone back to the Maset? Maybe he found something? Did you see him actually enter the church?'

'You couldn't see anything in that bedlam.'

Instinctively, without saying a word to each other, they turned down the Avenue Léon Gambetta towards the Plage des Amphores and the horses.

Sabir glanced across at Yola. 'You did brilliantly by the way. I just wanted to tell you that. You're a born agent provocateur.'

'Agent provocatrice. Who taught you your French?'

Sabir laughed. 'My mother. But her heart wasn't in it. She wanted me to be an All-American, like my father. But I let her down. I turned into an All-or-Nothing instead.'

'I don't understand.'

'Neither do I.'

They'd reached Bouboul's caravan. The picket where the three horses should have been tethered was conspicuously empty.

'Great. Someone's made off with the bloody lot. Or maybe Bouboul's sold them for dog meat? Do you know what Shanks's pony is, Yola?'

'Wait. There's Bouboul. I'll ask him what happened to them.'

Yola hurried across the road. Watching her, Sabir realised that he was missing something – some clue that she had already picked up. He crossed the road behind her.

Bouboul threw his hands up in the air. He was talking in Sinti. Sabir tried to follow but was unable to do more than understand that something unexpected had happened, and that Bouboul was loudly disclaiming any responsibility for it.

Finally, tiring of Bouboul's harangue, Sabir drew Yola to one side. 'Translate, please. I can't make out a word of what this guy is saying.'

'It is bad, Damo. As bad as it could be.'

'Where have the horses gone?'

'Alexi took one. Twenty minutes ago. He was exhausted. He had been running. According to Bouboul he was so worn out he could hardly mount the horse. Thirty seconds later another man came running up. This man was not tired at all. He had strange eyes, according to Bouboul. He didn't look at anybody. Talk to anybody. He simply took the second horse and rode off after Alexi.'

'Jesus Christ. That's all we needed. Did Bouboul try and tangle with him?'

'Does he look like a fool? They were not Bouboul's horses. They weren't even ours. Why should he risk himself for someone else's property?'

'Why indeed?' Sabir was still trying to figure out what might have triggered the chase. 'Where is the third horse? And was Alexi carrying anything? Ask him.'

Yola turned to Bouboul. They exchanged a few brief sentences in Sinti. 'It's worse than I thought.'

'Worse? How can it be worse? You already said it was as bad as it could be.'

'Alexi was carrying something. You were right. A bamboo tube.'

'A bamboo tube?'

'Yes. He had it clutched to his chest like a baby.'

Sabir grabbed Yola's arm. 'Don't you see what that

269

means? He found the prophecies. Alexi found them.'

'But that is not all.'

Sabir closed his eyes. 'You don't need to tell me. I picked up the name while you were talking. Gavril.'

'Yes, Gavril. He was following both of them. He arrived about a minute after the eye-man. It was he who took the third horse.'

37

Gavril was twenty minutes out of Les Saintes-Maries when he remembered that he didn't have a weapon. He had thrown it at Stefan in the scuffle.

The thought struck him with such an impact that he actually stopped his horse, mid-canter, and spent a full half-minute debating with himself whether to turn back.

But the thought of Badu and Stefan persuaded him to continue. The pair of them would be baying for his blood. They would be out scouring the streets of Les Sainte-Maries for him at this very moment – or else having their knives sharpened at Nan Maximoff's pedal-stone. At least, on horseback, in the middle of the Marais, no one would have a hope in hell of catching him.

The two men in front of him had no idea that he was following them. In fact, now that they'd finally left the roadway, he didn't need to get within five hundred metres of them, such was the impact of the trail they were leaving behind them through the brush. Two galloping horses churned up the ground in a very satisfactory manner, and Gavril could easily tell new horse tracks from old ones.

He would simply follow Alexi and the *gadje*'s trail and see what occurred. If the worst came to the worst and he lost them, he could always ride on through to the outskirts of Arles and hop on a bus. Make himself scarce for a while.

After all, what did he have to lose?

38

Alexi was making up some ground ahead of the eye-man – but not quite as fast as he had hoped. The mare had had ample time to recuperate from that morning's ten-kilometre ride, but Alexi suspected that Bouboul had neither fed nor watered her, for her tongue was already hanging loose at the side of her mouth. She was clearly on her last legs.

His only comfort lay in the knowledge that the gelding the eye-man was riding would be in a similar condition. The thought of being forced back on foot, however, in such an isolated environment, and pursued through the marshes by a madman with a pistol, didn't bear contemplation.

So far he had stuck to the exact reverse of the path that they had followed that morning on their way from the house. But Alexi knew that he would soon have to veer off and strike out into the unknown. He couldn't risk leading the eye-man back to their base – for when

Sabir and Yola discovered the two horses gone, they would have no option but return to the one place they knew he might come back to.

His only hope lay in eluding the eye-man completely. To have any chance at all of doing this, Alexi knew that he needed to gather his wits about him. To control his rising sense of panic. To think clearly and constructively and at full gallop.

On his left, beyond the Etang des Launes, was the Le Petit Rhône. Alexi knew it well, having fished there with a succession of male relatives on and off since childhood. To his knowledge, there was only one ferry-crossing nearby – at the Bac du Sauvage. Saving that, you were forced to cross the long way round, by road, maybe ten kilometres further upriver, at the Pont du Sylvéréal. There was, quite literally, no other way into the Petite Camargue – unless you flew, of course.

If he could time the ferry exactly right, he might stand an outside chance. But what were the odds? The ferry made the trip every half-hour, on the half-hour. It might already be positioned on the far side of the river, gearing up for the return journey – in which case he was trapped. The river, as he remembered it, was about two hundred metres wide at that point, and flowed far too strongly for an exhausted horse to manage. And he didn't have a watch. Should he throw all his eggs into one basket and try for the ferry? Or was he mad?

The mare stumbled and then caught herself. Alexi knew that if he carried on in this way she would simply burst her heart – he had heard of horses doing this. She would drop like a stone and he would break his neck in a flat-out fall over her shoulders. At least that way the eye-man would be saved the trouble of having to torture him, as he'd obviously done with Babel.

Alexi was two minutes' ride from the ferry-crossing.

He simply had to chance it. He cast one final, despairing glance over his shoulder. The eye-man was fifty metres behind him and gaining. Perhaps the gelding had snatched a drink of water at Bouboul's? Perhaps that was why he wasn't tiring as fast as the mare?

The barriers were down at the ferry-crossing, and the ferry was just putting off from the shore. There were four cars and a small van on board. The crossing was so short that no one had bothered to climb out of their cars. Only the ticket collector saw Alexi coming.

The man raised a warning hand and shouted, '*Non! Non!*'

Alexi aimed the mare at the single barred barrier. There was a steep slope leading down to it. Perhaps she would be able to get a firm enough grip on the asphalt and launch herself over? Either way, he couldn't afford to let up his pace.

At the last possible moment the mare lost her nerve and jinked to the left. Her back legs slid out from under her and her hip dropped, exaggerated by the downward slope of the slipway. She slid underneath the barrier, all four legs thrown up into the air, shrieking. Alexi hit the barrier back-first. He tried to curl himself into a ball, but failed. He smashed into the pole, which partially broke his fall. Then he struck the asphalt with his right shoulder and side. Without allowing himself to think or to count the cost in pain, Alexi launched himself after the ferry. If he missed the metal landing plank, he knew that he would drown. Not only had he damaged himself, somewhere, somehow – but he couldn't swim.

The ticket collector had seen many crazy things in his life – what ferryman hadn't? – but this took the biscuit. A man on a horse trying to leap the barrier and get on board? He transported horses all the time. The ferry company had even set up a semi-permanent tether for the summer months – tilted away from the cars so that the horses wouldn't damage anyone's paintwork if they kicked out backwards. Perhaps this man was a horse thief? Either way, he'd lost his prize. The horse had shattered her leg in the fall, if he wasn't mistaken. The man, too, was probably injured.

The ticket collector reached down and unhooked the life ring. 'It's tied to the ferry! Grab it and hang on!'

He knew, now the ferry was under way, that it was all but impossible to stop the towing mechanism. The pull of the river was so strong that the ferry had to be anchored to a guiding chain, which prevented it spinning out of control and down towards the Grau d'Orgon. Once the mechanism was triggered, it became risky to stop it, thereby loading the long loop of the chain with the dead weight of the ferry, backed up by the full driving force of the river. In conditions of heavy rain, the ferry could even burst its stanchions and drift towards the open sea.

Alexi grabbed for the ring and slid it over his head.

'Turn around! Turn around in the water and let it drag you!'

Alexi turned around and let the ferry drag him along behind it. He was scared of swallowing water and maybe drowning like that. So he curved his neck forwards, until his chin lay flat on his chest and allowed the water to wash over his shoulders like a bow-wake. As he did so, it belatedly occurred to him to feel around in his shirt for the bamboo tube. It was gone.

He glanced back at the slipway. Had he lost it there, while falling? Or in the water? Would the eye-man see it and realise what it was?

The eye-man sat astride his horse at the barrier. As Alexi watched, the eye-man took out his pistol and shot the mare. Then he turned back towards the Pont de Gau and the Marais and disappeared into the underbrush.

Perhaps it was a mistake to instil so much fear in your enemies that they had nothing left to lose? What other motive could possibly have prompted the gypsy into taking such a ridiculous risk as leaping across a single-pole barrier on an exhausted horse? Everybody knew that horses hated seeing daylight between whatever they were jumping over and the ground. And the horse had known it was headed for deep water. You had to train horses specially for that sort of thing. It was madness. Sheer madness.

Still. Bale had to admire the man for attempting it. The gypsy had known, after all, just what awaited him at Bale's hands. Shame about the horse, though. But it had shattered its leg in the fall, and Bale hated to see an animal suffer.

Bale gave the worn-out gelding its head. Instinctively, the gelding started back along the trail by which they had come. First stop on the return trip would be the gypsy who had been looking after the horses. Get some information there. Then a cast around town for the blond Viking. Failing that, his girlfriend.

Either way, Bale would pick up Sabir's trail some-where – somehow. He knew it. He always did.

Gavril slowed his horse to a walk. The animal was on its last legs. He didn't want to risk killing it, and then find himself stuck, kilometres from nowhere, in the middle of the Marais.

Unlike Alexi, Gavril wasn't really a country boy. He was happiest lurking on the outskirts of town, where the action was. Until now, Gavril's idea of a good time had involved the active trading of stolen cellphones. Gavril didn't steal them himself, of course – his face and hair were far too memorable for that. He simply acted as the middleman, moving from café to café, and from bar to bar, selling them on for a few euros' profit per pop. It kept him in beer and clothes, and there was the added attraction of knocking off the occasional *payo* girl, when he struck lucky. His hair always provided the guaranteed first topic of conversation. How can you be a gypsy with hair that colour? So his blondness wasn't all bad.

Almost without realising it, Gavril drifted to a halt. Did he really want to chase after Alexi and the *gadje*? And what would he do when he caught up with them? Frighten them into submission? Perhaps he should simply view the stealing of the horse as a clever way out of an impossible situation. It had at least guaranteed that Badu and Stefan couldn't pursue him and wreak whatever vengeance their perverted minds could conjure up. He would be happy never to see them or Bazena again in his entire life.

And what of Yola? Did he really want her that much? There were other fish in the sea. It might be best to leave the whole thing alone. Make himself scarce for a while. He could rest the horse, and then make his way slowly north. Abandon it somewhere near a train depot. Hitch a ride on a freight car to Toulouse. He had family there. They would put him up.

Secure in his new plan, Gavril turned away from the river and towards the Panperdu.

41
—

Bale chose to wait for Gavril behind an abandoned *gardien's cabane*. He and the gelding blended in perfectly beside the deep-shelved thatching of the roof, which was capped in white, like the keel of an upturned rowing boat.

Bale had been standing in the lee of the *cabane* for the past ten minutes, watching Gavril approach. Once or twice he had even shaken his head, bemused by the man's persistent blindness to whatever was going on around him. Had the gypsy fallen asleep? Was that why he had so arbitrarily decided to abandon a trail which had been clearly blazed through the marshgrass for everyone to see? It had been absurd good luck that Bale had caught sight of Gavril mere moments before the latter had had time to disappear for ever beyond the treeline.

At the last possible moment Bale stepped out from behind the *cabane*, leading his horse. He untied the handkerchief from around the horse's mouth, and replaced it in his pocket – it was a trick he'd learned with Berber pack camels in the Legion. He hadn't wanted the horse to whinny when it heard its companion approaching, and give away the game.

'Get down.' Bale waved his pistol encouragingly.

Gavril glanced over Bale's head towards the edge of the nearby woodland.

'Don't even think about it. I've just shot one horse. Another will make no difference to me. But I've got nothing against the animal. Shooting it unnecessarily would be guaranteed to make me very angry indeed.'

Gavril cocked his leg over the saddle and slid down the horse's flank. He automatically stood with the reins held in his hands, as if he had merely come to pay Bale a courtesy call, rather than to find himself the victim of an ambush. He looked bewildered – as if he were seven years old again – and his father had just landed him a clout for something he hadn't done. 'Did you shoot Alexi?'

'Why would I do that?'

Bale approached Gavril and took the horse from him. He tethered it at the hitching post outside the *cabane*. Then he unknotted the lariat from around the pommel of the saddle. 'Lie down.'

'What do you want? What are you going to do?'

'I'm going to tie you up. Lie down.'

Gavril lay on his back, looking up at the sky.

'No. Turn over.'

'You're not going to knife me again?'

'No. Not that.' Bale stretched both of Gavril's arms out beyond his head and guided them through the loop of the lariat. Then he fastened the other end in a temporary slip knot to the hitching post. He walked across to the gelding and unknotted the lariat from around the gelding's pommel. Then he walked back and knotted Gavril's feet together, leaving the trailing rope-end on the ground. 'We're alone here. You've probably realised that by now. Nothing but horses, bulls and bloody pink flamingos in any direction.'

'I'm no threat to you. I just now decided to head north. To steer clear of you and Sabir and Yola for good.'

'Ah. She's called Yola, is she? I did wonder. What's the other gypsy called? The one whose horse I shot?'

'Alexi. Alexi Dufontaine.'

'And your name?'

'Gavril. La Roupie.' Gavril cleared his throat. He was having difficulty in concentrating. His mind kept moving on to irrelevant details. Like the time of day. Or the consistency of the scrub grass a few inches in front of his eyes. 'What did you do to him? To Alexi?'

Bale was walking the gelding around to where Gavril was lying. 'Do to him? I didn't do anything to him. He fell off his horse. Managed to scramble into the river and hitch a lift on a ferry. It's a misfortune for you that he got away.'

Gavril started to weep. He hadn't consciously wept since childhood, and now it was as if all the misery and hurt that he had stored up in himself since that time had finally overflowed its borders. 'Please let me go. Please.'

Bale hitched the gelding to the rope-end tied around Gavril's feet. 'I can't do that. You've seen me. You've had a chance to mark me down. And you've got a grudge. I never let men go who hold grudges against me.'

'But I don't have any grudge.'

'Your leg. I gouged your leg with my knife. Back in Gourdon.'

'I've already forgotten that.'

'So you forgive me? That's kind. Why did you come after me then?' Bale had untied Gavril's horse from the hitching post and was leading it around in front of him. Now he unhitched the loose rope-end attaching Gavril's hands and knotted it to the pommel of Gavril's saddle.

'What are you doing?'

Bale tested both knots. Gavril was arching his neck backwards to see what was happening behind him. Bale walked to the edge of the nearby marsh and cut himself a handful of dried reeds, about three feet in length. He cut another, single reed, and looped it into a noose. Then he knotted the ends of the reeds together, until they took on the shape of a besom head. One of the horses began to snort.

'Did you say something just then?'

'I asked what you are doing?' The words came out as a sob.

'I'm making myself a whip. Out of these reeds. Do-it-yourself.'

'My God. Are you going to whip me?'

'Whip you? No. I'm going to whip the horses.'

Gavril started to howl. It was not a noise he had ever made before in his life. But it was a noise Bale was familiar with. He had heard it time and again when people felt themselves to be *in extremis*. It was as if they were trying to block off reality with sound.

'An ancestor of mine was hung, drawn and quartered once. Way back in medieval times. Do you know what that involves, Gavril?'

Gavril was shrieking now.

'It involves being put on a gibbet and having a noose placed around your neck. Then you are pulled up, sometimes as high as fifty feet, and displayed to the crowd. Surprisingly, this rarely kills you.'

Gavril was hammering his head against the earth. The horses were becoming restless with the unexpected noise and one of them even walked a few paces, tightening the tension on Gavril's rope.

'Then you are let down, and the noose is loosened.

You are revived. The executioner now takes a hooked implement – a little like a corkscrew – and makes an incision in your stomach. Here.' He bent down, turned Gavril partially over, and prodded him just above the appendix. 'By this time you are half strangled, but still able to appreciate what is happening. The hooked implement is then inserted in your stomach sack, and your intestines are pulled out like a steaming string of sausages. The crowd is cheering by this time, grateful, no doubt, that it is not all happening to them.'

Gavril had fallen silent. His breath was coming in tubercular gulps, as if he had the whooping cough.

'Then, just before you are dead, they attach you to four horses, placed in each quarter of the square like compass points. North, south, east and west. This is a symbolical punishment, as I'm sure you'll understand.'

'What do you want?' Gavril's voice came out unexpectedly clearly, as if he had come to a formal decision and intended to fulfil its contractual requirements in as serious a manner as possible.

'Excellent. I knew you'd see reason. I'll tell you what. I won't hang you. And I won't draw out your intestines. I've got nothing against you personally. You've doubtless led a hard life. A bit of a struggle. I don't want to make your death an unnecessarily painful or a lingering one. And I won't quarter you. I'm two horses short for that sort of flourish.' Bale patted Gavril on the head. 'So I shall halve you instead. Unless you talk, of course. I should tell you that these horses are tired. The halving may prove a bit of a strain for them. But it's extraordinary what a little whipping can do to galvanise a weary animal.'

'What is it? What do you want to know?'

'Well, I'll tell you. I want to know where Sabir and . . . Yola was it? Was that the name you said? I want to know where they are hiding.'

'But I don't know.'

'Yes you do. They'll be in a place Yola knows. A place she and her family may have used before, while they were visiting here. A place known to you gypsies but which no one else will think of. To encourage your creative juices, I am going to stir these horses up a little. Give them a taste of the lash.'

'No. No. I do know of such a place.'

'Really? That was quick.'

'Yes. Yes it was. Yola's father won it in a card game. They always used to stay there. But I forgot about it. I didn't need to think about it.'

'Where is this place?'

'Will you let me go if I tell you?'

Bale gave the gelding a taste of the switch. The gelding jerked forward, tightening the rope. The second horse was tempted to follow in the same direction but Bale shushed it away.

'Aiee. Stop it! Stop it!'

'Where is this place?'

'It's called the Maset de la Marais.'

'What Marais?'

'The Marais de la Sigoulette.'

'Where's that?'

'Please. Make them stop.'

Bale gentled the horses. 'You were saying?'

'Just off the D85. The one that runs beside the Departmental Park. I can't remember what it's called. It's the small park, though. Before you get to the salt workings.'

'Can you read a map?'

'Yes. Yes.'

'Then point it out for me.' Bale crouched down beside Gavril. He opened a local map. 'The scale on this is one centimetre for every 500 metres. That means that the house should be marked on it. It better be, for your sake.'

'Can you untie me?'

'No.'

Gavril started sobbing again.

'Just a moment. I'll fire up the horses.'

'No. Please. I can see it. It's marked. There.' He indicated with his elbow.

'Any other houses nearby?'

'I've never been there. I only heard about it. Everybody heard about it. They say Yola's father must have cheated to have won the right to use it off Dadul Gavriloff.'

Bale stood up. 'I'm not interested in folk tales. Have you anything else to tell me?'

Gavril turned his head back towards the ground.

Bale strolled a few yards until he found a twenty-pound rock. He hefted it under his arm and returned to Gavril's side. 'This is how you died. You fell off your horse, with your foot twisted inside your stirrup, and you smashed your face against this rock.'

Gavril half turned his head to see what Bale was doing.

Bale brought the rock down on Gavril's face. He hesitated, wondering whether to do it a second time, but the cerebrospinal fluid was already leaking out through Gavril's nose – if he wasn't dead, he was certainly dying. Pointless spoiling the set-up. He placed the rock carefully at the side of the track.

He unlooped the lariat and dragged Gavril by one foot towards his horse. Taking Gavril's left foot in his hand, he twisted it around in the stirrup, until the foot was inextricably caught, leaving Gavril half trailing along the ground. Then he retied the lariat to the pommel.

The horse had begun grazing again by this time,

calmed by the methodical pace with which Bale had conducted his chores. Bale rubbed its ears.

Then he mounted his own horse and rode away.

42

Calque looked around the Place de l'Eglise. He checked out the cafés and the shopfronts and the scattered benches. 'So this is where it happened?'

'Yes, Sir.' The auxiliary motorcycle gendarme had just been made aware that he was being asked these questions as part of an ongoing murder inquiry. His face had instantly taken on a more serious cast, as though he were being quizzed about the likely shortcomings of his family's health insurance cover.

'And you were first on the scene?'

'Yes, Sir. My colleague and I.'

'And what did you see?'

'Very little, Sir. The gypsies were impeding us on purpose.'

'Typical.' Macron glared around the square. 'I'm surprised they get any tourists at all in this place. Look at the filth around here.'

Calque cleared his throat – it was a habit he had recently got into whenever Macron made one of his more offensive public observations. After all, he couldn't actually tie the man's bootlaces for him, could he? Couldn't tell him what – or what not – to think? 'What did you deduce, then, Officer? If you couldn't see.'

'That the perpetrator, La Roupie, had thrown his knife at the victim, Angelo, catching him in the eye.'

'Alexi Angelo?'

'No, Sir. Stefan Angelo. There was no Alexi involved, as far as I understand it.'

'Is Monsieur Angelo pressing charges?'

'No, Sir. These people never press charges against one of their own. They sort out their differences privately.'

'And of course Monsieur Angelo was no longer carrying his own knife when you went to his assistance? Someone had divested him of it? Am I right?'

'I don't know that for certain, Sir. But yes. In all probability he'd palmed it off on to someone else.'

'I told you.' Macron stabbed his finger in the air. 'I told you this wouldn't get us anywhere.'

Calque glanced across at the church. 'Anything else of note?'

'What do you mean, Sir?'

'I mean did anyone notice anything else happening at the same time? Thefts? A chase? Another attack? Could it have been a diversion, in other words?'

'No, Sir. Nothing of that sort was brought to my attention.'

'Very well. You can go.'

The gendarme saluted and returned to his motor-cycle.

'Shall we go and interview Angelo? He'll still be in hospital.'

'No. No need. It would be an irrelevance.'

Macron made a face. 'How do you work that one out?' He seemed disappointed that his initiative over La Roupie had led them to a dead end.

But Calque's attention was elsewhere. 'What is actually going on here?'

'I'm sorry, Sir?'

'Why are all these gypsies here? Now? This minute? What is happening? Why have they come? It's not another wedding, is it?'

Macron looked in amazement at his chief. Well. The man was a Parisian. But still. 'It's the annual festival of Sainte Sara, Sir. It takes place tomorrow. The gypsies follow the statue of their patron saint down to the sea, where it is immersed in the water. It's been going on for decades.'

'The statue? What statue?'

'It's in the church, Sir. It's . . .' Macron hesitated.

'Is it black, Macron? Is the statue black?'

Macron breathed deeply through his nose. Here we go again, he thought. He's going to scold me for being an idiot. Why can't I think laterally, like him? Why do I always go everywhere in straight lines? 'I was going to mention it, Sir. I was going to make that suggestion. That we look at the statue. See if it has any connection with what Sabir is after.'

Calque was already striding towards the church. 'Good thinking, Macron. I'm so glad that I can count on you. Two minds are always better than one, are they not?'

～

The crypt was packed with acolytes. Candle smoke and incense were thick in the air, and there was the continual murmur of people at prayer.

Calque made a quick appraisal. 'Over there. Security. Yes? The one in plain clothes? With the name tag?'

'I should think so, Sir. I'll go and check.'

Calque moved to the side of the crypt, while Macron picked his way forwards through the crowd. In the dim, flickering light, Sainte Sara seemed almost disembodied beneath her many layers of clothing. It was next to impossible that anyone could get to her under these conditions. A hundred pairs of eyes were fixed on her at all times. The security guard was a massive irrelevance. If someone had the temerity to run across and molest her, they would probably be lynched.

Macron was returning with the security guard. Calque exchanged identity details and then motioned the man up the stairs towards the main body of the church.

'I can't leave. We'll have to stay in here.'

'Don't you ever leave?'

'Not during the festival. We take four-hour shifts. *Pari passu.*'

'How many of you are there?'

'Two, Sir. One on, one off. With a standby in case of illness.'

'Were you in here when the knifing occurred?'

'Yes, Sir.'

'What did you see?'

'I didn't see anything at all. I was down here in the crypt.'

'What? Nothing at all? You didn't go out in the square?'

'More than my job's worth, Sir. I stayed in here.'

'And what about the congregation? Did they all stay?'

The security guard hesitated.

'You're not trying to tell me that with a near riot going on outside in the square, everybody simply stayed in here and kept on praying?'

'No, Sir. Most of them went out.'

'Most of them?'

'Well. All of them.'

'And you followed, of course?'

Silence.

Calque sighed. 'Look here, Monsieur . . .'

'Alberti.'

'. . . Monsieur Alberti. I'm not criticising you. And I'm not here on behalf of your employers at the Town Council. What you say to me will not go any further.'

Alberti hesitated. Then he shrugged. 'Okay. When the crypt emptied, I did go up for a short look-see. I stood right outside the church door so that no one could come past me, though. I thought it might be a matter for Security. I thought I ought to look.'

'And you were right. It might very well have been a matter for Security. I would have done the same.'

Alberti didn't seem convinced.

'And when you came back. Still empty?'

Alberti blew out his cheeks.

Calque felt around in his pockets and offered him a cigarette.

'We can't smoke in here, Sir. It's a church.'

Calque cast a jaundiced eye at the plumes of candle smoke rising towards the low-slung ceiling of the crypt. 'Answer my question then. Was the crypt still empty when you came back inside?'

'As good as. There was just one man here. Stretched out in front of the statue. Praying.'

'One man, you say? And you definitely hadn't seen him when you left?'

'No, Sir. I'd missed him.'

'Right, Macron. Hold this man here while I check out the statue.'

'But you can't, Sir. This is a religious festival. Nobody touches the statue until tomorrow.'

But Calque was already striding through the massed phalanx of penitents like Old Father Time with his scythe.

43

—

Calque stood outside the church, squinting into the late-afternoon sunshine. 'I want six detectives. You can second them from Marseille.'

'But that'll take time, Sir.'

'I don't care how long it takes. Or how unpopular it makes us. They are to visit every *chef de famille* amongst these gypsies. Every caravan. Every lean-to, tent and *cabanon*. And I want them to ask these questions . . .', he scribbled rapidly on a sheet of paper and handed it to Macron, '. . . these specific questions.'

Macron eyed the sheet. 'What did you find, Sir?'

'I found a hole in the base of the statue. And fresh shavings scattered in and amongst the knickknacks surrounding it. Also this piece of linen. See how it curls up when you let it hang free? Not surprising, really, seeing as it's been shoved inside a statue for the past five hundred years and used as a stopper.'

Macron whistled through his teeth. 'So Sabir finally found what he's been looking for?'

'And what the eye-man is looking for. Yes. Almost certainly.'

'Won't he get in touch with you, Sir?' Macron couldn't quite keep the sarcastic undertone out of his voice.

'Of course he won't. The man has no idea who he is really dealing with.'

'And we do?'

'We are beginning to. Yes.'

Macron started back towards the car.

'Macron.'

'Yes, Sir?'

'You wanted to know what I was up to? Back at the Domaine de Seyème? With the Countess?'

'I did. Yes.' Macron was uncomfortably aware that he was missing something again. Something his boss had managed to tease out, and which he had misapprehended altogether.

'Tell the pinheads back in Paris that I've got a little test for them. If they succeed at it, I'll acknowledge that computers might be of some use after all. I'll even agree to carry a mobile telephone whilst on duty.'

Macron widened his eyes. 'And what test might that be, Sir?'

'I want them to trace the Countess's eldest adopted son. Bale. Or de Bale. Firstly, through the nuns at the orphanage – that should be easy enough. The boy was already twelve when he was adopted. Secondly, I want them to get me a full run-down of any career he might have had with the Foreign Legion, including a complete physical description, with particular attention paid to his eyes. And if they find that he did belong to the Legion, I want someone to go and talk personally to his commanding officer, and ask him – no, tell him – that we want access to the man's military records. As well as to his own personal summing-up.'

'But, Sir . . .'

'They are not to take no for an answer. This is a murder inquiry. I want no nonsense from the Legion about security, and promises they may or may not make to their men on sign-up.'

'You'll be lucky, Sir. I know for a fact that they never share their records with anyone. I come from Marseille, remember – I grew up with stories of the Legion.'

'Go on.'

'Their HQ is at Aubagne, only fifteen kilometres from

where my parents live. My second cousin even became a Legionnaire after he was let out of prison. He told me that they sometimes bend the rules and let French people join under a false nationality. They even change the men's names when they join. They get a new Legion name by which they're known throughout their tour of duty. Then, unless they are shot, and become *Français par le sang versé* – meaning French by virtue of spilled blood – or unless they take advantage of the right to become French citizens after three years' service, their own names are buried for ever. You'll never find him. For all we know he might even have become French for a second time around, but under a new identity.'

'I don't believe it, Macron. Their own names are not lost for ever. And certainly not to records. This is France. The Legion are like any other godforsaken bureaucracy. Up their own arses with paperwork.'

'As you say, Sir.'

'Look, Macron. I know you don't agree with some of my methods. Or some of my decisions. That's inevitable. It's what hierarchies are for. But you're a lieutenant and I'm a captain. That makes whether you agree or disagree with me irrelevant. We need to find Sabir and the two gypsies. Nothing else counts. If we don't, the eye-man will kill them. It's as simple – and as fundamental – as that.'

44

The ticket collector gazed down at Alexi as if he were an injured wild animal unexpectedly encountered on an afternoon's stroll. He was joined by the river pilot and the occupants of the van and two of the cars. The other two cars had driven off the ferry, obviously preferring to avoid a scene. The river pilot was preparing to use his cellphone.

Alexi struggled out of the life ring and threw it on to the deck. He bent forwards at the waist and cradled his ribs in his arms. 'Please don't call the police.'

The pilot hesitated, the phone halfway to his ear. 'It's not the police you need, my boy. It's an ambulance, a hospital bed and some morphine. And maybe a set of dry clothes.'

'Not them either.'

'Explain yourself.'

'Can you take me back across?'

'Take you back across?'

'I've dropped something.'

'What? You mean your horse?' Both men laughed.

Alexi sensed that if he stuck to concrete facts and flippancy, he might just be able to gather himself on firmer ground – dilute the men's memory of the event and turn it into a prank that had gone wrong, rather than into the near-tragedy it so obviously was. 'Don't worry. I can arrange for the horse carcase to be taken away. There's a lot of fresh meat there. I know people in Les Saintes-Marie who will come to pick it up.'

'What about our barrier?'

'I will pay you whatever I get for the meat. Cash. You can tell your employers that someone drove into the barrier and then skedaddled.'

The pilot squinted at the ticket collector. Already, three cars were waiting to board the ferry for the return journey across. Both men knew that the barrier got belted three or four times a year at least – usually by drunks. Or foreigners in rented cars. The repairman was on a rolling contract.

The van driver and the occupants of the two incoming cars had detected the wind-down in tension. They drifted away to get on with their journeys. The injured man was only a stupid gypsy, after all. And gypsies were all crazy, weren't they? Lived by different rules.

'You can keep your cash. We'll take you back across. But get rid of that horse carcase, do you understand? I don't want it stinking up the terminus for the next two weeks.'

'I'll call now. Can I use your phone?'

'All right. But no international calls, mind? Do you hear me?' The pilot handed Alexi his cellphone. 'I still think you're crazy not to go in for a check-up. You've probably got a rack of cracked ribs after that fall. And concussion, maybe.'

'We've got our own doctors. We don't like going to hospitals.'

The pilot shrugged. The ticket collector was already waving his new customers aboard.

Alexi punched in a number at random and pretended to make arrangements about the horse.

～

Alexi had never known such pain as he was feeling now. Cracked ribs? Concussion? He felt as if both his lungs

293

had been punctured with an awl, and then stretched out on an anvil and pounded with a mallet for good measure. Each breath he took was agony. Each step he took echoed through his right hip and shoulder like an electric shock.

He squatted down on the concrete slope of the ferry slipway and began searching for the bamboo tube. People gave him curious glances as they drove past him in their cars. If the eye-man comes back now, Alexi thought, I will simply lie down and surrender. He can do whatever he wants with me. O Del, please take this pain away. Please give me a break.

The bamboo tube was nowhere to be seen. Alexi struggled to his feet. The ferry was full. It was leaving once again on its outward journey. He limped off the slipway and began following the course of the river, his eyes fixed on the waterline nearest to the bank. The bamboo tube might have floated downstream. With luck, it might even be caught up in the vegetation at the edge of the flow.

Or it might have sunk. If it had sunk, the verses would be spoiled – Alexi knew that much. He would break open the tube and out would come a wadge of damp paper blotted with ink. He wouldn't simply have the eye-man to fear under those circumstances – Sabir and Yola would slaughter him personally.

For some time now Alexi had been feeling some discomfort in his right leg, just above the ankle. He had chosen to ignore it, assuming that it was merely part and parcel of his larger injuries. Now he stopped abruptly and reached down to pull up his trousers. Please God he hadn't broken something. His ankle bone, perhaps – or his shin.

There was a solid object jutting out of the gaping top of his cowboy boots. Alexi felt inside and brought out the bamboo tube. He had stuck the tube into his belt and it had been funnelled down inside his trousers by the force of the water, and from there into his boots. The wax seal holding both halves of the tube together was still intact, thank God.

He looked up at the sky and laughed. Then he moaned in pain as the laughter tore at his damaged ribs.

Clutching his stomach, Alexi began to trudge slowly back in the direction of the Maset de la Marais.

45

Thirty minutes into his walk he saw the saddled horse. It was standing near one of the *gardien*'s cabins, grazing.

Alexi fell back behind a nearby tree. Sweat dripped down his forehead and across his eyes. He had walked right into the trap. It had never occurred to him that the eye-man might be lying in wait for him again on this side of the bank. What had been the chances that he would return across the river after escaping on the Bac? One in a million? The man was crazy.

Alexi peered out from behind the tree. There was something strange about the horse. Something not quite right.

He squinted into the sunset. What was that darker mass lying near the horse's feet? Was it a figure? Had the eye-man fallen off and knocked himself unconscious? Or was it a trap, and the eye-man was simply waiting for Alexi to blunder over before finishing him off?

Alexi hesitated, thinking things through. Then he crouched down and buried the bamboo tube behind the tree. He took a few tentative paces and checked back to see if he could still mark its location. No problem. The tree was a cypress. Visible for miles.

He stumbled on for a few yards and then paused, rustling his pockets as if he were feeling for a titbit. The horse nickered at him. The figure at its feet didn't move. Maybe the eye-man had broken his neck? Maybe O Del had listened to his prayer and settled the bastard for good?

Alexi shuffled forwards again, talking quietly to the horse – gentling it. He could see that the figure's foot was twisted through one stirrup. If the horse walked towards him, and all of a sudden felt the dead weight of the body holding it back, it would panic. And Alexi needed that horse. He wouldn't make it back to the Maset otherwise – that much had become obvious in the last twenty minutes.

With each step he was becoming weaker and more desperate. His clothes had dried on him, stiffening his wounds. His right shoulder had seized up, and he could no longer raise it further than his navel. In his present condition, he wouldn't be able to outrun a tortoise.

Alexi reached the gelding and allowed it to nuzzle him – it was obvious that it was disturbed by the presence of the body, but that the grazing, and Alexi's whistling had temporarily calmed it. Alexi took the reins and knelt down beside the horse. He already knew by the clothes who he was dealing with. Nobody else wore belts that big or buckles that showy. Gavril. Jesus. He must have tried to follow them, and then somehow fallen off his horse and struck his head. Or else he had run into the eye-man coming back from the ferry, and the eye-man had assumed that he knew more than he did. Alexi retched, and spat out the excess saliva. Flies were already congregating around Gavril's nostrils. Talk about being in the wrong place at the wrong time.

Alexi unhooked Gavril's foot from the stirrup. He attached the horse to the hitching post and glanced around, searching for something capable of inflicting such a crippling wound. The gelding couldn't have strayed far, weighed down with Gavril's body.

He hobbled over to the stone. Yes. It was covered in blood. He lifted it up in his arms, using only his sleeves – he knew enough not to smear any fingerprints. He returned and placed the stone near Gavril's head. He was briefly tempted to feel inside Gavril's pocket for any spare cash, but decided not to. He didn't want to provide the police with a possible false motive.

When he was satisfied with his scene-setting, Alexi levered himself up on to the gelding. He swayed in the saddle, the blood pulsing round his head like a ball bearing in a pinball machine.

Two-to-one the eye-man was responsible for the killing – it was too much of a coincidence otherwise. He'd obviously run into Gavril on his way back. Questioned him. Killed him. In which case there was an outside chance that he now knew of the Maset, for Gavril, like any other gypsy his age who regularly visited the Camargue, would have known of the famous card game between Dadul Gavriloff and Aristeo Samana, Yola's father. He might not know exactly where the house was, but he'd sure as hell have known of its existence.

For one brief instant of uncertainty Alexi had been tempted to head back to the tree and retrieve the bamboo tube. But caution finally won out over vainglory. Now, setting the gelding's reins, he allowed it to follow its head back towards the house.

46

Yola had devised a novel way of hitchhiking. She waited until she saw a likely gypsy-owned vehicle approaching, made a snake-like sign with her left hand – followed immediately by the sign of the cross – and then walked out into the middle of the road to where the driver's window would be. The vehicles nearly always stopped.

Yola would then lean in and discuss where she wanted to go. If the driver was travelling in a different direction – or not far enough – she would wave him impatiently on. The fourth vehicle she flagged down fitted her parameters perfectly.

Feeling like Clark Gable to Yola's Claudette Colbert, Sabir followed her into the straw-littered rear of the *bétaillère*. He had to admit that even a stinking Citroën H van was marginally better than walking. He had originally tried persuading Yola that they ought to cut corners and take a taxi back to the Maset, but she had insisted that, this way, no one would have a record of where they had gone. She had been ahead of him, as usual.

Sabir leaned against the lath-framed interior of the H van and toyed with the Spanish-made Aitor lock-bladed knife that he was hiding in his pocket. He had bought the knife off Bouboul, twenty minutes earlier, for fifty euros. It had a four-and-a-half inch razor-sharp cutting edge, which latched into place with a comforting click when you swung it open. It was clearly a fighting knife, for it had an indentation for the thumb about half an inch behind the blade – which Sabir presumed was to allow the knife to be stuck into one's enemy without the disadvantage of cutting off one's own finger in the process.

Bouboul had been reluctant to part with the knife, but greed – he had probably bought it for the equivalent of about five euros thirty years before – and being on the receiving end of one of Yola's tongue-lashings, had been enough to force him to capitulate. She had claimed to hold him personally responsible for the loss of the horses – and, anyway, in her opinion, he was far too old to carry a knife. Did he want to end up like Stefan, with his eye hanging out on a string? Best get rid of the thing.

It was late afternoon by the time Yola and Sabir made it back to the Maset de la Marais. Predictably, the place was empty.

'What do we do now, Damo?'

'We wait.'

'But how will we know if the eye-man catches Alexi? Once the eye-man has the prophecies, he will leave. We will never know what happened.'

'What do you expect me to do, Yola? Wander out into the Marais and yell out Alexi's name? I'd lose myself in no time. There's three hundred square kilometres of absolutely nothing beyond that treeline.'

'You could steal another horse. That's what Alexi would do.'

Sabir felt himself reddening. Yola appeared to understand how men ought to behave, *in extremis,* somewhat better than he did. 'Would you wait here? Would you be prepared to do that? Not go gallivanting off so that I've got two people to find?'

'No. I would stay here. Alexi might come back. He might need me. I shall make some soup.'

'Soup?'

Yola stood and watched him, a disbelieving expression on her face. 'Men always forget that people need to eat. Alexi has been on the run since this morning. If he manages to get back here alive, he will be hungry. We must have something for him to eat.'

Sabir hurried around to the outhouse to see if he could find another saddle, a rope, and some more tack. With Yola in this sort of mood, he understood exactly how Alexi felt about marriage.

~

Within fifteen minutes of starting his horse hunt, Sabir realised that he was not going to get anywhere fast. He wasn't trained in the use of the lariat, like Alexi, and the horses were becoming more skittish the closer dusk approached. Each time he lined one up it would watch him trustingly until he came to within about ten feet, upon which it would twist around on its hind legs and disappear, farting and kicking, into the undergrowth.

Sabir dumped the saddle and bridle at the edge of the Clos, and started back along the trail in disgust. When he came to the junction that led towards the house he hesitated, then struck out to the left, down the track all three of them had taken that morning to get to Les Saintes-Maries.

He was deeply worried about Alexi. But there was also something about the man which inspired confidence, especially when it came to managing out in the wild. True – according to Bouboul's version of the story, the eye-man had been a bare minute's ride behind Alexi when they had left town at the gallop. But a minute was a long time on horseback, and Sabir had seen Alexi dealing with the ponies that morning, and the way that he rode . . . well, suffice it to say that he was a natural. Plus he knew the marshes like the back of his hand. If his horse held up, Sabir would bet good money on Alexi giving the eye-man the slip.

In Sabir's view, therefore, it was only a matter of time before Alexi came riding down the track, the prophecies raised triumphantly in one hand. Sabir would then retire to some quiet spot – preferably near to a good restaurant – to translate them, while the police did what the police were paid to do, and dealt with the eye-man.

In due course he would contact his publishers. They would put the prophecies out to tender. Money would come flooding in – money he would share with Yola and Alexi.

And then, finally, the nightmare would be over.

47

Achor Bale decided that he would approach the house from the east, via an old drainage ditch that ran the length of one untended field. With Alexi away, Sabir and the girl would be on the lookout – on the *qui vive*. Perhaps there was even a shotgun in the house? Or an old rifle? Wouldn't do to take unnecessary risks.

He was fleetingly tempted to return for the horse, which he had left tethered in a clump of trees a hundred metres or so behind the property. The horse would follow him perfectly easily along the ditch, and the sound of its hoofs might even mask his approach. Perhaps the pair of them might emerge from the house, thinking Alexi had returned? But no. Why complicate matters unnecessarily?

For Alexi would return. Bale was certain of that. He

had seen the gypsy risking his life for the girl at Espalion, when she had collapsed in the road. If she was inside the Maset, the gypsy would home in on her like a wasp to a honey-pot. He had only to kill Sabir, put the girl out as bait, and conjure up some creative way to pass the time.

He edged towards one of the main windows. Dusk was falling. Someone had lit an oil lamp and a pair of candles. Thin slivers of light emerged through the closed shutters. Bale smiled. Thanks to the residual glow of the lamps, there was no chance whatsoever of anyone making him out from inside the house. Even as close as six feet from the window, and with their eyes glued to the slats, he would be next to invisible.

Bale listened out for voices. But there was only silence. He moved across to the kitchen window. That, too, was shuttered. So Gavril had been right. If this house were conventionally occupied, there was no way the shutters would be closed so early in the evening. One only had to look around at the yard and the outbuildings to see that the house had been abandoned for years. No wonder the gypsies valued it. It would be like a free hotel to them.

For a moment he was almost tempted to enter by the front door. If Sabir and the girl were acting in character, it would doubtless be unlatched. There were times when Bale felt almost irritated by the unprofessionalism of his opponents. Take the case of the Remington, for instance. Why had Sabir agreed to give it back to him? It had been madness. Did he really believe that Bale would have fired at him, with the Redhawk, on the outskirts of a town blessed with only two main exits, and two relatively minor ones? And before checking out the Black Virgin? That single decision of Sabir's had left the three of them unarmed, and without the slightest clue to Bale's real identity, thanks to his unforgivable – but happily rectified – mistake about the serial number. It had been slack thinking on Sabir's part to overlook where the serial number could potentially have led them. Monsieur, his father, would have had something to say about that.

For Monsieur had always abhorred slack thinking. He had taken the cane to slack thinkers. There were days when he had beaten all thirteen children in a row, one after the other, starting with the largest. That way, when he came to the smallest – and factoring into account his advanced age and his medical condition – he would already be tired, and the blows wouldn't be nearly so painful. Now *there* was consideration for you.

Madame, his mother, had not been so thoughtful. With her, punishment had always been a one-on-one affair. That's why – after Monsieur, his father's, death – Bale had run away to join the Legion. Later, the move had proved unexpectedly useful and she had forgiven him. But for two years they had not spoken and he had been forced to carry out the duties of the Corpus Maleficus in isolation – without management or regulation. He had developed tastes, during that anarchic period, which Madame, his mother, later considered at variance with the movement's aims. That was why he still hid things from her. Unfortunate details. Unavoidable deaths. Things like that.

But Bale didn't enjoy causing pain. No. It certainly wasn't that. As with the horse at the ferry, he loathed seeing the suffering of animals. Animals couldn't protect themselves. They couldn't think. People could. When Bale asked questions of people, he expected answers. He might not have been born to his position in terms of blood but he had certainly been born to it in terms of character. He was proud of the ancient title of nobility, Monsieur, his father, had passed down to him. Proud of his family's record in anticipating – and thereby counteracting – the Devil's work.

For the Corpus Maleficus had a long and noble history. It had included amongst its rank of central adepts the papal inquisitors Conrad of Marburg and Hugo de Beniols; Prince Vlad Drăculea III; the Marquis de Sade; Prince Carlo Gesualdo; Tsar Ivan Grozny (The Terrible); Niccolò Machiavelli; Roderigo, Lucrezia and Cesare Borgia; Count Alessandro di Cagliostro; Grigori Rasputin; the Maréchal Gilles de Rais; Giacomo Casanova; and the Countess Erzsébet Báthory. All had been grossly and continually misrepresented by succeeding generations of cavalier historians.

In Bale's view – imbrued from countless hours of history lessons learned at the feet, and at the behest, of Monsieur and Madame, his parents – Marburg and de Beniols had been falsely labelled as sadistic and vainglorious persecutors of the innocent when they had simply been carrying out the orders of the Mother Church; Vlad 'the Impaler' had been incorrectly accused of turning torture into an art, whilst he had, in reality, been defending – in whatever way was deemed expedient at the time – his beloved Wallachia against the horrors of Ottoman expansion; the Marquis de Sade had been unfairly charged by his detractors with libertinism and the fomentation of sexual anarchy, whereas, in the view of the Corpus, he had simply been promulgating an advanced philosophy of extreme freedom and tolerance designed to liberate the world from moral tyranny; the composer Prince Carlo Gesùaldo had been wrongly castigated as a wife- and child-killer by his no doubt prejudiced accusers, merely as a result of defending the sanctity of his marital home against unwanted interference; history had tarred Tsar Ivan Grozny with the brush of 'filicidal tyrant' and 'The Terrible', whereas, to many of his countrymen, and in the view of the Corpus, he had been the saviour of Slavonic

Russia; Niccolò Machiavelli had been described by his critics as a teleological absolutist and a perpetrator of the politics of fear, labels designed to detract from the fact that he was also a brilliant diplomat, a poet, a playwright, and an inspirational political philosopher; the entire Borgia family had been branded as both criminally corrupt and morally insane, whereas, in the Corpus's view, they had (bar a few trifling infelicities) been enlightened popes, mighty lawmakers, and inspired art lovers, deeply concerned with the supranational promulgation of the glories of the Italian High Renaissance; Count Alessandro di Cagliostro had been called both a charlatan and a master forger – in fact he was an alchemist and a Kabbalist of the highest order, desperate to illuminate the as yet largely unplumbed depths of the occult; naturopath healer and visionary mystic Grigori Rasputin had been described by his critics as a lubriciously prepotent 'mad monk' who was single-handedly responsible for the destruction of the entrenched and moribund Russian monarchy – but who, Bale felt, could blame him? – who, in retrospect, would dare to cast the first stone?; Le Maréchal Gilles de Rais had been called a paedophile, a cannibal and a torturer of children, but he had also been an early supporter of Joan of Arc, a brilliant soldier and an enlightened theatrical promoter whose hobbies, in certain specific and unimportant spheres, might occasionally have got the better of him – but did that discount his greater acts? The larger lived life? No. Of course not – and neither should it; Giacomo Casanova was considered by posterity to be both spiritually and ethically degraded, whereas he had, in reality, been an advanced liberal thinker, an inspired historian, and a diarist of genius; and Countess Erzsébet Báthory, judged a vampirical mass murderess by her peers, had in fact been an educated, multilingual woman who had not only defended her husband's castle during the Long War of 1593–1606, but had also frequently intervened on behalf of destitute women who had been captured and raped by the Turks – the fact that she had later exsanguinated certain of the more severely traumatised of her charges had been deemed by the Corpus (although largely with tongue firmly thrust into cheek) to be empirically necessary for the furtherance and secure propagation of the now all-consuming twenty-first century science of cosmetic enhancement. All had been 'people of the fly', inducted by their parents, grandparents, teachers or advisers, into the secret hermetic cabal of the Corpus – a cabal designed to protect and insulate the world from its own misguided instincts. As Monsieur, his father, had put it: 'In a world of black and white, the Devil rules. Paint the world grey – muddy the boundaries of accepted morality – and the Devil loses his finger-hold.'

Later, what the Count had called the 'natural' adepts had come along – those with an innately destructive gene but who would not necessarily have recognised that what they were doing was in any way a part of a larger or more significant whole. Men and women like Catherine de Medici, Oliver Cromwell, Napoleon Bonaparte, Queen Ranavalona, Kaiser Wilhelm II, Vladimir Lenin, Adolf Hitler, Joseph Stalin, Benito Mussolini, Mao Zedong, Idi Amin Dada and Pol Pot. Each, in their turn, had been a diminisher of the status quo. A challenger of moral precepts. A shaker of the tree of civilisation. Natural adepts of the Corpus, fulfilling its aims despite – or perhaps even because of – their own self-styled agendas.

Such tyrants drew acolytes to them like a bug-zapper draws flies. They acted as recruiting grounds for the weak, the halt, and the morally insane – just the category of people the Corpus needed in order to fulfil its aims. And the greatest and most successful of these – thus far at least – had been the first two Antichrists predicted in Revelations: Napoleon Bonaparte and Adolf Hitler. Unlike their predecessors, both men had acted globally, and not merely nationally. They had functioned as catalysts for a greater evil – one designed to placate the Devil, and keep him from permanently investing the earth with his incubi and succubae.

Bale knew instinctively that the Third Antichrist spoken of in Revelations – the 'One Still To Come' – would easily outdo both his predecessors in the grandeur of his achievements. For chaos, the Corpus believed, was in everyone's best interests – because it forced people to conspire against it. To act communally, and with dynamic creativity. All the greatest inventions – all civilisation's mightiest leaps – had occurred during periods of flux. The earth needed the Dionysian, and must cold-shoulder the Apollonian. The alternative led only to damnation – and to the turning away of God.

What was it that John the Divine had written in his Apocalyptic Book of Revelation, following his exile to the island of Patmos, courtesy of the Emperor Nero?

And I saw an angel come down from heaven, having the key to the bottomless pit and a great chain in his hand. And he laid hold on the dragon, that old serpent, which is the Devil, and Satan, and bound him a thousand years. And cast him into the bottomless pit, and shut him up, and set a seal upon him, that he should deceive the nations no more, till the thousand years should be fulfilled: and after that he must be loosed a little season . . . And when the thousand years are expired, Satan shall be loosed out of his prison; And shall go out to deceive the nations which are in the four quarters of the earth, Gog and Magog, to gather them together to battle: the number of whom *is* as the sand of the sea.

AND AFTER THAT HE MUST BE LOOSED A LITTLE SEASON . . .

It was unfortunate that the numerological sum of Achor Bale's name added up to the Kabbalistic number two. This gave him a steady, even disposition, but also guaranteed that he would always remain subordinate and over-sensitive – a perpetual henchman, rather than a leader. Some fools even called it a malevolent, evil number, falling within the negative female spectrum and rendering its adherents prey to doubts and vacillations and uncertainties of focus.

Unless, of course, their characters were infused and strengthened by strong direction and a fundamental core belief from a suitably early age.

Bale felt that he owed this all-redeeming, positive aspect of his nature to Monsieur, his father's, influence. If Bale could not be an instigator, then he would be a follower. A loyal follower. A crucial cog in the outplaying of the infernal machine.

Now that he had forced the girl's name from that fool Gavril, Bale decided that it might be amusing to try the Kabbalistic test on her – and also on the gypsy, Alexi Dufontaine. It would help him to deal with them. It would give him insights into their character that he would not otherwise have access to.

He conducted the calculations swiftly in his head. Both came out as eights. Usually an auspicious number, and linked in some ways to his own. But when holders of the number persisted in following courses of action simply out of stubbornness or mere pig-headedness, the number turned negative, dooming its possessor. This, Bale decided, must be the case with the gypsies.

What was Sabir's number? Now that would be interesting. Bale thought it through. A. D. A. M. S. A. B. I. R. What did that give in terms of Kabbalistic numerology? 1, 4, 1, 4, 3, 1, 2, 1, 2. Making 19. Add 1 and 9, making 10. That's 1 + 0. Meaning Sabir was a number one. Powerful. Ambitious. Dominant. An easy friend-maker and an influencer of people. A 'righteous man' personality. Someone, in other words, who cannot admit that they are ever in the wrong. An Alpha male.

Bale smiled. He would enjoy tormenting and killing Sabir. It would come as such a shock to the man.

For Sabir had drained his good luck to the lees, and it was time to make an end of the matter.

18

When Sabir heard the shuffle of Alexi's horse, he refused, at first, to believe his ears. It was a stray from the neighbouring *domaine*. Or an escaped Camarguais bull, out looking for a mate.

He drew in for protection behind a clump of acacia trees, trusting that the outline of the branches would muddy his silhouette in the rapidly encroaching dusk. Carefully, painstakingly, he took the knife out of his pocket and extended the blade. Despite all his best efforts, it made a definite snick when opened.

'Who's there?'

Sabir hadn't realised that he had been holding his breath. He exhaled in one grateful, exultant whoosh. 'Alexi? It's me. Damo. Thank God you're all right.'

Alexi swayed in the saddle. 'I thought you were the eye-man. When I heard that click, I thought I was done for. I thought you were going to shoot me.'

Sabir scrambled up the bank. He clung on to Alexi's stirrup. 'So you have it? You have the prophecies?'

'I think so. Yes.'

'You think so?'

'I've buried them. The eye-man . . .' Alexi tilted forwards and began to slide down the side of the gelding's neck.

Sabir had been so wound up with his own excitement about the prophecies that it had not occurred to him to check on Alexi's physical condition. He caught Alexi under both arms, and eased him off the gelding. 'What's the matter? Are you injured?'

Alexi curled up into a ball on the ground. 'I fell. Hard. On to a barrier. Then some concrete. Escaping from the eye-man. It's been getting worse. The last half-hour. I don't think I will be able to make it back to the house.'

'Where is he? Where is the eye-man?'

'I don't know. I lost him. But he killed Gavril. Smashed in his head with a stone and made it look like an accident. I put everything back in place to incriminate him. Took Gavril's horse. My own horse was killed. Now you have to go back to the house. The eye-man might know about the Maset.'

'How could he know about the Maset? It's impossible.'

'No. Not impossible. He might have got it from Gavril. That fool followed us. The eye-man caught up with him. But I told you this already. I'm too tired to repeat myself. Listen to me, Damo. Leave me here. Take the horse. Go back to the Maset. Get Yola. Only then come back. Tomorrow, when I am better, I will show you where the prophecies are.'

'The prophecies. You've seen them?'

'Go, Damo. Take the horse. Fetch Yola. The prophecies don't matter any more. You understand? It is only writing. Not worth a single life.'

49

Bale located the defective shutter – the defective shutter that was always to be found in old houses if you had the patience to look for it. He levered the shutter gently open. Then he inserted his knife into the warped sash of the window frame and seesawed it from side to side. The window opened with a noise like the riffling of a deck of cards.

Bale paused, listening. The house was as silent as the grave. Bale allowed his eyes to focus in the gloom. When he could see again, he checked out the room. The place stank of dried rodent corpses and the accumulated dust of years of benign neglect.

He moved to the hallway and then down towards the kitchen. It had been there that he had seen the oil lamps and the candles burning. Strange that there were no voices. In Bale's experience, people nearly always talked in abandoned houses – it was a means of keeping the ghouls at bay. Of pricking the silence.

He reached the kitchen door and glanced inside.

Nothing. He twitched one nostril. Soup. He could smell soup. So the girl was here, at the very least. Was she outside, perhaps, using nature's closet? In which case he had been very lucky indeed not to run into her and risk losing her in the dark.

Or perhaps she had heard him? Warned Sabir? And they were lying in wait for him somewhere in the house. Bale smiled. That would make things a little more amusing. Give things a little more edge.

'Your soup's boiling over.' His voice echoed through the house as through a cathedral.

Had there been a rustling in the far corner of the salon? Over there behind the bergère sofa? Where the tired old curtains hung down? Bale picked up one of a pair of bronze knickknacks and lobbed it at the front door. The clatter it made seemed obscenely loud in the sound-dampened room.

A figure darted from behind the sofa and began levering wildly at the shutters. Bale picked up the second bronze statuette and flung it at the figure. There was a cry, and the figure fell.

Bale stayed where he was – listening – breathing only through his mouth. Had anyone else made a sound? Or had there only ever been that single person in the house? The girl – he sensed now that it had been the girl.

He walked back into the kitchen and fetched the oil lamp. Holding it out ahead of him, he walked over to the main shuttered window. The girl was curled up on the floor. Had he killed her? That would be inconvenient. He had certainly thrown the bronze statuette as hard as he had been able. But it might have been Sabir. He couldn't afford to take any chances at this late stage in the game.

As he reached down for her, the girl slithered away from his grasp and ran wildly down the corridor.

Had she heard him breaking in? Was she heading for

312

the back window? Bale ran in the opposite direction to the one she had taken. He threw himself through the front door and then curved left around the house.

He slowed down as he approached the window. Yes. There was her foot. Now she was pulling herself through.

Bale lifted her bodily out of the window and dropped her on the ground. He cuffed her once around the head and she lay still. Bale straightened up and listened. Nothing. No other sound. She had been the only one in the house.

Reaching down, he felt through her clothes and up between her legs for a knife or other concealed weapon. When he was sure that she was unarmed, he lifted her up like a sack of grain, draped her around his shoulders, and headed back towards the salon.

50
—

Bale helped himself to some soup. For the love of Mike, it was good! He hadn't eaten anything at all in twelve hours. He could feel the richness of the broth replenishing his powers – rekindling his depleted energy.

He drank some wine, too, and ate a little bread. But the bread proved stale and he was forced to dunk it in the soup to make it palatable. Well. You couldn't have everything.

'Are you getting tired, my dear?' He glanced across at the girl.

She was standing on a three-legged stool in the centre of the room, a bread sack over her head, and with her neck infibulated through a noose which Bale had constructed from a cowhide lariat. The stool was just wide enough to give her a fair base on which to stand, but the blow to her head had obviously weakened her, and from time to time she swayed awkwardly against the rope, which, within reason, acted as a support for her neck.

'Why are you doing this? I have nothing you want. I know nothing you want to know.'

Earlier, Bale had thrown open the salon shutters and the front door of the Maset to the night. He had also surrounded the stool with candles and oil lamps, so that the girl stood as if floodlit – visible for fifty metres in any direction except to the north.

Now he reclined as if on a divan, the saucepan of soup on his lap, the outlines of his body lost in the darkness outside the pool of candlelight, well out of any sight-lines afforded by the opened windows and front door. At his right side lay the Redhawk, its butt conveniently angled towards his hand.

He had chosen the three-legged stool because one shot from the Redhawk would be enough to topple the girl into the air. All he had to do was to shatter a single leg of the stool. True, she would kick and jerk for a minute or two, as the fall would be nowhere near long enough to break her neck – but she would eventually asphyxiate, leaving Bale ample time to make his getaway by the rear window while Sabir and the gypsy were occupied with trying to save her life.

None of this would be necessary, of course, if Sabir would simply come to terms. And Bale hoped that the sight of the girl would concentrate his mind on just that necessity. A simple transfer of the prophecies would do the trick. Then Bale would leave. Sabir and the gypsy could have the wretched girl. They were welcome to her. Bale never reneged on a deal.

In the unlikely eventuality that they came after him, however, he would kill them – but he was as certain as he was of anything that Sabir would capitulate. What did he have to lose? Some cash and a little fleeting fame. And to gain? Everything.

51

'Tell me again what time he left.'

Yola groaned. She had been standing on the stool for over an hour now, and her blouse was drenched in sweat. Her legs felt as if they were filled with crawling parasites that paraded up and down her thighs and calves, nibbling as they went. Her hands were tied behind her, and thus her only means of controlling her ever-wider swings was by means of her chin. When she sensed that she was on the verge of swaying, she would clamp the rope tightly to her shoulder with the underside of her jaw, counting on the tension of the lariat to keep her upright.

For some time now she had been wondering whether it would be worth testing the eye-man – letting herself fall on purpose. He was obviously waiting for Sabir and Alexi. So if they weren't there to see her strangle, would the eye-man scoop her up and save her? Untie her, while she recovered, before using her again? Relax his attention for a moment? It would be her only chance of escape. But it would be an awful risk to take.

Maybe he would just amuse himself by watching her die? Then he might tie her back up – string her from the noose – and nobody, at a distance, would realise that she was already dead.

'I asked you a question. At what time did Sabir leave?'

'I don't use a watch. I don't know the time.'

'How far off from dusk was it?'

Yola didn't want to antagonise him. He had already struck her once, after pulling her from the window. She was scared of him. Scared of what he was capable of doing. Scared that he might remember what he had threatened to do to her the first time they had met, and repeat the threat to amuse himself. She was certain that the information she was giving merely confirmed what he already knew. That there was nothing new about it – nothing that could in any way prejudice Alexi and Damo's chances of survival. 'About an hour. I sent him off to catch another horse. He would have ridden off looking for Alexi.'

'And Alexi would come back here?'

'Yes. Without a doubt.'

'And Alexi knows his way about the marshes? Knows enough to find his way back here in the dark?'

'Yes. He knows the marshes well.'

Bale nodded. That much had been obvious. That had made all the difference. If Alexi had been travelling blind, Bale would have caught him. If only he hadn't known about the Bac – then this entire charade would have been unnecessary. Bale could have taken the prophecies back to Madame, his mother, and been acclaimed as a hero. The Corpus Maleficus would have honoured him. He, personally, might have been placed in charge of protecting the next Antichrist. Or of eradicating the bloodline of the New Messiah *before the event*. Bale was good at such things. His mind functioned in a methodical way. Give him a goal and he would steadily and painstakingly work towards it – just as he had done with the prophecies, over the past few weeks.

'Are you going to kill them?'

Bale glanced up. 'I'm sorry. What did you say?'

'I said are you going to kill them?'

Bale smiled. 'Maybe. Maybe not. It all depends on how they respond to the picture I have created of you dangling from the end of a rope. You'd better hope they understand exactly what I am trying to communicate to them with my little piece of theatre. That they come in of their own free will. That they don't force me to shoot out one of those stool legs.'

'Why do you do all this?'

'Do all what?'

'You know what I mean. Torment people. Pursue them. Kill them.'

Bale let out an amused snort. 'Because it is my sworn duty to do so. It can be of no possible interest to you – or concern – but back in the thirteenth century, my family, and the larger brotherhood to which it belongs, was given a task by King Louis IX of France.' Bale made a reverse cross, which began at his crotch and ended behind his head. 'I am talking of Saint Louis, *Rex Francorum et Rex Christianissimus*, Lieutenant of God on Earth.' He mirrored the sign of the reverse cross with the sign of the six-sided Pentacle, again going from the bottom to the top of his body. 'The task he gave us was to be ours in perpetuity, and consisted, quite simply, of protecting the French people from the machinations of the Devil – or Satan, Azazel, Typhon, Ahriman, Angra Mainyu, Asmodai, Lucifer, Belail, Beelzebub, Iblis, Shaitan, Alichino, Barbariccia, Calcobrina, Caynazzo,

317

Ciriato Sannuto, Draghignazzo, Farfarello, Grafficane, Libicocco, Rubicante, Scarmiglione, or whatever else stupid people choose to call him. We have fulfilled this bond for over nine centuries – often at the cost of our lives. And we shall fulfil it until Ragnarök – until the End of Days, and the coming of Vidar of Vali.'

'Why do we need you to protect us?'

'I refuse to answer that question.'

'Why did you kill my brother, then?'

'Whatever gave you the idea that I killed your brother?'

'They found him hanging from a bed frame. You had stabbed him through the cheek with a knife. You had broken his neck.'

'The bit with the knife. The puncture wound. That was me. I admit it. Samana wouldn't understand that I meant what I said. I needed to show him that I was serious. But your brother killed himself.'

'How? That is impossible.'

'I thought so too. But I asked him something – something that would have led directly to you. I think he realised, in his heart of hearts, that he would eventually talk. Everybody does. The human mind cannot conceive how much punishment the human body can actually take. The mind intervenes considerably before it needs to – it trawls through what it knows and it jumps to conclusions. It is unaware that – unless a vital organ is damaged – nearly all physical functions may eventually be regained. But the thought of all the damage being inflicted acts as a temporary catalyst. The mind abandons hope – and at that particular point, and at that point only, death becomes preferable to life. That is the crucial moment for the tormentor – when the fulcrum point has been reached.'

Bale hunched forward in his enthusiasm. 'I have made

something of a study of this, you know. The greatest torturers – those from the Inquisition, say, like the Hangman of Dreissigacker, or Heinrich Institoris and Jacob Sprenger – even Chinese Masters like Zhou Xing and Suo Yuanli, who transacted their business during the reign of Wu Zetian – brought people back from the brink many times over. Here. I can see by your posture that you don't believe me. Let me read something to you. To pass the time, as it were – for it must be very uncomfortable for you, balancing on that stool. It's from a cutting I always carry about my person. I have read it to many of my . . .' Bale hesitated, as if he had been about to utter some infelicity. 'Shall we call them my clients? It concerns the first man I mentioned to you in my list of torturers – he was called the Hangman of Dreissigacker. A true adept of the art of pain. You will be impressed, I promise.'

'You make me sick. Sick to my heart. I wish that you would kill me now.'

'No. No. Listen to this. It really is quite extraordinary.'

There was the sound of a piece of paper being straightened. Yola tried to shut her ears to the sound of the eye-man's voice, but all that she succeeded in doing was to reinforce the thrumming of blood through her head, so that the eye man's voice intensified inside her like the clapping of a thousand hands.

'You must try to imagine your way back to the year 1631. To the time of the Catholic Inquisition. Such a leap of the imagination is probably an easy thing for you to do inside that sack, is it not? A pregnant woman has just been accused of witchcraft by the established Church authorities – a body of men with the weight of both religious and secular law on their side. She is to be questioned – a perfectly reasonable course of action to take in the circumstances, you might agree?

It is the very first day of her trial. What I am about to read to you now is how the great humanist, B. Emil König, describes the formal investigative processes of the Inquisition in his catchily titled *Ausgeburten des Menschenwahns im Spiegel der Hexenprozesse und der Aoto da Fés Historische Handsaülen des Aberglaubens, Eine Geschichte des After-Und Aberglaubens bis auf die Gegenwart*:

'In the first place, the Hangman bound the woman, who was pregnant, and placed her on the rack. Then he racked her till her heart would fain break, but had no compassion. When she did not confess, the torture was repeated. Then the Hangman tied her hands, cut off her hair, poured brandy over her head and burned it. He also placed sulphur in her armpits and burned it. Then her hands were tied behind her, and she was hauled up to the ceiling and suddenly dropped down. This hauling up and dropping down was repeated for some hours, until the Hangman and his helpers went to dinner. When they returned, the Master-Hangman tied her feet and hands upon her back; brandy was poured on her back and burned. Then heavy weights were placed on her back and she was pulled up. After this she was again stretched on the rack. A spiked board is placed on her back, and she is again hauled up to the ceiling. The Master again ties her feet and hangs on them a block of fifty pounds, which makes her think that her heart will burst. This proved insufficient; therefore the Master unties her feet and fixes her legs in a vice, tightening the jaws until the blood oozes out at the toes. Nor was this sufficient; therefore she was stretched and pinched again in various ways. Now the Hangman of Dreissigacker began the third grade of torture. When he placed her on the bench and put the I shirt on her, he said: 'I do not take you for one, two, three, not for eight days, nor for a few weeks, but for half a year or a year, for your whole life, until you confess: and if you will not confess, I shall torture you to death, and you shall be burned after all.' The Hangman's son-in-law then hauled her up to the ceiling by her hands. The Hangman of Dreissigacker whipped her with a horsewhip. She was placed in a vice where she remained for six hours. After that she was again mercilessly horsewhipped. This was all that was done on the first day.'

The room was silent. Outside, the wind soughed through the trees. An owl called in the far distance, and its call was answered from one of the barns, nearer to the house.

Bale cleared his throat. There was the sound of paper being put away. 'I misread your brother. I hadn't realised how devoted he was to you. How fearful he was of losing face in front of his community. Few people, you see, enjoy the benefits of community any more. They only have themselves to think of – or their immediate family. Rationalisations are possible. Shortcuts a temptation. But when wider communion is at stake, other factors become apparent. Martyrdom is one option. People are once more willing to die for an ideal. Your brother, in his way, was such an idealist. He used the position I had tied him in – the downward weight of gravity I had engineered – to break his own neck. I've never seen anything like it. It was most impressive. By the end of her first day of questioning, this self-evidently innocent woman whose ordeal I have just been describing to you would no doubt have willingly sold her soul to the Devil for the simple secret of its consummation.' Bale glanced across at Yola's standing figure. 'One man in a million would have been capable of pulling off such a magnificent physical feat as the giving of death to oneself whilst in suspensory bondage. And your brother was such a man. I shall never forget him. Does that answer your question?'

Yola stood silently on the stool. The angles of her face were distorted by the sack. It was impossible to tell what she was thinking.

52

—

'I'm not leaving you. If you stand up and lean against me, I will try to shunt you on to the horse. When we get to the Maset you can rest. Yola has made soup.'

'Damo. You're not listening to me.'

'I am listening, Alexi. But I don't think the eye-man is some sort of super-being. The chances are that Gavril fell off his horse unaided – that he struck his head on the rock by accident.'

'He had ligature marks on his hands and feet.'

'He had what?'

'The eye-man had tied him up before smashing in his face. He had hurt him. At least it seemed that way to me. The police will realise what has happened, even if you don't.'

'Since when have you become such a fan of the police, Alexi?'

'The police deal in facts. Sometimes facts are good. Even I am not so ignorant that I don't realise that.' With Sabir's help, Alexi pulled himself back across the saddle. He rested wearily forward on the horse's poll. 'I don't know what has come over you recently, Damo. The prophecies seem to have hypnotised you. I wish now that I had not found them. Then you would remember your brother and sister again.'

Sabir led the gelding in the direction of the house. Its hoofs made pelting noises in the dew-sodden sand. Apart from that and the *scurr* of the mosquitoes, the two men were surrounded, like a cloak, by the silence of the marshes.

Alexi cursed long-sufferingly. He stretched out a hand and touched Sabir lightly on the shoulder. 'I'm sorry, Damo. Sorry for what I just said. I'm tired. And I'm in pain. If anything happens to me, of course I want you to know where the prophecies are buried.'

'Nothing's going to happen to you, Alexi. You are safe now. And to hell with the prophecies.'

Alexi levered himself upright. 'No. This is important. I was wrong to say those things to you, Damo. I am frightened for Yola. It makes my tongue misbehave. There is a gypsy saying: "Everybody sees only his own dish." '

'So now you're viewing Yola as a dish?'

Alexi sighed. 'You are purposely misunderstanding me, Damo. Maybe this is an easier expression for you to understand: "When you are given, eat. When you are beaten, run away." '

'I get what you are saying, Alexi. I'm not trying to misunderstand you.'

'The thought of bad things happening to her makes me sick with fear, Damo. I even dream of her – of pulling her from evil places. Or from out of mud-holes and quicksands that try to take her back from me. Dreams are important, Damo. As a community, the Manouche have always believed in the *cacipen* – in the truth of dreams.'

'Nothing bad is going to happen to her.'

'Damo. Listen to me. Listen carefully, or I will shit on your head.'

'Don't tell me. That's another of your gypsy sayings.'

Alexi's eyes were focused on the back of Sabir's neck. He was willing himself not to pass out. 'To recover the prophecies, you must go to where I found Gavril. It is a twenty minute ride north of the Bac. Just before you get to the Panperdu. There is a *gardien*'s *cabane* there. It, too, faces north, as protection against the blowing of the Mistral. You can't miss it. It is thatched with *la sagno* and has a plastered and tiled roof and a chimney-stack. No windows. Just a door. With a hitching rail in front of it and a viewing pole behind it, where the *gardiens* can climb up and see far across the marshes.'

'Plus, according to you, it will soon become a crime scene. With police seething around everywhere with their sniffer dogs and their metal detectors and their plastic BVDs.'

'That doesn't matter. You don't need to be seen when you pick up the prophecies.'

'How come?'

'Hide yourself. Then pretend as if you are at the *cabane*, and turn to look south. You will see a single cypress tree standing out from the nearby wood. The prophecies are buried directly behind that, about two feet from the trunk. Not deep. I was already too weak for that. But deep enough. You will soon see that the earth has been disturbed.'

'They'll rot. In the first rain. They'll become illegible. And all this will have been for nothing.'

'No, Damo. They are contained in a bamboo tube. The tube is sealed in the middle with hard wax. Or tree sap. Something like that. Nothing can get in.'

An unknown horse suddenly whinnied ahead of them, the noise of its cry echoing through the marshes like a lament for the dead. Their own horse was about to answer but some belated survival instinct caused Sabir to clamp the gelding's nostrils shut just as the animal was taking a preparatory breath. He stood, the gelding's nose locked beneath his arm, listening.

'I told you.' Alexi was whispering. 'It is the eye-man. I told you he tortured Gavril. Got the location of the Maset off him.'

'I can see lights through the trees. Why would the eye-man switch on a bunch of lights? It doesn't make sense. It's more likely that Yola has received a visit from some of her girlfriends from the town. Everybody knows about this place – you told me so yourself.' Despite his apparent confidence, Sabir stripped off his shirt and wrapped it tightly around the gelding's nose. Then he led him on through the willow copse and down towards the rear of the barn. 'Look. The doors and windows are wide open. The place is lit up like a cathedral. Has Yola gone mad? Perhaps she wanted to guide us in?'

'It's the eye-man. I tell you, Damo. You must listen to me. Don't go straight towards the lights. You must check the place out from the outside first. Perhaps Yola had time to run away? Either that, or she's in there with him.'

Sabir looked up at him. 'You're serious?'

'You heard his horse.'

'It could be any horse.'

'There was only Gavril's and the eye-man's left. I have Gavril's. And the third horse is dead. The horses know each other, Damo. They know the sound of each other's steps. They recognise each other's whinny. And there aren't any other horses within half a kilometre of here.'

Sabir attached the reins to a bush. 'You've convinced me, Alexi. Now wait here and don't move. I will go and reconnoitre the house.'

53

'What are you burning? I can smell burning.' Yola instinctively turned her face away from the light and towards the darkness behind her.

'It's all right. I'm not setting fire to the house. Or heating up the pinching tongs like the Hangman of Dreissigacker. I'm merely burning cork. To blacken my face.'

Yola knew that she was perilously close to exhaustion. She didn't know how much longer she could hold her position. 'I'm going to fall.'

'No you're not.'

'Please. You have to help me.'

'If you ask me again, I will sharpen a broom handle and shove it up your arse. That'll keep you upright.'

Yola hung her head. This man was impossible to touch. All her life she had been able to manipulate, and thus to dominate, men. Gypsy men were easy game that way. If you said what you had to say with enough conviction, they would usually give in. Their mothers had trained them well. This man was cold, however. Not amenable to the feminine. Yola decided that there must be a very bad woman in his life to make him this way. 'Why do you hate women?'

'I don't hate women. I hate everybody who gets in the way of what I am doing.'

'If you have a mother, she must be ashamed of you.'

'Madame, my mother, is very proud of me. She has told me so.'

'Then she must be evil too.'

For a moment there was dead silence. Then a movement. Yola wondered whether she had finally gone too far. Whether he was coming across to get her.

But Bale was only stowing away the remainder of the soup in order to give himself a clearer line of movement. 'If you say more, I shall whip the back of your legs with my belt.'

'Then Alexi and Damo will see you.'

'What do I care. They don't have guns.'

'But they have knives. Alexi can throw a knife more accurately than any man I know.'

In the distance a horse whinnied. Bale hesitated for a moment, listening. Then, satisfied that it had been his own horse, and that there had been no answering call, he resumed their conversation. 'He missed Sabir. That time in the clearing.'

'You saw that?'

'I see everything.'

Yola wondered whether to tell him that Alexi had missed on purpose. But then she thought that it would be a good idea if he continued to underestimate his opponents. Even the smallest thing might be enough to give Alexi or Damo a crucial edge. 'Why do you want these writings? These prophecies?'

Bale paused, considering. At first Yola expected him to ignore her question but he suddenly appeared to make up his mind about something. In doing so, however, his tone changed infinitesimally. Thanks to the claustrophobic intensity inside the bread bag, Yola had become morbidly sensitive to each and every nuance in the eye-man's voice – it was thus at that exact moment that she understood, with total certainty, that he intended to kill her whichever way the handover went.

'I want the writings because they tell of things that are going to happen. Important things. Things that will change the world. The man who wrote them has been proved right many times over. There are codes and secrets hidden within what he writes. My colleagues and I understand how to break these codes. We have been trying to lay our hands on the missing prophecies for centuries. We have followed countless false trails. Finally, thanks to you and your brother, we have found the true one.'

'If I had these prophecies I would destroy them.'

'But you don't have them. And you will soon be dead. So it is all an irrelevance to you.'

54

Sabir lay on his belly at the edge of the stand of trees, watching. The horror of his position was leaching through his body like a cancer.

Yola was standing on a three-legged stool. A bread sack covered her head, and a noose had been slipped around her neck. Sabir was certain that it was Yola by her clothes and by the timbre of her voice. She was talking to someone and this person was answering her – a deeper, more dominant timbre. Not up and down, like a woman, but flat – all on one note. Like a priest intoning the liturgy.

It didn't take a genius to realise that the eye-man had staked Yola out as bait to catch him and Alexi. Nor to realise that the minute that they showed themselves, or came within range, they would be dead meat – and

Yola with them. The fact that the eye-man would thereby inadvertently lose the best chance he had ever had to discover the location of the prophecies was yet another of life's tender little ironies.

Sabir made up his mind. He squirrelled himself backwards through the undergrowth towards Alexi. This time he would not blunder in and risk everybody's lives. This time he would use his head.

55

When Macron's cellphone rang, he was interviewing three reluctant *gitans*, who had only just crossed the Catalonian border that morning, near Perpignan. They had obviously never heard of Sabir, Alexi or Yola, and didn't object to making this clear. One of them, sensing Macron's ill-concealed hostility, even pretended to fend him off with the flat of his forearm – just as if he had the 'evil eye'. Macron might have ignored the insult in the normal run of things. Now he responded angrily, the concentrated memory banks of his mother's ingrained superstitious beliefs erupting, uncalled for, through the habitually dormant surface of his own sensibilities.

The truth was that he felt disheartened and bone-weary. All his injuries seemed to have compounded themselves into one all-encompassing ache, and, to cap it all, Calque seemed to be favouring one of the new detectives to make the real running in the investigation. Macron felt humiliated and isolated – all the more so as he considered himself a local lad, whilst the six *pandores* Calque had seconded from Marseille – his home town, for Christ's sake! – still insisted on treating him like a pariah. Like a sailor who has abandoned ship and is busily swimming towards the enemy, hoping to give himself up in exchange for preferential treatment. Like a Parisian.

'Yes?'

Five hundred metres from the Maset Sabir nodded gratefully to the motorist who had lent him the phone. Five minutes earlier he had leapt in front of the man's car, waving dramatically. Even then the man hadn't halted, but had veered over on to the hard shoulder, missing Sabir by inches. Fifty metres further up the road he had changed his mind and stopped the car, doubtless imagining that there had been an accident somewhere in amongst the marshes. Sabir couldn't blame him. In his panic, he had forgotten all about his shirt, which was still wrapped around the gelding's nose – he must have presented a disturbing sight, lurching out of the undergrowth on a minor country road, half naked, and in the pitch darkness.

'This is Sabir.'

'You've got to be joking.'

'Who is this?'

'Lieutenant Macron. Captain Calque's assistant. We haven't met, unfortunately, but I know all about you. You've been running us a merry little dance across most of France. You and your two Magi.'

'Pass me Calque. I have to talk to him. Urgently.'

'Captain Calque is conducting interviews. Tell me where you are and we'll send a stretch limousine out to collect you. How's that for starters?'

'I know where the eye-man is.'

'What?'

330

'He's holed up in a house, not far from where I am speaking to you. He is holding a hostage, Yola Samana. He has her standing on a stool, with a noose around her neck. She's lit up like a *son et lumière*. The eye-man is presumably hiding in the shadows with a pistol, waiting for Alexi and me to show ourselves. As far as armament is concerned, Alexi and I have got exactly one knife between us. We don't stand a chance in hell. If your precious Captain Calque can get some paramilitaries in place, and if he can guarantee me that he will prioritise Yola's safety – and not the capture of the eye-man – I'll tell you where I am. If not, you can both go and piss against a drystone wall. I'll go in myself.'

'Stop. Stop. Wait. Are you still in the Camargue?'

'Yes. That much I'll tell you. Is it agreed? Otherwise I'll switch this phone off right now.'

'It's agreed. I'll go and fetch Calque. There are CRS paramilitaries on permanent standby in Marseille. They can be deployed straight away. By helicopter, if necessary. It will take no more than an hour.'

'Too long.'

'Less. Less than an hour. If you can be accurate about the location. Give me an exact map reference. The CRS will have to work out where to land the helicopter without giving away their presence. And then approach by foot.'

'The man I borrowed the cellphone from may have a map. Go get Calque. I'll stay online.'

'No. No. We can't risk your battery running out. I have your number. When I've reached Calque I will call you back. Get me that map reference.'

As Macron ran to where he knew Calque was conducting his interviews, he was already scrolling down for the code to their Paris headquarters. 'André. It's Paul. I have a cellphone number for you. We need an instant GPS. It's urgent. Code One.'

'Code One? You're joking.'

'This is a hostage situation. The man holding the hostage killed the security guard in Rocamadour. Get me that GPS. We're in the Camargue. If any other part of France comes up on your gizmo, you've got interference or a malfunction. Get me the exact position of that cellphone. To within five metres. And inside five minutes. I can't afford to blow this.'

~

Within thirty seconds of Macron explaining the situation to him, Calque was on the phone to Marseille.

'This is a Code One priority. I will identify myself.' He read out the number on his identity card. 'You will see a ten-letter cipher when you type in my name on the computer. It is this. HKL481GYP7. Do you have that? Does it match the code on the national database? It does? Good. Hand me over to your supervisor immediately.'

Calque spent an intense five minutes talking down the phone. Then he turned to Macron.

'Have Paris come back to you with Sabir's GPS?'

'Yes, Sir.'

'Now phone him. Compare it with the map reference he gives you.'

Macron got back on the phone to Sabir. 'Do you have a map reference for us? Yes? Give it to me.' He marked it down in his notebook, then ran across and showed it to Calque.

'It matches. Tell him to wait exactly where he is until you arrive. Then get into place yourself and call the situation in to me at this number.' He scribbled down a number on Macron's pad. 'It is the number of the local Gendarmerie. I will base myself there, coordinating the operation between Paris, Marseille and

Les Saintes-Maries. I have been reliably informed that it will take at least fifty minutes to get the paramilitaries in place. You can be at the Maset in thirty. Twenty-five, even. Stop Sabir and the gypsy from panicking into any precipitate action. If it looks as though the girl is being imminently threatened, intervene. If not, keep your head down. Do you have your pistol?'

'Yes, Sir.'

'Take any of the detectives that you can find with you. If you can't find any, go alone. I will send them on behind you.'

'Yes, Sir.'

'And Macron?

'Yes, Sir?'

'No unnecessary heroics. There are lives at stake here.'

The life-transforming idea came to Macron about six minutes into his journey. It seemed so simple – and so logical – that he was sorely tempted to pull the car over on to the hard shoulder to afford himself a little extra elbow room to consider it.

Why not think outside the loop for a change? Use his initiative? Why not take advantage of the eye-man's ignorance about the secret connection between Sabir and the police? It was the single edge they had on him. He would be expecting only Sabir and the gypsy to come riding to the girl's rescue. Why not make use of that very fact to pull off an ambush?

Macron had been present at only one police siege during the course of his career. He had just turned twenty and had passed his police primaries six days before. Neighbours had reported seeing a man threatening his wife with a gun. A building in the 13th arrondissement had been sealed off. Macron had been all but forgotten about. His police mentor at the time had been a trained negotiator and had been called in at the very last moment to defuse the situation. Macron had asked if he might come along as an observer. The man had said yes. Just so long as he kept out of the way. Far out of the way.

Five minutes into the siege the negotiations had broken down. The wife had made a comment to her husband which had driven him over the brink. He had killed her, killed the negotiator, and then killed himself.

It was the very first time that Macron had seen and understood the innate fallibility of the police machine, which was only as good as the cogs that made it up. If one of the cogs skipped a ratchet, the whole machine could go kaput. Faster than the *Titanic*.

He had liked that mentor. Macron had counted on the man to monitor and encourage his career. Shepherd him through his rookie-ship.

After the siege he had been forgotten about a second time. As good as abandoned. No more mentors. No more helping hands up the greasy pole. And now it was all happening again. The Marseillais detectives would come in and take over his case. Cosy up to Calque. Shunt Macron to the sidelines. Take all the credit that was his by right.

The eye-man had hurt him. Once, personally, out in the field, and once, professionally, on the road to Millau. And now the man was sitting, like a staked-out pigeon, in a partially lit room, expecting to dominate proceedings for the third time.

But Macron would be the spoke in his machine. He had a gun. He had the crucial element of surprise. The eye-man had made himself a sitting duck. Who would know, in the chaos of a shootout, what had really gone down?

If he killed the eye-man, his career would be made. He would forever remain the man who had cracked the twin fatalities of the Paris gypsy case. The gypsy didn't matter, of course. But security guards were honorary police – at least when it came to being murdered. Macron could already imagine the envy of his peers; the admiration of his fiancée; the grudging respect from his normally detached father; the triumphant revenge of his downtrodden mother who had fought long and hard for his right to leave the bakery and attend police college.

Yes. This was it. This would be Paul Eric Macron's moment of truth.

57
—

Sabir was standing by the side of the road, just as arranged. Macron recognised him immediately from the image he kept on his cellphone. Sabir had lost weight in the intervening period, and his expression lacked some of the bumptious self-confidence he exuded in the publicity photograph they had downloaded from his agency website. Now his face looked washed out in the artificial light from the stationary Simca's headlights – an airport face – the face of a man in endless transit.

The idiot was even stripped to the waist. Why had the other motorist stopped? If Macron, as a civilian, had happened upon a half naked-man, in the middle of a lonely road, at dusk, he would have hurried on past and left him to the next fool down the line. Or called the police. Not risked a mugging or a car-napping by stopping to pick him up. People were strange, sometimes.

Macron drew up beside the Simca, his eyes scanning the road for traps. At this stage he wouldn't put anything past the eye-man. Even setting up an ambush, with Sabir as the bait, in order to procure himself a police hostage. 'Are you alone? Is it just you two here? Where's the other gypsy?'

'You mean Alexi? Alexi Dufontaine? He's injured. I've left him with the horse.'

'The horse?'

'We rode in. At least Alexi did.'

Macron sifted a little air through his front teeth. 'And you, Monsieur. You decided to lend this man your phone?'

The farmer ducked his head. 'Yes. Yes. He was standing in the road with his hands held up. I nearly struck him with my car. He said he had to call the police. Are you the police? What is going on here?'

Macron showed the man his warrant card. 'I'm going to record your name and address on my cellphone and take a picture of you. With your permission, of course. Then you may go. We will contact you later if we need to.'

'What's happening here?'

'Your name, Sir?'

Once the formalities were over, Sabir and Macron watched the Simca disappear into the darkness.

Sabir turned towards the policeman. 'When is Captain Calque coming?'

'Captain Calque is not coming. He is coordinating the operation from the *gendarmerie* in Les Saintes-Maries. The paramilitaries will be here in two hours.'

'The hell you say? You told me fifty minutes. You people must be crazy. The eye-man has had Yola standing on a stool for God knows how long, with a noose around her neck and a sack covering her head. She must be scared witless. She'll fall. We need an ambulance on standby. Paramedics. A fucking helicopter.'

'Calm yourself, Sabir. There's an ongoing crisis in Marseille. The detachment of CRS we would normally be counting on for operations of this nature are fully occupied with other matters. We have had to address ourselves to Montpellier instead. Permissions have had to be given. Identities checked. That all adds to the time frame.' Macron was astonished at how easily the lies tripped off his tongue.

'What are we going to do then? Just wait? She'll never hold out that long. And neither will Alexi. He'll crack and go powering in. And so will I. If he goes, I go.'

'No you won't.' Macron tapped the waist of his blouson, just above the hip. 'I have a pistol. If necessary, I will handcuff both of you to my car and leave you for my colleagues to find. You, Sabir, are still wanted for murder. And I have reason to suspect that your companions – Dufontaine and the girl – have been using this house illegally. Have you any idea who it actually belongs to? Or have you just been house-sitting on spec?'

Sabir ignored him. He pointed up the track leading towards the house. 'When's your local back-up coming? You need to cut through all this bullshit, surround the place, and make immediate contact with the eye-man. The sooner you start putting pressure on him, the better.

Make it clear that he will gain nothing by harming Yola. That was the deal we had. The deal I made with your boss.'

'My local back-up will be here in fifteen minutes. Twenty at the outside. They know exactly where to go and what to do. Show me the situation, Sabir. Explain to me exactly what trouble you have all managed to get yourselves into. And then we will see what we can do to get you out of it.'

58

Macron had settled on his plan. It was absurdly simple. He had reconnoitred the house and understood the layout perfectly. A wide-open window led to the back of the Maset. He would wait for Sabir and Alexi to show themselves, and then he would pass through it, counting on their voices – and the eye-man's concentration on them – to mask the sound of his movements. The minute he had a clear sight of the eye-man he would take him out – a shot to the right shoulder ought to do it.

For Macron wanted his day in court. It wouldn't be enough just to kill the eye-man – he wanted the bastard to suffer. Just as he had suffered with his feet. And his back. And his neck. And the muscle at the top of his buttock that had been crushed by the car seat and which ticked incessantly since the accident – particularly when he was attempting to drift off to sleep.

He wanted the eye-man to suffer all the tiny

humiliations of bureaucratic procedure that he, Macron, had to suffer in his position as a junior police officer. All the stone walls, and the Chinese whispers, and the unintentionally intentional mortifications. He wanted the eye-man to rot for thirty years in a ten foot by six foot jail cell, and to come out an old man, with no friends, no future, and with his health in tatters.

Sabir had been telling the truth after all. This was a crisis. The girl was obviously on her last legs. She was swinging around like a rag doll on a light bracket. She couldn't possibly hold out for the twenty-five minutes necessary for the CRS to land a helicopter the full kilometre and a half away from the Maset needed for effective sound containment – and then to hurry into position.

This had become his call. He was the man the service had in place. Any hesitation would only lead to tragedy.

Macron squatted down beside Sabir and Alexi. He checked the loads in his pistol, enjoying the feeling of power it gave him over the other two men. 'Give me three minutes to get round to the back of the house, and then show yourselves. But don't come within the eye-man's range. Stay near the trees and tantalise him. Draw him out. I want him framed against the front door.'

'If you see him, will you take him out? Not hesitate? The man's a psychopath. He'll kill Yola without a second thought. God alone knows what he's put her through already.'

'I'll shoot. I've done it before. It wouldn't be the first time. Our part of Paris is no nursery. There are shootings nearly every day.'

Macron's words didn't ring true somehow – Sabir couldn't quite get himself to believe in them. There was something fervid about the man – something just a little fake. As though he were a civilian who had wandered into a police operation and had decided, off the cuff, to act the part of a participating officer simply for the hell of it. 'Are you sure Captain Calque's okayed this?'

'I've just this moment called him. I've explained that a further wait might be fatal. My back-up are still a good fifteen minutes away. Anything could happen in that time. Are you with me on this?'

'I say go in now.' Alexi pushed himself up on his knees. 'Look at her. I can't bear watching this any more.'

Given the tenor of Alexi's words and the urgency of the situation confronting them, Sabir decided to ditch his reservations too. 'All right, then. We'll do as you say.'

'Three minutes. Give me three minutes.' Macron slithered through the undergrowth towards the back of the Maset.

59

—

The second he heard Sabir's voice, Bale played the fire extinguisher over the candles and oil lamps surrounding Yola. He had caught sight of the extinguisher as he was fetching soup from the kitchen, and had immediately decided how best to use it. Now he screwed his eyes shut and waited for them to readjust to the darkness.

Yola called out in her terror, 'What was that? What did you just do? Why did the lights go out?'

'I'm pleased you've finally turned up, Sabir. The girl's

been complaining that her legs are tired. Have you got the prophecies with you? If not, she swings.'

'Yes. Yes. We've got the prophecies. I have them on me.'

'Bring them over here.'

'No. Let the girl go first. Then you get them.'

Bale knocked the stool away with a backward flick of his leg. 'She's swinging. I warned you of this. You've got about thirty seconds before her windpipe crushes. After that you could try an emergency tracheotomy. I'll even lend you a pencil to stick her with.'

Sabir felt rather than saw Alexi gliding past him. Five seconds earlier the man had been on his knees. Now he was running straight for the entrance to the Maset.

'Alexi. No. He'll kill you.'

There was a flash of light from inside the house. Alexi's running figure was briefly lit up. Then darkness fell again.

Sabir started running. It didn't matter that he would die. He had to save Yola. Alexi had shamed him by running in first. Now he was probably dead.

As he ran, he dragged the clasp knife from his pocket and locked open the blade. There were more flashes of light from inside the Maset. Oh Christh.

~

On the first note of Sabir's voice, Macron ducked in through the back window of the Maset. He would guide himself by the lights in the front room – that ought to do it. But as he made his way up the hall, the lights were suddenly extinguished.

Bale's voice was coming from the left of the open door. Now it was moving across the room. Macron could just make out a darker silhouette against the faint light coming in from outside.

He tried for a snap shot. Please God he hadn't shot the girl. The sudden flash of light was just enough to warn him of the barricade of chairs and tables Bale had set up across the face of the corridor. Macron tripped over the first chair and began to fall. In desperate slow motion he twisted over on to his back and endeavoured to kick his way out of the mess – but he only managed to sink deeper inside the morass of wooden slats.

He still had his gun in his hand. But by this time he was lying on his back like a stranded cockroach. He shot wildly over his head, hoping, in that way, to keep Bale's head down until he was able to disentangle himself.

It didn't work.

The last sensation Macron had on earth was of Bale kneeling on his gun-hand, levering his mouth open, and forcing a pistol barrel across the swollen barrier of his tongue.

~

Bale had instantly moved away from the girl after kicking out the stool legs. The Legion had taught him never to stand for too long in one place during a firefight. His drill instructor had drummed into him that you always move about a battlefield in a series of four-second bursts, to the tune of an internal rhythm that you keep on repeating in your head: *You Run – They See You – They Lock and Load – You Drop*. The old discipline saved his life.

Macron's snap shot passed through Bale's neck, puncturing his trapezius muscle, just missing his subclavian artery, and shattering his clavicle. Bale immediately felt his left hand and arm go numb.

He twisted towards the danger, his gun arm rising.

There was a crash, as whoever had come in by the back way encountered his barricade. Then a second shot smashed into the ceiling above Bale's head, showering him with plaster.

Still pulsing with adrenalin, Bale darted towards the shooter. He had seen the man silhouetted in the light of the gun flash. Knew where his head was. Knew what a mess he had got himself into with the barricade. Knew where the man's pistol was instinctively aiming.

He speared the man's gun-hand with his knee. Levered the man's mouth open with the barrel of the Redhawk. Then shot.

Police. It had to be the police. Who else would have a pistol?

Bale ran for the back window, his left arm hanging loose. Civilian clothes. The man had been in civilian clothes – not paramilitary kit. So it wasn't a siege.

He levered himself backwards through the window and fell to the ground, cursing. Blood was cascading down his shirt. If the bullet had nicked his carotid artery, he was done for.

Once out of the Maset, he cut to the right, towards the stand of trees in which he'd tethered the horse.

No other way out. No other way to go.

60

—

Alexi was holding Yola up in his arms, taking all her weight. Protecting her from the certain death that her own body mass would inevitably have afforded her.

Sabir felt blindly above her head until he encountered

the rope. Then he followed it down with his fingers until he was able to undo the noose that had tightened around her throat. She drew in a great, ragged breath – the very inverse of a death rattle. This was the sound of life returning. Of the body succouring itself after a great trauma.

Where was Bale? And Macron? Surely they hadn't killed each other? Part of Sabir was still expecting the fourth bullet.

He helped Alexi lay Yola out on the floor. He could feel the warmth of her breath against his hand. Hear Alexi's sobs of pain.

Alexi lay down beside her, with Yola's head cradled against his chest.

Sabir navigated his way by feel across to the fireplace. He recalled seeing a box of matches on the left, near the fire tongs. He felt around with his fingers until he encountered them. While he did this, he listened with all his concentration for any alien sounds inside the house. But the place was silent. Only the murmur of Alexi's voice broke the hush.

Sabir put a match to the fire. It flared into life. He was able, by its light, to focus on the rest of the room. It was empty.

He moved across to the fallen footstool, dried off one or two of the candles and lit them. The shadows played off the walls above him. He was consciously having to control the panic that was threatening to send him at a flat run back out of the room and towards the welcoming darkness outside. 'Let's take her over to the fire. She's drenched. I'll get a blanket and some towels from one of the bedrooms.'

Sabir had a fair idea by now of what he would find out in the corridor. There had been blood all over the floor near the stool. Thick gouts of it. As though the eye-man had blown an artery. He followed its trail until he came to the tangle of chairs encircling Macron's body.

The top of the policeman's head had been blown off. A flap of skin covered his one remaining eye. Dry-gagging, Sabir levered the gun out of Macron's hand. Averting his eyes from the rest of the mess, he felt blindly around for the cellphone he knew Macron kept in the front pocket of his *blouson*. He straightened up and continued on down the corridor. He stood for a while contemplating the fresh blood trail where it crossed the ledge of the rear window.

Then, glancing down at the illuminated VDU of the cellphone, he walked into the first available bedroom in search of blankets.

61

—

'I'll take that.' Calque held his hand out for Macron's gun.

Sabir tendered him the pistol. 'Whenever we meet, I always seem to be passing you firearms.'

'The mobile phone, too.'

Calque pocketed the gun and the cellphone and moved towards the corridor. He shouted back over his shoulder: 'Can we get the electricity reconnected here? Someone call the company. Either that, or hitch up a generator. I can't see to think.' He stood for a moment over Macron's body, playing his torch over what remained of his assistant's face.

Sabir moved up behind him.

'No. Stand back. This is a crime scene now. I want your friends to remain by the fireplace until the ambulance comes. Not wash their hands. Not tread in anything. Not touch anything. You, Sabir, will come outside with me. You've got some explaining to do.'

Sabir followed Calque out of the front door. Temporary spotlights were being levered into place outside, giving the area the look of a floodlit, all-weather football pitch.

'I'm sorry. Sorry about your assistant.'

Calque glanced at the surrounding trees and breathed in deeply. He felt in his pockets for a cigarette. When he didn't find one he looked temporarily bereft – as if it was the lack of a cigarette he was mourning and not his partner. 'It's a funny thing. I didn't even like the man. But now he's dead I miss him. Whatever he might have been – whatever he might have done – he was mine. Do you understand that? My problem.' Calque's face was a frozen mask. Impossible to read. Impossible to touch.

A passing CRS officer, noting Calque's search for a cigarette, offered him one of his own. Calque's eyes flared angrily in the rush of the lighter flame – an anger that was just as suddenly extinguished. Catching sight of Calque's expression, the man gave an embarrassed salute and passed on.

Sabir shrugged his shoulders in a vain effort to mitigate the effect of what he was about to say. 'Macron called it off his own bat, didn't he? Your people were here ten minutes after he moved in. He should have waited, shouldn't he? He told us the shooters would take two hours. That they had to come from Montpellier and not Marseille. He was lying, wasn't he?'

Calque turned away, grinding out his freshly lit cigarette in the same fluid motion. 'The girl is alive.

346

My assistant secured her life at the cost of his own.' He glared at Sabir. 'He injured the eye-man. The man is now on horseback, spewing blood, in an area bounded by two rarely used roads and a river. Once daylight comes, he will stick out like an ant on a blank sheet of paper. He will be caught – either from the air or in the land net. The area is already ninety per cent sealed off. In under an hour, we will have made it a hundred.'

'I know that, but . . .'

'My assistant is dead, Monsieur Sabir. He sacrificed himself for you and the girl. First thing tomorrow morning I will have to go and explain his death to his family. How it could possibly have happened on my watch. How I let it happen. Are you sure you heard him right? About Montpellier, I mean? And the two hours?'

Sabir held Calque's eyes with his own. Then he allowed his gaze to slide back towards the house. The distant sound of an ambulance cut through the night air like a lament.

'You're right, Captain Calque. I'm just a stupid Yank. My French is a little rusty. Montpellier. Marseille. They all sound the same to me.'

62

'I'm not going to the hospital. And neither is Alexi.' Yola watched Sabir warily. She was not sure how far she could go with him – how deep his *gadje*hood really reached. She had taken him aside for this one purpose. But now she was concerned that his fractured male pride would make him that much harder to convince.

'What do you mean? You came this close to being strangled.' Sabir slid one of his hands inside the other and then twisted. 'And Alexi fell from his horse on to a steel barrier and some concrete. He could have internal injuries. You need a complete medical check-up and he needs intensive care. In a hospital. Not in a caravan.'

Yola modulated the tone of her voice, consciously playing up her femininity – playing on the affection she knew Sabir felt for her. His susceptibility to the distaff side. 'There is a man at Les Saintes-Maries. A *curandero*. One of our own people. He will look after us better than any *gadje* doctor.'

'Don't tell me. He's your cousin. And he uses plants.'

'He is the cousin of my father. And he uses more than plants. He uses the *cacipen*. He uses the knowledge of cures that have been passed down to him in dreams.'

'Oh. Well. That's all right then.' Sabir watched as a woman in a plastic suit began photographing the interior of the Maset. 'Let me get this straight. You want me to convince Calque to let you into this man's care? To save Alexi from the sawbones? Is that it?'

Yola made her decision. 'You have not told the policeman about Gavril yet, have you?'

Sabir flushed. 'I thought Alexi was sick. I didn't realise he had brought you so swiftly up to date.'

'Alexi tells me everything.'

Sabir allowed his gaze to wander somewhere over Yola's right shoulder. 'Well, Calque's got enough on his plate. Gavril can wait. He's going nowhere fast.'

'Calque will blame you for holding out on him. You know that. He will blame Alexi, too, when he discovers who really found the body.'

Sabir shrugged. 'Maybe so. But why should he ever

find out? We're the only three who know what Alexi stumbled on. And I'm damned sure Alexi won't tell him. You know how he feels about cops.'

Yola stepped around and placed herself firmly in Sabir's sight-line. 'You have not told him because you want to retrieve the prophecies first.'

A rush of outraged virtue triumphed over Sabir's instinctive sense of moral discretion. 'What's wrong with that? It would be madness to lose them at this stage.'

'Even so, Damo, you must tell the policeman. Tell him now. Gavril has a mother who is still living. A good woman. It is not her fault that her son was a bad person. Whatever he was, whatever he did, he must not lie any longer unmourned – like an animal. The Manouche believe that a person's wrong actions are cancelled out by their death. For us there is no hell. No evil place that people go to when they are dead. Gavril was one of us. It would not be right. Do this thing and I will retrieve the prophecies for you. Secretly. While the policeman watches over you and Alexi.'

Sabir threw back his head. 'You're crazy, Yola. The eye-man is still out there somewhere. How can you even think of such a thing?'

Yola took another step towards him. She was consciously forcing herself into his space. Making it impossible for Sabir to ignore her – to write her off as a mere woman, braving waters better suited to men. 'I know him now, Damo. The eye-man has spoken privately to me. Revealed something of himself. I can combat him. I shall take with me a secret. Passed down to the *curandero* from the snake woman, Lilith, many mothers ago, when she gave the chosen ones of our family the second sight.'

'Oh, for Christ's sake, Yola. Death is the only thing

349

that will defeat the eye-man. Not second sight.'

'And it is death that I shall carry with me.'

—

The gelding had quailed at the scent of Bale's blood. Its legs had splayed as if it did not know in which direction it intended going. When Bale had tried to approach it, the gelding had thrown back its head in panic and dragged against its reins, which were tied in a bunch to a branch of the tree. The reins had snapped and the gelding had backed wildly away, then twisted on its haunches and galloped frantically up the track towards the main road.

Bale glanced back towards the house. The agony in his neck and arm cancelled out the sounds of the night. He was losing blood fast. Without the horse, they would catch him within the hour. Any minute now they would be here, with their helicopters, and their searchlights, and their infrared night glasses. They would dirty him. Tarnish him with their fingers and with their hands.

Clutching his left arm to his side to prevent it swinging, Bale did the only thing he could possibly do.

He began to retrace his steps towards the Maset.

Sabir watched the police car take Yola and Alexi away. He supposed that it was a deal that he had reluctantly cut with Calque, but words like 'rat' and 'trap' kept interposing themselves between him and any satisfaction that he might have taken in its inception.

The only edge that he had possessed with which to counter Calque's anger at his holding out about Gavril, lay in his by now tacit agreement to keep quiet about Macron's criminal impetuosity. Ironically, though, he hadn't dared mention Macron again in case he inflamed Calque way beyond rationality and ended up counting bricks in a jail cell – so *that* particular bargaining counter had proved less than worthless.

This way, at any rate, he remained useful to the man and capable of maintaining at least some degree of free movement. If Yola did what she'd said she'd do, they would still be ahead of the game. If the gouts of blood left in the Maset salon were anything to go by, it couldn't be long, surely, before the French police ran the eye-man down and either killed him or took him into custody?

Calque crooked a finger at Sabir. 'Get into the car.'

Sabir seated himself next to a CRS officer in a bullet-proof vest. He smiled but the officer refused to respond. The man was going to a potential crime scene. He was in official mode.

Hardly surprising, thought Sabir to himself – he was still a suspect in nearly everybody's eyes. The cause, if not exactly the perpetrator, of a colleague's violent death.

Calque spread himself out across the front seat. 'I'm

right, am I not? La Roupie's body is lying outside a *gardien*'s *cabane*, twenty minutes north of the Bac, just before you get to the Panperdu? That's what you told me, isn't it? That's where you came across it while you were out searching for the gypsy Dufontaine?'

'Alexi Dufontaine. Yes.'

'Do you have a problem with the word gypsy?'

'When used in that way, yes.'

Calque acknowledged the validity of Sabir's point without actually bothering to turn his head. 'You're loyal to your friends, aren't you, Monsieur Sabir?'

'They saved my life. They believed in me when no one else did. Am I loyal to them? Yes. Does that surprise you? It shouldn't.'

Calque twisted in his seat. 'I ask you this only because I am having difficulty in tallying up what you have just told me about your discovery of La Roupie's body and the fact that you declared quite clearly, when I questioned you earlier, that you went off in search of Dufontaine by foot. The distances involved seem quite unrealistic.' Calque nodded to the driver, who swung the car away from the Maset and down the drive. 'Do me a favour and look at this map, will you? I'm sure you will be able to put me right.'

Sabir took the map, his expression neutral.

'You will see, marked on the map, the only *cabane* you could possibly mean. I have highlighted it with a large red circle. There. You see it? Are we in agreement that this is the place?'

The unsmiling CRS officer reached across and switched on the interior light for Sabir's convenience.

Sabir glanced dutifully down at the map. 'Yes. That would seem to be the place.'

'Are you an Olympic sprinter, Monsieur Sabir?'

Sabir switched the interior light back off. 'Captain.

352

Do me a favour. Just get whatever it is you want to tell me off you're chest. This atmosphere is murder.'

Calque retrieved the map. He nodded to the driver, who set the siren in motion. 'I have only one thing to tell you, Mister Sabir. If Dufontaine does a vanishing act before I have a chance to question him and take his statement, I will hold you and the girl in his place – as accessories before the fact – for as long as I deem it necessary. Do you understand me? Or shall I get on to the radio this minute and tell the car that is delivering your two gypsy friends to the *curandero* at Les Saintes-Maries to turn around and come straight back?'

65

—

Bale eased himself back through the rear window of the Maset a maximum of three minutes after the sound of his final shot. So far so good. There would be no new blood trails to give his position away. He had merely been going over old ground.

But from here on in he must be more careful. Any minute now the 7th Cavalry would be arriving, and the place would revert to bedlam. Before that happened, he needed to find somewhere safe to lie up and nurse his shoulder. If he was caught out in the open, come first light, he might as well cash in his cards and cry *caprivi*.

Clutching his left arm to his side, Bale moved into one of the downstairs bedrooms. He was just about to snatch the coverlet off the bed in an effort to contain his bleeding when he caught the sound of footfalls approaching along the corridor.

Bale looked wildly around him. His eyesight had accustomed itself to the darkness by now and he was able to make out the silhouettes of all the major pieces of furniture. Not for a second was he tempted to ambush whoever was approaching. His main job now was to avoid the attentions of the police. The rest would come later.

He ducked in behind the bedroom door and pulled it tightly against his body. A man entered the bedroom immediately behind him. It was Sabir. Bale's senses were so hyper-alert that he could almost smell him, even in the dark.

He picked up the sound of rummaging. Was Sabir taking the blankets off the bed? Yes. To cover the girl of course.

Now he was using a cellphone. Bale recognised the particular timbre of Sabir's voice. The casually inflected, just so slightly mid-Atlantic, French. Sabir was speaking to a police officer. Explaining what he thought had happened. Telling him about the death.

Someone called the 'eye-man' was on the run, apparently. The 'eye-man'? Bale grinned. Well, it made sense, in an off-beam sort of a way. At least it confirmed that the police didn't yet know his name. Which also meant that Madame, his mother's, house might still be a safe place to retreat to. The only problem would lie in getting there.

Sabir walked back towards the door behind which Bale was hiding. For a split second Bale was tempted to smash the door into his face. Even with one arm, he was more than a match for a man like Sabir.

But the loss of blood from his neck had weakened him. And the other gypsy was still out there – the one who had sprinted into the house just a few seconds after Bale had set the girl on the dangle. That had taken balls. If the plain-clothes policeman hadn't neck-shot him, Bale would have picked off the gypsy a good twenty metres before he reached his target. The man must have a guardian fucking angel.

Bale waited for Sabir's footfalls to diminish down the corridor – yes, there was the expected hesitation near the policeman's body. Then the manoeuvring around the furniture. Sabir would want to avoid stepping in the man's blood – he was a gringo, after all. Far too squeamish.

Hardly breathing, Bale eased himself out into the corridor.

In the salon there was a red glow as the fire in the grate gradually took hold. Now Sabir was lighting more candles. Good. No one would be able to make Bale out beyond the immediate axis of the light.

Keeping his back tight against the wall, Bale sidestepped towards the rear stairs. He reached down. Good again. They were stone, not wood. No creaking.

A drop of blood plopped on to the step beside him. He felt around and scrubbed it off with his sleeve. He'd best make it fast. Before he left a blood trail any idiot could follow – let alone a policeman.

At the top of the stairs Bale decided that it was safe enough to risk his pocket torch. Shading the beam with his fingers, he played the torch down the disused corridor and then up along the ceiling. He was looking for an attic or a loft space.

Nothing. He moved into the first bedroom. Junk everywhere. When had this house last been lived in? Anybody's guess.

He tried the ceiling again. Nothing.

Two bedrooms further down the corridor he found it.

A loft hatch, consisting of a hole with a board laid across it. But no ladder.

Bale shone the torch around the room. There was a chair. A chest. A table. A bed with a distressed, motheaten coverlet. That would do.

Bale set the chair underneath the loft space. He knotted the coverlet around the spine of the chair, and then tied the other end of the coverlet through his belt.

He tested the chair for weight. It held.

Bale eased himself up on to the chair and reached up with his one good arm for the loft cover. The sweat began popping out on his forehead. For a second he felt faint and as though about to fall, but he refused to countenance such a possibility. He let his arm drop and took a few deep breaths until his condition returned to normal.

Bale realised that he would have to conduct the thing in one explosive movement, or else his strength would leave him and he would be unable to achieve his end.

He closed his eyes and began, quite consciously, to regulate his breathing once more. He started by telling his body that it was okay. That any trauma that had occurred to it was trivial. Not worth compensating for in terms of weakness.

When he felt his heart rate return to near normal, he reached up, slid the loft cover to the left, and hooked his good arm up over the lip. Using the chair as a fulcrum, he swung himself up and out, taking the full weight of his body on to his good arm. He would have only one chance at this. He had better make it good.

Scissoring himself upwards, he swung first one leg, then the other, over the lip of the loft space. For a moment he hung there, his bad arm flailing down, his legs and half his upper body eaten by the space. Kicking forwards, he managed to get the back of his right upper thigh across the hatch.

Now he was hanging with the coverlet trailing from his belt and still attached to the chair. He scissored his way further into the loft space, transferring the entire weight of his body on to his thighs.

With one final twist he launched himself over the edge of the loft hatch and lay there, cursing silently through clenched teeth.

When he had sufficient control of himself again, he untied the coverlet from around his waist and pulled the chair up behind him.

For one dreadful moment he thought that he had misjudged the size of the hatch and that the chair was not going to pass through. But then he had it. Out of sight, out of mind.

He shone his torch down on to the floor to check for blood loss. No. All the blood had landed on the chair. By morning, any other spots would have dried anyway and be virtually indistinguishable from the filth already covering the oak boards.

Bale hefted the lid back across the loft hatch, untied the coverlet from the chair, and collapsed.

66

He awoke to a fearful, nagging pain in his left shoulder. Daylight had found its way through a thousand inadvertent chinks in the roof, and one chink had been shining fully on to his face.

He could hear voices outside the house – shouts,

orders, the hefting of large objects and the firing-up of engines.

Bale crawled out of the light, dragging the coverlet behind him. He would have to do something about his shoulder. The pain of his shattered collarbone was close to unbearable and he didn't wish to pass out, with the risk that he might call out in his delirium and alert the police below.

He found himself an isolated corner, well out of the way of any boxes and bric-a-brac that might be susceptible to a kick or to toppling over. Any noise at all – any unexpected crashes – and the enemy would find him.

He constructed a pad for himself with the coverlet, forcing it under his armpit and then tying it back around his shoulder blades. Then he lay flat on the planking, with his legs stretched out and his arms down by his sides.

Slowly, incrementally, he began inhaling in a series of deep breaths and as he took each breath he allowed the words 'sleep, deep sleep' to echo through the inside of his head. Once he'd got a satisfactory rhythm going, Bale opened his eyes as wide as he could manage and rotated them backwards, until he was staring at a point on the ceiling way beyond his forehead. With his eyes fixed in that position, he deepened his breathing, all the while maintaining the rhythms of his internal chant.

When he could feel himself drifting into a pre-hypnotic state, he began to suggest certain things to himself. Things like 'in thirty breaths, you will fall asleep', followed by 'in thirty breaths you will do exactly as I tell you' – and then, later, 'in thirty breaths you will no longer feel any pain' – culminating with 'in thirty breaths your collarbone will begin to heal itself and your strength will return to you'.

Bale understood only too well the potential shortcomings of self-hypnosis. But he also knew that it was the only possible way that he could dominate his body and return it to a state bordering on the functional.

If he was to last out in this loft space – with no food and with no medical attention – for the day or two that it would take the police to complete their enquiries, he knew that he must focus all his resources on the conservation and cultivation of his essential energies.

All he had was what he came in with. And those assets would diminish with each passing hour, until either an infection, an unforced error, or an unintended noise could bring him low.

67

—

Gavril's body lay exactly where Alexi had said it would be. Sabir glanced idly towards the woodland – yes, there was the solitary cypress tree, just as Alexi had described it. But it might as well have been on Mars for all the good it would do him at this moment.

Calque seemed to be deriving keen pleasure from rubbing salt into Sabir's wounds. 'Is this how you remembered it from yesterday afternoon?'

Sabir wondered if he might get away with asking to take a leak? But a fifty-metre walk towards the woods might seem just a little suspicious in the circumstances.

When it became obvious that Sabir had no intention

of responding to his digs, Calque tried a different tack. 'Tell me again how Dufontaine lost the prophecies?'

'Escaping from the eye-man. On the Bac. He lost them in the water. You can confirm his story with the pilot and the ticket collector.'

'Oh, believe me, Mister Sabir, I will.' Calque mispronounced the Mister as Miss-tear.

Sabir decided that Calque was mispronouncing Miss-tear on purpose, simply in order to needle him. The man was obviously sore about Sabir's breaking their previous agreement over the tracking device. That and the minor matter of the death of his assistant.

'You don't seem at all disappointed about the loss of the prophecies. If I were a writer, I would be very angry indeed at my friend having mislaid such a potential gold mine as that.'

Sabir contrived a shrug. It was meant to convey that losing a couple of a million bucks was an everyday occurrence with him. 'If it's all right with you, Captain, I'd like to go back to Les Saintes-Maries and check up on my friends. I could also do with a little sleep.'

Calque made a big show of weighing up Sabir's request. In reality, he had decided on his plan of action some time before. 'I shall send Sergeant Spola back to the gypsy camp with you. Both you and Dufontaine will remain within his sight at all times. I am not finished with you both yet.'

'And Mademoiselle Samana?'

Calque made a face. 'She is free to go about her business. Frankly, I would like to hold her too. But I have no grounds. Something, though, may occur to me, should you and Dufontaine give my subordinate any difficulties whatsoever. But she is to confine herself within the precincts of the town. Do I make myself clear?'

'Quite clear.'

'We are in agreement, therefore?'

'Perfectly.'

Calque flashed Sabir an old-fashioned look. He beckoned to Sergeant Spola. 'Drive Mister Sabir back into town. Then find Dufontaine. Stay with them both. You are not to let either one of them out of your sight for even an instant. If one man wants to go to the washroom, they both go – with you stationed outside holding their free hands. Do you understand me?'

'Yes, Sir.'

Calque glanced at Sabir, frowning. There was something still niggling him about Sabir's part in the proceedings – but he couldn't put his finger on it. With the eye-man still on the loose, however, any misgivings about Sabir could wait. The eye-man's horse had turned up unexpectedly, in a lather, twenty minutes ago, a little less than five kilometres down the road to Port St-Louis. Could the eye-man really have escaped that easily? And with Macron's bullet still inside him?

Calque signalled to one of his assistants for a cellphone. As he dialled, he glanced across at Sabir's retreating back. The man was still holding out – that much was obvious. But why? For what? No one was accusing him of anything. And he didn't look the sort of a man to be consumed by thoughts of revenge.

'Who found the horse?' Calque angled his head towards the ground, as if he felt that such a movement would in some way improve reception – transform the cellphone back into its more efficient cousin, the landline. 'Well, put him on.' He waited, his eyes drinking in the dawn-lit landscape. 'Officer Michelot? Is that you? I want you to describe the condition of the horse to me. Exactly as it was.' Calque listened intently. 'Was there blood on the horse's flanks? Or on the saddle?' Calque sucked a little air through his teeth. 'Anything else you noticed? Anything at all? The reins, for instance? They were broken, you say? Could they have been broken by the horse treading on them after it had been abandoned?' He paused. 'What do you mean, how can you tell? It's simple. If the reins are broken at their furthest extent, then it suggests that the horse trod on them. If they are broken farther up – at a weak point, say, or near the bit – then it means that the horse probably broke away from the eye-man and we still have the bastard inside our net. Did you check this out? No? Well go and check it out this instant.'

68
—

Sergeant Spola had never been inside a gypsy caravan before. Even though this one was of the mechanised variety, he looked cautiously around himself, as if he had unexpectedly blundered his way on to an alien spaceship, rocketing towards a planet where intimate experiments were about to be conducted on his person.

Alexi was lying on the master bed, with his shirt off. The *curandero* was standing above him, a bunch of lighted twigs in one hand, chanting. The room was suffused with the scent of burning sage and rosemary.

Spola screwed up his eyes against the acrid smoke. 'What's he doing?'

Yola, who was sitting on a chair near the bed, put a finger to her lips.

Spola had the good grace to hitch his shoulders apologetically and retreat outside.

Sabir hunched down beside Yola. He looked quizzically at her, but her concentration was all on Alexi. Without looking at him, she pointed briefly to her head and then to that of the *curandero*, making a circular movement with her hands to encompass both as one entity; to Sabir, she seemed to be implying that she was helping the *curandero* in some way, possibly along telepathic lines.

Sabir decided to let her get on with it. Alexi didn't look good and Sabir made up his mind that once all the mumbo-jumbo was over, he would exert as much pressure as he reasonably could to persuade Yola to allow Alexi to be treated in a hospital.

The *curandero* laid his burning twigs aside in a dish and moved to the end of the bed. He took Alexi's head in his hands and stood silently, with his eyes shut, in an attitude of intense concentration.

Sabir, who was not used to squatting, could feel his thighs beginning to constrict with the tension. He didn't dare to move, though, for fear of breaking the *curandero*'s trance. He glanced at Yola, hoping that she might somehow deduce his problem and offer him some guidance, but her gaze remained firmly fixed on the *curandero*.

Eventually, Sabir allowed himself to slide backwards down the wall of the caravan until he ended up with his rump on the floor and his legs stretched out beneath the bed. Nobody noticed him. He began to breathe more freely again. Then the cramp hit him.

Grasping his left thigh with both hands, he squeezed for all he was worth, writhing away from the bed, his teeth locked together in a rictus of pain. He wanted to yell but didn't dare to disrupt proceedings any further than he already had.

Like a plastic match unravelling, he turned first on

to his front, one leg stretched out behind him, and then jack-knifed over on to his side when the cramp came back.

He was beyond caring what anybody else thought of him by this time, and began to drag himself, like a slug, towards the door, beyond which the ever-watchful Sergeant Spola no doubt awaited him.

～

'I'm sorry. I didn't mean to disrupt proceedings like that. Only I got the cramp.'

Yola sat down beside him and began rubbing at his leg. Sabir was by now so far indoctrinated by gypsy custom that he looked guiltily around in case any of her women friends might see her and be outraged at her polluting – or being polluted by (he still didn't quite understand which) – a *gadje*.

'It's all right. The *curandero* is very happy. You took away much of Alexi's pain.'

'*I* took away Alexi's pain? You've got to be joking.'

'Yes. Under the *curandero*'s hands it transferred itself to you. You must feel very close to Alexi. I had thought that it would transfer to me.'

Sabir was still in far too much pain to even consider laughing. 'How long does this transfer last?'

'Oh, a few minutes only. You are a . . .' Yola hesitated.

'No. Don't tell me. A conduit?'

'What is that?'

'Something which leads to something else.'

She nodded. 'Yes. You are a conduit. Unless the pain finds somewhere else to go, it will stay with Alexi. That was why I came to help. But the pain would not necessarily find me. It might find another target, that could not deal with it. Then it would return, much stronger, and Alexi might die. The *curandero* is very pleased with you.'

'That's big of him.'

'No. Don't laugh, Damo. The *curandero* is a wise man. He is my teacher. But he says you, too, could be a *curandero*. A shaman. You have the capacity inside you. You only lack the will.'

'And any understanding of what the heck he's talking about.'

Yola smiled. She was beginning to understand Sabir's *gadje* diffidence by this time and to attribute less importance to it than heretofore. 'When he's finished with Alexi he wants to give you something.'

'Give me something?'

'Yes. I have explained to him about the eye-man, and he is very worried for us both. He picked up the evil on me that the eye-man left, and he has cleaned me free of it.'

'What? Like he was cleaning Alexi?'

'Yes. The Spanish call it *una limpia* – a cleansing. We don't really have a word for it, as no gypsy can be cleaned of their ability to pollute. But evil that another has planted on us may be taken off.'

'And the eye-man planted evil on you?'

'No. But his own evil was so strong that his connection to me – the relationship he forged with me when I was standing on the stool, waiting to be hanged – this was enough to pollute me.'

Sabir shook his head in disbelief.

'Listen, Damo. The eye-man read a story to me at that time. A story of a woman being tortured by the Inquisition. This was a terrible thing to hear. The evil of this story settled on me like dust. I could feel it sifting through the bag covering my head, and settling about my shoulders. I could feel it eating into my soul and blanketing it with darkness. If I had died straight after hearing this story, as the eye-man intended, my *lacha* would have been tarnished, and my soul would have been sick before God.'

'Yola, how can someone else do such a thing to you? Your soul is your own.'

'Oh, no, Damo. No. No one owns their own soul. It is a gift. A part of God. And we take it back to Him when we die and offer it to Him as our sacrifice. Then we are judged on the strength of it. That is why the *curandero* needed to clean me. God works through him, without the *curandero* knowing how or why it is done, or why he has been chosen – just as God worked through the prophet Nostradamus, who was chosen to see things that other men could not. The same thing happened with your cramp. God chose you to take Alexi's pain away. He will be well now. You've no need to worry any more.'

Sabir watched Yola walk away from him and back towards the caravan.

One day he'd understand all this, surely? One day he'd re-attain the simplicity that he'd lost as a child – the simplicity that these people he loved appeared to have held on to in the face of every last obstruction that life cared to put in their way.

69

The *curandero* still travelled by horse-drawn caravan. He had found himself a pitch at a riding stables about two kilometres out of town, on the right bank of the Etang des Launes. His horse presented an unnatural slash of brown amidst the predominant white of the *gardien* ponies in the corral.

As Sabir approached, the *curandero* pointed to the ground outside his front steps. Yola was already squatting there, an expectant expression on her face.

Sabir gave a vehement shake of the head, one eye still fixed on Sergeant Spola who was lurking near his car at the roadside. 'I'm not squatting anywhere. Believe me. I've never had cramp like that before. And I don't want it again.'

The *curandero* hesitated, smiling, as if he didn't quite understand Sabir's use of the vernacular. Then he disappeared inside the caravan.

'He understands French, doesn't he?' Sabir whispered.

'He speaks Sinto, Calo, Spanish and Romani-Cib. French is his fifth language.' Yola looked embarrassed, as if the mere subject of how much the *curandero* might or might not be able to understand was subtly out of order.

'What's his name?'

'You never use his name. People just call him *curandero*. When he became a shaman, he lost his name, his family, and all that connected him to the tribe.'

'But I thought you said he was the cousin of your father?'

'He is the cousin of my father. He was that before he became a shaman. And my father is dead. So he is still the cousin of my father. They called him Alfego, back then. Alfego Zenavir. Now he is simply *curandero*.'

Sabir was saved from further bewilderment when the *curandero* re-emerged, brandishing a stool. 'Sit. Sit here. No cramp. Ha ha!'

'Yes. No cramp. Cramp a bad thing.' Sabir looked uncertainly at the stool.

'Bad thing? No. A good thing. You take pain from Alexi. Very good. Cramp not hurt you. You a young man. Soon gone.'

'Soon gone. Yes.' Sabir didn't sound convinced. He backed on to the stool, stretching his leg carefully out ahead of him like a gout victim.

'You married already?'

Sabir glanced at Yola, unsure what the *curandero* was getting at. But Yola was doing her usual trick of concentrating intensely on the *curandero*, and pointedly refusing to notice any strategies Sabir might care to use to gain her attention.

'No. Not married. No.'

'Good. Good. This is good. A shaman should never marry.'

'But I'm not a shaman.'

'Not yet. Not yet. Ho ho.'

Sabir was beginning to wonder whether the *curandero* might not in fact be short of a few marbles – but the stern expression on Yola's face was enough to disabuse him of that notion.

After a short pause for prayer, the *curandero* felt inside his shirt and drew out a necklet, which he placed around Yola's neck. He touched her once with his finger, along the parting of her hair. Sabir realised that he was speaking to her in Sinto.

Then the *curandero* moved across to him. After another pause for prayer, the man felt around inside his shirt and drew out a second necklet. He placed it around Sabir's neck and then took Sabir's head in both his hands. He stood for a long time, his eyes shut, holding Sabir's head. After a while Sabir felt his eyes closing and a rather comforting darkness obtrude itself upon the surrounding day.

With no apparent effort, Sabir suddenly found himself watching the back of his own eyes – rather as an intruder in a cinema might find himself staring at the reverse image on the rear of a projection screen. First, the approaching darkness turned to a roseate hue, like water that has been imbrued with blood. Then a tiny face seemed to form itself a long way away from him. As he watched, the face slowly began to approach, gaining in precision the closer it came, until Sabir was able to make out his own features clearly imprinted on its physiognomy. The face came closer still, until it passed clean through the notional screen in front of him, to disappear via the rear of Sabir's own head.

The *curandero* moved away from him, nodding in satisfaction.

Sabir opened his eyes as wide as they would go. He felt tempted to stretch himself – rather like a cormorant drying its wings on a rock – but for some reason he felt physically abashed in front of the *curandero* and contented himself with a series of small circular movements of the shoulders. 'I saw my own face approaching me. Then it seemed to pass right through me. Is that normal?'

The *curandero* nodded again, as if what Sabir said did not surprise him. But he seemed in no mood to speak.

'What is this?' Sabir pointed to the necklet resting just above his sternum.

'Samana's daughter will tell you. I am tired. I will

sleep.' The *curandero* raised a hand in farewell and ducked in through the doorway of his caravan.

Sabir glanced down at Yola to see what effect the *curandero*'s strange behaviour might be having on her. To his astonishment, she was crying. 'What is it? What did he say to you?'

Yola shook her head. She ran the back of her hand across her eyes like a child.

'Come on. Please tell me. I'm completely out of my depth here. That much must be obvious.'

Yola sighed. She took a deep breath. 'The *curandero* told me that I would never make a shamaness. That God had chosen another path for me – a path that was harder to accept, more humbling, and with no certainty of achievement. That I wasn't to question this path in any way. I was simply to follow it.'

'What does he know? Why would he tell you such a thing? What gives him the right?'

Yola looked at Sabir in shock. 'Oh, the *curandero* knows. He is taken away in his dreams by an animal spirit. He is shown many things. He may not influence events, however, but only prepare people to accept them. That is his function.'

Sabir masked his bewilderment with enquiry. 'Why did he touch you like that? Along the hairline? It seemed to hold some significance for him.'

'He was cementing both halves of my body together.'

'I'm sorry?'

'If I am to succeed in what I have been chosen to do, the two halves of my body must not be split one from another.'

'I'm sorry, Yola. But I still don't understand.'

Yola stood up. She glanced uncertainly towards Sergeant Spola, then allowed her voice to drop to a whisper. 'We are all made in two halves, Damo. When God cooked us in His oven, He fused the two parts together into one mould. But each part still looked in a different direction – one to the past and one to the future. When both parts are reversed and brought back together – by illness, perhaps, or by the actions of a *curandero* – then this person, from that moment onwards, will look only to the present. They will live entirely in the present.' Yola searched for the right words to convey her meaning. 'They will be of service. Yes. That is it. They will be able to be of service.'

Sensing that they were finally aware of him once again, the ever-courteous Sergeant Spola raised his shoulders quizzically from over by the road. He had long acknowledged that he was way out of his depth with these gypsies, but as time trickled past, he was increasingly dreading the somewhat inevitable call from Captain Calque about his charges.

For Sergeant Spola had belatedly realised that he could never satisfactorily explain how he had allowed the girl to persuade him to abandon Alexi to his sickbed in favour of this visit to the *curandero*. Not even to himself could he explain it.

As he stood by his car, willing the gypsies to give up what they were doing and hurry back to him, he experienced a sudden desperate urge to return and check on his other charge in case someone, somewhere, had taken advantage of his good nature and was planning to land him in the horseshit.

Sabir raised a placatory hand. Then he turned his attention back to Yola. 'And these things around our necks?'

'They are for killing ourselves.'

'What?'

'The *curandero* fears for our lives against the eye-

371

man. He senses that the eye-man will hurt us simply out of anger if we fall into his hands again. Inside this vial is the distilled venom of the Couleuvre de Montpellier. That is a poisonous snake that lives in the south-western part of France. Injected into the bloodstream, it will kill in under a minute. Taken by the throat . . .'

'Taken by the throat?'

'Swallowed. Drunk like a liquid. Imbibed. Then it will take fifteen minutes.'

'You can't mean it. Are you seriously telling me that the *curandero* has provided us with a poison? Like the sort they used to give spies who risked torture by the Gestapo?'

'I don't know who the Gestapo are, Damo, but I doubt very much that they are as terrible as the eye-man. If he takes me again, I will drink this. I will go to God intact and with my *lacha* untarnished. You must promise me that you will do the same.'

70
—

Joris Calque was a deeply unhappy man. Only once in his life had he been responsible for breaking the news to a family of the death of their only son, and that time he had been covering for another officer who was injured in the same engagement. He had been in no way responsible. Far from it, in fact.

This was another matter entirely. His proximity to Marseille, Macron's home town, and the fact that

Macron had died violently, at the hands of a murderer, and on his watch, made Calque's job all the harder. It had somehow become a priority for him to deliver the news personally.

It was obvious to everyone now that the eye-man had somehow escaped the net. Helicopters and spotter-planes had criss-crossed the entire area below the N572 Arles to Vauvert road – including the vast span of country delimited by the Parc Naturel Régional de Camargue – and they had found nothing. The eye-man appeared to be a wraith. CRS units had inspected every building, every *bergerie*, and every ruin. They had stopped every car going either in or out of the Parc Naturel. It was an easy place to seal off. You had the sea on one side and the marshes on the other. Few roads bisected it and those that did were flat, with traffic visible for miles in every direction. It should have been child's play. Instead, Calque could feel his position as chief coordinator of the investigation becoming more precarious by the minute.

Macron's family were waiting for him at the family bakery. A female police officer had gathered them all together, without being allowed to tell them the exact reason for their convocation. This was established practice. Dread, in consequence, laced the atmosphere like ether.

Calque was visibly surprised to find that not only were Macron's father, mother and sister present, but also a bevy of aunts, uncles, cousins, and even, or so it appeared, three out of four of his grandparents. It occurred to Calque that the smell of freshly baking bread would be forever linked in his mind with images of Macron's death.

'I am grateful that you are all here together. It will make what I have to tell you easier to bear.'

'Our son. He is dead.' It was Macron's father. He was

still wearing his bakery whites and a hairnet. As he spoke he took off the hairnet, as though it were in some way disrespectful.

'Yes. He was killed late last night.' Calque paused. He needed a cigarette badly. He wanted to be able to lean over and light it, and then to use the movement as a convenient means of masking the vast sea of faces that were now focusing on him with the greediness of anticipated grief. 'He was killed by a murderer who was holding a woman hostage. Paul arrived a little before the main body of the force. The woman was in imminent danger. She had a rope around her neck, and her kidnapper was threatening to hang her. Paul knew that the man had killed before. A security guard, up in Rocamadour. And another man. In Paris. He therefore decided to intervene.'

'What happened to Paul's killer? Do you have him?' This, from one of the cousins.

Calque realised that he had been casting his seed on stony ground. Macron's family must inevitably have heard about the possible death of a police officer on the radio or TV, and have come to their own conclusions when the Police Nationale had convoked them. They hadn't needed his rubber-stamping. All he could reasonably do, in the circumstances, was to provide them with any information they needed, and then abandon them to the grieving process. He certainly couldn't use them to rinse out his conscience. 'No. We don't have him yet. But we soon will. Before he died, Paul was able to get off two shots. It is not public knowledge yet – and we would prefer that you keep the information to yourselves – but the killer was badly injured by one of Paul's bullets. He is on the run somewhere inside the Parc Naturel. The whole place is sealed off. More than a hundred policemen are out there searching for him as we speak.' Calque was desperately

374

trying to look away from the scenes in front of him – to concentrate on the questions that the peripheral family were firing off at him. But he was unable to take his eyes off Macron's mother.

She resembled her son in an uncanny way. Upon hearing the confirmation of her boy's death, she had instantly turned for comfort to her husband, and now she clung to his waist, crying silently, the baking dust from his apron coating her face like whitewash.

When Calque was finally able to withdraw, one of Macron's male relatives followed him out into the street. Calque turned to face him, half prepared for a physical assault. The man looked hard and fit. He had a razor-strop haircut. Indeterminate tattoo-ends burst from his sleeves to scatter out across the backs of his hands like varicose veins.

Calque regretted that the policewoman had remained inside with the rest of the family – the presence of a uniform might have acted as something of a curb.

But the man did not approach Calque in an aggressive manner. In fact he screwed his face up questioningly, and Calque soon realised that something other than Macron's death was foremost on his mind.

'Paul telephoned me yesterday. Did you know that? But I wasn't there. My mother took the message. I'm a joiner, these days. I have a lot of work on.'

'Yes? You are a joiner these days? An excellent profession.' Calque had not intended to sound abrupt but the words came out defensively, despite his best intentions.

The man narrowed his eyes. 'He said you were looking for a man who was in the Legion. A killer. That you thought the Legion would hold back the information that you needed. That they would force you to go through the usual fucking bureaucratic hoops they always use to protect their people with. That was what he said.'

Calque nodded in sudden understanding. 'Paul told me about you. You are the cousin who was in the Legion. I should have realised.' He was on the verge of saying 'because you people get a particular look – like a walking slab of testosterone – and because you use "fucking" every other word', but he somehow managed to control himself. 'You were also in prison, were you not?'

The man looked away up the street. Something seemed to be irritating him. After a moment he turned back to Calque. He forced his hands inside his pockets, as if he felt that the material itself might prevent them from rioting – but still the hands thrust themselves towards Calque as if they wished to break through the cloth and throttle him. 'I'm going to forget you said that. And that you're a fucking policeman. I don't like fucking policemen. For the most part they're no fucking better than the cunts they bang up.' He clamped his mouth tightly shut. Then he snorted long-sufferingly and glanced back down the street. 'Paul was my cousin, even though he was a fucking *bédi*. This shit-heap killed him, you say? I was in the Legion for twenty fucking years. I ended up a fucking quartermaster. Do you want to ask me anything? Or do you want to scuttle back to fucking Headquarters and check out my criminal fucking record first?'

Calque's decision was instantaneous. 'I want to ask you something.'

The man's face changed – becoming lighter, less enclosed. 'Fire away then.'

'Do you remember a man with strange eyes? Eyes with no whites to them?'

'Go on.'

'This man may be French. But he might also have been pretending to be a foreigner to get into the ranks of the Legion as a soldier, and not an officer.'

'Give me more.'

Calque shrugged. 'I know people change their names when they enter the Legion. But this man was a Count. Brought up as an aristocrat. In a family with servants and money. His original name may have been de Bale. Rocha de Bale. He would not have fitted easily into the role of a common soldier. He would have stuck out. Not only because of his eyes, but also on account of his attitude. He would have been used to leading, not being led. To giving orders, not taking them.' Calque's head snapped back like a turtle's. 'You know him, don't you?'

The man nodded. 'Forget Rocha de Bale. And forget leading. This cunt called himself Achor Bale. And he was a loner. He pronounced his name like an Englishman would. We never knew where he came from. He was crazy. You didn't want to get on the wrong side of him. We're tough in the Legion. That's normal. But he was tougher. I never thought I'd ever have to think about the cocksucker again.'

'What do you mean?'

'In Chad. During the 1980s. The fucker started a riot. On purpose, I would say. But the authorities exonerated him because no one dared to testify against him. A friend of mine was killed during that action. I would have testified. But I wasn't there. I was at the *baisodrome*, wasting my pay on porking blood sausage. You know what I mean? So I knew nothing about it. The cunts wouldn't listen to me. But I knew. He was an evil fucking bastard. Not quite right in the head. Too much interested in guns and killing. Even for a fucking soldier.'

Calque put away his notebook. 'And the eyes? That's true? That he has no whites to his eyes?'

Macron's cousin turned on his heel and walked back inside the bakery.

71

Bale awoke shivering. He had been dreaming, and in his dream, Madame, his mother, was beating him about the shoulders with a coat hanger for some imagined slight. He kept on crying out – 'No, Madame, no!' – but still she continued hitting him.

It was dark. There were no other sounds from inside the house.

Bale shunted himself backwards, until he was able to prop himself against a beam. His fist was sore, where he had lashed out to defend himself during the dreamed attack, and his neck and his shoulder felt raw – as if they had been scalded with boiling water and then scrubbed with an emery board.

He cracked on his torch and checked out the loft. Perhaps he could kill a rat or a squirrel and eat it? But no. He wouldn't be quick enough any more.

He knew that he didn't dare venture downstairs yet to check out whether any food had been left in the kitchen, or to draw some water. The *flics* might have left a watchman behind to protect their crime scene from ghouls and curiosity seekers – it was comforting to think that such people still existed, and that not everything in this life had been relegated to normalisation and mediocrity.

But water he did need. And urgently. He had drunk his own urine on three occasions now, and had used the residue to disinfect his wounds, but he knew, from lectures with the Legion, that there was no earthly sense in doing that again. He would be contributing to his own certain death.

How many hours had he been up here? How many days? Bale had no idea of time any more.

Why was he here? Ah yes. The prophecies. He needed to find the prophecies.

He allowed his head to drop back on to his chest. By now the blanket he had been using as a pressure pad had congealed to his wound – he didn't dare separate the two for fear of starting the blood flow up again.

For the first time in many years he wanted to go home. He wanted the comfort of his own bedroom, and not the anonymous hotels that he had been forced to live in for so long. He wanted the respect and the support of the brothers and sisters that he had grown up with. And he wanted Madame, his mother, to publicly acknowledge his achievements for the Corpus Maleficus, and to give him his due.

Bale was tired. He needed rest. And treatment for his wound. He was fed up with being hard, and living like a wolf. Fed up with being hunted by people who were not worthy to tie his bootlaces.

He lay on his belly and dragged himself towards the hatch cover. If he didn't move now, he would die. It was as simple as that.

For he had suddenly understood that he was hallucinating. That this temporary helplessness of his was just another strategy of the Devil's to unman him – to make him weak.

Bale reached the hatch cover and dragged it to one side. He stared down into the empty bedroom.

It was dark in there. The shutters were open and it was night. There were no lights anywhere. The police had left. Surely they had left.

He listened, through the rushing of blood in his head, for any inexplicable sounds.

There were none.

He eased his legs through the hatch cover. For a long time he sat on the lip of the hatch staring down at the floor. Finally he cracked on his torch and tried to estimate the total drop.

Ten feet. Enough to break a leg or sprain an ankle.

But he didn't have the strength left to let down the chair. Didn't have the agility to hang from the hatch and feel for it with his legs.

He switched off his torch and slid it back inside his shirt.

Then he twisted on his good arm and dropped into the void.

72
—

Yola watched the two policemen from her hiding place at the edge of the wood. They were huddled in the shelter of the *gardien*'s *cabane*, smoking and talking. So this is what the *flics* call a search, she thought to herself. No wonder the eye-man hasn't been found. Satisfied that the two men could not possibly see her, she settled down to wait for the further twenty minutes or so until full dusk.

Bouboul had dropped Yola at the Bac, thirty minutes before, and had then driven on to Arles, with his son-in-law, Rezso, to retrieve Sabir's Audi. Later, Rezso would come back with the Audi to pick her up.

At first Sabir had refused to allow Yola to go and collect the prophecies. It was too dangerous. The job should be his. He was head of the family now. His word should count for something. But Sergeant Spola's stolid and ever-watchful presence had eventually decided the matter – there was no way Sabir could go anywhere without his say-so.

Night-time would be different, though. The man had to sleep. If Sabir could manage to give Spola the slip, Bouboul had agreed to drive him back to the Maset, where Yola and Reszo would arrange to meet him with the prophecies. Sabir would then have both the time and the privacy necessary to translate them.

Before dawn, Reszo would come back with the car and collect Sabir and deliver him back to the caravan, just in time to meet an awaking Sergeant Spola. This was the plan, anyway. It had the virtue of simplicity, it protected the prophecies, and it would serve to keep the police nicely out of the frame.

Yola had already established that the investigation had moved on, and that the Maset would be empty. Sergeant Spola was a man who respected his stomach. Yola had offered him wild boar stew with dumplings for his lunch, instead of his customary chicken sandwich. Spola had proved particularly amenable after that – especially as the wild boar was twinned with about a litre and a half of Costières de Nîmes, and a follow-up cognac. He had confirmed to her that by now, a day and a half after the attack, the Maset would be bolted and sealed with police tape, and to all intents and purposes abandoned until next needed. All available manpower would be seconded in the search for the eye-man. What did she think? That the police left people dotted around the countryside guarding old crime scenes?

The two *flics* at the *cabane* got up and stretched themselves. One of them walked a few yards, unzipped his fly and took a leak. The other flashed his torch around the clearing, lingering on the security tape marking the spot where Gavril had been found.

'Do you think murderers really come back to the spot they've offed someone?'

'Shit, no. And particularly not when they've got a bullet in them, they're hungry, and they've got sniffer dogs chewing up their arses. The bastard's probably lying dead behind a bush. Or else he fell off his horse into a bog and drowned. That's why we can't find him. The wild pigs probably got him. They can eat a man, teeth and all, in under an hour. Did you know that? All the murderer has to do is to get rid of the spleen. They don't like that for some reason.'

'Bullshit.'

'Yes. I thought so too.'

Yola had walked into the wood by the path, just as Alexi had described it to her, leaving strips of white paper at five-metre intervals to guide herself back to the road when it was dark. In her head she had marked the position of the solitary cypress tree beneath which the prophecies lay buried. If the police stayed where they were, however, she would have no possibility – even if she used the woodland as cover – of reaching the prophecies unseen. The cypress tree was far too exposed.

'Shall we take a turn about the forest?'

'Fuck that. Let's go back to the *cabane*. Light a fire. I forgot my gloves and it's getting cold.'

Yola could see their silhouettes approaching her. What were they after? Wood? How could she explain away her presence if they stumbled on her? They'd be so keen to get gold stars from Calque that they'd probably bundle her back with them in their *poullailler ambulant* – their travelling henhouse. Wasn't that what Alexi called Black Marias? And Calque was certainly no fool. He would smell a rat straight away. It wouldn't take him long to

382

figure out that she was after the prophecies and that they weren't lost at all.

As the policemen approached, Yola pressed herself into the ground and began to pray.

The first policeman stopped three or four feet away from her. 'Can you see any dead trees? We just need a branch or two.'

The second policeman switched on his torch and swung it in an arc above their heads. At that exact moment his cellphone rang. He tossed the torch to his companion and felt for the phone. As the torch passed near her head, Yola could feel the light from its beam skimming across her body. She stiffened, sure of discovery.

'What's that you say? We've got to pull out? What are you talking about?' The second policeman was listening intently to the voice at the other end of the line. He grunted from time to time, and Yola could almost sense him glancing across at the first policeman, who was holding the lighted torch with its beam focused down along the seam of his trousers.

The second policeman snapped the cellphone shut. 'That Parisian Captain they've sicced on us thinks he's found out where the guy lives. Reckons, if he really has slipped the net, that he's sure to make for there. We're all wanted. This time all we've got to do is seal off the whole of the St-Tropez peninsula, from just outside Cavalaire-sur-Mer, via La Croix-Valmer and Cogolin, to Port Grimaud. Can you credit it? That's sixty fucking kilometres.'

'More like thirty.'

'What do you care? There's no sleep for us tonight.'

Yola turned on to her back, when they eventually walked away, and gazed up in wonder at the first star of the evening.

73

Somewhat to his surprise Calque found himself regretting the lack of Macron's presence as he made his way across the courtyard and back towards the Comtesse de Bale's house. Calque did not consider himself a sentimental man, and Macron had, after all, largely brought his death upon himself – but there had been something magnificently irritating about him as a person, an irritation which had, in its turn, fed Calque's over-emphatic sense of self. He concluded that Macron had acted as a kind of straight man to his iconoclast, and that he was missing having an excuse for being grumpy.

He recalled, too, his delight when Macron had leapt to his defence when the Countess had questioned his knowledge about the Pairs de France and the French nobility. You had to hand it to the man – he might have been a bigot but he had never been predictable.

The *soignée* private secretary in the tweed and cashmere twinset emerged from the house to greet him – this time, though, she was wearing a silk one-piece dress in burgundy, which made her look even more like a countess than the Countess herself. Calque searched through his memory banks for her name. 'Madame Mastigou?'

'Captain Calque.' Her eyes skated over his shoulders to take in the detachment of eight police officers bringing up his rear. 'And your assistant?'

'Dead, Madame. Killed by the adopted son of your employer.'

Madame Mastigou took an inadvertent pace backwards. 'I am sure that cannot be so.'

'I, too, trust that I have been misinformed. I have a search warrant, however, for these premises, which I intend to exercise immediately. These officers will accompany me inside. They will obviously respect both Madame la Comtesse's property and her privacy. But I must ask that no one interfere with them during the course of their duties.'

'I must go and warn Madame la Comtesse.'

'I shall accompany you.'

Madame Mastigou hesitated. 'May I see the warrant?'

'Of course.' Calque felt in his pocket and handed her the document.

'May I copy this?'

'No, Madame. A copy will be made available to Madame la Comtesse's lawyers when and if they desire it.'

'Very well then. Please come with me.'

Calque nodded to his officers. They fanned out across the courtyard. Four of the officers waited patiently at the foot of the stairs for Calque and Madame Mastigou to enter the house, before clattering up the steps behind them to begin their search.

'Do you seriously intend to implicate the Count in the killing of your assistant?'

'When did you last see the Count, Madame?'

Madame Mastigou hesitated. 'Some years ago now.'

'Then you may take it from me. He has changed.'

~

'I see that you have discarded the arm sling, Captain Calque. And your nose. It is healing. A great improvement.'

'It is kind of you to notice, Countess.'

The Countess sat down. Madame Mastigou fetched a chair and placed it behind the Countess and a little to one side – she seated herself demurely, both knees pressed together, her ankles tucked beneath her and lightly crossed. Finishing school, thought Calque. Switzerland, probably. She sits just like the Queen of England.

This time, the Countess waved the footman away without bothering to order coffee. 'It is nonsense, of course, to suspect my son of violence.'

'I don't suspect your son of violence, Countess. I formally accuse him of it. We have witnesses. In fact I am one myself. Thanks to the condition of his eyes, he does, after all, stand out from the crowd, does he not?' He glanced across at her, his head tilted to one side in polite enquiry. With no answer forthcoming, Calque decided to press his luck. 'The question I must ask – the question that really troubles me – is not whether he has done these things, but why?'

'Whatever he has done he has done for the best.'

Calque sat up straighter, his antennae flaring. 'You cannot be serious, Madame. He has tortured and killed a gypsy in Paris. Committed grievous bodily harm on three people, including a Spanish policeman and two casual passers-by. He has killed a security guard at the shrine at Rocamadour. Tortured and killed another gypsy in the Camargue, and two days ago he shot dead my assistant during a siege in which he was threatening to hang the sister of the man he killed in Paris. And all this to discover some prophecies that may or may not be true – that may or may not be by the prophet Nostradamus. I suspect, Madame, that you are not as unaware as you would have me believe of the true reasons behind this horrendous chain of events.'

'Is that another of your formal accusations, Captain?

If so, I would remind you that there is a third party present.'

'That was not a formal accusation, Madame. Formal accusations are for the courts. I am conducting an investigation. I need to stop your son before he can do any more harm.'

'What you say about my son is grotesque. Your accusations are entirely without foundation.'

'And you, Madame Mastigou? Have you anything at all to add?'

'Nothing, Captain. Madame la Comtesse is not well. I consider it in the worst possible taste that you continue this investigation under such conditions.'

The Countess stood up. 'I have decided what I shall do, Mathilde. I shall telephone the Minister of the Interior. He is a cousin of my friend, Babette de Montmorigny. We shall soon have this state of affairs rectified.'

Calque also stood up. 'You must do as you see fit, Madame.'

One of the uniformed officers burst into the room. 'Captain, I think you should see this.'

Calque shot the man a scowl. 'See what? I am conducting an interview.'

'A room, Sir. A secret room. Monceau found it by accident when he was investigating the library.'

Calque turned to the Countess, his eyes glittering.

'It is not a secret room, Captain Calque. Everyone in my household knows about it. Had you asked me, I would have directed you to it.'

'Of course, Countess. I understand that.' With both hands anchored firmly behind his back, Calque followed his subordinate out of the door.

74

The room was approached through a tailored entrance, masterfully concealed within the library shelving.

'Who discovered this?'

'I did, Sir.'

'How does it open?'

The officer swung the door shut. It sealed itself flush against the stacks. The officer then bent forwards and pressed against the ribbed spine of three books, situated near the floor. The door sprung back open again.

'How did you know which books to press?'

'I watched the footman, Sir. He came in here when he thought we weren't looking and fiddled with the catch. I think he was trying to lock it so that no one could inadvertently trigger the mechanism. At least that's what he told me.'

'Do you mean he was worried for our safety? That the door might spring back and strike one of us unexpectedly?'

'That was most likely it, Sir.'

Calque smiled. If he had read the Countess's character rightly, that footman was for the chop. It was always a good thing to have a disgruntled employee cannoning around. Valuable information could be gleaned. Backs might be stabbed.

Calque ducked through the entranceway. He straightened up inside the room, then gave a low, appreciative whistle.

A large rectangular table formed the centrepiece of the room. Thirteen chairs were collected around it. On the wall behind each chair was a coat of arms and a series of quarterings. Calque recognised some of them. But they were not those of the twelve Pairs de France one would have expected, given the tenor of his present company.

'This room hasn't been opened since my husband's death. There is nothing in here of any interest to your people.'

Calque ran his hand across the table. 'Dusted, though. Someone must have been in here a good deal more recently than your husband's death.'

'My footman. Of course. Keeping the room tidy would form part of his duties.'

'As would locking the doors if strangers come around?'

The Countess looked away. Madame Mastigou tried to take hold of her hand but found herself brushed off.

'Lavigny, I want these heraldic shields photographed.'

'I would rather you didn't do that, Captain. They have nothing whatsoever to do with your investigation.'

'On the contrary, Madame. I believe they have every thing to do with my investigation.'

'This room is a private place, Captain. A club room. A place where people of like minds used to meet to discuss serious issues in discreet and conducive surroundings. As I said, the room has not been used since my husband's death. Some of the families to whom these coats of arms belong may even be ignorant of their presence in this room. I would be grateful for that state of affairs to continue.'

'I see no billiard table. No bar. It's a funny type of club room. What's this, for instance?' Calque pointed to a chalice, locked inside its very own tantalus. 'And these initials engraved on it? CM.'

The Countess looked as though she had been bitten by an adder.

'Sir?'

'Yes.'

'There's a roll of parchment here. With seals on it. It's heavy, too. It must have wooden rollers or something.'

Calque indicated that the parchment should be spread out on the table.

'Please don't touch that, Captain. It is very valuable.'

'I have a search warrant, Madame. I may touch anything I please. I will endeavour not to smear it with my fingers however.' Calque bent forwards and perused the document.

The Countess and Madame Mastigou stood frozen against the interior wall of the sanctum.

'Lavigny. Would you kindly escort the Countess and Madame Mastigou out of the room. This may take some time. And fetch me a magnifying glass.'

75

The first thing Sabir did when Bouboul dropped him back at the Maset was to light the fire for comfort. The night was cold, and he felt an indefinable frisson overtake his body as he glanced up the corridor towards the place where Macron's body had lain. Shaking his head in disgust at his own susceptibilities, he began the search for candles.

The old house seemed to echo back his footfalls as he padded round the room – so much so that he found himself curiously unwilling to venture further up the corridor towards the kitchen. After a desultory five-minute search he was relieved to discover three candles still lying on the floor, where they had been overset by the eye-man's use of the fire extinguisher, two nights before.

Lighting them, and then seeing his shadow reflected around the room like a torchlit *danse macabre*, Sabir wondered, not for the first time, how he had ever allowed Yola to persuade him to come back and use the Maset? The rationale was certainly there – for Les Saintes-Maries remained tightly sealed by the police in their search for the eye-man, with egress relatively easy, and ingress more controlled.

But since he had last been here the Maset seemed to have transformed itself into a place of doom. Sabir now felt distinctly uncomfortable in using the location of someone's brutal murder for what he understood might well turn out to be a flippant journey up a no-through-road. In fact it brought home to him, yet again, just how differently the Manouche viewed death when compared to the rather sentimental, post-Victorian way he still viewed it himself.

It was all very well for him to sit here and fantasise about the nature of the prophecies – in reality there was a fair chance that the bamboo tube didn't even contain them, and would instead prove full of dust. What if the weevils had got in? Four hundred and fifty years was a long time for anything to survive, much less parchment.

He sat down on the sofa. After a moment he straightened up the French dictionary which he had brought with him until its edges accorded with the border of the table. Then he lined up his pen and paper beside the dictionary. Bouboul had loaned him a large-faced, gaudy watch, and Sabir now laid this on the table next to the other accoutrements. The familiar movements provided him with some measure of comfort.

He glanced back over his shoulder towards the corridor. The fire was burning well by this time and he began to feel a little more secure in his isolation. Yola would find the prophecies, if anyone could. When she arrived at the Maset, he would take the prophecies from her and send her straight back to Les Saintes-Maries with Reszo. He was fine alone here. He would have the rest of the night in which to translate and copy the prophecies. From that moment on he would not let them out of his sight.

Come morning, he would send the originals by courier to his publisher in New York. Then he would work on the copies until he had milked out their full meaning. With the prophecies skilfully interleaved with the story of their discovery, he would have a sure-fire bestseller on his hands. It would easily bring in enough to make them all rich. Alexi could marry Yola and end up Bulibasha, and Sabir could write his own ticket.

Twenty more minutes. It couldn't take longer than that. Then he would have one of the great untold secrets of the world within his grasp.

There was a crash from upstairs. Then silence.

Sabir sprang to his feet. The hairs on the back of his neck stood erect, like the spine fur of a dog. Holy heck, what had that been? He stood listening, but there was only silence. Then, in the distance, he heard the approaching drone of a car.

With a final, furtive glance over his shoulder, Sabir hurried outside. It had probably only been a cupboard door falling open. Or maybe the police had moved something – a mosquito screen, perhaps? – and the wretched thing had stood there, teetering, until a gust of wind had finally finished off the job and blown it over. Perhaps the noise had even come from outside? From the roof, maybe?

He glanced up at the house as he stood waiting for the Audi to make its way up the track towards him. Hell. And now here was another thing – he'd have to come to a reckoning sooner or later with his friend John Tone about the theft of his car.

Sabir squinted into the headlights. Yes, there was Yola's outline in the passenger seat. And that of Bouboul's nephew in the driving seat beside her. Alexi was safely tucked up in his bed back in Les Saintes-Maries, with Sabir next door, in the guest bunk. Or at least that was what Sergeant Spola had been persuaded to think.

Sabir walked towards the car. He could feel the night wind pick at his hair. He motioned downwards with his hands, indicating that Reszo should douse the lights. As far as he knew, there were still policemen dotted all around the marshes and he didn't want to draw anyone's attention back to the Maset.

'Do you have them?'

Yola felt inside her coat. Her face looked small and vulnerable in the light of Sabir's torch. She handed Sabir the bamboo tube. Then she glanced towards the house and shivered.

'Did you have any trouble?'

'Two policemen. They were using the *cabane* for shelter. They nearly found me. But they were called away at the last moment.'

'Called away?'

'I overheard one of them talking on his cellphone. Captain Calque knows where the eye-man has escaped to. It is somewhere over towards St-Tropez. All the police are going there now. They aren't interested in here any longer.'

'Thank God for that.'

'Do you want me to come in with you?'

'No. I have the fire going. And some candles. I'll be all right.'

'Bouboul will collect you just before dawn. Are you sure you don't want to come back with us now?'

'Too dangerous. Sergeant Spola might smell a rat. He's not as stupid as he looks.'

'Yes he is.'

Sabir laughed.

Yola glanced once more towards the house. Then she climbed back inside the car. 'I don't like this place. It was wrong of me to suggest it as a rendezvous.'

'Where else could we have used? This is by far the most convenient.'

'I suppose so.' She raised her hand uncertainly. 'Are you sure you won't change your mind?'

Sabir shook his head.

Reszo eased the car back down the track. When he was near the road he switched the lights back on.

Sabir watched their glow as it disappeared over the horizon. Then he turned back towards the house.

76

—

Captain Calque leaned back in his chair. The document laid out before him made no earthly sense. It purported to have been written on the express instructions of King Louis IX of France – and it was, indeed, dated 1228, two years after Louis had ascended to the throne, aged eleven. Which made him just thirteen or fourteen years old at the time he was credited with its conception. The seals, however, were definitely those of Saint Louis himself, and of his mother, Blanche of Castile; in those days, trying to fake such a thing as a royal seal would have seen you hung, drawn and quartered, with your ashes used for soap.

Three other signatures were appended beneath those of the King and his mother: Jean de Joinville, the King's counsellor (and, alongside Villehardouin and Froissart, one of France's greatest early historians); Geoffrey of Beaulieu, the King's confessor; and William of Chartres, the King's chaplain. Calque shook his head. He had studied de Joinville's *Histoire do Saint Louis* at university, and he knew for a fact that de Joinville would have been no more than four years old in 1228 – the others, well, it wouldn't take him long to find out their ages. But it suggested that the document – which appeared to grant a charter and cognisance to an association called the Corpus Maleficus – had been, in some sense at least, post-dated.

It was at that point that Calque remembered the chalice locked inside the tantalus, with its initials of CM. The coincidence, particularly in this hidden room, with its revocations of secrets, plots and cabals, struck him as an unlikely one. He glanced again at the document in front of him.

Grunting with concentration, he turned the document over and scrutinised its reverse side through the magnifying glass. Yes. Just as he'd suspected. There was the faint imprint of writing on the back. Backwards writing. The sort a left-hander might engineer if called upon to write in the manner of an Arab – that is to say from right to left. Calque knew that in medieval times the left side was considered the side of the Devil. *Sinister* in connotation as well as in Latin nomenclature, the concept had been carried across from the early Greek augurs, who believed that signs seen over the left shoulder foretold evil to come.

Calque drew the document nearer to the light. Finally, frustrated, he held it up in front of him. No dice. The writing was indecipherable – it would take an electron microscope to make any sense of it.

He cast his mind back to the Countess's words during their first meeting. Calque had asked her what the thirteenth Pair de France would have carried during the Coronation and she had answered: 'He wouldn't have carried anything, Captain. He would have protected.'

'Protected? Protected from whom?'

The Countess had given him an elliptical smile. 'From the Devil, of course.'

But how could a mere mortal be expected to protect the French Crown from the Devil?

Calque could feel the gradual dawning of some sort of understanding. The Corpus Maleficus. What did it mean? He summoned up his schoolboy Latin. *Corpus* meant body. It could also mean an association of people dedicated to achieving one end. And *Maleficus*? Mischief. Evildoing.

A body devoted to mischief and evildoing, then? Impossible, surely. And certainly not under the aegis of the saintly Louis, a man so pious that he felt that he had wasted his day if he hadn't attended two full Masses (plus all the offices), and who would then drag himself out of bed once again at midnight to dress for matins.

Then it must mean a body devoted to the eradication of such things. A body devoted to undermining the Devil. But how would one go about such a thing? Surely not homeopathically?

Calque stood up. It was time to talk to the Countess again.

77

Achor Bale lay where he had fallen. His wound had opened again and he could feel the blood pulsing weakly down his neck. In a moment he would move. There might be something in the kitchen with which to staunch the bleeding. Failing that, he could go out to the marshes and collect some sphagnum moss. In the meantime he would lie here on the floor and recuperate. Where was the hurry? No one knew he was here. No one was waiting for him.

Outside the house there was the crunch and hiss of a car.

The police. They'd sent a watchman after all. He and his partner would be almost certain to check through all the rooms before settling down for the night. Men did that sort of thing. It was a kind of superstition. A marching of the bounds. Something inherited from their caveman ancestors.

Bale dragged himself angrily towards the bed. He would lie underneath it. Whoever drew the short straw for upstairs would probably content himself with flashing his torch about inside the room. He'd be unlikely to bother with more. Why should he? It was only a crime scene.

Bale eased the Redhawk out of its holster. Maybe there would only be one of them? In that case he would overpower him and take the car. The Maset was so isolated that no one could possibly hear the shot.

His hand brushed against the cellphone concealed in his inside pocket. It might still have some juice left in it, if it hadn't been damaged in the fall. Perhaps he should call Madame, his mother, after all? Tell her he was coming home.

Or would the *flics* be monitoring the frequencies? Could they do that? He thought not. And they had no reason to suspect Madame, his mother, anyway.

No sounds from downstairs. The coppers were still outside. Probably checking the periphery.

Bale keyed in the number. He waited for the tone. The number took.

'Who is this?'

'It's the Count, Milouins. I need to speak to the Countess. Urgently.'

'The police, Sir. They know who you are. They are here.'

Bale closed his eyes. Had he expected this? Some fatalistic djinn whispered into his ear that he had. 'Did she give you a message for me? In case I called?'

'One word, Sir. *Fertigmachen*.'

'*Fertigmachen*?'

'She said you would understand, Sir. I must put the phone down now. They are coming.'

78

——

Bale slept for a little after that. He seemed to drift in and out of consciousness like a man given too little ether before an operation.

At one point he thought he heard footsteps coming up

the stairs and he pulled himself up on the side of the bed and waited, for five endless minutes, with his pistol at the ready. Then he slipped back into unconsciousness.

He awoke to a noise in the kitchen. This time it was certain. The rattling of pots. Someone was making themselves coffee. Bale could almost hear the pop of the butane gas. Smell the grounds.

He had to eat. To drink. The noise in the kitchen would disguise his footsteps. If there were two of them, *tant pis*. He would kill them both. He had the element of surprise on his side. The *flics* apparently thought he was on his way to Cap Camarat. That was a good thing. They must figure he had escaped their *cordon sanitaire*. They would be standing down in their dozens.

If he drove out in a police car, they would be flummoxed. He could dress up in one of their uniforms. Wear sunglasses.

In the middle of the night?

Bale shook his head slowly. Why did he have no energy any more? Why did he doze so much?

Water. He needed water. He would die without water. The blood loss had merely compounded the issue.

He forced himself to his feet. Then, holding the Redhawk down by his side, he stumbled towards the stairs.

Sabir held the bamboo tube out in front of him and cracked the wax seal. A strange odour assailed his nostrils. He allowed his mind to wander for a moment. The scent was sweet, and warm, and earthy at the same time. Frankincense? Yes, that was it. He held the tube to his nose and inhaled. Incredible. How had the scent stayed sealed inside the tube so long?

Sabir tapped the tube on the table. Some resin fell out. He felt the first pinpricks of anxiety. Could the frankincense have been used as a conservation agent? Or was the tube merely an incense container? Sabir tapped the tube again, this time a little harder and a little more fretfully. A thin roll of parchment tumbled on to his lap.

Sabir unrolled the parchment and spread it hastily out on to the table. It covered an area approximately six inches by eight. There was writing on both sides. In groups of four lines. It *was* the quatrains.

Sabir began the count. Twenty-six quatrains on one side. A further twenty-six on the other. He could feel the tension building inside his chest.

He pulled a sheet of paper towards him. Adhering scrupulously to the text, he copied down the first quatrain. Then he began his first tentative translation.

Calque looked across at the Countess. They were alone in the room, just as the Countess had insisted when Calque had requested the interview. 'So your son wants to come home?'

The Countess waved her hand in irritation, like someone trying to disperse a bad smell. 'I don't know what you're talking about.'

Calque sighed. 'My people intercepted a telephone call, Madame. Between your son and your footman, Milouins. The same footman found attempting to lock your secret meeting chamber. Your son used Milouins' name, so we are certain of our facts.'

'How do you know it was my son? Milouins may receive calls from whomever he likes. I am extremely tolerant with my servants. Unlike some people I know.'

'Your son introduced himself as the Count.'

The Countess's eyes went dead. 'I've never heard anything so absurd. My son has not called here for years. I told you. He left to join the Legion. Against my express instructions, I should add. I can't understand why you are harassing us in this manner.'

'Milouins passed your son a message.'

'Don't be so silly.'

'The message consisted of one word. A German word. *Fertigmachen.*'

'I don't speak German. Neither, I believe, does Milouins.'

'*Fertigmachen* means to end something. Or someone.'

'Really?'

'Yes. It can also mean to kill oneself.'

'Are you accusing me of asking my son to kill himself? Please, Captain. Give me credit for a modicum of maternal solicitude.'

'No. I believe you were asking your son to kill someone else. A man named Sabir. To kill Sabir and to make an end of the matter. I should tell you now that Sabir is in our protective custody. If your son attempts to murder him, he will be caught.'

'You said "to kill Sabir and to make an end of the matter". What matter can you possibly be referring to?'

'I know about the Corpus Maleficus, Madame. I've read the document you keep in the hidden room.'

'You know nothing about the Corpus Maleficus, Captain. And you did not read the document you cite. It is in cipher. You are trying to bluff me and I won't have it.'

'Aren't you concerned about your son's actions?'

'Deeply concerned, Captain. Is that what you want me to say? Deeply concerned.'

'Cipher experts will soon decrypt the parchment.'

'I think not.'

'But you know what it says?'

'Of course. My husband taught it to me verbatim when we first married. It is written in a language known only to an inner circle of chosen adepts. But I am an old woman now. I have entirely forgotten both the contents and the language. Just as I have forgotten the content of this conversation.'

'I think you are an evil woman, Madame. I think you are behind whatever your son is doing, and that you are happy to consign him to the Devil, if that accords with your and your society's interests.'

'You are talking nonsense, Captain. And you are entirely

402

out of your depth. What you say is pure speculation. Any jury would laugh you out of court.'

Calque stood up.

A strange look passed over the Countess's face. 'And you are wrong in another thing as well. I would never consign my son to the Devil, Captain. Never to the Devil. I can assure you of that.'

81

As he approached the final step in the seemingly endless line of stone steps leading to the ground floor, Bale slipped. He fell heavily against the wall – so heavily that he grunted in surprise when his shattered shoulder was caught a glancing blow by the balustrade.

Sabir sat up straighter in his chair. The police. They must have left someone here after all. Perhaps the man had simply crept upstairs to take a nap? It had been incredibly stupid of him not to have checked the house out before he settled down to start work.

Sabir gathered his papers together and went to stand with his back to the fire. There wasn't time to make for the door. Best to bluff it out. He could always claim that he had needed to come back for some of his belongings. The dictionary and the wad of papers would bear him out.

Bale emerged around the corner of the living-room door like an apparition fresh from the grave. His face was deathly pale, and his clotted eyes, in the light cast by the candles, resembled those of a demon. There was blood splattered down his front, and more blood smeared like an oil slick across his neck and shoulder. He held a pistol in his left hand, and as Sabir watched, horror-struck, Bale raised the pistol and brought it to bear on him.

For probably the first and only time in his life, Sabir acted entirely on impulse. He threw the dictionary at Bale, and in the exact same movement he twisted in place until he was on his knees, facing the fire. A split second before the sound of the shot, Sabir thrust the original parchment and his paper copy deep into the flames.

82

Sabir awoke with no idea of where he was. He tried to move but could not. A fearful, noxious odour assailed his nostrils. He attempted to free his arms but they were immersed in a kind of mud. The mud reached to just above his collarbone, leaving his head free. Sabir frantically tried to lever himself out, but he only slipped deeper into the morass.

'I wouldn't do that if I were you.'

Sabir looked up.

Bale was squatting above him. Six inches above Sabir's head was a small hole, little more than the width of man. Bale was balancing the trapdoor that normally sealed the hole against his side. He shone his torch directly down on Sabir's face. 'You're in a cesspit. An old one. This house has obviously never been on mains sewerage. It took me a while to find it. But you'll have to admit that it's perfect of its kind. There's ten inches between the level of the shit and the roof of the pit. That's just about the size of your head, Sabir, with a couple of inches left over for wastage. When I close and seal this trap you'll have enough air for, oh, half an hour? That's if the carbon monoxide from the decomposition of the food sugars doesn't kill you first.'

Sabir became aware of a pain in his right temple. He wanted to put up his hand to feel for damage, but could not. 'What have you done to me?'

'I haven't done anything to you. Yet. The damage to your face was from a ricochet. My bullet struck the fireplace just as you were turning to destroy the prophecies. The deformed slug sprang back and took part of your ear off. It also knocked you cold. Sorry for that.'

Sabir could feel the claustrophobia begin to take hold of him. He tried to breathe normally but found himself entirely incapable of that measure of control. He began to whoop, like the victim of an asthma attack.

Bale tapped Sabir lightly across the bridge of the nose with the barrel of his pistol. 'Don't go hysterical on me. I want you to listen. To listen carefully. You're already a dead man. Whatever happens, I will kill you. You will die in this place. No one will ever find you in here.'

Sabir's nose had begun to bleed. He tried to turn his head away from Bale's pistol, fearing a second blow, but the sudden admixture of blood and excrement triggered his gag reflex. It took him some minutes to regain control of himself and stop retching. Eventually, when the fit was over, he raised his head as far as he could and dragged in some marginally fresh air from above. 'Why are you still speaking to me? Why don't you just get on with whatever you are intending to do?'

405

Bale winced. 'Patience, Sabir. Patience. I am still speaking to you because you have a weakness. A fatal weakness that I intend to use against you. I was there when they put you in the wood-box back at Samois. And I saw your condition when they brought you out. Claustrophobia is what you fear most in this world. So I offer it to you. In exactly sixty seconds' time I shall lock and seal this place, and leave you here to rot. But you have one chance to buy back the girl's life. The girl's – not your own. You can dictate to me all that you know of the prophecies. No. Don't pretend you don't know what I'm talking about. You had more than enough time to copy down the verses and translate them. I found the dictionary you threw at me. I heard your car arrive. I have estimated how long you were down in the sitting room, and it runs into hours. Dictate what you know to me, and I will shoot you through the head. That way you won't die of suffocation. And I will promise to spare the girl.'

'I didn't . . .' Sabir had trouble getting the words out. 'I didn't . . .'

'Yes you did. I have the pad you were pressing on. You wrote many lines. You translated many lines. Later, I will have the pad analysed. But first you will give me what I want. If you fail to do this, I will find the girl, and I will do to her exactly what was done to the pregnant woman by the Hangman of Dreissigacker. Right down to the very last lash – the very last scalding – the very last screw of the rack. She told you about that, didn't she, your little Yola? The bedtime story that I read to her while she was waiting to die? I can see by your face that she did. Haunting, wasn't it? You can save her from that, Sabir. You can die a hero.' Bale levered himself up on to his feet. 'Think about it.'

The trapdoor slammed shut, returning the cesspit to a condition of total darkness.

83

Sabir started to scream. It wasn't a rational sound, based on a desire to get out. It was an animal sound, dragged from some doomed place deep inside him – a place in which hope no longer had a foothold.

There was a noise above him of something heavy being dragged across the trapdoor. Sabir fell silent, like a wild animal sensing the approaching line of beaters. The darkness in which he found himself was absolute – so dark, in fact, that the blackness seemed almost purple to his wildly staring eyes.

The gag reflex began again, and he could feel his heart clenching in his chest with each explosive expectoration. He tried to focus his mind on the outside world. To take himself beyond the cesspit and this hideous darkness which threatened to engulf him and drive him mad. But the darkness was so complete, and his fear so acute, that he could no longer dominate his own thoughts.

He tried to drag his arms up from beneath him. Were they tied? Had Bale done even that to him?

With each movement he sank deeper into the sump. Now it was up to his chin and threatening to invade his mouth. He began to wail, his arms flapping like chicken wings in the viscous liquid below him.

Bale would come back. He had said he would come back. He would come back to ask Sabir about the prophecies. That would afford Sabir the crucial leverage he needed. He would get Bale to pull him out of the cesspit so that he could write down all that he knew. Then he would overpower him. No power on earth would ever get Sabir back inside here once he was out. He would die if necessary. Kill himself.

It was then that Sabir remembered Bale's useless left arm. It would be physically impossible for Bale ever to pull him out. Drag him to the cesspit he could. Control an unconscious man's slide into the sump he could – that would simply have been a matter of leverage, and of snagging his inert body by the collar and allowing gravity to do the rest. But there was no way on God's earth that Bale could ever get him back out again.

Slowly, incrementally, the gases in the cesspit were having their effect. Sabir imagined himself drawn upwards as if by an outside force. At first his entire body seemed driven against the sealed cover of the cesspit like a man sucked against the porthole of a depressurised plane. Then he burst through and up into the air, his body bent into the shape of a U by the centrifugal throw-out. He threw his arms as wide as he was able, and his body-shape reversed itself, until he was rocketing upwards in the shape of a C – in the shape of a skydiver – but with the force and speed of his ascension having no discernible effect.

He looked down at the earth below him with a sublime detachment, as if this expulsive exodus was in no way part of his own experience.

Then, deep inside his hallucination, his body began a gradual process of discombobulation. First his arms were torn off – he saw them swirling away from him on a current of air. Then his legs.

Sabir began to moan.

With a frightful wrench, his lower torso, from his waist down to his upper thighs, ripped apart from his body, dragging intestines, lights, bowel and bladder in its wake. His chest burst apart, and his heart, lungs and ribs shredded from his body. He tried to snatch at them but he had no arms. He was powerless to control his body's liquefaction, and soon all that was left of him was his head, just as it had been in his shamanic dream – his head approaching him, face on, its eyes dead.

As the head came closer its mouth opened, and from inside a snake began to issue – a thick, uncoiling python of a snake, with scales like those of a fish, and staring eyes, and a mouth that seemed to unhinge itself, becoming ever larger. The python turned and swallowed Sabir's head – Sabir could see the shape of his head moving down the python's body, driven by its myosin-fuelled muscles.

Then the python turned, and its face was his face, even down to his newly damaged ear. The face tried to talk to him, but Sabir could no longer make out the sound of his own voice. It was as if he was both inside and outside the snake's body at one and the same time. Somehow, though, Sabir sensed that his incapacity to hear came from the internal head, which was being drawn like forcemeat through the lozenge of the snake's body.

It's like a birth, Sabir decided. It's like coming down through the birth canal. That's why I'm claustrophobic. It's my birth. Something to do with my birth.

Now Sabir could see through the snake's eyes, feel through the snake's skin. He was the snake, and it was him.

His hand burst out of the sump near to his face. He felt the hand reach for his neck, as though it were still not part of him.

He was still the snake. He had no hands.

The hand reached for the necklet the shaman had given him.

Snake. There was snake in the necklet.

Poison. There was poison in the necklet.

He must take it. Kill himself. Surely that was what the dream had been telling him?

Suddenly he was back in the reality of the cesspit. There was a scraping sound above him. In a moment Bale would be opening the hatch.

With his free hand Sabir tore a wad of fabric off the front of his shirt and rammed it into his mouth. He thrust it down his throat, blocking off all access to his windpipe.

He felt the gag reflex trigger, but ignored it.

Bale was sliding the hatch open.

Sabir broke the vial of poison into his mouth. He was breathing only through his nose now. He could feel the poison lying on his tongue. Dispersing against the roof of his mouth. Filtering up his nasal passages and through his sinuses.

When the hatch slid back, Sabir played dead. In the split second before the light struck him, he allowed his head to drop forward and rest on the surface of the scum, so that Bale would imagine he had drowned himself.

Bale grunted in irritation. He reached down to raise Sabir's head.

Sabir grabbed the collar of Bale's shirt with his free hand. Temporarily unbalanced, Bale started to topple.

Using the impetus of the downward movement, Sabir steered Bale's head through the hatch. His eyes fixed themselves on the open wound on Bale's neck.

As Bale's head came briefly parallel with his own, Sabir sank his teeth into the wound, forcing his tongue inside the bullet hole, dispersing the poison deep into Bale's veins.

Then he spat what remained of the poison into the cesspool surrounding him and prepared to die.

84

Joris Calque's interview with the Countess had proved
to be the equivalent of a *coitus reservatus* – in other
words he had delayed completion for so long that the
final effect had been little more satisfying than a wet
dream.

He had convinced himself before the interview that it
was he who held the upper hand. The Countess, surely,
must be on the defensive? She was an old woman – why
didn't she simply open up and have done with it? There
was no capital punishment in France any more. In fact the
Count would most probably be carted off to an asylum,
where he could play dynastic games to his heart's content
in the sure and certain knowledge that after fifteen or
twenty years he would be ejected back into the system
with a 'harmless' label tagged around his neck.

Instead, Calque had found himself facing the human
equivalent of a brick wall. Rarely in his career had he
encountered a person so sure of the moral justifications
of their actions. Calque knew that the Countess was the
driving force behind her son's behaviour – he simply
knew it. But he couldn't remotely prove it.

～

'Is that you, Spola?' Calque held the cellphone six inches
in front of his mouth, as one would hold a microphone.
'Where are Sabir and Dufontaine now?'

'Sleeping, Sir. It is two o'clock in the morning.'

'Have you checked on them recently? Within the last
hour, say?'

'No, Sir.'

'Well do so now.'

'Shall I call you back?'

'No. Take the telephone with you. That's what these things are for, isn't it?'

Sergeant Spola eased himself up from the back seat of his police meat-wagon. He had made himself a comfortable nest out of a few borrowed blankets and a chair cushion which Yola had purloined for him. What was Calque thinking of? This was the middle of the night. Why would Sabir or the gypsy want to go anywhere? They weren't being accused of anything. If Calque asked his opinion, he would tell him that there was no sense at all in wasting police manpower trailing non-suspects around in the enjoyment of their lawful rights. Spola had a lovely warm wife waiting for him at home. And a lovely warm bed. Those constituted his lawful rights. And, typically, they were in the process of being violated.

'I'm looking at the gypsy now. He's fast asleep.'

'Check on Sabir.'

'Yes, Sir.' Spola eased the internal door of the caravan open. Such bloody nonsense. 'He's lying in his bed. He's . . .' Spola stopped. He took a further step inside the room and switched on the light. 'He's gone, Sir. They packed his bed full of cushions to make it look as if he was asleep. I'm sorry, Sir.'

'Where's the girl?'

'Sleeping with the women, Sir. Across the way.'

'Get her.'

'But I can't, Sir. You know what these gypsy women are like. If I go blundering in there . . .'

'Get her. Then put her on the phone.'

85

Spola squinted through the windscreen at the passing trees. It had started to rain, and the police car's headlights were reflecting back off the road, making it difficult to judge distances.

Yola fidgeted anxiously beside him, her face taut in the reflected glare.

Spola flicked on the rear wipers. 'That was a rotten trick to play on me, you know. I could lose my job over this.'

'You shouldn't have been told to watch us in the first place. It's only because we're gypsies. You people treat us like dirt.'

Spola sat up straighter in his seat. 'That's not true. I've tried to be reasonable with you – cut you some slack. I even let you visit the *curandero* with Sabir. That's what's got me into all this trouble.'

Yola flashed a glance at him. 'You're all right. It's the others that make me sick.'

'Well. Yes. There are some people who have unjustifiable prejudices. I don't deny it. But I'm not one of them.' He reached forwards and scrubbed at the inside of the windscreen with his sleeve. 'If only they'd give us cars with air conditioning, we might see where we are going. Are we nearly there?'

'It's here. Turn left. And go on up the drive. The house will appear in a few moments.'

Spola eased the car up the rutted track. He glanced down at the clock. It would take Calque at least another hour to get here – unless he hijacked a police helicopter. Another night's sleep lost.

He pulled the car up in front of the Maset. 'So this is where it all happened?'

Yola got out and ran towards the front door. There was no solid basis to her anxiety, but Calque's call, warning them that the eye-man was still after Sabir, had upset her equanimity. She had thought that the eye-man was out of their lives for ever. And now here she was, in the middle of the night, aiding and abetting the police.

'Damo?' She looked around the room. The fire was almost out. One of the candles was guttering, and another was only ten minutes away from extinction. There was hardly enough light to see by, let alone transcribe detailed text. She turned to Sergeant Spola. 'Have you a torch?'

He clicked it on. 'Perhaps he's in the kitchen?'

Yola shook her head. Her face looked pinched and anxious in the artificial light. She hurried down the corridor. 'Damo?' She hesitated at the spot where Macron had been killed. 'Damo?'

Had she heard a noise? She placed one hand on her heart and took a step forwards.

The sound of a gunshot echoed through the empty building. Yola screamed. Sergeant Spola ran towards her. 'What was that? Did you hear a shot?'

'It was down in the cellar.' Yola had her hand to her throat.

Spola cursed, and manhandled his pistol out of its holster. He was not an active man. Gunplay was not in his nature. In fact he had never needed to use violence in over thirty years of police work. 'Stay here, Mademoiselle. If you hear more shots, run out to the police car and drive it away. Do you hear me?'

'I can't drive.'

Spola handed her his cellphone. 'I've put in a call to Captain Calque. Tell him what is happening. Tell him he must call an ambulance. I must go now.' Spola ran through the back of the house towards the cellar, his torch casting wild shadows on the walls. Without pausing to think, he threw open the cellar door and clattered down, his pistol held awkwardly in one hand, his torch in the other.

A man's feet projected from the lip of what appeared to be an old water cistern or cesspit. As Spola watched, the feet slithered down into the pit. Crazed sounds were coming from inside the sump, and Spola stood, for one wild moment, fixed to the spot in shock and consternation. Then he crept forwards and shone his torch inside the pit.

Sabir had his head craned back and his mouth open, in a sort of silent rictus. In his free hand he held Bale's fist, with the Redhawk anchored between them. As Spola watched, Bale's head emerged from the cesspool, the clotted eyes turned up further than it seemed possible for human eyes to go. The gun rocked forwards, and there was a vivid flash.

Spola fell to one knee. A numbness spread across his chest and down through his belly in the direction of his genitals. He tried to raise his pistol but was unable to do so. He coughed once, and then fell over on to his side.

A figure darted past him. He felt the pistol being wrenched from his hand. Then his torch was taken. He placed both his free hands on his belly. He had a sudden, exquisite image of his wife lying on their bed, waiting for him, her eyes burning into his.

The gun flashes became more intense, lighting up the cellar like the repeated strikes of a tornadic lightning storm. Spola was aware of movement way out beyond him. Far away. Then someone was gently separating his hands. Was it his wife? Had they brought his wife to look after him? Spola tried to speak to her, but the oxygen mask cut off his words.

86

'You owe the girl your life.'

'I know I do.' Sabir twisted his head until he was staring at the tips of the pine trees just visible outside the window of his hospital room. 'I owe her more than that, if the truth be told.'

The remark passed Calque by. He was concentrating on something else altogether. 'How did she know that you had taken poison? How did she know that you needed an emetic?'

'What emetic?'

'She fed you mustard and salt water until you brought up what was left of the poison. She saved Sergeant Spola's life, too. The eye-man gutshot him. With gutshot victims, if they go to sleep, they die. She kept him talking while she lay with one hand hanging down into the cesspit, holding you upright – out of the sump. Without her, you would have drowned.'

'I told you she was a special person. But, like everybody else, you distrust gypsies. It's simply not rational. You ought to be ashamed of yourself.'

'I didn't come here to receive a lecture.'

'What did you come here for, then?'

Calque sat back in his chair. He felt around in his pockets for a cigarette, and then remembered that he was in a hospital. 'For answers, I suppose.'

'What do I know? We were pursued by a madman. He's dead. Now we get on with our lives.'

'That's not enough.'

'What do you mean?'

'I want to know what it was all for. Why Paul Macron was killed. And the others. Bale wasn't mad. He was the sanest one amongst us. He knew exactly what he wanted and why he wanted it.'

'Ask his mother.'

'I have. It's like kicking a dead tree. She denies everything. The manuscript we found in her hidden room is indecipherable, and my superior considers it a waste of police time to pursue it any further. She's got away scot free. She and her aristocratic band of Devil-fanciers.'

'What do you want from me, then?'

'Yola admitted to Sergeant Spola that the prophecies weren't lost. That you had secured them, and were translating them at the Maset. I think she has a soft spot for Sergeant Spola.'

'And you want to know what was in the prophecies?'

'Yes.'

'And what if I were to publish them?'

'No one would listen. You would be like King Priam's daughter, Cassandra, who was given the gift of prophecy by her suitor Apollo. Only when she refused to go to bed with him, he varied the gift so that, although her prophecies were invariably true, no one would ever believe them.' Calque held up three fingers to silence Sabir's inevitable riposte. He began to count off the points he wished to make by gripping each finger in the palm of his free hand. 'One – you don't have the originals. Two – you don't even have a copy of the originals. You burned them. We found the ashes in the fireplace. Five million dollars' worth of ashes. Three – it would simply be your word against the rest of the world. Anyone could say they found them. What you have is valueless, Sabir.'

'Then why do you want it?'

417

'Because I need to know.'

Sabir closed his eyes. 'And why should I tell you?'

Calque shrugged his shoulders. 'I can't answer that.' He hunched forwards. 'But if I were in your shoes, I'd want to tell someone. I wouldn't want to carry whatever it is you're carrying to the grave with me. I'd want to get it off my chest.'

'Why you in particular?'

'For Christ's sake, Sabir!' Calque started up from his chair. Then he changed his mind and sat down again. 'You owe me. And you owe Macron. You played me for a sucker after I trusted you.'

'You shouldn't have trusted me.'

Calque gave the ghost of a smile. 'I didn't. There were two trackers in the car. We knew if we lost one, that we could pick you up again with the other. I'm a policeman, not a social worker, Sabir.'

Sabir shook his head sadly. He was watching Calque, his eyes dark in contrast to the pristine white bandage that was protecting the side of his face. 'Something happened to me in there, Captain.'

'I know it did.'

'No. Not what you are thinking. Something else. It was like a transformation. I changed. Became something other. The *curandero* warned me that it happens when you are about to become a shaman. A healer.'

'I don't know what the hell you're talking about.'

'I don't either.'

Calque sat back in his armchair. 'Do you remember any of it? Or am I just wasting my time?'

'I remember all of it.'

Calque's body stiffened like a bird dog scenting its prey. 'You can't be serious.'

'I told you that some change had occurred in me. Some transformation. I don't know what it was or why it happened, but even now I can bring up every word of the French text that I saw. Like a photograph. I just have to close my eyes and it comes back. I spent six hours in that house, Captain. Reading those quatrains over and over again. Translating them. Trying to understand their significance.'

'Have you written them down?'

'I don't need to. And I don't want to.'

Calque stood up. 'Fine. It was stupid of me to even ask. Why should you tell me? What can I do about anything? I'm an old man. I should retire. But I hang on in the police force because I don't have anything else to do with my life. That's about the sum of it. Goodbye, Mister Sabir. I'm glad the bastard didn't get you.'

Sabir watched Calque shuffle towards the door. There was something about the man – an integrity, perhaps – that raised him above the common run of humanity. Calque had been honest according to his own lights during the investigation. He had cut Sabir far more slack than he had any right to expect. And he hadn't blamed him for Macron's death or Sergeant Spola's wounding. No. He had taken those things on himself. 'Wait.'

'For what?'

Sabir held Calque's eyes with his own. 'Sit down, Captain. I'm going to tell you part of the story. The part that will not compromise any third parties. Will you be satisfied with that?'

Calque returned Sabir's glance. Then he settled himself cautiously back in his seat. 'I shall have to be, won't I? If that's all you feel you can give me.'

Sabir shrugged. Then he inclined his head questioningly. 'Secrets of the confessional?'

Calque sighed. 'Secrets of the confessional.'

87

'There were only fifty-two quatrains on the parchment I retrieved from the bamboo tubing. I had initially assumed there would be fifty-eight, because that is the exact number needed to make up Nostradamus's original ten centuries. But six are still missing. I now think that they are scattered around, like the ones at Rocamadour and Montserrat, and designed to serve as clues to the main caucus.'

'Go on.'

'As far as I can work out, each of the fifty-two remaining quatrains describes a particular year. A year in the run-up to the End of Days. The Apocalypse. Ragnarök. The Mayan Great Change. Whatever you choose to call it.'

'What do you mean, describes a year?'

'Each one acts as a pointer. It describes some event that will take place in that year – and each event is significant in some way.'

'So the end isn't dated?'

'It doesn't need to be – even Nostradamus didn't know the exact date of Armageddon. He only knew what preceded it. So the date becomes obvious the nearer we get to it. In increments.'

'I still don't understand.'

Sabir sat up straighter in his bed. 'It's simple. Nostradamus wants mankind to escape the final holocaust. He feels that if the world can change its behaviour by acknowledging the Second Coming – by rejecting the Third Antichrist – then we might stand a faint chance of avoiding annihilation. That's why he's given us the clues, year by year and event by event. We're to correlate the quatrains with the events. When each event occurs just as Nostradamus predicted, the quatrains will increase in importance and we can tick them off. The closer we get to Armageddon, the more obvious the starting date and the end date will be, for the simple reason that the events predicted for the last few years in the run-up to the End of Days haven't happened yet. Then people will start to believe. And maybe change their behaviour. To all intents and purposes Nostradamus was giving us a fifty-two-year warning.'

Calque made a face.

'Look, the first clue, in what I now believe to be the first quatrain, runs like this:

> *"The African desert will melt into glass*
> *False freedoms will torment the French*
> *The great empire of the islands will shrink*
> *Its hands, feet, and elbows shun the head."*

'That means nothing. It gets us nowhere.'

'On the contrary. Look at it again. "The African desert will melt into glass." In 1960 the French conducted their first ever nuclear test in south western Algeria. In the Sahara Desert. They called it the Gerboise Bleu – the Blue Jerboa.'

'You're stretching, Sabir.'

'Try the next line, then: "False freedoms will torment the French." In 1960 France granted – or was forced to grant – independence to French Cameroon, French Togoland, Madagascar, Dahomey, Burkina Faso, Upper Volta, Ivory Coast, Chad, the Central African Republic, Congo-Brazzaville, Gabon, Mali, Niger, Senegal, and Mauritania. But still they persisted with their war in Algeria. "False freedom" is when you give with one hand

and you take back with another. Now lines three and four: "The great empire of the islands will shrink. Its hands, feet, and elbows shun the head." Great Britain was always the "great empire of the islands" to Nostradamus. He uses the image on numerous occasions and it was always specific to Britain. In 1960 the British granted independence to Cyprus. Also to British Somaliland. Ghana. Nigeria. These are the extremities. Queen Elizabeth II was the head. By achieving independence, they shun her.'

'Not enough.'

'Try the next one then:

"*Germany will be strangled and Africa retaken*
A young leader will emerge: he will retain his youth
Men will raise their eyes towards the battlefield
A star will shine that is no star."'

'According to your theory, Sabir, this quatrain should then refer to 1961. Does it? I don't see that.'

'Why don't you? Take the first half of the first line: "Germany will be strangled." Nostradamus uses the phrase *envoyer le cordon*, meaning to "send the bowstring". In other words to "order to be strangled". And what happened in 1961? The border was closed between East and West Berlin, and the Wall was built – a concrete cordon, effectively separating and strangling Germany. Now the second part of the first line: "And Africa retaken." On the 21st of April 1961 rebellious members of the OAS took Algiers, in an effort to stop General de Gaulle from granting Algerian independence. You remember that, don't you, Calque? You were probably still busy cutting your milk teeth on the beat as a *pandore*.'

'Pah.'

'"Men will raise their eyes towards the battlefield."

Does that remind you of anything? On the 12 th of April 1961 Yuri Gagarin became the first ever man to enter space – in the *Vostok I* – thereby launching the space race and further aggravating the Cold War between the United States, NATO and the Soviet Union. "A star will shine that is no star." That's a pretty damned good description of an orbiting spacecraft, isn't it? Especially when you figure that Nostradamus was writing 450 years before any such thing had even been envisaged.'

'What about "A young leader will emerge: he will retain his youth"? I suppose you're going to tell me that describes John F. Kennedy.'

'Of course it does. Kennedy first took over the US Presidential office on the 20th of January 1961. "A young leader will emerge" – Kennedy became the leader of the Western world when he took the Oath of Allegiance. He will "retain his youth" because he will be assassinated, two years later.'

'I suppose Nostradamus calls that one, too.'

'Yes. I have it as "The pale carriage of the young King turns black." The second line goes: "The Queen must mourn; the King's crown will be sundered." Kennedy was shot in the head, on the 22nd of November 1963, in Dallas, Texas. Robert McClelland, MD, described the wound in his testimony at Parkland before Arlen Specter on the 21st of March 1964. He said that the brain tissue had been blasted out through the top of the President's skull. Look. I've printed his testimony off the internet. Let me read it to you: "I could very closely examine the head wound, and I noted that the right posterior portion of the skull had been extremely blasted. It had been shattered . . . so that the parietal bone was protruded up through the scalp and seemed to be fractured almost along its right posterior half, as well as some of the occipital bone being fractured in its lateral half, and this sprung open the bones that I mentioned in such a way that you could actually look down into the skull cavity itself and see that probably a third or so, at least, of the brain tissue, posterior cerebral tissue and some of the cerebellar tissue had been blasted out . . ." That seems to me to accord pretty clearly with "the King's crown will be sundered". Don't you think?'

'No one will take this seriously. You realise that?'

'No one will have the chance to take it seriously. Because I am not going to make these prophecies public. You yourself explained why, with your Cassandra parallel. I don't have the originals. No one will believe me. And there are things in here that the Corpus Maleficus still want to know.'

'But Bale is dead.'

'So he is.'

'There's more, isn't there?'

'The proof of the pudding, you mean? Well that comes next year. And the year after that. And the year after that.'

'What are you talking about?'

'Think about it, Calque. We have the starting date to the countdown as 1960. That's clear. Even you can't dispute that. And I have forty-nine quatrains moving on from that year, describing an event or events in each succeeding year which pinpoints that year as part of the cycle. They're not all in order, but when you spread them out, they tally. I've got the US defeat in Vietnam. The Chinese Cultural Revolution. The Arab-Israeli War. The Cambodian Genocide. The Mexico City Earthquake. The First and Second Gulf Wars. 9/11. The New Orleans Floods. The Indian Ocean Tsunami. And that's just the tip of the iceberg. There are dozens of smaller events which seem to tally too. It's beyond the realms of happenstance.'

'So what are you telling me?'

'I'm telling you that the Mayans were right. According to the Mayan Long Calendar, they have the Great Change as occurring in 2012. On the 21st of December, to be precise. 5126 years – that's thirteen baktuns, each comprising twenty katuns – from the calendar's inception. That tallies precisely with Nostradamus's own index dates. Except that he starts in 1960, at the exact turn of the Age of Aquarius. And he gives us fifty-two quatrains, and a fifty-two-year warning. That's 2012 too. It couldn't be clearer.'

'And you have the prophecies for the succeeding years?'

'Yes. I've isolated them by default. It's exactly those prophecies that Bale wanted so badly. One describes the Third Antichrist. The one who will bring the world to the abyss. Another describes the Second Coming. And another describes the location of a new visionary who will either confirm or deny the date – who can see into the future and channel the information. Only this person can tell us what awaits – regeneration or apocalypse. But all will ultimately depend on whether we are prepared to recognise the Second Coming. Recognise it universally. See it as something beyond religion, in other words – as a universal blessing. Nostradamus believes that only by bringing the world together – in the communal worship of one entity – can we be saved.'

'You can't be serious.'

'Deadly serious.'

'The Third Antichrist, then. Who is he?'

Sabir turned away. 'He is with us now. He was born under the number seven. Ten seven ten seven. He has the name of the Great Whore. He already holds high office. He will hold higher. His numerological number is one, indicating ruthlessness and an obsessive desire for power. Nostradamus calls him the "scorpion ascending". That is all I can tell you.'

'But that is nothing.'

'Oh, it is.'

Calque looked searchingly at him. 'So you know his name?'

'Yes. And so do you.'

Calque shrugged. But he had gone pale beneath his temporary Camargue tan. 'Don't think I won't try to work it out. I'm a detective. Numerology isn't an entirely alien concept. Even to me.'

'I expected nothing less.'

'And the Second Coming?'

'I will tell no one of that. It was the real purpose of Nostradamus's gift to his daughter. It is a secret that men and women would die for. A secret that could change the world. You are the only person on earth who knows that I have it. I am content for things to remain that way. Are you?'

Calque watched Sabir silently for some minutes. Finally, awkwardly, he stood up. He nodded his head.

POSTSCRIPT

———————

Alexi kidnapped Yola when the summer was at its height. They ran away to Corsica and Alexi took her virginity on the beach near Cargèse. As he made love to her for the first time, a flight of ducks travelled over them, casting their shadow across the mating couple. Yola sat up the moment he withdrew from her body and told him she was pregnant.

'This is impossible. How can you know?'

'I know.'

Alexi never doubted her. To him, Yola possessed a mysterious understanding of secrets beyond his ken. This suited him, as someone out there needed to know such things – and to carry their weight – if Alexi was to be allowed to live his life in the present, with neither a backward nor a forward glance.

The moment Sabir heard of Yola's kidnap, he took a plane across to Europe and waited for the couple at the camp in Samois. In his new position as Yola's brother and the titular head of her family, it was inconceivable that she should be allowed to marry without his presence and permission. He knew that this was the one final thing he needed to do for her, and that his appearance at her wedding would at last free her of the blood taint from her brother's death.

Yola had kept the towel she had lain on when Alexi made love to her for the very first time on the beach at Cargèse, and when this was displayed before the wedding guests, Sabir formally acknowledged that she had been a virgin before her kidnapping, and that her *lacha* was untarnished. He agreed to pay Alexi her bride-price.

Later, after the ceremony was over, Yola told him that she was pregnant, and asked him if he would be *kirvo* to her son.

'You know it's a son?'

'After Alexi plucked out my eyes, a male dog ran up to us on the beach and licked my hand.'

Sabir shook his head. 'It's crazy. But I believe you.'

'You are correct to do so. The *curandero* was right. You are a wiser man now. Something happened to you while you were dying. I don't want to know what it was. But I feel that you can see things sometimes, just as I can, after the eye-man gave me my two half-deaths. Are you a shaman now?'

Sabir shook his head. 'I'm a nothing. Nothing's changed. I'm just happy to be here, and to see you married. And of course I'll be *kirvo* to your son.'

Yola watched him for a few seconds, hoping for something more. But then a sudden understanding dawned across her face. 'You know, don't you, Damo? What the *curandero* told me about my child? About the *Parousia*? It was all written on those pages that you burned. This was why the secret of the prophecies was given to my family for safe keeping? That was why you burned them at the risk of your life?'

'Yes. It was written.'

Yola pressed her stomach with her hands. 'Was anything else written? Things I should know? Things I should fear for my son?'

Sabir smiled. 'Nothing else was written, Yola. What will be will be. The die is cast, and the future written only on the stars.'